A NOVEL

INFORMED CONSENT

SANDRA GLAHN

David C Cook

transforming lives together

INFORMED CONSENT
Published by David C. Cook
4050 Lee Vance View
Colorado Springs, CO 80918 U.S.A.

David C. Cook Distribution Canada
55 Woodslee Avenue, Paris, Ontario, Canada N3L 3E5

David C. Cook U.K., Kingsway Communications
Eastbourne, East Sussex BN23 6NT, England

David C. Cook and the graphic circle C logo
are registered trademarks of Cook Communications Ministries.

The Web site addresses listed in the back of this book are
offered as a resource to you. These Web sites are not intended in any way
to be or imply an endorsement on the part of David C. Cook, nor do we vouch for their content.

This story is a work of fiction. All characters and events are the product of the author's imagination.
Any resemblance to any person, living or dead, is coincidental.

All Scripture quotations, unless otherwise noted, are taken from the *Holy Bible,
New International Version*®. *NIV*®. Copyright © 1973, 1978, 1984 by International
Bible Society. Used by permission of Zondervan. All rights reserved.

LCCN 2007931293
ISBN 978-1-58919-109-9

© 2007 Sandra Glahn
Published in association with the literary agency of Chip MacGregor,
2373 NW 185th Ave., Suite 165, Hillsboro, OR 97124.

Cover Design: The DesignWorks Group, Jason Gabbert
Cover Photos: © Photodisc Illustration/Veer; © Stockbyte Photography/Veer
Interior Design: Karen Athen

Printed in the United States of America
First Edition 2007

1 2 3 4 5 6 7 8 9 10

062707

THANK YOU...

Bill Cutrer, MD – For your brilliant medical insights, rich imagination for plot options, and knack for storytelling that includes a gift for hyperbole. You kept me from impossibilities such as patients who talk while intubated, and you made me laugh in the process.

Clay Reynolds, PhD – For your astute critique from the beginning, for helping me find my narrative voice, and for shaping me as a writer. You tirelessly waded through many drafts, for which I'm grateful. I appreciate the sacrifices of time you made to coach me.

Reg Grant, PhD – For teaching me to love "story" with its layers of narrative voice, point of view, plot, setting, characterization, and word crafting. I know you've opened more doors for me than even I realize, and I'm grateful.

Kenn Gangel, ThD – For instilling in me a distain for wimpy verbs and love for strong ones.

Chip MacGregor, PhD – For representing me, intervening for me, and providing banter along the way.

Don Pape – For publishing, agenting, and publishing again. Thank you, friend.

Traci DePree – For your careful editor's eye that understood my characters and for helping me help them express emotion.

Benji Brunel, my teaching assistant – For your help on all my projects (including a fine editor's eye on this one), which allowed me to carve out more time to write.

Kelley Mathews – For thorough editing on more than one draft and for tenacity in a temporarily one-sided friendship.

Justin Brumit – For your rich textual insights and abundant encouragement from the beginning.

My readers in the A&H program at the University of Texas at Dallas: Jaena Almallah, Catherine Berg, Marilyn Bland, Kim DeLauro, J. P. Fassler, Chris Foltz, Melissa Gravely, Vivian Jones, Serenity

King, Rachel Maverick, Awista Ramyar, Meghan Rennie, Greg Shows, Jeremy Skinner, Jeanne Smith, Kristin van Namen, Desireé Ward, and James Welch IV – For all of your feedback and for challenging me to grow as a writer.

Jacob Glidewell – For coming up with the word-count race that helped me make deadline. (Yes, I won, but don't you think, really, we both did?)

Vicki Caswell – For reading an early draft and cheering me on.

Virginia Swint – For your shameless love and support without which I would dread opening my daily email. Thanks, too, for your thoughts on this manuscript.

Jack Campbell – For guiding and editing the manuscript through its final stages of production.

Lance and Jeni, the Kirsteins, Rhonda, Erin, Eva, Tim and Beverly – You know why. The secret things will be rewarded in the open.

Gary and Alexandra – "When every family member contributes, all celebrate the result." I love you! We did it!

For Kelley
φίλη in Light Supreme and story

PROLOGUE

Like most children, Jeremy Cramer thought his father would never die. Some nights when Jeremy had trouble forcing his ten-year-old eyes to sleep, his mind drifted to what he'd do if anything ever happened to his parents. But he relegated such thoughts to the world of disbelief—the same world he entered when his dad read *The Runaway Bunny* to him. His parents could no more die than rabbits could talk.

To conceive of his parents' passing was rare enough. But that his father would die the way he did had never entered Jeremy's imagination, rich as it was. He allowed passing thoughts of motorcycle accidents and biking mishaps and even falls off the sides of mountains during ski runs. But never what actually happened.

EVERY MORNING EXCEPT Sunday, Jeremy's father, Randall, roused his son at 5:00 a.m. Then Randall pulled swim trunks over muscular legs, sipped black coffee by the pool as he read the paper, and waited for Jeremy to finish his oatmeal.

On a hook beside the water hung a stopwatch, a whistle, and a towel. A clipboard lay on an ironwork table at the pool's edge. It contained each day's times recorded in green ink with the shortest circled in black. Flipping back through the records of the past two months alone, anyone could see Randall had good reason to believe in Jeremy's potential.

Randall's blond hair and physique seemed godlike to Jeremy compared to his own scrawny, dark body. Never mind that Jeremy's mother said he had enchanting eyes that would someday break hearts. Girls didn't interest him; he just wanted the build of an athlete. He worked to increase his muscles and endurance, but speed came naturally. He could slice through the water like sharpened cutlery.

From what Jeremy's fifth-grade teacher taught him about family trees, he knew he inherited most of his physical features from his mother, who was Asian Indian, and few from his Caucasian American father. But the invisible parts—Jeremy's drive, his speed, his style in the water—these came undiluted from his dad.

Randall pressed hard, but he praised generously, and that combination motivated Jeremy. He pushed himself to earn a black circle, ever striving to beat the previous day's speed. He usually accomplished what he set out to do, driven by his father's smile and the word Jeremy loved to hear him emphasize—that's *my* boy!

But this day differed from the usual routine because it was Sunday. Sundays in the Cramer household were for sleeping in and eating pancakes. Jeremy glanced at his digital clock, congratulated himself for slumbering through the equivalent of twenty laps, and dozed off again.

When the blaze shining through the window hurt his eyes and the aroma coming from the kitchen overpowered him, he obeyed the rumbling in his stomach and padded off to join his family. He found his mother bent over the stove, his father reading the *Denver Post,* and his little sister, Gloria, drowning her pancakes in blueberry syrup. As she sawed her cakes into sloppy squares, she sang an alphabet song learned from endless loopings of her preschool video.

"You left out 'v,'" Jeremy corrected. He reached for the plate of hotcakes on the table, but he stopped when he noticed his father's attire. Though his mother stood wrapped in her usual satin robe, his dad had on swim trunks. And deck shoes. Normally on Sundays everybody lounged until noon in their pajamas.

"Up for a rafting trip?" His father winked at him.

"Yes!" Jeremy glanced over at his sister and tempered his joy. "The whole family?"

"Just us. Your mom's taking Gloria to a movie this afternoon."

That was fine with Jeremy. He would have more fun without Gloria whining about getting wet.

"I reserved a place in the noon group. I wanted us to make the first run of the season," his dad told him. "It'll take about two hours to get there, and we'll need some time to gear up. We leave in thirty minutes."

His dad was always early. And even though Jeremy knew they had plenty of time, he shoveled and gulped the rest of his food and tore off to get ready. He'd waited all spring for this—school was finally out, and it was warm enough. The only thing better than the pool was the river.

Jeremy had vivid memories of the conversation at breakfast that morning. And an uneventful drive to the Arkansas River. But after that it got foggy.

Jeremy didn't recall putting on a life preserver, but the photos produced later left no doubt that everyone suited up in proper gear. Apparently the guide gave plenty of instructions—two witnesses testified to that. Jeremy remembered only that the water splashed up and numbed his hands as he pulled his oar through the water. Had he turned around to complain and distracted his father? He was supposed to paddle hard to move the boat away from the rocks. Had he shirked his responsibility because he was too cold? He wasn't sure. But the icy feeling in his fingers had been minor compared to the shock of having his entire body cast into the roaring waves. He felt his father grasping his arm, but shortly after that the gripping sensation ceased. A wave pushed Jeremy under, but he resurfaced to float in the sea of frigid motion. Then he watched horrorstruck as he saw the back of his father's head bobbing down the rapids. After that, Jeremy lost consciousness.

A FEW DAYS later when the hospital released Jeremy, his mother and Gloria accompanied him on the eternal two-hour drive home. He learned later what the police report said—that the boat hit the rapids at the wrong angle and capsized. Of the six people on board, Jeremy and another child survived, but the four adults—including the guide—died. Without the help of some photographers downriver, none of them would have made it.

Jeremy was submerged for longer than his father in the bitter cold, yet he survived. And though his dad was a strong man and a great swimmer, he died. His head hit a rock, and they thought the impact killed him. But then the autopsy revealed a reality more horrible to Jeremy than his worst fear. The blow wasn't fatal. His father drowned.

CHAPTER 1

The ringing phone jarred Jeremy out of a deep sleep. "Yes." It was more a groan than a question.

"Sorry to disturb you, Dr. Cramer," the head nurse said.

"What is it, Dev?"

"We need you in the ER."

He sat up and turned on the call-room light. "What's up?"

"Bus crash."

He sighed. "Be right there."

Jeremy hung up and looked at the clock. It was 10:08 p.m. Only one hour of sleep in the past day. *This residency is killing me*, he thought.

With a couple of gulps, he drained the half-cup of cold coffee on the nightstand and tossed the Styrofoam in the trash on his way out the door. Shoving a stick of gum into his mouth to mask the nasty taste, he exited the room and jogged down the hall to the ER. As he went, he ran his fingers through tangled brown hair and retied the drawstring that passed for a belt on his scrubs.

Devin Garrigues stood waiting at her station. A tall, slender black woman from Antigua or Aruba—Jeremy could never remember which—she was at least ten years his senior.

"What's the story?" he asked.

She pointed up. When he drew closer, she said, "Helo's due in a minute or so." They strode toward the roof elevators and Devin explained, "Bus in the lake near Fossil Bends."

Jeremy felt a cold surge. "Submersions?"

Devin nodded and entered the code to call the elevator. "Seven adults, nine kids."

"All fourteen coming *here*?"

She shook her head. "No. And seven plus nine's sixteen—sorry, man." She spoke in the easy tones of an islander, even when she was in a hurry. "I let you sleep as long as I could." The door opened and they boarded. Devin lowered her voice. "We have two incoming—mother and daughter."

"Injuries?"

"Not sure. But they were under for five to ten minutes."

Jeremy whistled.

"Right—slim chance," she said. "Kid's about eleven. Mom's late thirties—one of the only two adults they haven't already pronounced dead. Dad died along with four other adults and four kids."

Jeremy's stomach tightened.

At 10:12, the stench of helicopter fuel came at them in wind pulses of cool June air that blew their hair back. A pilot and two EMTs threw open the doors. Leaving the mother to Devin by default, Jeremy instinctively raced toward the little girl. He knew something of the terror she'd just lived through, and he had to help her if he could.

One of the EMTs yelled over the roar of the engine, "Female child—pulse slow and thready, weak at sixty. Body temp down to ninety-six. Pupils fixed and dilated when we got there. Started CPR. The woman—lost pulse en route. We did external compressions most of the way here. Body temp down to ninety-five."

Not good, Jeremy thought. His patient was in a coma and unresponsive to light. Jeremy raced the little ashen-faced blonde into an ER room where three nurses stood ready to assist. He pulled the curtains and took over compressing the girl's chest while a nurse ventilated the child with the oxygen mask from the helicopter. Another nurse hooked the girl up to the EKG pads already in place.

"Cut her out of these clothes. Get some heat on her," Jeremy ordered. The damp smell evoked memories he had no intention of revisiting. He watched as a nurse with bandage scissors cut off the girl's wet pants and shirt. Then she replaced the helicopter blankets with heated ones.

Jeremy glanced up at the heart monitor. *Not a great rate,* he thought, *but there was a beat.* He looked at the wet-haired girl's pale face. Her round nose reminded him of Ravi—another memory he didn't want to think about. Jeremy bit his lip.

Someone pulled back the curtain, and Jeremy looked up to see the stethoscope-yoked, attending physician, Nate Barlow, a pediatric intensivist. Jeremy didn't know him well, but pediatrics wasn't Jeremy's specialty, so the sight of Barlow's face brought relief.

Jeremy filled Barlow in on the girl's status, and Barlow took charge. "I need a complete blood cell count and serum electrolytes. Let's get a pulse oximeter on this kid. Keep the blankets and warmed IV fluids coming. And we need an ET—*stat.*" He took over the chest compressions and watched as a nurse removed the helicopter's oxygen mask. Then he put a laryngoscope and inserted an endotracheal tube through the girl's mouth and down into the large airway to the lungs.

Jeremy shot a look at the clock—10:18 p.m. He slid a laryngoscope into the patient's mouth to view the vocal cords. The water on the patient's lungs made her cords frothy, so it was hard to see. After placing a tube into her windpipe, he slid it through the space between the cords. To the other end he hooked up an Ambu bag for manual breathing and gave it a couple of squeezes to make sure the lungs inflated. Then he took his stethoscope and listened. When he realized he'd intubated the girl's stomach, he cursed.

"Blowing up the stomach, Doctor?"

Jeremy couldn't tell if Barlow was impatient or amused. "Give me some suction," Jeremy said. He waited for the nurse to assist and took another look. It was much clearer this time, and the tube slid right in. He listened again, this time to the welcome sound of both lungs filling with air. "There. Got it."

"Good job," Barlow said.

Jeremy glanced over and, seeing that Barlow's smile was genuine, felt his confidence returning. He eyeballed the monitor. The girl's heart rate was improving. A nurse swiped an alcohol prep pad across a spot on the child's arm, and the sharp smell of alcohol replaced the soggy-clothing odor that permeated the room. The nurse stuck a vein and drew blood. Then she hooked the IV to the same needle. The pediatric urinary catheter revealed no blood in the urine—a good sign.

Jeremy checked the pulse oximeter clamped on the girl's chipped-polished fingernail. "We're at ninety-one now," he said, referring to the blood oxygen level. "Up from the low eighties." He glanced at her face. Was it wishful thinking, or was the color in her cheeks improving?

The girl stirred, and two of the nurses hurried to tie her arms with cloth bindings so she couldn't pull out her IV. When her temperature reached ninety-seven, Jeremy and Barlow exchanged smiles. The girl thrashed about, struggling without success to break free. She opened her green eyes. At 10:32, she made her first sound—a moan—and continued to struggle.

One of the nurses rested a hand on the girl's arm. The other nurse leaned down to speak in her ear. "It'll be all right, honey. You're doing fine. You're in the hospital. We'll take good care of you." The girl shivered. She looked around and her eyes grew so wide Jeremy could see the whites completely surrounding the irises. With her growing awareness of her surroundings, her fear increased. Jeremy recognized in her a terror he had once felt and would never forget.

"Can you understand me?" Barlow asked her. She gave him a timid nod. "You can't talk because of a tube in your throat that's helping you breathe. I'll bet you want it out." She nodded vigorously.

Barlow looked over at Jeremy. They would need to check her muscle strength first.

The moment Jeremy took her hand, his paternal instinct kicked in, and he had to will himself to stay focused on her medical need. "Squeeze hard for me," he said. She had a good grip. "Great job." When she relaxed, he didn't let go.

Barlow turned to the tech, who was wheeling in a portable X-ray machine. "We need to rule out neck injuries before we remove the ET tube." The tech shot a C-spine and rushed off to get the films developed.

Time, which had rushed by, now seemed to loiter as everyone waited for the tech. Jeremy's eyes wandered from the gray streaks in Barlow's otherwise brown hair to a stack of Q-Tips that had spilled on the floor in the rush. He walked over to pick them up and caught his reflection in the metal canister—his short hair, round face, tired brown eyes—and saw something in his own features that reminded him of his dad.

At the thought of his father, memories he'd tried to suppress flooded into his consciousness. Icy water. The sight of a head bobbing down the river. The fright of waking up alone in a hospital. He wondered if he could have prevented that accident. Forcing himself out of his reverie, he gazed down at the patient.

Eleven years old, alone, where no one knew her name, in a hospital without a father and probably without a mother or maybe without even anyone else in the world. He wanted desperately to protect her from the pain. Jeremy had lost both of his own parents—his mother died shortly before he married Angie. And his second-born—Ravi—had died too. Jeremy shuddered when he considered the future this girl would face. He knew only too well the sadness and grief—and especially the guilt—she would bear.

He leaned close to whisper. "Scary, isn't it?" She focused on his face and nodded slightly. "I'd be scared too," he said, "but you're going to be fine." He took her hand again.

The tech returned with the radiologist, who hung the pictures on a view box and switched on the light. "Neck looks fine," the radiologist told Barlow.

Barlow studied the X-rays for himself and then leaned toward the girl. "Can you lift your head off the pillow?" She let go of Jeremy and raised herself up. "Good."

Barlow looked in Jeremy's direction, signaling for him to take off the Ambu bag that was helping the girl breathe. Then Barlow spoke to her again. "Take a couple of good, deep breaths for me. Okay?" She complied. "Good. Another?" After she breathed again, she closed her eyes and seemed to drift off. Jeremy deflated the cuff and slid out the tube. "Another," Barlow insisted. She coughed. "Again, please." She took another breath, this time deeper, followed by more coughing.

"It hurts! Daddy, it hurts!" Jeremy realized she didn't know her father was dead, and the revelation sent a jolt through him like an electrical current. She lay with her eyes still closed, but the volume in her voice increased. "Daddy! Don't let go!"

Jeremy swallowed hard and looked away. When he did, he saw Devin poking her head through an opening in the curtain. "How's the mom?" he whispered.

Devin glanced at the girl then back at Jeremy. She pursed her lips, shook her head, and mouthed, "Gone."

Moments that change your life forever, Jeremy thought. It was one of those phrases the ER staff tossed around as they steadied themselves to break news to families. When you know your words will crush them, you feel no urge to rush. You rehearse—at least the more compassionate doctors do—selecting every phrase with care, preparing to break news and hearts gently.

The girl opened her eyes again and looked around. "It hurts," she whispered.

"Where?" Barlow asked.

Her gaze came to rest on Devin. "It hurts …"

"I know, sweetie," Devin said, stepping inside. She moved closer to the girl and rubbed her arm. Devin cocked her head and locked her deep-set eyes on the child. "We'll get you feeling better as fast as we can. What's your name, honey?"

"It hurts!"

"That's a funny name," Devin teased in a voice that bordered on baby talk. Jeremy admired how Devin, with her twenty years' experience, worked her charms on patients, drawing from a seemingly unlimited cache.

"What hurts?" Barlow asked. The girl didn't answer.

Devin stroked the small cheek with an index finger. "I have a little girl who's just about your size and she's very, very brave—just like you."

"Amy," the girl said.

"Your name's Amy?" Devin asked.

"Uh-huh. Amy Black."

Devin brushed tresses from the girl's cheek and looped them behind her ear. "How old are you, Amy?"

Amy coughed hard. "Ten and a half."

She's lucky to be alive, Jeremy thought. *Yet so unlucky.* Devin rested a hand on the girl's shoulder and Jeremy took her hand again. He could feel her trembling.

Devin soothed with her unique brand of vocal anesthesia. "We know you're hurting, so we'll give you some medicine to help that real soon, little missy. Where does it hurt? You can tell it all to Nurse Devin. What happened?"

"My leg." The girl let go and pointed to her right side. Jeremy pulled back the blanket to have a close look. A small patch of semi-dried blood covered the inside of her right leg. Amy spoke slowly. "I thought I was gonna die. I don't know how to swim. Not really." She coughed hard again.

"I'll bet that was *very* scary then." Devin's brown eyes exuded empathy.

Amy nodded. "The bus was sinking. Dad kicked out the window so me and Mom could get out."

"Were you in pain then?"

"When we crashed, something banged my leg. And then I drunk a ton of water. It tasted dis-*gusting!*"

The sweet smell of Betadine filled the room as a nurse cleaned the wound. The blood on the leg disappeared, revealing a laceration. Jeremy caught the attention of Barlow, who had been focusing on the girl's words, and pointed to the injury. Barlow nodded and told the tech, "I need an X-ray."

"I'm only up to intermediate in swimming," Amy continued. "I never had to keep my head up that long before." *Sometimes knowing how to swim doesn't help*, Jeremy thought. "How long were you under?" Devin asked.

"I dunno. Maybe three hours." The team members exchanged glances and suppressed smiles. "Dad got me and Mom out of the bus and up where we could try to breathe. He was helping us, but we got tired."

Jeremy felt a rush of heat. Suddenly he was short of breath. He turned his head away, trying to shake the image of his own father's struggle.

"Dad was under us," she continued. "He pushed me and Mom up above the water. But then he let go."

Then he let go. Jeremy wanted to step out and catch some air, but he was trapped.

"That must have been so scary," Devin said.

"Yeah, that was the scariest of all. But after that it was like—it got pretty ... kind of purple. And then ... I don't remember."

Jeremy glanced at the heart monitor once again. As Amy's heartbeat slowly returned to normal, so did his.

By MIDNIGHT JEREMY had treated five kids, and all of them looked as though they were going to make it. Neither of the adults survived. He recalled what he'd learned from experience and later in med school—that in cold-water submersions, kids fared better than adults. Far better. Adults could make it only a couple of minutes, tops. But kids? They could survive after more than ten minutes under the surface if the water was cold. He wondered why. Textbooks attributed it to the resiliency of youth, but he wondered—as he had many times since med school—what factors actually made youngsters more resilient.

On his way to the morgue, Jeremy stopped by Devin's station. "How's Amy?" he asked.

Devin looked up, concern lining her dark forehead. "Physically she'll be okay. But …" She shook her head.

"I know what you mean," Jeremy said.

"Social services got us a counselor who specializes in pediatric trauma. They sent her to see Amy after the docs told her. Her mom's sister is on her way. Sad."

Jeremy couldn't imagine losing both parents at once. One at a time was bad enough. "Her leg's all right, then?"

"A little banged up, but no breaks. She may be asleep now with the help of some Stadol."

"What room's she in?"

"Room 703."

Jeremy made a mental note and leaned on the counter. "What do we know about the rest of the victims?"

"Not much. But they transported all the bodies here for autopsy. Morgue has its hands full."

Typical for a research hospital, Jeremy thought. "Ward X" always filled up when multiple-death accidents occurred. The demand for autopsies rose, especially if some of the victims donated their bodies to science.

"Listen, I'll be down in the morgue if you need me."

Devin's eyes widened. "Why down there?"

"I want to ask the coroner pathologist for samples on all the victims."

"Samples?"

Jeremy hesitated, but saw no harm in telling Devin. "Blood. Spinal fluid. Urine. And I want them marked for cause of death—which ones from trauma, which drowned." Jeremy had a hunch that some chemical factor or something genetic or some physiological reason accounted for why kids handled submersions better.

Devin stared at him. "What're you looking for now?"

"Just something I'm curious about. But I'm tired and not thinking straight, so it may be harebrained."

"C'mon, tell me, man."

He shook his head. "I don't want to risk you mocking me tomorrow when I wake up and it makes no sense."

"You mean the part where I say, 'Hey, brain-dead flatliner, you can't even add! What were you thinking?'"

"Right."

Devin shot him a wicked smile. "You do have a point."

Jeremy went to the elevator banks and reached out for the Down button, but he changed his mind and pressed Up. When the doors opened, he got on and punched 7. All the way to Room 703 he resisted the urge to turn back. He handled patient care just fine when it came to ordering blood work and diagnosing diseases, but when it came to actually caring, to empathy, he usually left that to the patients' families. Or to nurses like Devin. He rarely made casual visits, but tonight he felt compelled. He figured he'd find Amy asleep, but he had to check on her. Reaching her room, he gave the door a tap.

"Yes?" The voice of a grown woman came from the other side.

He cracked the door wide enough to look in. Amy lay staring out the window, as if to disconnect herself from the woman whom Jeremy recognized as a member of the hospital's psychiatric staff. She was patting Amy's arm.

Jeremy couldn't blame Amy. He wouldn't have wanted to be with a stranger either. But then he reminded himself that he was a stranger too. A moment of insecurity held him back until Amy gave him a slight smile and said, "Hi." He hadn't been sure she would recognize him from the ER—she'd been so out of it—but she seemed to know who he was.

"Okay if I come in?" he asked.

"Uh-huh," Amy said. Her eyes followed him as he came over to the side of her bed and stood with his hands folded.

The counselor gestured toward the chart, but Jeremy shook his head. "I'm just here to tell Amy how sorry I am." The woman nodded, got up, and slipped outside.

Amy blew her nose and wiped her eyes. "Did you hear my mom and dad are …?"

Jeremy sat on the side of the bed, remembering how that felt. "Yeah," he said. "I heard. There's nothing I can do, but I wanted to tell you I'm sorry." The silence felt awkward. "My dad drowned too when I was about your age."

Jeremy reached for her hand, but Amy grabbed him and clung to him wailing. He patted her back as she cried and cried, digging her nails into his arms. He wrapped her in a hug as he often did with his own kids, and though she got snot all over the front of his scrubs, he didn't care.

She choked out, "It's not true!"

Jeremy knew she would spend her life thinking of what she might have done to save her parents, and he wished he could help her.

"I know it's awful, sweetie," he said.

"Will you …?" She asked something, but it was too garbled for him to understand.

He leaned back so he could see her thin lips as she spoke. "What?"

"Will you stay until Aunt Julie gets here?" Her wide eyes pleaded.

"Certainly," he said. He squeezed her hand. It could be hours and he was already running on one hour of sleep, but how could he say no?

Amy leaned against him again. "I want my daddy," she said through muffled sobs. *I know what you mean,* he thought.

Her sobbing tapered off followed by short bursts of sporadic sighs. Eventually she lay back down. When he saw that her eyes were more shut than open, he slid over to the phone and pressed the morgue's number. He asked them to start collecting samples immediately.

Within the hour Amy's aunt showed up. Jeremy expressed his condolences, briefed her, and excused himself. Then he slipped out of the room and headed straight for the morgue.

CHAPTER 2

The following morning, shortly after Jeremy arrived home, he stood making an omelet when Angie approached the back door of their suburban Denver ranch house. She had four-month-old Ainsley strapped to her front and a bag of groceries in her arms. Seeing Angie through the window wearing capri pants and one of his T-shirts, Jeremy thought she looked great, though he knew she was still self-conscious about her postbaby figure. Her new short cut with highlights in her already blonde hair had grown on him. Now he liked it better than the way she used to wear it.

He opened the door, took the bag from her, and gave her a peck on the lips. "Hi, baby," he said. He set the bag on the counter, put the milk in the refrigerator, and returned to the omelet he was making. "What's up?"

"I have a writing deadline this week, so Mom's coming to help. But don't worry—we'll be quiet." She unstrapped Ainsley and fastened her into the infant seat on the table. Then Angie leaned over his shoulder and looked into the pan. "Smells great."

"I'm making some for you, too," he told her.

"Thanks. I probably shouldn't eat any, but …" She put away the rest of the groceries. Then she reached in the refrigerator for a baby-food jar and plopped down to feed Ainsley some strained spinach.

Jeremy placed an omelet in front of Angie and set his own down next to hers.

She savored several bites with closed eyes and then looked at him. "How was work?"

"Way too much excitement. Way."

"What happened?"

He took another bite and swallowed to delay answering. "Bunch of people drowned." He looked away to avoid the sympathetic look he knew would follow. He was glad when she remained silent and didn't touch him. He shoved another forkful of egg into his mouth and got up. "Gonna catch some z's now," he said. He put his unfinished omelet in the fridge. "Wake me in about seven hours, okay?"

JEREMY USUALLY STAYED home on his day off, but an eagerness to get started drove him. He took the skywalk from the doctors' garage to the hospital and caught the elevator to the basement. Winding down the corridors past the morgue and central supply, his quick footsteps echoed. Once in the research wing, he reached the door to the laboratory—where he spent most of his time—and pressed the numbers of the security code. They corresponded to the month and day of his anniversary followed by the star key. Though December was six months away, the code reminded him that Angie's twenty-ninth birthday was coming up in July. He made a mental note to take her someplace nice.

When he pulled open the heavy door, he inhaled a draft of the anesthetic agent. Most people disliked the smell, but to Jeremy it was the aroma of work he loved. The lab was a large room with cement walls and tile floors. Tables and equipment were organized for optimum traffic flow, and refrigerators lined hallways going off the main room. Operating lights hung from the ceiling in the center, and a draped operating microscope sat on a small table nearby. Three researchers bent over smaller microscopes, seemingly oblivious to his entry.

Jeremy donned his lab coat and pulled from the refrigerator a tray full of the victims' urine and blood samples. He separated them according to children and adult, living and dead. He was still waiting for the rest of the spinal fluid samples, but he could at least get started.

He sat and outlined on a legal pad the steps he would have to take to narrow the options. What, if anything, did the survivors have that those who died lacked?

He ordered complete blood counts—CBCs—on all the samples, along with a differential. The differential indicated the various kinds of white blood cells, including the average infection fighters—the leukocytes. In addition he wanted to know more about what interested him most as a specialist in infectious disease—the lymphocytes. Of particular interest to him was how these nearly colorless cells functioned in T cells, which played a role in cellular immunity.

Since immunology was his forte, the easiest starting point would be to screen for bacteria and viruses. If that turned up nothing, he could move to adding pulmonary research, but for now he would focus on the white blood cells and explore the role short peptides played.

Some peptides caused illness; some didn't. No one knew yet why most of the body's T cells flunked out of "illness-recognition school" right after birth. Jeremy hoped he might someday find answers to this and other questions if he doggedly pursued the questions. He wondered if the way the body reacted to drowning was more similar to how it handled illness than researchers had explored. He wrote pages of questions, possible answers, and the research steps necessary to eliminate possibilities.

When he heard the research assistants returning from a break, he looked up at the clock and realized his work had consumed several hours. He called the lab assistants over and laid out what he needed from each—one would set up the microscopes; another would prepare petri dishes; the other would do some preliminary paperwork. Once he dispatched them to their various tasks, Jeremy headed off to the morgue to see if he could expedite the processing of spinal fluid samples. All the way there he considered the ramifications if his hypothesis turned out to be right. What if …? Maybe one day he could find a way to improve survival rates for adult submersion victims—for people like his dad.

FOR THE NEXT two weeks Jeremy spent every free minute in the lab. One morning as he peered into his microscope, Devin phoned, "I have a shivering patient up here in screamin' head pain."

"Be right there." Suspecting meningitis, Jeremy rushed upstairs. He hated to stop what he was doing—he was finally getting somewhere—but meningitis was a true medical emergency that could leave a patient blind, brain damaged, or even dead.

Devin met him in the hall with the chart, which he scanned. Then she led him into the examination room. There lay a slender, frail-looking young man curled into a ball with his chin vibrating so hard his teeth chattered. He let out a moan when his squinting eyes met Jeremy's.

Devin slid a thermometer in the patient's ear and waited for it to beep. She read the numbers to Jeremy. "A hundred four, point eight."

Jeremy skipped the introductions, knowing the patient was probably in too much pain for formalities. "Try to move your neck for me," he said gently. The man complied and cried out. "Definite meningeal signs and nuchal rigidity," Jeremy observed. He wanted to be sure Devin clued in on the infectious-disease risk, yet he didn't want to say "meningitis" in the patient's presence—not until he had more evidence. But the rigid neck supported his initial hunch. Jeremy leaned down and shined the ophthalmoscope in his eyes. Tears appeared, indicating discomfort. Jeremy turned to Devin. "We'll need some blood work, and start an IV—Ringer's lactate at 150 cc's per hour." She nodded and left the room.

Jeremy glanced again at the chart and got the patient's name and age: Jim Dennison, twenty-four. "Mr. Dennison, I know you're in a lot of pain and I'm sorry. We'll get you comfortable as soon as possible. But first we need your permission to run a bunch of tests, and we'll have to do a lumbar puncture. Do you know what that is?"

He moaned. "No."

"We need to check for an infection in your brain and spinal fluid. Then we'll identify the cause and start you on treatment. I'll need to insert a needle in your spine," Jeremy said.

The patient lay perfectly still, making no response. Jeremy resisted the impulse to pat his back, knowing the patient was probably in too much pain to appreciate the gesture.

Devin returned with another nurse—Jordan, a short, wide woman with a gap between her front teeth and a penchant for wearing deep-purple scrubs. While Jordan explained the consent forms and obtained the patient's signature, Devin drew blood, hooked up the IV, and prepared a lumbar-puncture tray for the spinal tap. Next, with Jeremy's help, Devin positioned the patient on his left side.

"Bring your knees to your chest," she said. She stood in front of him, her dark, strong hands guiding him to hug his legs so he was in the best position to open the spaces between the vertebrae in his spine. "Okay, a little more—all the way up to your chin." Jordan helped hold him in place. He moaned again.

"Doing great," Jeremy said. He stood on the side of the patient opposite Devin and offered an explanation. "First we need to wash your back. All you have to do is lie still—*very* still. I'll tell you everything we're doing."

The man mumbled, "Okay."

Devin opened a packet and set its contents on the chrome-plated instrument stand. Jeremy pulled on gloves and opened the package to remove a stick sponge. He dipped it in the solution that came with the kit and cleansed the patient's back.

Devin handed Jeremy a sterile drape—a plastic-covered paper with a hole in the center. Jeremy placed it over the patient's back and located the spot where the needle should enter. He pressed on it with his thumb. "You'll feel a little pressure," he said. "That's just my thumb finding the perfect place. Okay, I'm wiping off the soap and I'm going to numb the skin. You'll feel a little twinge. Now hold still—*very* still." The patient held his breath and so did Jeremy. One wrong move on his part—or the patient's—could damage the spinal cord.

Jeremy stuck him and injected the numbing agent. "First part done," Jeremy said. "We'll give that a moment to take effect. I need to numb it a bit deeper, but all you should feel is some pressure from my pushing. You okay so far?"

"My head … oh-h-h."

"We'll get you something for pain in just a minute. Now hold still." Jeremy held his breath again. He placed a large-bore needle on the right spot and stuck it in. Advancing the needle until he felt the *pop*, he knew he'd reached fluid. He removed the stylet, confident it would drip back. "Got it."

Jeremy took the reading. "Only slightly elevated," he said. He collected the fluid, taking plastic tubes from the tray and filling each one. "Jordan, record the pressure and the fluid clarity, please."

She walked over to the chart and picked up a pen.

Jeremy got a closing reading. "The same," he called out. He withdrew the needle and pressed on the site. "Okay, Mr. Dennison. You did great." Jeremy put a dressing on the patient's back and told Devin, "If you'll clean him up, I'll mark the tubes."

The nurses cleaned off the soap, secured the dressing with a Band-Aid, and helped the patient return to lying on his back. Devin got a needle ready and gave an injection for pain. She was steadying the cap to snap it back on for disposal when she dropped it. She leaned down to pick it up. Jeremy, whose back had been to her, turned to go. He took a step, but didn't see her.

"Watch out!" Jordan called out.

But it was too late—Jeremy stumbled. He recovered fast enough to keep the vials from falling, but he accidentally knocked against Devin. When he did, the needle she was holding stuck her in the index finger. Hard. They all froze.

Jordan took charge, "I'll finish up here. You two—go!"

Devin yanked the needle from her finger. Still holding the vials with one gloved hand, Jeremy grabbed her elbow with the other and ushered her outside. At first both were too stunned to speak. Her brown eyes looked wild as she stared at him.

"I'm so sorry!" Jeremy said.

"Meningitis!" she whispered.

Let's hope that's all, Jeremy thought.

CHAPTER 3

The hospital protocol for inadvertent needle contamination called for washing the wound copiously, culturing needle and fluid, and testing both the patient and Devin for a variety of diseases. The initial tests came back with the patient positive for meningitis, and to everyone's relief, Devin tested negative.

The next step was to repeat tests on both the patient and Devin at two weeks, again at two months, and finally at five months. That way they would know if the patient served as a carrier for disease before it showed up on initial tests. But the likelihood of Devin falling ill diminished significantly after the first "all clear."

The patient agreed to follow-up testing while confined to the hospital, but by the two-week mark, he didn't return to the clinic. Jeremy tried to track him down, only to learn that the man had left the state.

Still, at two weeks and later at the four-week mark, Devin was fine.

FOR THE NEXT few months Jeremy virtually lived in the lab. Though he knew he was gone from home too much, the research was progressing rapidly—with a possible announcement imminent—and the thrill of it drove him.

One Saturday the week before Christmas, Angie's eyes flashed when she saw him put his beeper into his scrubs' pocket. She jumped out of bed. "You're going to the lab—again?" Jeremy turned his back to her as he put on his shoes. She pleaded, "Please don't go! I was hoping we could take the kids to the mall today to get their picture made with Santa."

Jeremy still didn't answer her. He was trying to think of the best answer when a pillow hit him in the back of his neck. He spun around.

"Answer me!" She stood there with a hand planted firmly on her slender waist.

"What do you want me to say?"

"You're shutting me out again."

"It's just that I'm finally getting somewhere." *At least, I hope I am,* he told himself. The lonely look in her eyes added to the guilt he already felt.

"But when you get a break from the ER—which is rare—you always go back to the hospital now."

He knew he should at least apologize for neglecting her—them. He'd been lonely for her last night, but Angie was sound asleep by the time he got home. Now her hair was uncombed and yesterday's makeup smeared, but she still looked good to him.

"It's like—ever since that bus crash we've been replaced by your research."

That was why he pursued the MD/PhD—because he excelled at medical research. "The ER's not my favorite place. You know that. But the lab ..."

She sat on the bed staring at him as if she expected more.

"You know why I went into research," he said. He couldn't look at her anymore, so he fiddled with the drawstring on his scrub pants. "And I finally have a chance to do what I trained for."

"But it never used to be like this. I'm used to both of us parenting our kids, not doing it by myself. I thought we'd all be together today."

Jeremy forced himself to consider her words. She wanted him around, didn't she? Wasn't that good? If he were in her place, he'd be frustrated too. They'd been happy until Ravi died. After that Angie had been depressed. And now that he was gone all the time, he had to admit to himself it was easier to handle her sadness. "Hey, why don't you grab some burgers and bring the kids at lunchtime?" he asked.

Her expression softened, but then his beeper went off. Angie sighed heavily, then stood and stalked out of the room.

Jeremy looked down to see that somebody in ER needed him. He pulled his cell phone from his pocket and punched in the auto dial for the hospital. "Dr. Cramer here," he said. "Somebody paged me."

"Just a minute," a female voice told him, before putting him on hold.

"Thank you for calling back, Doctor." It was Devin. "I got some results we need to discuss."

Jeremy wondered why she was being so formal and why the urgency. "What kind of results?"

"Mine."

His mind swam with the possibilities of all the infectious diseases he'd treated—and a few he'd yet to encounter. "What did you find out?" he asked.

"I'd rather talk in person." Did he imagine it, or did her voice waver?

"I'm on my way to the lab. I'll stop by and see you first. Be there in fifteen."

The line went dead. He snapped the phone shut and put it in his pocket as he sat on the bed. Resting his elbows on his knees, he pressed his temples with his palms. Calling him on his day off—and needing to tell him in person—meant only one thing: bad news.

He wondered, *What does she have? Will she survive? Will I be legally liable? Will the hospital hold me accountable? Will I lose my license? Will everyone blame me for tripping over her?* He wanted to think positively, but when he tried out more optimistic scenarios, he didn't believe them.

His immediate concern, however, was Angie. He walked down the hall and found her changing Ainsley's diaper. Standing in the doorway, he struggled to find words but none came. She kept her back to him and sighed. "Go ahead," she said softly. "I know how important this is to you. It's just difficult for the rest of us, that's all."

"Can you bring the kids down later?" he asked. "Maybe we can have lunch?"

"I don't know. I'll have to think about it."

WHEN JEREMY GOT to the hospital, he found Devin at her desk. Seeing him, her worry lines disappeared and tears welled in her eyes. She stood to greet him. "Thanks for coming so fast."

Jeremy was glad that—whatever the news was—she didn't seem angry. But then, she wasn't the kind to get angry, even when wronged. He'd never heard her utter a critical word about another human being.

"C'mere," he said. He led the way to the doctor's lounge. Finding it full of people, he looked for a call room. The call rooms, where doctors caught snippets of sleep between cases, suggested more intimacy than he wanted. But he suspected this conversation would require absolute privacy. Finding an empty room, though it meant sitting on an unmade bed, he motioned for her to enter ahead of him. He gestured toward the crumpled sheets and sat next to her with several inches between them. He knew not to say anything, waiting until she was ready to talk.

She blew her nose and then drew a deep breath. "You know that meningitis patient ..."

He felt a sudden tightness in his throat. The room shrank around him.

"Well, I had my final blood work.... And I really didn't expect a problem. Especially because I feel fine."

"But ...?" He braced himself for what was coming and wished she wouldn't answer him. Everything would change.

"But I tested positive—for HIV."

HIV? The news hit him like buckshot through the brain. He wanted to let loose a string of expletives, but he held back. For some reason cursing around Devin felt ungentlemanly.

But how could she know she'd tested positive when he, the infectious-disease resident himself, didn't know? He reminded himself that they probably got the results this morning—his day off. His mind bounced between Devin's condition and the ramifications for his own responsibility.

Her voice wavered as she said, "You of all people know what this means. And I have a husband and girls at home ..."

Staring into the dark brown eyes of his friend, Jeremy blinked rapidly to keep his own from clouding over. He failed. He wanted to exude confidence. He knew he should say or do something kind, something reassuring, but comforting was her strength, not his. He reached over and touched her shoulder. "I'm so sorry."

"If only I hadn't dropped the cap."

"If only I hadn't tripped."

"That, too."

There it was. Her acknowledgment that he had some responsibility, the hint told him that in at least a small corner of her heart, she blamed him. "I'm sorry," he said again. "How's your husband taking it?"

"I haven't told him yet." When she looked at Jeremy, he saw deep worry lines on her forehead. "I needed to know something first."

"What's that?"

"Does the fact that I got HIV at the five-month mark—despite taking antivirals—mean I probably have the superstrain?"

"Not necessarily," he said, more confidently than he felt. "While it's rare, the risk is greater when it's a large-bore needle. Which it was ..."

Devin got up and pounded a fist against the wall. "Why, why, why?" Jeremy jerked back, stunned by the sudden outburst. Her teeth were clamped together. She erupted with sobs as she stood resting her forehead on her forearm. "Why?" she wailed.

Jeremy had no clue. Fate? God? Karma? He didn't have an answer. He pursed his lips and shook his head. But she wasn't looking at him anyway. She wasn't asking him.

Jeremy stood and laid a hand on her shoulder. He didn't know what else to do. He didn't want to just sit there, but this felt awkward.

"How could we both have been so careless?" Her voice broke as she asked the question. She shook her head. Settling down, she sat at the end of the bed, and he sat next to her. Several minutes passed with her weeping and him wishing he could think of something fitting to say. Nothing came to mind. He handed her a tissue from a box on the nightstand and mopped his own face with another.

"I don't blame you if you hate me," he whispered.

"It's not your fault. Not really." Her words sounded reassuring, but her tone was anything but.

Jeremy knew what she meant. It seemed to him that trying to assign fault in this situation was like trying to figure out which of two scissors blades did the cutting. But still—he was one of the blades.

She clamped her teeth together again. "Give me a little time, okay?" Devin said. "I'll be okay. God'll get me through. I just need some time."

Jeremy nodded.

"Starting tomorrow," she went on, "when the news will have leaked all over this place, we have to be the strongest of allies. You'll have to be the best doc you've ever been."

"So you don't want somebody different to handle your case?"

"Don't be ridiculous." She cast him a sideways glance. "That's the dumbest thing I've ever heard you say."

JEREMY DROVE HIS Saab around Denver for an hour before stopping at a park. When he left the hospital, the day had been overcast but unseasonably warm. Now, silver drops of rain formed beads like mercury on his windshield. He stared through them toward mountains hidden behind clouds and chided himself for his inability to come up with words to match the magnitude of Devin's horror. If only he hadn't tripped in the first place. If only she hadn't dropped the cap. And the patient hadn't been sick. If only they had been more careful. If only …

As streaks of rain slithered down the windshield, a lifetime of guilt washed over him. His responsibility for others' suffering stabbed at him with every tap that pelted against the glass. The death of his father. Ravi. His neglect of Angie. And now Devin.

Eventually he saw this was getting him nowhere. It was illogical to sit here feeling sorry for himself when he could try to do something about it in the lab. Maybe he couldn't bring back his dad, but he could do the next best thing—honor his father's legacy through his research. Maybe he could keep some other kid from a lifetime of blaming himself. And if Devin needed him to be the best doc he'd ever been, he would start now, not tomorrow.

He drove back to the hospital, and when he returned to the lab, he found Nate Barlow waiting for him. The pediatric doctor motioned with a coffee cup toward the office of Bonnie Dylan, head of research. "She said you'd probably show up soon."

"Been waiting long?" Jeremy asked him.

"Five minutes, max," Barlow said. The tall senior physician shoved his hand in a front hip pocket, suggesting to Jeremy that he was in no hurry. "I was going to give you three more minutes. I assumed you were serious when you said to stop by sometime so we could talk about your discovery."

"Possible discovery," Jeremy corrected. "And yes, sir, I was. No question."

Barlow shrugged. "I finished rounds and figured I'd have a look."

The image of Devin asking, "Why? Why? Why?" drifted through Jeremy's mind, but he forced it aside. He rolled up a stool and motioned for Barlow to do the same.

"You okay, man?" Barlow was tilting his head, sizing Jeremy up.

"Why? Do I look bad?" Jeremy asked, forcing a grin.

"That's not what I—"

"You know the Fossil Bends accident?" Jeremy asked. Barlow thought a minute, took a seat, and shook his head. Jeremy prompted him. "Bus in a lake? A bunch of drownings?"

Barlow squinted, but then the wrinkle lines disappeared. "Oh, right. A lot of kids."

"Uh-huh. A lot of kids *survived*. But no adults. And do you ever wonder why adults and kids submerged for the same amount of time end up with different outcomes?"

Barlow shrugged. He was looking into his coffee cup, swirling the remaining liquid. "The resiliency of youth, I suppose."

"Precisely. Textbook answer. But what about youth makes them so resilient?"

Barlow looked up and touched his lips with his index finger. He sat for a full half-minute and his blue eyes grew wide. "You think you might know of a specific factor? Something that gives a survival advantage?"

"Maybe." Jeremy pulled a drawer of vials from the refrigerator and pointed as he explained. "I've isolated something all the surviving kids had but none of the adults did. And with only one exception I also found it in greater quantities in the kids who survived than in the kids who didn't."

Barlow scooted closer, his eyes on the vials. "What is it? What have you isolated?"

"The lymphocytes were slightly elevated in all the survivors, but only one of the deceased."

Barlow lowered his voice and, with furrowed brows, echoed Jeremy. "Lymphocytes ...?"

"Yes," Jeremy said. "It might be a coincidence, since I'm working with such a small test group. I'm still not positive that it's significant, but when I subjected the results to further analysis, I found that the cells unique to the survivors were actually immature lymphocytes."

"Wow." Barlow's grin revealed a perfect smile. "So you think the immature immune system may have certain protective effects?"

Jeremy didn't want to overpromise, so he played it down. "I wish I *knew* what I think."

"Got any hunches?" Barlow asked, optimism in his eyes. "A favorite theory?"

Jeremy shut the drawer and rolled back on his chair. Sure, he wanted to avoid overpromising, but he also needed to justify Barlow's help. "It's puzzling. The substance seems related to T cells that we follow in HIV patients, though it's not exactly the same. It has a chemical marker we don't routinely test for."

"Fascinating. So where do I come in?" Barlow took a last gulp of coffee and tossed his cup into the trash.

Jeremy hesitated. "I need access to some patients—to children." Barlow raised an eyebrow. "Well, not the children *themselves*. Their labs. When you order tests, I need some extra blood. I know that'll mean parental consent, but I could sure use the samples." Jeremy studied Barlow's expression. He seemed interested, even fascinated. But whether he'd give the authorization necessary—that remained a mystery.

"Help me understand exactly how having more blood from my kids would help."

"Now that I've isolated the cells of interest," Jeremy said, "I can stimulate and grow them with a technique I borrowed from our adult stem-cell guys. But I need more cells. Lots more."

Barlow crossed his arms and stroked his clean-shaven chin. Then he gave Jeremy a sly smile. "You know, there's a much easier way to keep adults from drowning."

"Really?"

"Sure. Keep 'em out of the water."

Very funny, Jeremy thought, even though he grinned. He had a hunch the humor was a delay tactic.

Barlow grew serious. "Listen, I need a little time to think on it. I'll get back to you."

Jeremy hoped a "little time" meant hours not weeks.

<hr />

FOR THE REST of that day, Devin Garrigues fought vertigo from the shock of her test results. Every time she thought of her future, she had to grab on to something. She tried to pray, but she had no words. And the only Scripture that came to mind was "My God, my God, why hast thou forsaken me?" The clock on the institutional-green wall above her desk ticked off the minutes as they crawled by. She chose to stay at work rather than go home, where she feared the dizziness would overcome her.

She fought her way home through rush hour and endured dinner, picking at her macaroni and cheese, and forcing herself to interact with her girls. She was glad her husband, Terren, a commercial real estate agent, was dining with clients. One look from him during their meal and she would have lost it.

When she and Terren actually had sex following the needle mishap, they had used double condoms. He said he hated feeling gift-wrapped in a suit of armor, but it beat abstinence.

Devin had taken antiviral meds to ward off infection. *What a waste*, she thought. She lay staring at the textured ceiling above her bed. Everything around her felt surreal. Soft light emanated from an antique lamp illuminating the dark green master bedroom with its king-size bed, massive antique wardrobe, and marble-topped bed stand. "God, help me!" she prayed. "I need the words. How can I tell him? Help him!"

She lay waiting for him to get home. Finally she heard the garage door open and shut, then the door leading from garage to house. Her heart beat faster at the sound of his footsteps. At last he came into the bedroom. But before she could say anything, he entered the bathroom and shut the door.

A few long minutes later he slipped between the sheets and gave her a kiss. A retired Denver Bronco, Terren was a big man whom she met when she worked as a sports-therapy nurse.

She looked into the familiar brown eyes and clean-shaven face. How would she tell him? She ran her fingertips over the dense curly fuzz on the back of his head. "I got some results today." Her voice broke as she said it.

He studied her face and read her eyes. "What? What's wrong?"

She couldn't look at him. "HIV," she whispered.

He lay frozen. Then he cursed so loudly she feared the girls would hear. He flipped over and lay facedown next to her, cradling his forehead in his palms.

She felt compelled to fill the glacial silence. "A lot of people live long lives with HIV. I'm not planning on going anywhere anytime soon." She wiped a tear with the back of her hand.

Terren shifted to look at her, shaking the bed when he moved. He reached over and pulled her close. "I don't want to lose you." A moment later he added, "But I thought you said this almost never happens. That HIV was extremely unlikely."

Devin studied his dark eyes and inhaled his fear. "Apparently it's more likely if the needle is a large-bore—which it was."

Terren banged his fist against the mattress. "We shouldn't have been making love at all."

It sounded like an accusation. Devin cringed. She felt fragile and afraid—she was too weak to deal with this being her fault. She lay in silence wondering if her marriage would survive as long as she would. She flashed back to the lowest point in their twenty-year relationship and imagined him kissing that Broncos cheerleader she'd caught him with. When she felt the throb of her elevated pulse, she reminded herself that he'd apologized. And by God's grace she chose to forgive him again, as she had chosen to do every day for the past six years. But with this diagnosis, all her insecurities returned.

The couple's Shih Tzu, Champ, jumped up on the bed, reminding Devin that she'd forgotten to give him his after-dinner treat. She'd never done that before, but then she'd never had news like this. She shooed him away, and he skulked off with a whimper.

She lay wondering if she would survive. If not, would Terren remarry? Had she already given him HIV? Who would take care of the girls once she was gone? What if she and Terren both died? Would she trust God to take care of them? The same worries she'd pushed away since the accident forced their way into her consciousness once again, only with more force now that fear had become reality.

Terren reached out and interlocked her long, dark fingers with his. He pulled her close and held on tight. "I'll be hugging you all the time—count on it...."

She rested in his arms, grateful for his loving words.

"... but scared to do much more than that," he added.

Devin sighed. "We need to tell the girls."

"I could already have HIV," Terren said. Devin understood his focus on himself, but she had hoped he might think of her a little more. "So how long are we talking here?" he asked.

They'd already had "what-if" discussions several times. She pulled away and sat up. She wished somebody would comfort her the way she wanted to be comforted. "I have no idea. We've made a lot of progress, but there's still no cure—only meds that slow the progression. Yet even patients with the regular strain find the meds don't work half the time." She shifted to get comfortable, but no position felt right.

"Is it like chemotherapy? Will you lose your hair?"

Devin shook her head. "No. Antivirals just slow the virus—keep it from wreaking havoc on the immune system."

"You didn't get meningitis. You're strong. They'll work for you. I know they will. They have to." That was better. Not great, but better. "What's it going to cost?" Terren asked.

Devin sighed. Ever since she'd known him—since a sports injury ruined his football career—he'd worried about money. "Cost?" she asked. "For most patients—like buying a new car every year. For us—nothing. The hospital has good insurance, and worker's comp will surely cover me. Plus I have an infectious-disease team that cares."

He pulled himself up and rested on his elbow. "Nobody cares more than I do."

"That's nice to hear. Because I feel like you're angry with me."

"Angry, yes. But not at you. You know I love you ... and I'll be here for you."

It was true—he did love her. And he meant what he said. She knew he believed himself. But if she looked emaciated and wasn't meeting his needs, she also feared his love might have its limits.

BY LATE DECEMBER most Denver residents had grown weary of seeing overcast skies, shoveling the unusually heavy snow, and prying open frozen doors. But not Jeremy. He'd spent so little time outside between September and December that he hardly noticed the empty expanse of gray. Dreary days didn't bother him, but the darkness of December's short days did. In the dark the past had a stronger hold on him than the present. It was then that he thought of his parents. And Ravi. And lately of Devin, too.

Jeremy awoke from a night full of tormenting dreams to welcome a New Year's Eve day aglow with sunshine. He surveyed with delight the fresh blanket of snow that covered the backyard. He'd promised Angie on their anniversary that they'd spend the day together, so he planned to cook her favorite recipe for spicy butter chicken after the kids went to sleep.

Following a leisurely breakfast and a morning spent replacing lightbulbs and doing odd jobs, he settled onto the couch and picked up the remote. Rajak, his six-year-old son, ran up to him. He tugged at Jeremy's sleeve. "Please, Daddy, can't we have just a little snowball fight?" It was his fourth request.

Can't a guy just veg out and channel surf? Jeremy wondered. He sank deeply into the cushion. "C'mon, Jak, gimme a break. I never get to watch TV."

"But I *never* get to play with you, Daddy. Never, ever, ever!" Jak crawled into Jeremy's lap and stared eyeball-to-eyeball, his brown eyes pleading.

From behind Jak, Jeremy saw Angie shooting him what he termed the don't-suck-as-a-dad look. He was outnumbered, so he might as well do it. What chance did he stand of watching a show in peace?

"Okay, sport. We'll have a big snowball fight. You and me— against Mommy."

Angie pointed to their ten-month-old who was sitting in her high chair. "Uh, Mommy needs to keep an eye on Ainsley."

Jak hopped off Jeremy's lap, jumped up and down, up and down, and ran in circles like a puppy on amphetamines.

Jeremy looked at Jak. "Guess it's just us guys, buddy."

"Ainsley and I will come out," Angie said. "But I can't fight."

Before long Angie strapped Ainsley in a kangaroo pouch and the entire family wore down coats, bright hats, and scarves. They headed out of the house and into the sloping yard that backed up to one of Denver's many hills. Jak ran in circles again.

Angie seemed happier than she'd been lately. Sometimes Jeremy wondered if she was anemic—she seemed so pale and unenergetic. But today she seemed stronger. He wondered if his being home had something to do with that.

Within half an hour their footprints transformed seamless snowdrifts into trails lined with holes. Forts stashed with piles of snowballs stood like bookends at the yard's extremities.

Then the fight started. In full view of Jeremy, Angie helped Jak pack some snowballs with ice, laughing as she did so. Jeremy wanted to tackle her for that. "Thought you said you couldn't fight! No fair hiding behind a baby!" he chided. But when Angie turned her back, he ran as fast as he could and aimed a hard-packed snowball at her left buttock. It exploded at close range.

"Ow! You'll hurt Ainsley—and I'll have a bruise!" She seemed mad at first, but then she fought back with a vengeance, though the weight around her middle slowed her down. She seemed pleased with herself when she landed a spray of cold, wet snow squarely on the back of his neck. It dripped down inside his coat and made him squirm.

Just about the time Jeremy wanted to call it quits, Jak's pleading eyes again compelled him. So off they went, this time with the sled, for a few runs.

As they trudged uphill for one last joyride, panting and laughing like errant kids as they went, Jeremy heard Angie calling from the back door.

"I'll put Ainsley down and make some cocoa."

"Trade you places," Jeremy called back. "You take the sled, I'll make the cocoa?"

"Fat chance, Nanook." Angie laughed and disappeared inside.

Jeremy felt Jak's hand in his. Smiling down at his son, he rubbed the top of Jak's cap. They took off, panting and laughing as they climbed the hill. The effort made Jeremy's lungs burn. Jeremy called out, "Last one to the top stinks like rotten broccoli!"

Jak won.

The final sled run was their fastest yet. Father and son yelled all the way down, as if noise increased their speed. It felt like it did.

When Angie called them in, Jak put up a little fight until she announced, "Hot chocolate's getting cold!"

Inside, the warm air and hot beverages made noses run. Angie, Jeremy, and Jak sat on kitchen barstools watching marshmallows melt, savoring their steaming drinks.

"Hey, about tomorrow …" Angie said.

Jeremy could tell from her tone she had something specific in mind. "Tomorrow?"

"Remember? My parents? Coming for New Year's brunch?"

Jeremy wanted to groan. But the day had gone well, and he wanted to avoid ruining his night with Angie, so he held his tongue. They had so little time as a family—though Jeremy knew that was his doing, not hers. But just once he'd like to spend a holiday alone.

PORTIA BARLOW KNEW how to throw a dinner party, and tonight's New Year's party was no exception. If her husband's colleagues wanted to peg her as a trophy wife, she was happy to play the part: the house right out of *Architectural Digest*, the well-toned size-four body, the French manicure, the designer clothes, and the long hair—wavy and red this year. She loved having all the trappings of success, even if that success was someone else's. When she married Nate Barlow a year earlier, she had happily left behind her job at a salon to spend her days redecorating his home with its cathedral ceilings, stainless steel appliances, and outdoor Jacuzzi.

She glanced around her crowded living room, pleased at the jovial postdinner mood. And she felt proud to be Nate's wife. She'd worked hard to attract and catch the distinguished-looking doctor. He was not only generous and well respected, he was kind. And what she sometimes lacked in tact, he covered with his good humor. She had only one complaint: She rarely saw him.

The gray-eyed cardiac surgeon with a sardonic smile who sat next to Portia at dinner teased Nate. "Did you choose pediatrics because you didn't want to grow up—a Peter Pan complex, maybe?"

"Nothing wrong with a little childlike wonder, is there?" Barlow asked.

"But wearing Mickey Mouse ties to work? What kind of taste is *that*?"

"Hey, I like designer stuff as much as the next guy," Barlow said with a confidence that lacked any hint of defensiveness. "My designers just have names like Warner and Disney."

"Why'd you pick pediatrics, anyway?" The surgeon turned to Portia. "I mean—does he talk to you in baby talk?"

"Sometimes, Doctor." She followed the purr in her voice with a seductive wink.

"Oh, baby!"

"Uh-huh!"

"Ye-ow."

Portia was glad to deflect the conversation. If Nate shared his reason for choosing pediatrics, it would definitely kill the mood.

"New Year's Day tomorrow," Nate said. "The one holiday celebrated almost worldwide." He looked around at the multiethnic group of twenty, made up of colleagues and their significant others. "How do you celebrate?"

Portia watched her husband. Maybe she was the one who could get the guests seated boy-girl-boy-girl to keep it interesting, but it took Nate to put everyone at ease. She was just discovering that if medicine had a caste system, pediatricians were at the bottom. But he never let his colleagues' pride raise his blood pressure. Of course, if she had her way, they'd all talk religion and politics. Really argue. Liven things up a bit. But her husband preferred peace, and it was his party.

Around 11:30 the phone rang. She assumed it was the answering service. No one else phoned this late, but Nate wasn't on call. Portia walked over to glance at the ID, pleasantly conscious of the cardiologist eyeing her shape-hugging dress pants. Sure enough, it was the hospital calling. She excused herself and walked into her husband's spacious office, where she could hear someone speaking into the machine. She picked up.

"This is Dr. Zoan. Sorry to call so late." She recognized the voice of one of the pediatric residents.

"Got an emergency?" She shuffled through the stacks on the desk to find pen and paper.

"Not exactly."

She stopped and stood straight. "No?"

"It's just that Dr. Barlow asked me to call if we got a case like this, and I wasn't sure if I should wait. It's not urgent, but he'll probably want to know about it before he gets here tomorrow."

"Can he call you back in an hour or so?"

"That'd be great. No rush. Oh, and happy New Year, Mrs. Barlow."

When Portia returned to the party, her husband looked over at her. She shook her head and mouthed, "Later."

At midnight their guests greeted the new year with glasses raised and couples kissing. Soon after that, in twosomes and foursomes, they said their good-byes. The cardiologist, who came without his wife—as he often did at social occasions—mentioned to Portia that he'd spied her swimming at the club and would welcome a game of handball sometime. Twenty minutes after that, Portia bid their last guest good night, told her husband about the call, and said, "I'm going to bed."

"Be right there," he told her.

She did her nightly routine, slid pedicured toes between thousand-thread-count sheets, and waited. And waited. *What's keeping him?* she wondered. She got up, threw a silk robe over her teddy, and found

Nate in his office with the phone against his ear. She stood in the doorway and listened.

"Yeah, we got a case in tonight like you're wanting," he said. "Care to join me in the morning for rounds?"

"Seven. Sorry. I know that's early and it's late now, but ..."

"Hey, you can stop calling me 'sir.'

"Barlow's fine. Or even Nate—just not in front of the other residents.

"Great. See you then. Good night."

———※———

JEREMY STOOD ACROSS the bed from Angie, who stood covering her front with a red sateen sheet and staring at him. He could see she was still breathing fast, as she had been in his arms only moments earlier. Her face was flushed, both with passion and anger.

"You're *what* tomorrow? You told Barlow yes?" Her eyes were misty.

Jeremy didn't want to talk about tomorrow. He didn't want to think about tomorrow.

"You took vacation time. We have a brunch. My parents ..."

Behind her in the mirror with a gold-gilded frame, he saw the reflection of a bruise where his snowball hit her. He told himself to go easier next time. When he didn't say anything, she turned her back to him.

"Wait, honey." He stepped around the bed, bare feet sinking into the plush carpet, and drew her to him. He knew she'd understand if he explained how important this case was, but he didn't want to do that right now. "I'm sorry."

She was tense, but she yielded to his touch. He could feel her heartbeat.

"For the past six months it's always the same." She didn't look at him. "I want to support you—I really do. But you're gone. Always gone."

"I know, honey. I'll be back by ten." He kissed her neck and again tasted her fragrance. "Gone just a few hours—three max. I promise," he whispered. He moved to her forehead and then her nose. "I just need to be there for rounds." When she exhaled, he smelled again the champagne they'd shared. It occurred to him that for the past few months, the only time they made love was when she'd had something to drink first. "I'll come straight home."

She didn't answer, but she eased herself down, sitting on the bed. He reached over and turned off the light. "C'mon—don't be mad. Please."

He felt her relax. Only when he kissed her full on the mouth again did he taste the saltwater on her lips.

CHAPTER 4

At 7:00 a.m. on New Year's Day, Jeremy stood among a small group of bleary-eyed residents and med students meeting for daily rounds in a hall painted with cartoon characters outside the pediatric intensive care unit. Unlike them, Jeremy was eager as a husky in a dogsled race. One sample from the new patient might yield valuable information. Jeremy sipped strong black coffee as the chief pediatric resident, a squatty young man with a deep drawl said, "Is Barlow wearing a Tweety Bird tie?" Jeremy followed his eyes and spotted Barlow coming down the hall.

"No, dude, that's your hangover talking," one of the other residents mumbled.

As Barlow drew closer, he looked serious. "Make a joke about the tie and you get an appointment with a nice fridge in the basement."

Jeremy knew Barlow was deadpanning, and the residents were amused, but some of the med students didn't catch on. They nodded anyway.

Groupies, Jeremy thought.

"The thing is, a patient presented late last night with a thymoma." Barlow revealed a cosmetically perfected gleam when he smiled. "And the head nurse told me the little girl's favorite character is Tweety." Barlow looked around. "Where are the others?

One of the residents said, "Finishing breakfast. They'll be here in a sec."

"All right, then—quiz time. Dr. Chan, what's a thymoma?"

Calling med students "doctor" was part of hospital protocol. It kept patients from worrying about students "practicing" on them, and the students liked the honor. They got so little of it from the residents.

"A thymoma? Uh … it's a tumor of the thymus—sir," Chan answered. "Usually benign."

"Duh." One of the residents rolled his eyes.

"Correct, but not very technical," Barlow said. "Dr. Nguyen, can you tell us more?"

"A thymoma is a tumor of epithelial cells of the thymus."

"Right. And back to you, Dr. Chan—what's the thymus?"

"A small organ between the breastbone and the heart that's responsible for producing T cells—important in the maturing of white blood cells. When it's removed from adults, we see few effects because other parts of the immune system can handle the load. But without a thymus, a baby's immune system collapses and the child dies."

"Better. Good." Barlow nodded.

The stragglers arrived and apologized for the delay, so Barlow motioned to the group to follow. He led them to the room of the patient with the thymoma, but a nurse told him the girl was in X-ray getting a scan of the chest.

Barlow told the group they'd have to come back later. That meant Jeremy had to go with everyone on rounds, going from room to room checking on patients. He suppressed the urge to groan.

As was his custom, Barlow taught his eager learners as they walked. They sometimes entered patients' rooms with him and sometimes waited in the hall. When they saw a patient with severe asthma, they got a review course in respiratory physiology. They met a patient with cystic fibrosis and learned about the latest medicines being used to treat it.

Jeremy wanted to get to the important stuff—the stuff that would help his research … the stuff big enough to risk upsetting Angie and to drag him out of a warm bed on New Year's.

Sandra Glahn

The group entered the room of a toddler with a fever of undetermined origin. Her parents, a young Latino couple, stood to greet
everyone. The husband removed a Tomateros team baseball cap and
shook everyone's hand.

Jeremy watched Barlow as he read the chart and then, speaking
Spanish, asked a series of questions. Jeremy didn't know Spanish, but
something was clearly amiss. He looked on as the conversation
between parents and doctor grew animated. The young mother's volume increased and she waved her hands around.

Back in the hall, Dr. Barlow raised his voice at Williams, a second-
year resident. "Am I to understand you arranged a repeat spinal tap on
that child?"

"Yessir," Williams said, his arms crossed and his tone defiant.

Jeremy pegged Williams long ago as a showboat inebriated with
the sense of his own significance. His arrogance was totally out of proportion to his competence.

"Even though the results of the original were sufficient for diagnosis
and treatment?" Barlow asked.

Williams shrugged. "The parents agreed to it."

Jeremy saw veins pop out on Barlow's neck.

"Of course they agreed, Williams," Barlow said. "The parents
would've agreed to let you shave their kid's head and dye it green if
you said she needed it. Do you even *speak* Spanish? How'd you get
informed consent, anyway? We've had this conversation before, and
you'd better be listening this time."

Everyone stood frozen. Jeremy had never seen Barlow so upset.

Barlow glared as he continued, "You may *not* treat patients like
your own personal lab rats or fodder for your experimentation and skill
development." The heating unit made the only sound. "Without solid justification for the procedure and permission from the consenting patient,
you have performed inexcusably. Be sure every procedure you recommend
will stand up to my scrutiny on rounds. I'm watching you, Doctor."

Williams opened his mouth, but Barlow held up a hand to silence him. "You have to have much more respect for patient well-being. The second spinal tap was more than unnecessary. It was exceptionally painful for that child. Not to mention risky!" Williams studied the floor. "I'm a pretty reasonable guy," Barlow continued, "but there's no way I'm tolerating this sort of crap. Don't think because this is a teaching institution you can play around with patients, especially my patients, as if they aren't human beings. We've all got our pet peeves, right? Mine is violating a patient's rights."

Williams mumbled, "Yessir."

Barlow looked over at Jeremy and shook his head as if to say what idiots rookies can be! He motioned for the group to proceed. Thick silence hung over them until they saw two more patients.

A nurse approached Barlow and told him the patient with the thymoma had returned. *Finally* Jeremy thought. They'd have to wait for another doctor to read the results, but at least they could see the patient.

The group proceeded to the room. Outside, Barlow signaled to everyone to move in close. "Some of you med students may not know that Dr. Cramer here is our third-year resident in infectious disease." When they looked at him, Jeremy nodded. Barlow continued, "He's doing some research on T cells that's of particular interest to me, especially as it may relate to our next patient."

Barlow looked around at the students. "Tell me, if you can, Dr. Chan—in accidents involving cold-water submersions, who is more likely to survive? Adults or children?"

Chan stood tall. "Given the same submersion times, the children have a much better chance of survival."

"Right." Barlow looked around. "Anyone want to tell me why?"

One of the med students offered an answer: "They're younger?"

"They *are* younger—correct," Dr. Barlow told him. "But can anyone tell me why their age is of benefit?" The students and residents whispered possibilities among themselves, but no one spoke up with a guess. "That's what Dr. Cramer's trying to help us find out," Barlow said. He crossed his arms. "He and I are about to see something unusual. Thymoma generally occurs only after the third decade—it's quite rare in children. We classify it according to four stages, but we'll wait until tomorrow to discuss those. Now then, any questions?"

A medical student asked, "The patient's presenting symptoms …?"

"Pain. Difficulty swallowing. Pressure in the chest," Dr. Barlow told him. He took off his expensive glasses and rubbed the bridge of his nose.

Jeremy hoped nobody would ask any more questions. Surely they wanted rounds to end as much as he did so they could get their scut work done and, if not on call, go home. *It's a holiday, people*, he thought.

Chan turned to Jeremy. "What's your hypothesis, Dr. Cramer?"

Jeremy determined to reveal nothing as elegantly as possible. "We're evaluating a number of hypotheses, trying to narrow the scope of the research."

Barlow put his glasses back on and looked around. Seeing no one else eager to voice questions, he addressed everyone again, "Perhaps later you all can meet our patient, but today we don't want to overwhelm her." He shot a hard glance at Williams. "As you can imagine, she and her parents are probably traumatized. Now, if you'll excuse us." Barlow looked at Jeremy and motioned with his head toward the door.

With Jeremy leading the way, the two doctors entered the patient's yellow room. Balloons filled every corner. A designer-label overnight bag and a top-of-the-line laptop on the table suggested to Jeremy that the family was well off.

A young girl with a smattering of freckles and brown shoulder-length hair—Jeremy guessed her age to be about seven—lay propped up in the massive hospital bed. Her parents sat across from each other at a bedside table eating breakfast from Styrofoam trays. Her father had a crew cut and he wore a polo shirt; her mother had on flared jeans and a denim jacket. They stood when the doctors entered and introduced themselves as the Bancrofts. Their daughter, they said, was Ninette.

Barlow told the parents to take their seats and turned to face Ninette. She zeroed in on his tie, her smile revealing a few gaps where she'd lost baby teeth. Without saying a word, she held a stuffed Tweety Bird doll out to Barlow.

Barlow shook Tweety's hand. With an exaggerated Cockney accent, he said, "Pleased to make your acquaintance. Nice bow tie, that." The girl's grin broadened and Jeremy marveled at how quickly Barlow captivated her.

Barlow glanced through the chart. Then he handed it over to Jeremy, who stood in the corner and studied the data.

After taking a tongue depressor from his pocket, Barlow looked into the girl's mouth. Then he withdrew it. "Is your throat sore?" he asked. She gave her head a vigorous shake. He tossed the depressor into the trash and felt her lymph nodes. "In any pain?" he asked.

"Only a little," she said. She put her palm on her chest.

Her mother said, "She's complained of chest pain on and off for a year, but I figured it was just part of growing up." The mother nibbled on her thumbnail while she kept her eyes on Ninette. "But then last night she had shortness of breath with it. Now I feel just terrible for not taking it more seriously."

Her father added, "She started coughing about a week ago. I wonder if that's significant." Jeremy glanced at him and noticed bags under his eyes.

Barlow listened to Ninette's lungs and felt her abdomen. When he finished, he turned to face the parents. "We'll have more information tomorrow. I know waiting's hard work. But we'll get answers as soon as we can." He leaned against the wall. "Right now, though, I'm sure you have more questions than we have answers."

"We have a thousand questions, Doctor," Mrs. Bancroft said. She looked tired and pale, but Jeremy figured with a little makeup and some rest, she was probably a pleasant-looking thirty-something woman. She pointed toward the door. "Could we, uh ... can we talk out there?"

"Sure," Barlow said. He waved to Ninette and pointed to the door with his thumb. "Time to go—I tawt I taw a puddy-tat." The little girl giggled and Barlow led the way out.

Finding the group waiting, Barlow asked them to move down the hall to allow for some privacy. The parents and doctors stood in a huddle. Barlow crossed his arms and lowered his head, listening with his full attention.

"They said Ninette has a tumor. Is she going to be okay?" Mrs. Bancroft asked, a worried expression on her face. "And ... what in the world is a thymus? How important is it?" Mr. Bancroft put an arm around his wife, and the corners of his mouth turned down in a helpless expression as they awaited an answer.

Barlow pointed to the knot on his tie. "The thymus is a flat, sort of pinkish-gray organ that sits about here, up high behind the breastbone. It extends into the lower neck behind the thyroid. That's why your daughter has had some discomfort in her neck."

"What does the thymus do?" Mrs. Bancroft asked.

"Aids in development of white blood cells, called lymphocytes—helps fight disease. And fighting disease is Dr. Cramer's forte." He extended a hand in Jeremy's direction.

That was Jeremy's cue to jump in. Conscious of the Bancrofts' anxiety, he spoke in his warmest voice. "People have two kinds of lymphocytes—both formed from cells in bone marrow. The T group travel to the thymus, where they're changed to T cells—or thymus-derived cells. T cells then go out to live in the blood, lymph nodes, and the spleen ..." Barlow shifted his weight and shot him a look. Jeremy knew his strength didn't lie in translating medicalese to everyday language, and Barlow's expression told him to stop sounding like an instructional video. "Uh ... bottom line: These defense cells protect us by destroying infections."

Barlow added, "And your daughter has a growth on her thymus, which we call a thymoma."

"Is it cancerous?" Mr. Bancroft wanted to know.

Barlow shook his head. "Hopefully not. We're waiting to find out."

"What if it is?" When Mr. Bancroft looked straight into Jeremy's eyes, he noticed how red they were. And he wondered if the forehead wrinkles were from age or worry.

"We have several options. One's to remove the thymus," Barlow said.

"And destroy her ability to fight disease?" Mr. Bancroft shuddered.

Barlow shook his head. "It's kind of a strange deal. It actually may not even have a noticeable effect. When we're born, the thymus weighs about half an ounce. But by age twelve it's doubled. Then the lymph nodes and spleen take over, and the thymus shrinks. By adulthood it's hard to tell it from the surrounding fatty tissue. Apparently adults don't even need a thymus—but we're getting ahead of ourselves."

Jeremy wanted to earn their trust, both so he could help them and so they'd let him work on the case. He could get their daughter's blood and urine samples, but what he really wanted—no, needed—was a bone marrow sample. He thought of how Barlow had barked at Williams, and getting a bone marrow sample was more painful for the patient than a spinal tap. But surely Barlow would want it, not just for research, but also to understand this odd tumor in such a young person. He hoped Barlow would agree.

AFTER THEY FINISHED rounds, Jeremy and Barlow grabbed some donuts in the doctors' lounge and sat at a table. They made small talk for a few minutes and then Jeremy got down to business. "How do you feel about getting a bone marrow sample from Ninette?" he asked.

Barlow traced the pattern in the carpet with the tip of his shoe. Finally he looked up. "Your question raises the whole patient autonomy issue for me." Barlow leaned forward on his elbows, revealing a Mickey Mouse watch. "Here's the thing—want to know why patients' rights are such a big deal to me?"

Jeremy just wanted an answer about the bone marrow so he could get home to Angie, but he knew better than to push. "Why's that?"

Barlow pressed his fingertips together. "Back in med school I did a rotation with a pediatric intensivist. I had no real interest in pediatrics—planned to specialize in reproductive endocrinology."

Jeremy was baffled. "Not even interested in pediatrics? How'd you make such a radical shift, then?"

"During the pediatric rotation I got pulled in on a case where they needed somebody to speak Spanish. And the case had some overlap with my interest in fertility."

"What happened?"

"Kids kept showing up violently ill after getting their DPT shots."

"Tainted immunizations?" Jeremy asked, wondering what that could possibly have to do with fertility.

Barlow gave him a jaded smile. "No, not the immunizations, though we thought so at first. But the strange thing—none of the kids died." He raised an eyebrow. "Only people around them died."

"Around them?"

"And all the kids had something in common—they were in-vitro babies conceived through a Massachusetts fertility clinic with ties to a doc in Mexico. Using frozen cord blood from some of the kids, our pediatrics guy figured out the virus was introduced before conception."

"No way!"

"Oh, yes. The Massachusetts doc got altered human eggs from a lab in Mexico City. The techs down there made stem-cell lines with viruses genetically engineered to attack the immune system. They'd take out the nucleus from the human eggs and graft the virus into the part of the cell that remained. When the eggs got cloned for a stem-cell line, the little cell bits were still there. They purposefully altered genetics—creating a genetic time bomb."

Jeremy whistled. His mind raced with all sorts of bad outcomes.

"And the DPT shot activated the virus."

Twisted as it was, Jeremy respected the technology. Brilliant.

"Once those kids got their shots, the virus spread by air like a cold," Barlow continued. "Kids would get immunized, get sick, and become very contagious. They could make their own antibodies, but everybody around them got the disease."

"But ... why? Why go to that much trouble?"

"What if they wanted to sell a vaccine that worked against the virus?" Barlow had the smug smile of someone who has solved a riddle. "Before the authorities closed the Mexico operation, the rogue researchers started to market a flu vaccine that precisely fit the renegade virus. Diabolical, eh?"

Jeremy slapped his forehead. "Why haven't I ever heard about this?"

"Oh-ho," Barlow leaned back and tapped his fingertips against each other again. "Our government caught wind of it after a couple hundred people died. Gave us a sobering gag order to avoid panic. NIH blamed the deaths on a bad strain of flu."

Jeremy shook his head and glanced down. When he did, he noticed the time—almost ten. But he had to secure permission to get the bone marrow. And now he wanted to know more about Barlow's story.

"That little development killed my desire to do fertility work," Barlow continued. "After that my heart was in pediatrics. People messing with patients' parts, even parts like eggs or sperm or even blood and urine ... well, I *react*."

"But why pediatrics? Why not protect grown-ups' parts?"

Barlow got up and threw away his used napkin. When he sat back down, it seemed to Jeremy that something in his mood had changed. Barlow looked at the wall as he answered, "Grown-ups can speak for themselves. But kids … they're helpless." He lowered his voice. "My first wife and I couldn't have kids, and I'm too old now."

Jeremy shook his head. "You're not too old."

"Yeah, I am—I'm fifty-four, and …" he turned to face Jeremy. "And as Portia frequently reminds me, I'm hardly ever home. No, my kids are here." He pointed in the general direction of the pediatric ward.

He said it firmly enough that Jeremy hesitated to argue. "But your wife—"

"Yeah, she's young enough—thirty-seven." He glanced off again. "But babies aren't really her thing."

Jeremy had heard something about Barlow's first wife leaving him, but he didn't know the specifics. A lot of the nurses—including some very attractive, single ones—talked about how handsome Barlow was, but he seemed oblivious.

Barlow placed both hands firmly on the table signaling that he was ready to change the subject. "Anyway, everything I told you—keep it under wraps. And don't get me wrong. I know you'd never do anything like that. But in case we end up working together a lot—and here lately it looks like we will—you need to know how essential informed consent and patient autonomy are for me. I wanted you to know why. Now, I told you I'd help you, and I will. But it needs to be balanced with accountability."

"Like a research grant?" Jeremy immediately kicked himself for making the suggestion. The money would be fabulous, but the application and approval processes would delay him.

Barlow shrugged and nodded. "I do think we need bone marrow on Ninette Bancroft soon. What she has is rare, and we need some answers. But if we're going to try out your theories with additional patients, I'm happy to oblige, as long as you have some oversight. And you'll also need some funding." He rubbed his temples. "And frankly, I'll sleep better if we have more accountability."

CHAPTER 5

Devin stood in front of the microwave in her bathrobe. She glanced at the clock and realized they'd all slept later than usual. But it was New Year's, so why not? Since everyone would be home, she figured the holiday offered the best chance she and Terren would have to tell the girls. But how?

Tory, her sixteen-year-old, sat at the kitchen table, her head buried behind the cereal box she was reading. As she slurped down cold cereal, she watched a parade on the countertop TV.

Why worry them? Devin asked herself. She stared out the window, weighing the pros and cons. Once the news was out, she reasoned, they couldn't "untell" it.

"'Scuse me, Mom." Tory was holding her half-filled bowl of milk. Devin moved aside, and Tory dumped the sugary liquid into the sink. Then she set the bowl down, not bothering to load it into the dishwasher. She wiped her mouth on the kitchen towel—something she'd been asked a thousand times to stop doing—and returned to the kitchen table.

Devin watched as her daughter plopped her slender frame onto a cushioned chair and opened a bottle of "Watermelon Sugar." The smell of nail polish filled the room.

Instantly, a wave of nausea washed over Devin, forcing her to grasp the counter. She leaned over the sink. Then the sound of footsteps bounding down the stairs made her straighten up. Kaylee, the Garrigues's third-grader, poked her face around the corner. She was petite for her age, and cornrows striped her head.

"Hey, Mom. Can I have a Pop-Tart?"

Devin shook her head.

"Why not?" Kaylee asked.

Devin told herself to inhale. The nausea had sucked away all her resolve. Who cared if her child had a toaster pastry?

"Cuz Mom said no that's why," Tory snapped at her little sister.

Kaylee wagged her head at Tory. "What? Are you Mom? You're not the boss of me."

"You're such a brat," Tory said.

"Cut it out, you two." Devin's voice sounded more breathy than normal.

Tory looked at her mother. Her eyes scanned from head to foot. "You okay, Mom? You look kind of bad."

Kaylee remained oblivious. Shoving her hands onto her hips, she said, "Mom, you told me Pop-Tarts are for special occasions, and today's a holiday."

The nausea subsided as suddenly as it hit. Devin ignored Tory's question and directed her words to Kaylee. "You're right—today's a holiday. But we'll eat lots of dessert today. So right now I want you to have something that's not sweet."

Kaylee exaggerated a sigh. "Like what?"

"Cheerios. Shredded Wheat. A banana," Devin offered. Kaylee muttered, turned around, and ran back upstairs. Tory cocked her head.

"What?" Devin asked.

"I asked if you're okay?"

"I'm fine." But the cramp twisting her intestines filled her with doubt. Devin hurried off.

Several minutes later she emerged from the bathroom and climbed the stairs. She found Terren in bed, still dozing. She cast off her robe and crawled in beside him. Resting her head on the pillowcase her mother embroidered two decades earlier, she closed her eyes.

She wondered which daughter should get the set of linens when the time came. She'd been thinking that way a lot. Tory would receive her mother's wedding ring; Kaylee would get the china—or maybe the girls should split it. If Terren remarried, which he probably would, Devin wanted to be sure the things from her own family stayed with the girls.

Terren stretched his legs, let out a little groan, and scratched his right ear. He exhaled, covering Devin in a warm blast. She altered her breathing to match his and lay looking at him.

Eventually Terren opened one eye, which met hers. Then he shut it again. "Hi, beautiful," he said. He reached over, his eyes still shut, and pulled her close. She tucked her head down, but he lifted her chin with his forefinger so their eyes met. "Feeling bad again?"

Her eyes avoided his gaze. "Yeah, but it's not that. We have to tell the girls. *Have* to."

Terren groaned, covering her again with his breath. "What's the rush?"

She pulled away. "They'll catch on that something's wrong—assuming they haven't already."

He sat up, propped a pillow against the headboard, and leaned back. After grasping the remote with his beefy hand, he turned on ESPN, but he left the volume muted. "How much should we tell them?"

Devin lay on her back and focused on a spot that stood out on the textured ceiling. She often focused there when she and Terren had difficult conversations. "I say I'm fine, but I'm not. Lately I've had G.I. symptoms. Maybe it's HIV-related; maybe it's stress. But I don't know how much longer I can pretend. They'll have to know at some point."

"What exactly do you think we should tell them?" he asked.

Devin had sought advice from a couple of the hospital's therapists, and she parroted back their recommendations: "I have a virus that makes it hard for my body to fight illnesses. So I'll probably be getting sick a lot."

Terren, now flipping through channels, said, "What do you expect the girls to do?"

Devin had recognized long ago the pointlessness of objecting to his channel flipping, even though it annoyed her. As long as he muted the sound, she had at least a fraction of his attention. "You mean how do I expect them to *help*? Or how do I expect them to *respond*?"

"Respond."

Devin imagined what she would have done as a young woman if her mother announced she had a serious illness, but Devin was much different from her girls. From her youth she always wanted to know medical details, but her daughters seemed more concerned with fashion and nail polish. "Tory will probably fall apart. Kaylee will only want to know whether I'll be okay."

Terren pressed a button and the picture on the TV vanished. "Why don't you let me handle it?" he offered. "I can take the girls out to lunch and break it to them."

Devin, moved by his rare gesture, scooted up and kissed his cheek. Fresh tears clouded her view. She appreciated his offer—but there was no way. When it came to relationships, Terren had the gentleness of an offensive tackle. "No, we need to tell them together, and we need to do it here at home."

He shrugged—his way of saying "suit yourself."

"I know today's a holiday," she continued. "So it isn't the ideal time, but we're going to have to tell them at—"

"Tell us what?" Tory asked. She stood in their bedroom doorway, cell phone in hand, dressed in a tight sweater and hip-huggers low enough to reveal a press-on tattoo. "Brad wants to know if I can go to a matinee with him at two."

"Tell him you'll call back," Terren told her.

"What? *Why?*" she argued. When Terren glared, she stomped off. "Oh, all right. *Fine!*"

In Devin's weakened state she found it difficult to tolerate her daughters' attitudes. She gritted her teeth and got up. In her walk-in closet she changed from her robe into a work shirt and jeans. When she emerged, Terren was sitting on the edge of the bed.

"Let's get this over with," Terren said. He ran his hand over his hair and rubbed his eyes again.

After he dressed and ate some cold cereal, they called the girls into the den. At first both daughters resisted gathering for a family meeting. Kaylee, decked out in fake nails and a dress-up wedding veil, sat engrossed in a commercial. Tory furiously pressed the buttons on her phone as she composed a text message.

Instead of taking their usual places—Terren commanding control of the recliner and Devin on the couch in the nearest seat—the grown-ups sat side-by-side on the sofa.

When Terren raised his voice, Tory slammed the phone shut and stuffed it in her pocket. Then she plopped down hard. Folding her arms, she asked, "What's so important that it couldn't wait for me to finish?" Devin ignored her, reminding herself that her daughter would probably be sorry soon enough. Terren bared his teeth, but Devin placed a calming hand on his knee.

"You're not pregnant are you, Mom?" Tory asked her.

Devin took a couple of deep, cleansing breaths before answering. "No, Tory Janine, I'm *not*."

"Kaylee!" Tory yelled. "We're *wait*-ing!"

"You don't have to yell. I'm right here." Kaylee reached for the remote and clicked off the TV.

Ever since Devin got her test results, she had imagined this scene as a tragic but loving moment with a close-knit family, not as an inconvenience to kids with other priorities. She looked up at Terren, whose jaw was snapped tight. *Lord, give me strength,* she prayed.

Terren saw her looking at him, and turned to address the girls. "Your mother has—er, *we* have—something important to tell you." He glanced back at Devin.

That's it? she wondered. She had expected a longer introduction— perhaps something kind, maybe an exhortation to treat her right. Apparently not. Now all eyes focused on her. She felt her heart pounding and drew a slow, deep breath. "I got a dis—uh, a virus—from an accidental needle stick at the hospital." The girls blinked. She took another breath. "I got a virus that makes it more difficult for my body to fight infection. That's why I haven't had much energy lately." *Or patience,* she wanted to add. Terren squeezed her hand.

She gazed at each of the girls, nestled as they were on the couch engulfed in oversized pillows. Kaylee seemed clueless. But Tory sat up straight, the color in her cheeks disappearing.

"Mom, you don't have … AIDS … do you?" Tory lowered her voice to a whisper when she said "AIDS," as if the very word might jinx her mom.

"AIDS?" Kaylee blurted out. "No, Tory! Mom's not *gay.*"

Devin said, "Not AIDS, but, yes, I do have HIV. And Kaylee, you don't have to—"

"Same thing." Tory looked up at the ceiling.

Terren started to come out of his seat, but Devin's hand restrained him. "Not exactly!" he said.

"Well, okay, not *technically,*" Tory conceded.

Devin looked at Terren for support. He was casting a glance at Kaylee in an apparent effort to signal Tory to tone it down, but the teen remained oblivious.

It was too late, anyway. Kaylee sat wide-eyed with her jaw agape. Devin wondered why she hadn't thought to tell the girls separately. What kind of lamebrain would break it to a teen and an elementary- aged child in the same conversation? She cleared her throat and added, "HIV is *not* AIDS. But it *is* the virus that causes AIDS. It can lead to

AIDS, but they're not the same thing. And lots of people who aren't gay have it."

"But I thought only gay people get AIDS," Kaylee said.

Devin wondered just how much Kaylee actually knew about being gay and where she'd learned it. "That's not actually true, sweetie. Anybody can get it, but—"

"So I might catch it from you?" Kaylee shrieked.

"Girls! How about if you let your mother talk and ask questions *after* she's finished?" Terren said.

Tory and Kaylee obeyed, signaling their compliance by settling back into the cushions.

Devin, her elbows on her knees, rested her cheeks in her palms. She struggled to form the right words—as if there were any. "We had this sick patient, and I got stuck by accident with his needle." Her words came out feeling clumsy, but she pressed on. "I took medicine to keep me from getting what he had, and for a while we thought it helped, but it turns out I got sick anyway. That rarely happens, but once in a while it does. What I have is called HIV, and it can lead to AIDS, but medicines can help people with HIV—lots of medicines. I've been taking some of them. And many people can take them for a long time and it will keep them from getting AIDS."

"Can we get it, too?" Kaylee asked.

"You can't get it from being around me or using my hairbrush." Devin searched for a way to lighten the weight that had fallen over them. Motherly instinct made her long for a way to shield her girls from the pain. "And you can't get it by letting me hug or kiss you."

Kaylee's eyes brightened, but Tory sat frozen.

"But it's better if we don't drink out of the same cup. And if I cut myself, I'll get my own Band-Aids, okay? The big risk for me right now is getting stuff like the flu easier than usual. My body will have a harder time fighting than yours would. So we all need to be extra careful to keep our hands washed, and if I'm sick a lot, we'll need you to pitch in more."

"Is the ivy thing curable?" Kaylee asked.

"There's no cure for HIV, but that's true of *any* virus. The flu's a virus. A cold's a virus, and there's no cure for a cold, but doctors have ways to control most viruses. So someone with HIV can stay healthy longer than in the past."

Kaylee rose, walked over to Devin, and crawled into her mother's lap. Too big to fit, she wrapped slender arms around her neck anyway and leaned her head on her mother's shoulder. "Will you be okay, Mommy?"

Tory burst into tears, muffled her sobs with her hands, and ran from the room.

Terren started to go after her, but halfway out of his seat, he stopped. He sat back down, wrapped an arm around Devin's shoulder, and pecked her cheek.

6

Seeing his in-laws' car in front of his house, Jeremy felt a mild sense of dread. "Family maintenance," he called their time together. His mother-in-law, Joan, had been a blonde for as long as Jeremy had known her. She had a wide, toothy smile, and she always wore what he considered gaudy rings. It bugged him that she tried to make her lips look bigger by coloring outside her natural lines, but she had a cheerful personality.

Being a little over six feet tall, Jeremy thought of Tom, his father-in-law, as short, but at five-eleven, he was actually taller than most men. He had brown hair, graying only around his sideburns, and the way he sometimes formed his O's reminded Jeremy he was originally from British Columbia.

Angie's parents were in their midfifties and in great shape. Tom was an architect who collected rare books and played tennis. Joan, a CPA, was a power-walker who served on the board of an environmental advocacy organization in her free time. Jeremy didn't dislike Angie's parents outright, but the characteristics that most annoyed him in his wife sometimes came in stereo when her parents showed up for a visit. He also had an illogical prejudice against anyone who wore a sweater like a cape tied about the neck, which they both did—frequently. Besides, today he just wanted to enjoy some rare time alone with his wife and kids.

Opening the door that led from garage to kitchen, he felt a burst of warm air accompanied by the scent of bacon, cinnamon, and fresh-baked bread. He expected a tongue-lashing for being late, so he cast his eyes to the floor. "Smells great in here," he said to Angie.

She wiped her hands on a towel and slid on an oven mitt. "Hurry and clean up, honey. We'll eat in about ten minutes." She sounded happy enough—which relieved Jeremy.

"You don't want me comfy in scrubs?" He gave her an affectionate pat.

"Don't want you smelling like the lab." She said it matter-of-factly, with no hint of annoyance.

"Sorry. Where're your parents?"

"In the den with Jak watching the Rose Parade."

Jeremy found Tom and Joan snuggled comfortably with Jak on the sectional couch that formed an L-shape in front of the large-screen TV. "Gramps, Grandma." He greeted them with nods.

Tom stood to shake his hand, and Jeremy motioned to his mother-in-law, holding Ainsley, to stay seated. Her hair was a shade lighter today.

Jak hugged his dad enthusiastically, and Jeremy gave Jak's hair a tussle. "Hey, sport." Jeremy stood there, arms folded. When no one else said anything, he fixed his attention on the TV screen. "Check out that Bart Simpson balloon." The adults looked but made no response.

"I like Batman better," Jak said. "You missed him."

Joan stole a peek at her watch, and Jeremy felt a surge of guilt for being late. "I, uh—let me go shower and change so we can eat. Excuse me."

He hurried to clean up and appeared fifteen minutes later wearing dress jeans, a rugby shirt, and Nikes. After taking his place at the head of the table, he shifted awkwardly, wondering if his in-laws would expect him to ask the blessing. Whenever the question of religion came up, he always answered that he was a Hindodist, since his mother was

Hindu and his father, Methodist. He was pretty sure he believed in a higher power, but he felt prayers were better offered in private. When Tom volunteered to do the honors, Jeremy exhaled a little sigh of relief.

Then, before anyone passed food, Tom pulled a package from under his chair and handed it to Angie. "Brought you a gift, sweetheart. Happy New Year."

"Just a little something for the hostess," her mother chimed in.

While some people preferred touch and others preferred words, Angie's love language was "gifts." Jeremy had learned long ago that even a magazine or a candy bar could be enough to make an average day great for her. He felt a pang of guilt that he hadn't brought her anything like that in months.

Angie grasped the brightly wrapped package and fondled its edges. "Definitely a book," she said. Jeremy noticed she wasn't keeping her nails as nicely as she had in the past, and he wondered why. She untied the silver string bow and tore through the wrapping.

"A first edition," her mother told her.

Angie turned to the title page and read aloud, "*The Man Born to Be King*, written for broadcast by Dorothy L. Sayers. Presented by the BBC December 1941 to October 1942."

Her father beamed.

Angie looked puzzled. "Dorothy L. Sayers? *The* Dorothy L.? The mystery writer?"

Her mother placed a hand on her husband's forearm. "Your father remembered how much you loved her stories—"

He took it from there. "She was also one of the first women to do a major broadcast series with the BBC—an audience of millions. And that book sold over a hundred thousand copies."

"Thanks, Dad." Angie thumbed through it. "I do love her Lord Peter Wimsey stuff. Didn't know she did nonfiction."

Jak tickled Ainsley, and the two of them giggled.

"Actually, her nonfiction's pretty good, Ange," her father told her, oblivious to anyone but his daughter. Angie thanked her parents and went around to give each a kiss.

Tom took some coffeecake and passed it. "How's the freelance business going?" he asked Angie.

"Okay." She passed Jeremy the bacon. "Now I'm helping a client write a book about New York City's Canyon of Heroes."

"What's that?" Joan asked.

"The ticker-tape parades. The Canyon is a section of Broadway lined with high-rise office buildings, making it easy to throw paper out the window. The first parade was spontaneous—at the Statue of Liberty dedication." She handed Jeremy the scrambled eggs. "Blizzards of confetti have fallen on more than two hundred motorcades. Right now I'm researching parade seventy-six," she said. Glancing at Jeremy she added, "For Nehru. 1949."

"India's first prime minister ..." Jeremy said, raising an eyebrow.

"Yeah. I *thought* that might interest you."

"What did you find out?" Jeremy asked, suddenly self-conscious about his heritage, which had once been a touchy subject with the in-laws.

"Nehru said the reception at City Hall overwhelmed him." Angie seemed oblivious to his tension. "He said the people along the street looked at him with friendly eyes and faces, and that meant more to him than the ceremony. His daughter, Indira, accompanied him on that trip."

"Too bad her guards had to go and assassinate her later," Jeremy said. Everyone fell silent. *Way to kill a conversation*, he told himself.

Back when Angie and Jeremy first started dating, Tom had asked if Jeremy's Indian mother was "Sioux, Apache—or what?" One of Tom's sisters told him, "When a woman marries a man from India, she marries his whole family—parents, siblings, uncles, aunts, and cousins." Tom had retorted with "Lucky for Jeremy we don't have the same custom, eh?" Something about that whole interchange still bothered Jeremy.

"... some important research," Joan said.

Jeremy realized Joan was asking a question. "Excuse me?"

"Angie says you're doing some important research." The look on her face told Jeremy she expected more than a "yes, ma'am" reply. Jeremy glanced at his wife, who sat staring at her plate. "She said that's why you had to go in this morning," Joan continued.

"Right. We had a little girl with a disease we usually see only in adults."

"Really? What kind of disease? Something contagious?" Joan looked back and forth between her two grandchildren.

Jeremy shook his head and pointed to the top of his breastbone. "A tumor."

"Something serious?" Tom asked.

"Could be. We don't know yet," Jeremy said. "If it's really bad, we'll probably have to remove her thymus."

"Is that like the thyroid?" Joan asked.

"No. Sounds similar and it's located nearby, but not the same. The thymus affects the immune system."

"What happens if you take it out?" Joan wanted to know.

"Maybe not much. By the time we reach adulthood, adults don't even need a thymus." *Adults don't even need a thymus.* Jeremy dropped his fork. Those were the very words he'd heard Barlow say to Ninette's parents. He leaned down to pick up the utensil.

The revelation stunned him. Yet it was so simple. What would happen if he found a way to keep the thymus from disappearing with age? Could a working thymus be the childhood advantage in drowning cases? He had to find out.

***

THE FOLLOWING MORNING after rounds, Jeremy called to schedule an appointment with his boss, Beatrice Jasper, the head of Infectious Disease. The secretary told him to show up at 9:45.

When the time came, he sat outside Jasper's door fidgeting with a paper clip. He pulled it into a straight line. Then he twisted it into an S. After that he shaped a J. All the while he considered the big *what if*—what if an adult had a working thymus? What might that do to survival rates? Sure, if given enough time underwater, everyone will drown, working thymus or not. But kids could survive five times as long as grown-ups. Was the thymus their advantage?

"Dr. Jasper will see you now." The secretary's words jarred him out of his thoughts. He tossed the metal into the trash and strode into Jasper's office. It smelled of fresh paint and new carpet.

Jasper, a stout, muscular woman in her early sixties with fuzzy shoulder-length gray hair, sat behind her desk. Her cheeks were red, as they nearly always were, which made Jeremy wonder if Jasper had rosacea or—more likely from the way her breath sometimes smelled—a drinking problem.

She waved Jeremy in and pointed. "Take a seat, son. What's on your mind?"

Jeremy lowered himself into the high-backed chair and grasped its arms. "Dr. Jasper, you're aware of the research I've got going …?"

She nodded. "I assumed we'd have this conversation sooner or later."

"You did?"

"I keep up with your lab reports. Interesting approach. You want my help getting a grant—right?"

Jeremy appreciated how direct she was. "I'd like to take the research to the next level. And Dr. Barlow is happy to cooperate, but he'd like us to have some accountability if we're going to start using his kids. And I want to do T-cell research using samples from his patients—with your okay, of course."

Jasper leaned forward and rested her weight on her elbows. "Yes, I've talked with Barlow."

The pediatrics chief certainly hadn't wasted any time. Jeremy hoped that indicated a degree of enthusiasm on Barlow's part. Jeremy waited for more, but Jasper seemed deep in thought. Finally he couldn't stand it. "So what do you think?"

"I think … good news and bad news." He had trouble reading her face, but he raised his eyebrows to coax her on. "The good news? There's lots of grant money available—*lots*."

"And the bad?" he asked.

"Everybody wants to emphasize AIDS research. But that's not where you want to go, is it?"

He felt torn between his responsibility to Devin and his drive to find answers to the submersion question. "I think AIDS research is important, but—to be honest—no. Not exactly. I was wanting to focus on the thymus … in relation to drowning victims."

Her smile was condescending. "Let me ask you something," she said. "When was the last time you saw celebrities rally to raise funds to raise survival rates for drowning victims?" He felt as naïve as a first-year medical student. She had a point. "Still, your request comes at a significant time—so significant, in fact, that we can probably get you what you want. It'll just depend on how married you are to your original idea."

Jeremy had an empty feeling in the pit of his stomach. "What do you mean?"

"To get the funding and get it fast, you need to shift your focus to AIDS research."

"I see." He resisted the urge to slump in his seat. "And what's the significance in the timing?"

Jasper eyed her pale, stubby fingernails. "Devin Garrigues," she said. "Her infection gives us the chance to do some cutting-edge research." Jeremy couldn't believe Jasper would talk about Devin's illness opportunistically. "And as you know, we've seen a few cases of the superstrain of AIDS. The fact that Ms. Garrigues had all those medications and still got HIV concerns me. And now she's getting worse, despite the antiretrovirals. Anyway, the lab's nearly set up to deal with virulent, deadly strains. It just makes *sense* for us to gear up to research this virus. The advantage—we know the exact hour you stuck Ms. Garrigues and she contracted HIV. So we have the luxury of precision."

You stuck Ms. Garrigues. That was cold. The words sent a shot of pain like a toothache. What if he walked out now and told them where they could stuff their grant money?

"She took the viral meds," Jasper continued. "But nothing touched it. We know we have the pure, unadulterated, active virus. So, Doctor, the five-hundred-thousand-dollar question is …"

"Yes?"

"… whether you're willing to flex. Shift your focus to AIDS research. And lest you have any question about where I stand, I strongly urge you to do so." Her expression told him not to bother trying to negotiate.

Jeremy had arrived feeling as though he was on the research super-highway. Now he felt like roadkill on a dirt road. Yet what choice did he have? He was Jasper's research assistant. Besides, he owed it to Devin.

"You look less than thrilled." Jasper's eyes met his, expecting an answer.

"I'm all for working to fight AIDS," Jeremy said. "That's just not where I saw this going. Though I suppose with any T-cell research there's overlap."

Dr. Jasper came around her desk and slapped Jeremy on the back. "Now you're talking, son. So let's go see the big cheese." Jasper walked to her door and signaled for Jeremy to follow.

"Now?" She wanted him to tell the chief of staff now? This was happening too fast. He wanted to come up with a good compromise, but that would require more time.

"Sure. Wait out here while I call him." She pointed to the chair outside her door. "Dr. Castillo's always looking for projects to get his name on. But we use his big name, too, to get funds, so it's win-win. You do know he'll be listed first on whatever you publish, right?"

"Yes, ma'am." Jeremy hated that when he got upset he was slower on his feet.

"As long as you keep that straight, he'll bite like a hungry fish on a hook. So when we get up there, try to show a little enthusiasm."

Jeremy sat outside Jasper's door, which she shut. He hoped Castillo wouldn't be available. Maybe he'd be in a meeting, and that would give Jeremy more time. But he was stuck—his responsibility for Devin's illness put him at a clear disadvantage. Didn't he owe it to her to try to find a cure for her disease? But that would detract from solving the question he'd pursued since he was ten—finding a way for drowning victims to survive. And he was finally getting close to an answer. He was sure of it!

In less than a minute Jasper came out and said, "Let's go."

Jeremy walked with her in stony silence down the corridor to the elevator. Jasper punched sixteen, and the elevator whisked them to the top of the hospital's main tower. When they arrived at Castillo's office, a platinum blonde told them Castillo was out but he would be right back. She led them into his office and told them to help themselves to the coffee bar. Jeremy noticed silver-laced trim on her jacket and speculated that she probably made more money than he did.

Neither Jeremy nor Jasper wanted coffee. So they stepped over to the chief of staff's picture window to gaze at the cityscape. Looking straight down they could see the snow-covered jogging track lined with leafless willows and beyond it the members-only golf course offered as part of the hospital's benefits plan.

"Not a shabby view," Jeremy said.

"I predict the entire wing will be named after Castillo within five years," Jasper said.

Jeremy stared at the trees without seeing them. Instead he saw his own reflection—his round face, dark, angry eyes, and set jaw—staring back. Was his frustration that obvious? He concentrated on veiling it. Much depended on this conversation, and if he blew it now, he'd only make it tougher for himself later. He hated being the pawn. Still, maybe he could work this to his benefit. If he gave them what they asked for, played their politics, and tried to focus his research where their goals overlapped, it might work.

He turned and surveyed the office. A stack of journals lay piled high on a mahogany desk. A bathroom door behind the desk was cracked open widely enough for Jeremy to see that the room had a marble floor.

Photos of the Andes and the chief's hometown in Tierra del Fuego, Argentina's "land of fire," lined the walls. An upbeat song with singers repeating *"machina elevadora"* drifted out from the computer speakers. Ceiling-high bookshelves on two walls held volumes ranging from *Gray's Anatomy* to *The Odyssey*. Tastefully arranged amidst the books were awards, plaques, and photos. One of the shelves reminded Jeremy of restaurants that "name-drop" by featuring photos of famous patrons. The shelf included shots of nearly every newscaster and politician within a thousand-mile radius, and a few from beyond. Most impressive to Jeremy was the photo of the well-dressed, dark-haired Castillo playing golf with the vice president of the United States. A plaque on the desk read, "If you can dream it, you can do it."

"Sorry to keep you waiting," Castillo said. He breezed past them and headed straight for his executive chair. "Have a seat. Please." He waved toward the leather chairs facing his desk.

Jeremy and Jasper did as instructed. It occurred to Jeremy that for a man of such short stature, Castillo wielded a lot of personal power.

Castillo looked first at Jasper. He nodded at her and gave Jeremy a quick visual inspection. "Dr. Cramer. Nice to see you again. I understand you want a grant for some AIDS research."

"Uh, yessir." Jeremy regretted sounding unenthusiastic.

Castillo rested his elbows on the desk and peered at Jeremy above his reading glasses. "But your research to date has been unrelated to AIDS, right?"

"Correct."

"So what's your angle?"

Jeremy cleared his throat and sat up straight. "I'm actually interested in T cells in both groups. So if we could get a research grant for T cells, we could look into prolonging cell life, cell resistance."

Castillo grinned and winked at Jasper, then looked back at Jeremy. "Dr. Jasper here tells me you're our golden boy in the research department. And Dr. Barlow has mentioned you to me too. How fast can you get me a proposal?" When Castillo folded his hands, a Patek Philippe wristwatch peeked out from under his starched shirt.

Jeremy and Jasper exchanged glances.

Before they had a chance to answer, Castillo spoke again, "Just get me the proposal. Fast. I may have to reallocate some existing research resources, but we'll get you what you need."

CHAPTER 7

Two days before Valentine's Day, Jeremy arrived home to find Angie dozing on the bed with the Sayers book covering her face. The digital clock read 11:12 p.m.

Jeremy leaned down and whispered, "Wake up, hon. Good news. I brought you a present." Angie reached up, removed the book from her face, and opened one eye. He waved two airline tickets at her.

Angie sat up and tilted her head to see them better. "Where to?"

"Jamaica."

She cocked her head. "Jamaica?"

"You know ... warm waters, bathing suits, no kids. Sun. Surfing. Swimming up to the bar. You. Me." He leaned down and planted an enthusiastic kiss on her mouth. "What could be better?"

Angie stammered. "B-b-but I—"

"We leave in two days and stay for five," he said.

She shook her head. "Two days? But the carpool ..." She splayed her fingers at her midsection. "And this body! I need to hit the gym."

"You look fine." He patted her side, signaling for her to scoot over so he could sit next to her. "Your parents will keep the kids."

"You already talked to them?"

"Uh-huh. Your mom was really nice about it—even said she'll take off work to help." He'd wanted to do something like this for a long time, and he'd finally pulled it off.

Angie's mouth opened and shut. "But I thought you didn't get more vacation time until spring."

"Jasper gave me time off before we gear up. The grant came through, Angie. We got everything we wanted—everything. Five hundred thousand big ones! We're already redesigning the lab, ordering new equipment, and posting signs about new precautions." Angie opened and shut her mouth again. Jeremy loved that he'd totally stunned her. "Jasper called me in. She had this grin on her face and she said, 'We got it!' And here's the part you'll especially like—she got my rotations changed. No more night call."

Angie blinked. But then she shook her head. "They'll own you 24-7. You'll work nights anyway, because you'll *want* to. Besides, you've always wanted to do research about … about your dad … drowning."

Jeremy clenched his teeth. Unbelievable. "We both know AIDS research isn't my first choice. But I do care about it—and even more now that I'm responsible for Devin's condition. But frankly, AIDS research looks like the only door—albeit a back door—to where I want to end up. I'm trying to work it so I can focus on both at the same time. I have to compromise with the system. I hate the system, but I'm trying to make everybody happy."

Angie groaned. "But for the past eight months, we've hardly seen you."

Jeremy adopted a monotone to keep from raising his voice. "That is why, Angie, I bought us tickets to Jamaica—time together."

"I appreciate it, honey. I really do, but …"

"But …?" Jeremy threw the tickets on the bed and stormed out to the living room. He folded his arms across his chest and slumped on the couch staring at the picture window that overlooked the backyard. After a few minutes Angie joined him.

At first he thought she was there to reconcile. But she just sat in the dark saying nothing. Finally Jeremy told her, "This is the only way

I can get to the research I really want to do. And you know I have to do research, Angie. That's who I am."

She crossed her legs and leaned forward. He could see her lips pressed together. "That's the problem, Jeremy. It's your *first* love. The lab is your mistress. You're such a smart guy, so how can you not see it? Sure, they give you time off—so what? You'll live down there. You already do. You haven't taken a day off since New Year's six weeks ago—and even then you went to work for a while."

Jeremy shook his head. "Pick a night for us and a night for the kids. I'll stay home two nights a week—a regular night you can count on. I mean it." He heaved a sigh. "Look. We have about ten days while they refit the lab. And what's the first thing I do? Buy tickets to Jamaica with my wife—the same wife who is upset because we've had no time together. And is she happy about it? No!"

Angie held her cheeks in her hands. "You have a demanding job— I get that. Your bosses' expectations are just *crazy*. But I'm not cut out to be a single mom. I feel like I'm losing it. And ... Jamaica ... maybe a trip would do me good. But I worry about Jak. I hate to leave him. He's been through a lot too, you know."

It was the subject they never talked about—what they'd all been through when Ravi died. There was so *much* they never talked about. Jeremy knew what she meant, and he knew she needed him to bring it up. But he didn't want to get into it. Things between them were volatile enough already.

JEREMY STOOD WATCHING the tide erode the sand from under his feet each time it went out. It gave him a dizzy feeling but he kept looking down. He'd spent the past hour walking along the shore alone, deep in thought, but now he stood on the beach in front of the hotel. And the ground beneath his feet was eroding.

He and Angie had basked in the sun, sipped piña coladas, and sailed on catamarans. Yet surrounded by so many limbo-dancing couples, Jeremy felt his and Angie's own unhappiness more acutely. The azure waters and calypso music accentuated his emptiness. The only time he didn't feel the "disconnect" was when their bus to Ocho Rios passed through areas where villagers had constructed their homes out of refrigerator boxes. He felt a keener connection with suffering families than with celebrating couples.

Where was the lighthearted girl he'd married? The girl who used to laugh all the time. Now nothing he did ever seemed to evoke a smile. He used to have a sense of humor. So did Angie. She said she missed the kids, but he felt sure she had something else on her mind.

He made his way back to the room, still lost in his thoughts as he slid his card key in the lock and went inside. Didn't she want him to be the best doctor and researcher he could be? Would she want him to be any less?

He stretched out on the bed and turned on the TV. After a few minutes flipping between Book TV and C-SPAN, he heard Angie's cardkey in the door. She was back from getting a massage.

"Feel better?" he asked. She shrugged but didn't look at him. Jeremy stared at the wall. A long silence ensued.

"What's wrong?" she finally asked.

He turned to see her standing by the bathroom door staring at him. "I could ask you the same question."

"Why don't you, then?" She crossed tanned arms.

"All right. What's wrong, Angie?"

She walked over and sat on the end of the bed. "I did a lot of thinking while I was getting my back pounded. I guess it boils down to this. You can't figure out why I'm in pain, and I can't figure out why you're not." Jeremy squinted at her, trying to understand. "It's been two years and you expect me to be over it."

So that's what all this is about? He had assumed getting pregnant with Ainsley had helped Angie put her grief behind her. "No. I don't expect you ever to get over it. I know *I'll* never get over it. But you also have to move on."

"Move on?" Angie's voice cracked. "How can you say that? How can you believe that? You must—because you love your work so much. I wonder how you can love *anything* that much. How can you *feel* anything? I'm still numb. I think I'll always be numb."

"You're upset because I threw myself into work? Got any better options?"

"That's just it! When *I* work, I can hardly drag myself into my office. I still can't forget long enough to concentrate. But you—you adore your job."

"Hardly drag yourself? You have plenty of energy."

She raised her voice. "How would you know, Jeremy? You're never there!"

He pulled back from the force of her words. "Do you know how often I call my mom to come watch the kids so I can lie buried under the covers for a few more hours? I have no friends left. And you—" she continued. "You're all excited about how great your research is going. It makes me wonder if you really loved him—if you really miss him." Her words struck him as cruel, but her tone wasn't.

"How can you wonder that? My own son!"

"But you never *talk* about him." She broke into shoulder-quaking sobs. He reached toward her, but she pulled away, wounding him with her rejection. She got up, walked into the bathroom, and returned, wiping her nose. Then she came back over to the bed, sat down, and spoke barely above a whisper, "You don't even mention Ravi's name. You never even seem to think about him. We had him for three months, but you act like he was never here."

Remembering how it felt to hold his dead child in his arms after the accident, he wiped a tear of his own. "Maybe we cope differently, Angie."

"Maybe. But the lab. That *lab!* How can you not hate that lab?" She packed venom in her words.

Jeremy's thoughts swirled in a vortex of confusion. "Why should I hate the lab?"

"If I'd been headed to my precious *lab*-or-a-tory when somebody hit my car and killed my kid, I'd *never* want to go back. And that day—your day off. You didn't even have to go!"

He mentally repeated her words. *You didn't even have to go.* So that was it—she thought the accident was his fault!

"I know it was an accident," she said, her voice much softer than it had been only seconds earlier. "But ..."

He wanted to yell, but determined to remain calm. "But what?"

Tears streamed down her face. "But he's gone, and we can't ... can't get him back."

It was hard to read her. Did she regret being so cruel? Did she feel better now that she'd lashed out? At least now he understood—her distance, her hatred for the lab. She blamed him. "But it was an *accident,* Angie."

She looked at the ceiling and heaved an exasperated sigh. "I know. I just said that."

"Then how can you blame me? How?"

"I have three options. Either everything's random, or God caused it, or you did."

"What about the truck driver who broke the law? Where does he come into this?" Jeremy loathed the desperation in his own voice.

"It's his fault most of all," she said, her eyes squinting as they met his. "But you ... *you* could have prevented the whole thing. If only ..."

He rolled over so his back was to her and processed her words as he would any new piece of evidence. Her conclusion was faulty—she was wrong to blame him. But she was seeking a clear cause-and-effect relationship for the circumstances that ended in Ravi's death. "Control ... so this is about control?" he asked, still facing the wall.

"Stop analyzing me!" she screamed.

Her words jarred him. "What do you want me to do, Angie? And if it's my fault, why do you even *stay* with me?"

"I've already lost one family member," she said, sobs choking her as she formed the words. "I'm not losing the rest."

He wanted to tell her she was losing him anyway, creating vast continents between them, but he kept his thoughts to himself.

As HE WATCHED the island below shrink to a dot and disappear during the flight home the next day, Jeremy wondered about his own understanding of the "whys." Why wasn't he afraid tragedy would strike again? Sure, he'd had moments of trepidation, especially when he strapped one of the kids into a car seat. But he knew the slim odds of the same tragedy striking twice, especially if he took steps to minimize the risk. Still, just in case God existed, sometimes he also prayed.

He glanced over at Angie. She had cried half the night, but she seemed gentler this morning—as if she felt better after getting it off her chest. Maybe it was better this way if their argument shifted some of the load to him so Angie didn't have to carry it alone.

Her eyes met his and her lips parted in that smile he loved but had seen so infrequently of late. He admired her tan skin framed in blonde hair. If she was as depressed as she'd said, and he'd missed it, what else had he missed? It was true that she hadn't been out with friends in longer than he could remember. What did her parents know? And what did they think of him? Had she told them how she felt? If so, how had they counseled her?

When the captain gave permission, Jeremy adjusted his seatback to a reclining position. "I have a question for you," he said. "Do you think your parents really like me?"

"Sure. They always said if I found someone I loved, they were happy as long as I was happy."

Precisely. But he wondered, *What if you're not happy?*

She continued, "And the fact that you're a doctor—a really smart doctor—doesn't hurt, either."

He wanted to say, "Thanks for that vote of affirmation," but he bit his lip.

"When I dropped Ainsley off before we came, my mom said maybe someday you'll take me vacationing in an exotic place like the Nile. Ha! I told her the closest we'll probably ever get to the Nile will be when you discover a cure for the *West* Nile virus. Dad tells his friends he's sure you're going to cure cancer or something. It's very endearing."

Jeremy felt patronized. "*Endearing?* You don't think I'm capable of making a research breakthrough?"

The couple across the aisle looked over at them, but Angie didn't seem to notice. She chose her words carefully. "I never said that. And that's certainly not what I meant. I just said you'd probably cure West Nile. It's just that your discovering something is not that important to me."

"Curing disease … not important?"

"That's not what I meant and you know it." She talked a little too loudly for Jeremy's comfort. "Quit spinning everything I say to turn it into an insult. I just meant it's more important to me to have a happy, healthy family than it is for you to be a superstar. That may sound self-ish, but you're not around much, so maybe my perspective is distorted. I want you to be home for Ainsley and Jak and me, like my dad was for us. You have no idea how great it is to have a wonderful father who's around—"

Jeremy's blood boiled. "That's where you're wrong," He whispered through clenched teeth. What did she know about his childhood? And especially about his father? "I do have an idea. Before Dad died, he grilled me on my homework, ran me to the library, rented educational videos." It occurred to Jeremy that he was quite different from the father he had enjoyed in his childhood. "He took me wherever he traveled, coached my swim team ..." That last one always got him. When Jeremy's voice broke, he couldn't go on.

Ever since the bus accident, when he'd been so obsessed with his research, he knew he'd hardly resembled his father. But staying insanely busy had helped, actually. He spent less energy mourning Ravi and more doing something that would ultimately prevent a lot of others from such pain.

Right after Ravi's funeral Angie had wanted them to go to grief counseling, but he couldn't ever work out the hours. She wouldn't go alone. Was she paying the price for his decision?

He stared at his lap, thinking that a plane was the absolute worst place to have such a conversation. When he looked over at Angie, her head was leaned back into the headrest, her eyes closed. Tears flowed once again, only this time they streaked freshly applied makeup.

"I'm sorry," she whispered. "I never should have said anything. I never should have even brought it up."

CHAPTER 8

For the rest of February and the entire month of March, Jeremy
kept his promise to Angie. Though he worked double shifts for
five days straight, every Tuesday night he stayed home with his family.
Then he'd work late on Wednesdays, sometimes even sleeping over in
a call room, and then Thursday evening he appeared again to take
Angie out somewhere inexpensive for dinner while her mom kept the
kids.

For the first three weeks they stuck to safe topics—subjects they
explored with civility, even if impersonally. They talked about Jak and
Ainsley and Angie's writing clients and even Jeremy's research. But
never their relationship. Yet around the first of April, Angie's iciness
began to thaw. Jeremy couldn't put his finger on exactly what had
changed, but he noticed that she started polishing her nails again. She
had more energy. And she seemed more patient with the kids—and
him.

After a particularly long but exhilarating stretch in the lab the first
weekend in April, Jeremy massaged the back of his neck. He glanced
up from his test-tubes to the clock—8:00 p.m. No wonder hunger
twisted his insides. He got up to buy some crackers from the vending
machine when he heard a knock. Answering the door, he found
Barlow standing there wearing a grin.

"Thought I might find you down here," Barlow said, stepping

into the room. "I stopped by for an update. Jasper told me you've had enough success to submit something to the journals, so I came by to see for myself."

"Great," Jeremy said. "Come here. Let me show you." He led Barlow over to a refrigerator and removed a tray with a human liver on it. He placed it on the counter and pointed to the organ. "Will you look at that?" Jeremy asked.

"Uh … you created a human liver?"

Jeremy laughed. "No, man. It's a *healthy*-looking liver. And you know what's amazing? It's from a patient with end-stage AIDS."

A warming smile lit Barlow's face. "No way."

"I kid you not," Jeremy said, folding his arms over his chest.

"But how?" Barlow stroked the stubble starting to appear on his chin.

"The T-factor cells seem to resist the AIDS virus by acting young. So they make it harder for the virus to thrive. It seems so simple now that I see it at work."

"Amazing." Barlow studied the organ. "But he died of AIDS anyway?"

"No. Suicide."

Barlow looked up at Jeremy and grimaced. "You sure insanity isn't a side effect?"

"No. Not sure of anything," Jeremy said. "But I can only jump one hurdle at a time."

ANGIE GRABBED HER gym bag off the passenger seat and slung it over her shoulder. Unfastening Ainsley, Angie inhaled the faint scent of baby powder and felt a twinge of sadness that her girl was growing up so fast. She hugged her daughter close and toted her through the double doors that opened to the health club's glass atrium.

Angie fumbled for her access card. Though she swam in college, after she got married she always said her idea of exercise was fighting the current when she drained the tub. But lately she had taken advantage of the posh fitness center's free membership for doctors and their spouses. She wasn't sure what had changed lately, but she felt more like getting up and out. And the club's free child care allowed her time to think uninterrupted about writing projects as she biked or swam.

Balancing Ainsley on her hip, Angie handed her card to a sandy-haired young man at the desk. While he checked her in, she looked through the windows to the pool area. She thought she recognized Portia Barlow looking depressingly fantastic in a black bikini. She was heading into the sauna. The man at the desk gave Angie a hand towel and told her to have a nice workout.

After she dropped Ainsley off at the kids' care center, Angie changed into her one-piece, worn Nike swimsuit and took the requisite preswim shower. She found the pool area empty except for an overweight man in the hot tub. Opening the sauna door, she looked for Portia, but didn't see her. She glanced into the steam room, but the hot billows of steam blinded her.

"Hey, Angie!" Portia's voice called out.

Angie blinked several times and took a step closer. "I *thought* I saw you here, Portia."

"You know Alex Combs, right?"

Angie could barely make out two forms sitting on a bench. "Not sure I do." She took one more step and a toned, gray-eyed man with chestnut hair and a high forehead came into view. He sat next to Portia in a scarlet Speedo. Angie hated Speedos.

"Sure you know him. Cardiologist? Offices up on five." The doctor stood and took Angie's hand, and she suddenly felt funny standing there in her boring, old bathing suit.

"Yes, I recognize you now. Sorry I don't always have the name with the face," Angie said, thinking he held her hand longer than necessary.

"No problem," he said.

She couldn't remember when she'd met him, but his fine face was hard to forget. She looked at Portia. "Just wanted to say hi."

"I've never seen you here," Portia said. "Come often?"

"I started a couple months ago," Angie said. "Nothing like a Jamaican beach to make you feel your baby fat." She immediately regretted drawing attention to her own figure.

"Nonsense. You look fab," Portia said with a laugh.

The doctor looked Angie over and let a provocative smile speak his agreement. "Good to see you again," he said.

Angie exchanged niceties, excused herself, and hopped into the pool. She grabbed a kickboard and did a couple of laps while she tried to put her finger on what made her feel creepy about the interchange. It wasn't just her prejudice against men in Speedos.

As she returned from her second lap, she wondered how the two of them could stay in the suffocating heat so long. Angie could never stand a steam room for more than sixty seconds. She heard giggling coming through the door. After another minute the doctor emerged crimson-faced with a towel wrapped around his waist. He gave Angie a little wave and departed quickly for the men's locker room.

About thirty seconds later Portia came out, shining from head to toe, and grabbed her towel off of a peg on the wall. She slung it around her neck. Steam emanated from her head and shoulders. She spotted Angie, put the towel back on the peg, and slipped into the adjacent lane. "Br-r-r!"

Angie swam over to her. "Bet it's cold after being in the heat."

"Freezing! I was going to swim with you, but it's too frigid. Think I'll go hit the bikes instead. Sorry."

"Hang on, I'll join you," Angie said. She pulled herself up the steps, dried off quickly, and followed Portia to the women's locker-room. They grabbed their bags from the lockers and headed for separate changing rooms.

Minutes later Portia emerged in a Spandex outfit that looked as though it had yet to see its first wash cycle. Angie felt plain once again in shorts and one of Jeremy's old T-shirts.

They headed upstairs and found a couple of bikes overlooking the atrium below. Angie started pedaling lightly, and the digital numbers on the bike flashed on. Scrolling through the preset routines, Angie asked, "How long do you usually go? Twenty-four? Thirty minutes?"

"Twenty-four's about all I'm up for today," Portia said. "I have a lunch appointment."

"Works for me." Angie punched the code and pedaled harder. It was easy enough to talk without growing breathless for the first few minutes.

"So how often do you work out?" Angie asked.

"Just about every day, but usually later, around lunchtime—when it's more crowded."

"I like midmorning," Angie said. "I practically have the pool to myself. Feel free to join me, though. I come up here only a few times a week."

"I'd love to. I've been playing handball at lunchtime for the past couple of months," Portia said. "But I could use some female company."

Angie didn't want to ask who the handball partner was. When she followed Portia's eyes to the now-dressed and departing Dr. Combs in the atrium below, Angie thought she had a pretty good idea.

THE FOLLOWING MORNING Jeremy dashed from the lab to his car and headed straight for Starbucks. In his euphoria he noticed details he often missed. Seeing tulips, poppies, and other beauties blooming, he hoped the last frost—still a month away—wouldn't kill them all.

The fragrance of coffee met him when he opened the door, and he stopped to appreciate the rich aroma. Then he approached the counter and ordered a Frappuccino.

When he arrived back at the hospital with it, he moved the drink from hand to hand to minimize the icy discomfort as he carried the cup from the parking garage to Admitting.

As he approached Devin, she looked up from her desk. Recognition flashed across her face. He held out the beverage, and a broad smile replaced her worry lines.

"What's this?" she asked.

"Your favorite drink."

"Vodka?" She wore a wicked smile. He knew Devin didn't drink. She took the cup and drew a long sip. "Ah-h, just the way I like it. On the rocks."

Jeremy pulled up a chair and sat across from her at the desk. After the accident, the hospital transferred Devin to an office job. Jeremy understood the need to minimize risk, but the ER team felt the loss acutely. Devin claimed she liked the new job, but Jeremy thought that said more about her than it did about the job.

"Thanks. So what's the occasion?" she asked.

"No occasion."

Her eyes twinkled. "Liar." She drew another long sip without taking her deep brown eyes off him.

"You know me too well," he said. "I just got your lab results. And you definitely don't have the nastiest virulent strain, which buys us more time."

"Us? Who's us?"

"The lab rats."

She sat up straighter. "You referring to yourself or your subjects?"

"Very funny."

"Actually, I assumed it wasn't the worst strain, since most of the time I feel pretty good. But you think maybe you're on to something?" The eagerness in her eyes communicated her dependence on him, her "infector," as her "curer," and it sent a stab of guilt through him.

"I don't want to get your hopes up, but yes. It's going better than expected. I'll let you read my journal article when I finish writing it all up, but I'm pretty optimistic."

"Journal article?" She sat up straight and her voice took on a new eagerness. "Sounds serious."

"Uh-huh. So take care to stay well as much as possible, okay?" Jeremy said. "Because I think soon we may have some new ammo for fighting HIV. T-factor seems to rejuvenate diseased organs."

"Maybe you can reverse the death sentence?" she asked.

"Again, I don't want to give you—or anybody else—false hope. But that's my goal. Definitely," Jeremy said.

"Well, hallelujah!"

LATE THAT NIGHT Jeremy sat at his computer, putting the finishing touches on his submission. He added an en-dash here, a research date there, and the piece was finished. On the required form accompanying the article, he included each participant's full name, careful to list Castillo first. It occurred to Jeremy that Castillo had never actually wandered down to the lab, but he *had* secured the money. Hadn't Jasper predicted Jeremy would have to share credit? He told himself he would mind less if Castillo actually *did* something.

Jeremy swallowed his pride. He could hear his father saying, "You can accomplish twice as much if you don't care who gets the credit." Still, he resented Castillo's infringement on his intellectual property.

Jeremy printed and reread the article one last time looking for stray typos. His mood improved as he read. The piece detailed how he had used a stem cell line to replicate "T-factor"—which he wrote as "$T*$."

He'd read literature from fertility clinics that reported how human embryos thrived in tissue taken from fallopian tubes during hysterectomies. Then he coaxed his own adult stem-cell line to reproduce in a similar human-tissue culture. Using human rather than animal tissue eliminated concerns about animal/human disease transmission.

How many times had the kaleidoscope of color, symmetry, and precision beneath his microscope captivated him during that stage? He propped his feet on the desk and leaned back as he thought of how easy it all seemed, this side of the effort.

He read with satisfaction the summary of how, using animal models to test for preclinical efficacy and toxicity, his team established cell integration and migration. The T* lines clearly repaired animal tissue and prolonged organ viability.

Advancing to human studies, the researchers started with freshly harvested kidneys. When cadaver studies proved promising, his team located AIDS patients in end-stage disease who volunteered for experimental therapies. And though they were near death at the time they started therapy, most of their volunteers had rallied. As Jeremy reread his own story, he felt glad for the progress, but not thrilled. The discovery he still longed to make eluded him—that of survivability in drownings.

Seeing the time, he checked his watch to make sure the clock on the wall was right. Only then did he notice the hollow feeling in his stomach. Seven hours had passed since the ham-and-cheese sandwich he'd inhaled at 6:00 p.m.

Jeremy wondered how cutting-edge his research would be by the time the article made it through the turtle-slow process of passing muster with review committees. As directed, he e-mailed a copy to Castillo, in hopes that the chief's publication contacts equaled his grant connections.

Part of Jeremy felt the research would garner immediate honors, but his self-conscious side told him he'd no doubt lost perspective. Movie producers probably all thought their films would win Oscars, too.

Jeremy applied the address sticker and slid the manuscript inside the envelope along with an electronic copy. He pushed away from the table and rubbed his neck.

At a time like this any other researcher would break out some champagne. But the lab was empty and he had no one with whom to celebrate. He wanted to call Angie, but he knew she would have fallen asleep hours earlier and a phone call this late would only alarm her.

He printed out an extra copy of the article for Devin and stuck it in the interoffice mail with a note: "Once in a while even a flatliner has an original idea. You are hereby officially invited to Jak's future high school graduation."

———※———

ANGIE PUT AINSLEY down for her nap and willed herself to go into her office. She logged on to the Internet and pulled up her "favorites" menu, picking up where she left off in her research. Her client's book on the ticker-tape parades was missing a June 1963 celebration—parade number 173—for Sir Sarvepalli Radhakrishnan. Angie had promised a quick turnaround, and the research was going well. What she found about the Oxford don who went on to become second president of India fascinated her. In researching him, she discovered he espoused a modern form of Hinduism that attempted to reconcile the world's religions.

Angie considered such attempts ludicrous—like trying to make the world's races into one color. She questioned the wisdom of minimizing the distinctions, thinking that might be like forcing everyone to eat vanilla ice cream after raising them on thirty-one flavors.

Jeremy influenced her thinking, she knew. Early in their marriage when she had said, "We all worship the same God," he had responded with, "Ask any Hindu or Muslim what he thinks of one God in three persons, and you'll stop saying that."

The research captivated her, so she worked longer than intended and had to hurry to beat the lunch crowd to the club. She went religiously now. She and Jeremy had made an agreement—he'd committed to staying home two nights a week and she signed up for three mornings a week at the club. As a result she had more energy, and the endorphin rush was a great antidote for her depression. She also liked that she was trimming down. Now if she could just make some friends, she could hang out with someone other than her mother.

As she climbed out of the pool, she glanced through the interior window straight ahead and saw Portia Barlow checking in at the desk. She wore a perky red and black tennis number. Angie grabbed her towel and dried off as she watched Portia heading in the direction of the handball courts. Shortly after she disappeared from sight, Alex Combs arrived at the desk wearing his lab coat and toting a gym bag.

Angie showered, dressed, and dried her hair. On her way out she changed her mind about going straight home and headed up to watch through the glass walls that circled the running track above the courts.

She found Portia and Dr. Combs competing hard and sweating profusely in court three. Portia was fit, and her slender form proved more athletic than Angie would have guessed. For about ten minutes the only sounds were balls or bodies hitting the wall or each other, and an occasional "nice shot," or "interference" when one impeded the other's route.

But was it her imagination, Angie wondered, or was Alex eyeing Portia like a cold drink on a hot day whenever Portia wasn't looking?

CHAPTER 9

Eleven days after Jeremy sent his article, he stood peering down the throat of a child with an acute case of chicken pox. Suddenly he felt his beeper vibrate. Ten minutes later, while still tending to the same patient, he felt the motion again. Both calls were nonemergencies, but as soon as he finished with the patient, he walked over to the ER phone. He pulled out his beeper to study the numbers. He didn't recognize either, though one was a hospital extension. He punched that number in first.

"Communications," a bright voice answered.

"This is Dr. Cramer," Jeremy said. "Somebody paged me."

"Yes, sir. Media Relations needs to talk with you about the press conference tomorrow. I'll connect you."

What press conference? Following a click, Musak piped a few bars of Haydn into his ear.

A voice came on the line. "Congratulations, Dr. Cramer!" The speaker's Southern accent was unfamiliar to him.

"Thank you …?"

"Appreciate your getting back to me so quickly. I'm Gina LeBeaux, the hospital's director of corporate communications. I'm just putting finishing touches on the press release, and I need to verify a few details."

Jeremy suddenly noticed an extra thumping in his heart. Before he could ask what she was talking about, she continued, "But first, let me give you the twenty-four-hour media pager number in case—"

"Wait. May I ask what this is about?" Silence. "Hello?"

"I-I'm sorry, Dr. Cramer. You don't know?" He heard a little chuckle. "Oh my! I'm so sorry. I assumed you'd already spoken with the journal editor."

"Journal editor?" Surely she didn't mean what he hoped she meant.

"Yes. *The International Journal of HIV/AIDS Research.* They've bumped down their lead article to make room for ours. The magazine's online version is set to hit the e-waves tomorrow, and they expect all the major news outlets to pick it up. We've scheduled a press conference for nine in the morning."

Now it was Jeremy's turn to fall silent. He had never attended a press conference, let alone spoken at one.

She gave him the pager number and continued, "Let's start by verifying a few facts. I have that you're thirty-one and that you got your MD/PhD at the New York University School of Medicine. Where did you get your bachelor's?"

"Georgetown." He considered telling her about his fourth-grade report card that said he wouldn't go far because he "fails to take constructive criticism." If only that teacher could see him now.

"And you're our third-year infectious disease resident?"

"Indeed." He turned over the page where he'd written the media number and jotted down the second number that had appeared on his beeper. He figured that call was from the journal editor. He wished he'd phoned it first.

"How do I pronounce this T-asterisk you use throughout the article?"

"T-factor."

"Thank you. Where were you born?"

"India."

"Really? But you speak English so well!" Jeremy was used to this. India had the largest English-speaking population in the world—a third of its citizens spoke English—but most Americans had no clue. "How long have you lived in the States?"

"My family moved here when I was three. My father was American and my mother was Indian." Referring to his parents in the past tense still caught him off guard.

"Ha! You got here as soon as you could, right?" She laughed and Jeremy cast his eyes to the ceiling. Ms. LeBeaux verified a few more personal facts and then explained the setup for the press conference, mentioning that she would be there as well as Castillo and Jasper. The journal editor would join them by satellite. "Ever done a media interview, Dr. Cramer?" she asked.

"Not fully dressed."

"Excuse me?" She was exactly the sort of person he enjoyed shocking.

"My college swim team won some championships, so we did some TV interviews after successful meets."

"Well, I certainly hope you'll come dressed *tomorrow*. Please wear a suit. Avoid ties with stripes, patterns, or bright colors—especially red. They don't photograph or film well." Earlier when he heard *press*, he'd envisioned print media. Television was going to cramp his style. Jeremy lived in scrubs.

"Sit with good posture, don't talk with your hands," she continued. "Prepare a few key messages. Make them brief, to the point. Show how our hospital's fine research has the potential to benefit the average person. Think in terms of succinct talking points." *No pressure or anything*, Jeremy thought.

"The average reporter writes for a public that uses an eighth-grade vocabulary. That means lots of one- and two-syllable words. So simplify."

One- and two-syllable words? Guess that rules out studies on *animals, T^*, and immune deficiency*, Jeremy thought. Pretty much everything he'd have to say was excluded. Jeremy decided it was time

Castillo earned his credit. If the man liked the limelight so much, let him have it. Jeremy opened his mouth to ask if that was all.

"You might want to practice tonight in front of a mirror," she said.

The mental picture made him want to laugh. *Not a chance,* he thought.

"We're so proud of you, Dr. Cramer!" From the moment she picked up the phone, her speech sounded as if she'd given it a hundred times. It reminded him of why he usually disliked PR people. "You represent our hospital," she chirped on. "And even though you will discuss your own research, readers and viewers will identify you as representing us. So get out there and make *us* proud!" Then she hung up.

They could have their pride. After that conversation Jeremy just wanted to drink an ice-cold beer. Slowly. But once he was past the hill of instructions, he pondered the ramifications of the publicity. Now people would expect more. He'd rather keep quiet until he had more evidence. Better to under promise.

He knew he should tell Jasper in case Castillo hadn't already sent an email to her and all the other department heads. As soon as Jeremy returned the other call, he'd drop by her office.

He walked down the hall to get a Diet Coke, and on his way he passed the nurse's station. A pang of guilt yanked him out of his reverie as he regretted for the millionth time the needle incident. What a difference one careless moment could make in so many people's lives. He thought of his father's death, and Ravi, and now Devin. He couldn't help but wonder if his own carelessness was going to kill everyone who mattered to him.

Once he got his drink, he headed for the doctor's lounge. Assuming the second phone number belonged to the journal, he wanted a little privacy when he returned the call. He punched in the numbers and, when a woman answered on the second ring, identified himself. She put him right through.

"Dr. Cramer, Dr. Roberts here with the *Journal of HIV/AIDS*

Research," a man with a booming voice told him. "If you haven't already heard, your fine piece of work will hit all the major media outlets when we announce it tomorrow. Your hospital's holding a press conference in the morning, and I'll be joining you by video. Do you have any questions?"

So it was really true. "Questions? Uh, wow, no, none that I can think of. Thanks!"

"You're the one deserving thanks—you and Dr. Castillo's team. Good work. I look forward to meeting you—in a manner of speaking— tomorrow."

THE NEXT MORNING Angie accompanied Jeremy to the hospital. The thought of a press conference seemed to excite even her. And her enthusiasm evoked something long buried in him. He felt proud to have his young blonde wife by his side. He glanced over at her sitting in the passenger seat in her pale-blue suit and ivory silk blouse. She met his gaze with a smile. And that fragrance she sometimes wore—he could never remember the illegal substance it was named for. Heroin? Opium? At any rate he wanted to get lost in it.

They arrived an hour early and surveyed the room. It had lecture-hall seating with no tables except one at the front of the room with five chairs behind it. A starched white cloth covered the table, and on top of it were a pitcher of ice water, glasses, and nameplates. Each seat had a microphone in front of it, and several members of the media stood wiring their own equipment to the podium and setting up cameras in the back. The center place was reserved for the hospital system's president. Next to him were Castillo on one side and Jasper on the other. Jeremy was stuck at one end, Gina LeBeaux at the other. Next to the table sat a six-foot-high screen, presumably for the journal editor.

Jeremy had butterflies in his stomach, but he told himself to relax.

With this lineup, which included two peacocks—Dr. Castillo and Gina LeBeaux—Jeremy figured no one would ask him or Jasper a thing. He hoped to get by with a nod now and then.

A tall woman, wearing a suit that complemented her dark hair and a too-bright smile approached them. "I'm Gina LeBeaux," she said, her extended hand showing off salon-red nails and a crowded charm bracelet. "We spoke yesterday." Jeremy immediately recognized the drawl. He started to introduce her to Angie when Castillo made a grand entrance. Flanked by two secretaries in what Jeremy considered unprofessionally short skirts, the doctor caught LeBeaux's eye and waved her over. She excused herself.

"They deserve each other," Jeremy told Angie as Ms. LeBeaux walked away. Angie gave him an inquisitive look.

On each chair lay a folder bearing the hospital's logo. Jeremy took one and leafed through it. Inside he found a copy of the journal article, a summary about the research, a FAQ sheet about the hospital including a list of its research grants, and biographical summaries on each of the five speakers. He read over his own bio and handed it to Angie.

She skimmed it, and when she finished she lifted her head. "What do you think?" she asked.

"I'm thinking I doubt anybody other than a board member asks questions—and certainly not frequently—about all of our research grants. That FAQ page is typical PR junk."

She lowered her voice. "I meant about their write-up of your bio. Pretty impressive when you see it all shoved into two paragraphs."

"I think … my dad would have been proud, and my mom would have believed it," he said. She squeezed his hand and he studied her face. "You've made more sacrifices than I have," he told her.

She squeezed his hand again. "I don't know about that. But thanks for noticing."

Her warm hand reassured him. They both seemed swept up in the moment, and he wanted to make it last.

As the room filled, the noise of everyone's chatter made hearing difficult. When a group of the lab assistants showed up with Bonnie Dylan, head of research, Jeremy introduced Angie to them. He made a big deal over each, emphasizing how much help he'd had, deflecting praise back to whatever person offered it.

Jeremy was counting the number of TV crews at the back of the room when Angie pulled him aside. "Tell me about Dr. Dylan," she said.

"What about her?" It struck Jeremy as an odd question.

"What did you say she did?"

"She's head of the lab. Why?"

"Why doesn't she have a place on the stage?" Angie asked.

"I don't know. There's no room?"

"Hasn't she been more involved in the research than Castillo and Jasper?"

"Of course—she's head of research," Jeremy said.

"She didn't seem all that thrilled to meet me," Angie said.

"She's not too personable. And we have lots going on today," Jeremy said, his eyes on the door, where he saw Nate and Portia Barlow walking in. He felt someone tapping his back and turned around. It was Ms. LeBeaux.

"Time to take your seat up front," she said.

"I'll go sit with Nate and Portia," Angie said. "Good luck!"

Jeremy proceeded to his place on the platform and poured himself a glass of ice water. Ms. LeBeaux stood behind the podium and the crowd fell silent. She welcomed everyone. Then the hospital president did the same, and Jeremy doodled while the man droned on with a long hospital sales pitch. The president then made an official statement about the research and introduced everyone on the platform. After that he called on Castillo to make a statement.

The chief of staff adjusted his expensive-looking tie, approached the podium, and grasped both sides of it with the confidence of a practiced politician. "Good morning. I'm Dr. Jovi Castillo—that's C-A-S-T-I-L-L-O. As chief of staff here, I add my welcome to that of our distinguished president." He spoke with the subtlest hint of a Spanish accent. "Thank you so much for coming to hear about a major breakthrough our hospital has made in AIDS research. The past ten months have seen exciting times for our research team."

Jeremy stifled a smirk. He watched Castillo shift his weight to his back foot as if winding up for a pitch. *He probably* did *practice in front of a mirror*, Jeremy thought. Castillo leaned into the microphone and produced a grin that, to Jeremy, had a wooden effect. "I'm delighted to bring you our report, which appears in today's issue of the *Journal of HIV/AIDS Research*. With today's announcement, we see the first real hope we've had of eradicating the worst scourge on the face of our planet."

He paused and his smile morphed into pursed lips. "Forty million people live with HIV worldwide," he said solemnly. "That's more than 100 times the number of U.S. soldiers lost in World War II. About 25 million have already died of AIDS, and in Africa alone another 12 million children are orphaned." The room was dead quiet. "Researchers estimate that about a million Americans have HIV, and more than half a million have died—a disproportionate number of them black. About three million more will die this year worldwide because of HIV/AIDS."

Again he paused, his brown eyes measuring the crowd. Then he smiled. "But all that changes here! I am convinced"—he marked the beat of his words with his index finger—"that number will drop drastically in the foreseeable future thanks to a major discovery made right here in this hospital." The crowd whispered among themselves, and it seemed to Jeremy that Castillo was giving a campaign speech, not a press conference. "Our exciting breakthrough will change how the world looks at the AIDS crisis. Finally we have a cure in sight!"

When the room grew quiet again, Castillo gestured toward Dr. Jasper. "Here with us today," he said, "is Dr. Beatrice Jasper, head of

Infectious Disease. I want her to tell you about the timeline—and the process I led our team through. Dr. Jasper."

Unbelievable, Jeremy thought. He glanced over at Angie, who shook her head and cast her eyes upward. He looked away from her to keep from snickering.

Castillo took his seat and Jasper brought her stout frame to the podium, the hem of a long skirt flowing beneath her long, white coat and above her thick-soled tan shoes. Makeup muted the normal flush of her cheeks, and she had on lipstick—which she rarely wore.

"Thank you, Dr. Castillo. These are indeed exciting times. In the interest of time, I'll be brief. But to summarize the process, Dr. Cramer here"—she gestured toward Jeremy and nodded, "had somewhat of an epiphany a little over ten months ago after a bus accident that involved numerous fatalities. That event marked the start of his research on a stem-cell line to replicate a factor in T cells, which are essential to the immune system. Starting with animal models," she continued, "he determined that these T-factor cells—as he calls them—repaired animal tissue and prolonged organ function."

Jeremy noticed Dr. Castillo sucking on his thick lower lip, disapproval shrieking from his cold silence as he watched her. Jasper had attributed the research to Jeremy, and Castillo had surely picked up on it.

Jasper glanced at Castillo and then back at the crowd. "From there," she said, "we obtained special permission through Dr. Castillo's influence to use human studies and began with freshly harvested kidneys. Then AIDS patients in end-stage disease volunteered for experimental therapies. Most of those patients are still alive. The entire process has moved quite quickly, due in part to the astonishing success of the therapy—and the tremendous support of our administration."

When she finished, the journal editor gave a summary of the findings and directed everyone to a copy of the article in their packets. No one had asked Jeremy to prepare a statement, so they skipped him and went straight to Ms. LeBeaux, who provided contact information and again directed everyone's attention to their packets. Finally she opened the floor to questions.

Each time the reporters tried to seek out a human-interest angle, they came up short. *They have no stories,* Jeremy thought. No narratives. Only data. Report info.

One reporter tried again. "Dr. Castillo, perhaps you could tell us the greatest surprise in your research."

He hesitated before saying, "On the one hand, I expected this sort of success. But it's still gratifying." He looked down the table to Jeremy and hesitated. "Um, perhaps Dr. Cramer can tell us about one of the surprises in the lab."

To Jeremy that was a no-brainer. He leaned into the mic. "My greatest surprise? The time I obtained a freshly donated kidney and injected it with T* to see how long I could keep it going. When I connected it to a blood source, it started filtering."

"Filtering, Doctor?" the reporter asked.

"Yes. What I mean is, well, the thing urinated." Thunderous laughter followed.

A heavy-set reporter of average height and brown hair stood next. "Dr. Cramer, Dr. Jasper mentioned that last year's bus accident at Fossil Bends caused an epiphany for you. Can you tell us about that?"

Jeremy cleared his throat and shifted in his seat, conscious of the need to sound nontechnical. "When I was ten, my father drowned. And that motivated me to choose research as a profession. The victims in the Fossil Bends accident were adults, but the children survived—a phenomenon we see frequently in deaths by drowning when adults and kids have the same submersion times. So I was particularly interested to find out the childhood advantage in the survivors. The information happened to overlap with AIDS research, and that brought about a shift in our focus. But what happened when I was ten was the real influence on my thinking."

Another asked, "Dr. Cramer, is there one person you can say most influenced your thinking?"

"If you mean as a researcher, Louis Agassiz and his emphasis on observation. The man could stare at a dead fish for a year and discover something new every day."

"What about outside of research?" the same reporter asked.

Jeremy pondered the question. "Certainly my dad, but …" He pointed in Angie's direction. "The gorgeous blonde over there in the iceberg-blue suit who's going to expect me to take out the trash tomorrow. That'll influence you—keep you from getting the big head about your great credentials and fancy research." Everyone laughed again. "Other than my wife, I'd have to say Matt Biondi." Jeremy avoided eye contact with Gina LeBeaux.

"Excuse me, sir? You mean the swimmer?" The same reporter who lobbed the question kept after him for more.

"I do. Biondi qualified in the last position for one of the freestyle relays going into the '84 Olympics. When told the team makeup, the world-record holder—also a relay team member—asked 'Matt who?' And that team went on to win the gold medal and set the world record. Biondi proved you don't have to *be* somebody. You just have to be *good*. So I've made it my goal to be as good as possible. I'm not trying to be somebody. I'm just trying to be goo—"

"Thank you, Dr. Cramer," Castillo said. He then made a few quick concluding remarks, thanked the reporters for their time, and abruptly left the stage.

After the press conference members of the media lined up to talk to Jeremy. He kept looking around for Angie and he finally spotted her sitting patiently in the back of the room.

He kept his comments short to dispatch the reporters as soon as possible. Then he made his way over to her. He had to know her impressions.

As he approached, she stood. He couldn't read her expression. Was she annoyed? Glad? Neutral? Her face was hard to read. As he wiped sweaty palms on his dress pants, he realized he was as nervous as he'd been on their first date. He reached out and tentatively took her hand. Avoiding her gaze, he quickly ushered her out to a private hall.

When they stopped, she stood on tiptoes, put her palms on his cheeks, and leaned in so her lips were close to his. "You were ama-a-zing," she whispered. Then her lips brushed his with a light kiss.

A thrill like new love coursed through his veins. "Ya think?" He wanted her to do that again.

"Definitely." She stood facing him and took both of his hands. "And it's not *just* because you flattered me in front of everybody, though that didn't hurt. What made you particularly charming was that you were the only one who didn't seem to give a rip about being up there." Angie cocked her head. "You really don't care about the notoriety, do you, Jeremy?" She sounded a little surprised.

He shook his head. "Couldn't care less." He looked into her eyes. "Honestly, I just love the research—and I totally adore you." He smiled. "The promise of helping somebody. I know it sounds cheesy, honey, but it's the truth." Suddenly emboldened by her attitude, he laced his fingers with hers with one hand and guided her to the bank of elevators. He pressed the Down button.

"Where are we going?" she asked.

"I want to show you ..." he said, but then hesitated. "Do you mind? I know how you feel about ..."

"What?"

"I want you to see how we reconfigured the lab for our research. And to introduce you to the rats and the monkeys."

She cocked her head. "The people you work with or the animals?"

He laughed and motioned toward the room they'd just left. "You already met the human versions. Now for the real heroes of the research."

A bell rang and the light pointing down lit up. "I'm game," she said.

When the elevator closed with Angie and Jeremy inside, he yanked her playfully, pulled her close, and gave her a kiss.

———❈———

ANGIE EXPECTED TO see some of the researchers again, but none of them were there.

"Everybody's probably still schmoozing with the media," Jeremy told her. That seemed to suit him fine, as if he wanted to have her to himself. The smell bothered her—the same odor Jeremy's clothes bore when he arrived home late. But she was adjusting to it.

He seemed so excited to have her there. She'd often referred to this place as his mistress, but now that seemed unkind. What man would be this thrilled to introduce his wife to his mistress? His brown eyes with those long, perfect lashes seemed to study her, as if her approval was the most important thing to him. Maybe it really was.

The place was larger than she remembered, and she liked finding pictures of herself and the kids—including a baby picture of Ravi—on Jeremy's desk. In the past he'd not displayed them in his research pods. She felt a lump form in her throat. It never occurred to Angie that he might think of her and the kids while he slaved over microscopes.

The phone rang and he answered it. While he talked, she leaned down to study the pictures. There was the one she gave him their first Christmas—a framed shot of their college swim team holding trophies. They looked so young. The two of them met at the pool during their senior year and she instantly had a crush on him—the tall, muscular, quiet guy whom she thought was Italian. When word filtered to him through a friend, that was all the impetus he needed to ask her out. He cooked her dinner and took her to a planetarium on their first date—neither of which any guy had ever done. But the little kindness of buying her a favorite candy bar on the way home impressed her most. Angie had fallen hard. Six months later, the week after graduation, they married in a huge church wedding.

There was a shot of them dancing cheek-to-cheek on their honeymoon in Tahiti. Her parents sent them there as a wedding gift—as if the wedding itself and the reception at the country club had not been present enough. In the photo Jeremy was bronzed and bare-chested, his swimmer's physique shimmering with suntan oil. Angie was wearing a bikini with a pareu cover-up in the body she used to be proud of.

Another photo was of Jeremy holding Jak moments after Angie had given birth. Jeremy wore scrubs and leaned down as he smiled next to a tired-looking Angie. She didn't like how she looked with no makeup, but it was certainly a great moment.

Jeremy ended the call and motioned her over to a drawer of vials. He talked faster than usual as he told how he got the idea for the research after the bus crash. She didn't mind that he was telling her what she already knew. It was fun to see him like this. He led her past the petri dishes and microscopes to the animals. He explained which animal was testing what hypothesis. And all the while, he couldn't seem to take his eyes off her face, as if hoping to convince her of the importance of his work.

It was the first time she'd ever felt this way. Was it guilt? Why had she resisted so much? It wasn't a matter of winning or losing. It was about supporting her man in his dreams. She did want him to succeed, to be great at what he did. It had just been so hard to be alone so many nights over the past year. And hard to watch the kids miss their dad.

Angie told herself it might just be her pride in the moment—maybe she felt this way because the whole world seemed to love Jeremy. But she didn't think that was it. At least she hoped not. She preferred to think his enthusiasm, once encouraged a little, was contagious.

—✦—

THE FOLLOWING MORNING Jasper brought a newspaper down to the lab where Jeremy was injecting human organs with T*. "Have you seen the headlines today, Cramer?" she asked. He shook his head. She threw it down good-naturedly on the table beside him. Page one of the *Denver Post* read "AIDS Cure in Sight." She flipped to the inside. Jeremy's face smiled out from the front page of the metro section. The lead story was a personality profile about him with the headline: "Jeremy Who?"

"It's a great piece," she said. "All about how you and your research are going to cure AIDS."

"Thanks," Jeremy said, staring down at the paper.

When he looked up, he saw Jasper stroking her chin, which made him wonder about the source of her quandary. She finally spoke. "Of course both articles also mention the hospital—fortunately for you. But the second one doesn't mention either our distinguished president or Castillo. Now, just for the record, I thought you did a bang-up job yesterday, and I couldn't be prouder." She slapped him hard on the back. "But don't say I didn't warn you—Castillo is gonna be pissed."

CHAPTER 10

Jeremy stopped long enough for a cup of coffee in the doctor's lounge before heading up to the floors to do rounds. As he sipped the jet-black brew boiling hot—just the way he liked it—he massaged his neck. He hadn't noticed until now how taut the muscles felt.

One of the infectious-disease residents breezed through and grabbed a book she'd left on the table. Hearing her, Jeremy looked up and saw circles under the petite brunette's eyes.

"Glad I ran into you," she said. "We admitted Devin last night, and she's asking for you—actually more like demanding."

His heart thumped hard. "Admitted? Why?"

"Cramps, nausea, diarrhea, a little vomiting. The nodes in her armpits are enlarged and she's running a fever—almost a hundred and two."

Jeremy grimaced. "Thanks." What she described could be the usual HIV symptoms, but it could also be the flu. Still, for a patient with HIV, the flu could kill.

"You'd better go see her!" the resident called back "She might start throwing things if you don't get in there."

Jeremy thought about Devin. In all the publicity he had neglected her. Maybe guilt had kept him away from her desk. He hated that about himself—how he avoided people he loved when they hurt. He was a fixer, a doer—not a sitter. When his own child died, he appreciated friends who sat and said nothing. But he loathed doing the same for others. For one, it bored him. But he also felt useless as a bent needle.

When he arrived at the floor nurse's desk, he asked for Devin's file. The nurse handed it to him, and he read through the notes. Unable to keep fluids down, she got dehydrated, so she came to the hospital asking for IV fluids. The infectious-disease doc in ER admitted her. *Good call,* Jeremy thought.

Sometimes it was hard to convince medical people that their own home remedies and self-medicating had limits. He had admitted a colleague once before, and she fussed the whole time that the blood-pressure readings in the night contributed to fatigue more than her disease did.

"How restful is it to get going into a good REM-cycle only to get jolted awake by the boa constrictor?" she had asked. Since then many of the staff referred to the blood-pressure cuff as the snake.

Jeremy knocked lightly. Thinking he heard a weak "Come in," he peeked in to make sure. Devin waved him over. The last time he saw her, she still had a healthy thickness in her arms. She was slender before, but now she looked as thin as a ballerina, and the wrinkles around her mouth were more pronounced. But her disease had not diminished the wideness in her smile.

"Good morning." She seemed genuinely cheerful about his arrival. He told himself he didn't deserve her kindness. "About time you got here."

"I just found out. Feeling puny, eh?" He patted her shoulder.

She nodded. "Stupid snake kept me awake all night. I told them I'd rest better at home, but no-o-o. None of that ..." Her voice started strong but trailed off. She motioned for him to sit down.

"Sorry," Jeremy said. "I can't stay."

"Baloney. Sit," she ordered. He complied, feeling like an obedient dog. "Saw you on the news," she said. "Good job." He started to thank her, but she shushed him.

"I need to tell you something friend to friend," she said. "I've worked here a long time, and I've seen plenty of politics ruin some good people. So listen up."

"I think I know what you're going to say—"

"You bet you do. You need to fly below the radar when it comes to Castillo and the press."

"I know."

"Oh no you don't. If you did, I wouldn't have seen your sorry mug on TV. I would have seen *his*. Or if I *had* seen you, I would have seen *your* lips talking all about *his* research."

Of all the things she has to think about, he thought.

"The biggest card Castillo holds against you is me," she said. "Think about it. We certainly don't want him to play it. You take too much of the limelight, and he'll let out enough info to tarnish your image. If you think I'm trying to protect my family by keeping a low profile, you're wrong." Whatever was on her mind had her energized now. "This stinking, rotten virus has killed more than twenty million people. So stay out of the media and stay in the lab."

"But corporate communications—"

"Oh, communications-schlummunications. They hate his guts. They'll go out of their way to give you all the interviews."

"What should I do?"

"If you *must* talk to the news, always, *always* point the credit back to him."

Jeremy reached over and pressed her hand. "I appreciate you looking out for my backside."

Devin chortled. "You mean watching your back, don't you?"

"Sure, whatever." Jeremy felt a little stupid, but he couldn't suppress his grin. "Anyway, thanks." He got up to leave.

Her smile disappeared. "Sit back down, you flatliner."

He obeyed. "What? What did I do?"

"Your bedside manner, Doctor."

"What about it?"

"It sucks, that's what."

Jeremy was speechless.

"Here's how it works," she said. "You come to the bedside of a friend who's bored out of her mind. The few minutes you or any other visitor spend will get replayed in her mind during a day that drags on for a million miles, and all you want to do is split. Staying a few extra minutes means so much to the patient, and so little to you. Why can't you just waste a minute? Just one minute?"

"Are you talking about patients in general or yourself?"

"Both."

"I see. Sorry." Jeremy hung his head and considered her words. "Maybe I should start by saying thanks for calling me your friend."

"Don't be ridiculous. Of course you're my friend."

"Yeah, a lousy one. First I make you stick yourself with a needle. Then lately I desert—"

"Right. If you even drop by my desk or—in this case, my hospital bed—you leave twenty seconds later. And that hurts much more than the first." Jeremy squinted at her, trying to make sense of her words. "The needle stick was an accident," she said. "Avoiding me isn't." She seemed determined to cut him no slack. "Maybe you dropped by here today, but you were still in a hurry to leave."

He played with the drawstrings on his scrubs. "All right, I'll sit awhile. So ... what do you want to talk about?"

"Did I say you had to talk?" He shook his head. "All right then." She closed her eyes. Before long he heard the labored breathing that told him she had slipped off to sleep. But he determined not to run out. He walked over to her tray, picked up the pitcher, and refilled her water. He checked her chart to make sure nobody had fouled up. Then he returned to her bedside. In all he had been there five minutes at the most, but it felt much longer. He rested his head in his hands and thought hard. He bore too much guilt. Was it or wasn't it his fault that his father drowned? That Ravi died? That Devin contracted HIV?

Jeremy thought about what he believed. It wasn't karma—not exactly. Karma was too impersonal. He was pretty sure the force he believed in was a personal God. But did he want a helpless God—one who wouldn't keep a drunk driver from smashing up his son? If his father's three-personed God was in control, why did the world seem so out of control?

As a scientist Jeremy had no time for what he considered the silliness of those who said religious people didn't do science. If that were true, hospitals wouldn't have names like "Baptist," "Deaconess," "Mt. Sinai," "Presbyterian," and "Holy Cross." His training told him to believe in natural selection, but if Darwin was right, Jeremy wondered how to account for the existence of sacrificial love. He'd heard the arguments, but he remained unconvinced.

"You're a quick learner," Devin whispered.

He looked up. "Thanks." He scooted closer and said, "Can I ask you something?"

"Sure."

"You said the needle stick was an accident. Do you really believe that? I mean, somewhere deep, deep down, don't you really blame me?"

She considered his words for so long he feared the worst. Maybe she really did blame him and was trying to figure out how to say so with tact.

"I've replayed what happened a thousand times a day since it happened," she said. "I suppose you have too. I wish I'd stood somewhere else. I wish I'd been more careful. I wish the other nurse had moved over. I wish you hadn't been where you were and that you'd seen me when I leaned over. A million details could have gone differently ..." She licked her bottom lip. "But ultimately, I believe nothing happens unless it first passes through loving hands."

"What does that mean? That God caused it?"

"God permitted it."

That didn't fly with Jeremy. It still left the Almighty ultimately responsible. If God could have prevented what happened to Ravi, then he—or she—should have. Any good parent would have. "Caused or permitted, God could have prevented it," Jeremy said.

Devin nodded. "There's a big gap between what God allows and what we understand. And between the two lies a huge mystery that makes no sense to me. In this universe, awful, cruel, unspeakable evil passes through those permitting hands."

"But doesn't that make you angry?"

"Sure. Remember how I pounded the wall and asked *why* the day I got my results? There's a whole prayer book in the middle of the Bible full of rants by folks asking why."

"Then how do you reconcile this?" He gestured toward her IV pole and the blood pressure cuff.

Devin licked her lips again and seemed to weigh her response. "When my babies were little, and they'd crawl toward electric plugs, I'd pull them away. And what do you suppose they'd do?"

That's easy, Jeremy thought. The exact scenario had happened with Ainsley lots of times. "Scream. And then crawl back to it again."

"Right. Do babies understand? Of course not. Their intelligence isn't developed enough to comprehend our reasons."

Jeremy considered her words, but they left him unsatisfied. "You're assuming God is good," he said.

"You're right, I am," she said. Then she said something so softly he had to ask her to repeat herself. "You lost a child, right?" She spoke barely above a whisper. He swallowed hard and nodded, wondering what that had to do with it.

"He sent and sacrificed his only son ... can you imagine doing that as a parent?"

No way. Suddenly he wanted to change the subject. "So are you telling me you're a Republican?" He got up and checked her IV fluids.

"Not a chance. I'm a yellow-dog Democrat."

He hadn't expected that. He didn't know what he expected.

Lowering her voice again, she said, "I suspect a day is coming—sooner than either of us would like—when you'll attend my funeral and stand at my graveside. And in case there's some doubt, I do expect you to be there."

"Stop talking that way," Jeremy insisted. "There's not going to be any funeral or a gravesi—"

She held a finger to her lips to silence him. "When that day comes," she continued, "don't you dare sit there beating yourself up. And you can grieve for … for my … for *them* …" She stopped, unable to give voice to her family members' names. She inhaled deeply and seemed to regain her strength. "But don't you grieve for me."

CHAPTER 11

The next few days Jeremy spun in a whirlwind of interviews and calls as the hospital's communications department sent numerous media requests his way. He did his best to wiggle out of them, but when he had no choice, he tried to deflect the credit.

During a live conversation on NPR, Jeremy spoke of how Castillo's T* research prolonged organ viability.

Time was running a sidebar in one of their April editions on how the researchers moved quickly—perhaps too quickly?—from animal to human studies. So Jeremy explained to the magazine's reporter how the research had to shift from animals to humans when human protein in T* proved an obstacle. And Jeremy went on to credit Castillo's reputation with their ability to fast-track approvals.

With the *New York Times* and the *Washington Post,* Jeremy talked about how "Castillo's team" found that T*, derived from T cells, resisted the AIDS virus by acting young, which made it harder for the virus to infect. Using T cells, the researchers sought to extend the life spans of AIDS patients. It was too soon to tell the long-term effects, but the T* did seem to improve organ function.

In interviews with ABC and CNN, Jeremy told "the suicide story"—how the hospital pathologist did an autopsy on an AIDS patient who committed suicide. Jeremy had treated him with Castillo's team's T*, and the pathologist found the corpse's organs in great condition considering the ten-year duration of the disease.

With NBC, CBS, and FOX News, Jeremy told how Castillo's team found early on that AIDS patients with high levels of T* stayed healthier for longer than those with lower levels—or none—and how they progressed to using T* with volunteer end-stage AIDS patients.

Jeremy loved talking about the research—enjoying most the follow-up interview with *Newsweek* that focused entirely on the potential of T* to help water-submersion victims. But the people contact exhausted him. By the end of the week, he longed to escape to the lab and actually do some research.

LeBeaux scheduled him for an eight o'clock Friday night phone interview. At five thirty, he dashed home for dinner, stopping to pick up milk for Angie. On impulse he grabbed a copy of *Lucky* magazine for her. Then he hurried home to catch the six o'clock news so he could watch an interview he'd taped that morning.

Jak sat on his lap to watch. But seeing his father on TV, Jak ran to his room and returned with a party-favor noisemaker. He blew it in Jeremy's face, making it impossible to view or hear the TV.

"Wait until a commercial, okay? Please?" Jeremy asked.

"But I'm celebrating!" Jak blew it again. "You're famous!"

Angie got up, took Jak's hand, and pulled him toward his bedroom. "Come on, let's let Daddy watch in peace."

Jak resisted. "But I want to see too!"

"If it helps, I'm taping this," Angie told Jeremy.

"I'll be quiet. I promise. I want to stay!" Jak's voice was still too loud for Jeremy to hear himself talking to the reporter.

"Okay, but shh." He patted the spot next to him on the couch, and Jak settled in.

At the conclusion of the segment, Jeremy was satisfied that they'd at least kept the part where he mentioned Castillo. Jeremy clicked off the remote and glanced over at Angie. "I brought you a little something."

He pulled the sack with the magazine from under a couch cushion. The delight on her face and enthusiastic hug told him he should remember to bring such gifts more often.

"Mommy! Look! *MOM* upside down spells *WOW!*" They looked up to see Jak lying on the couch with his seat against the back cushion, his feet in the air and his head dangling off the edge. Jeremy followed Jak's eyes to a picture he'd drawn with the letters M-O-M hanging on a cabinet in the den.

"It's true, isn't it?" Jeremy said. He winked at Angie. "Mom, wow—they mean pretty much the same thing."

Jak righted himself and scooted over into Jeremy's lap. He held up the noisemaker in front of Jeremy's nose to show it off. Jeremy leaned back to bring it into focus. "See, Daddy? Cool, huh? I won it!"

"Yeah, really cool. Hey, buddy, I've missed you." Jeremy expected Jak to jump down and take off, but instead his son leaned his head against his chest. Ainsley lay on the couch next to him.

Jeremy looked over at Angie. "You're the only one missing here—well, you and the gerbil." Angie came closer and nestled in under Jeremy's arm.

"I'm really proud of you," she said. "When we were in Jamaica and you said you'd spend more time here, I thought you were just saying that to get me off your case. I've never felt so glad to be wrong, Jer. Sure wish you didn't have to go back tonight." She readjusted and leaned her head on his shoulder.

"You have to go?" Jak asked.

The look in his son's eyes brought a fresh wave of guilt. "Only for an hour or so," Jeremy said. "I'll come back as fast as possible, little buddy. Honest." Jeremy rubbed his knuckle gently against the top of Jak's head.

"Can I come with you, Daddy? I don't have school tomorrow."

"Sorry."

Angie shrugged. "Why don't you take him with you?"

Jeremy's stomach tightened at the remembrance of ambulances and lights flashing. He couldn't believe Angie was suggesting that he take Jak.

She seemed to read his mind. "You're going up to the tower, right?"

"Uh-huh." Jeremy took this as a very good sign. "He'd have to be super quiet."

Jak jumped up. "I will! I promise! I can be quiet."

"It's radio, right? Not TV?" Angie asked. "He's super quiet when I tell him it's important."

"Okay," Jeremy said solemnly. He gave Angie a kiss and Jak tore out to the car.

Five minutes later Jeremy helped Jak buckle himself into the backseat. His fingers shook as he put the key in the ignition. But he reminded himself that the risk was minimal. He took an alternate route, drove under the speed limit, and stopped for yellow lights.

Jak played with a handheld electronic game all the way there. Jeremy tried to suppress thoughts of the accident, but they kept coming back.

Once they arrived at the parking garage, he heaved a sigh of relief. From there father and son proceeded to the eighteenth floor. Jeremy got Jak settled in the waiting area with his game on mute and slipped into one of the offices to make the call.

The interview ended after only five minutes due to some breaking news—something about a commercial flight trying to get a restroom fire under control.

Jeremy walked into the lobby and felt a surge of pride when he found his son, as promised, sitting engrossed in his game, quiet as ultrasound. "All done," Jeremy told him. "Time to go."

Jak pouted. "But we just *got* here!"

His son's response caught him by surprise. "But I'm finished. We can go home to mommy now."

"I don't want to go home yet. Please, Daddy. I like it here with you."

Jeremy stood thinking. He knew he couldn't take his son onto any of the infectious-disease floors. "I suppose I could take you down to the lab for a few minutes." The minute he said it, Jeremy regretted it.

Jak jumped up. "Oh boy!"

"Wait. You know, son, that's not a good idea. Maybe we should just go home."

"No. The lab! The lab!"

Jeremy knew there'd be no stopping Jak now, so he gave in. "All right. C'mon. I'll show you where I do my research. It has lots of cool microscopes and even some mice and rabbits."

Jak ran ahead of Jeremy and punched the Down button for the elevator. When the door opened, to Jeremy's surprise, Castillo got off.

As he held the door so Jeremy and Jak could board, the chief's jaw tightened. "What are you doing up here so late?" He looked from father to son with furrowed brows.

"Radio interview."

"Ah, figures. You do enjoy the publicity, don't you, Doctor?" Castillo let the doors shut behind him.

The word *projection* came to Jeremy's mind.

Jak mashed as many numbers as he could with his fist until Jeremy stopped him. "No, son. We only need B for basement." Jak punched the *B* and down they went. They stopped on seventeen, sixteen, fifteen, fourteen, and twelve before proceeding smoothly.

"Somebody can't count," Jak observed. Jeremy didn't know what he meant. "See?" Jak pointed to the numbers. "Thirteen's missing."

"Ah, thirteen has air conditioners on it. Lots of buildings are set up that way. Sometimes people think thirteen brings bad luck, so there's no thirteenth floor."

Jak laughed at that. When the lift reached the basement, he bounded out and ran off in the wrong direction.

"This way, son," Jeremy told him.

Jak spun around and raced ahead again. Jeremy called after him, "Look for the door that has a word starting with L-A-B." Sure enough, Jak located the door and stood waiting as Jeremy strode down the hall.

"I can read *laboratory*, Daddy," Jak said. He stood beaming. "I can even spell *constitution*—C-O-N-S-T-I-T-U-T-I-O-N." Jeremy praised his son and mentally commended himself for having—and marrying— such good genes. He punched in the security code and turned the knob.

Jak took a whiff of the lab. "P-eeew!" The lab assistants all looked up. Jak announced, "It stinks like you when Mommy tells you to go take a shower!"

Jeremy pulled Jak back into the hall and let the door shut behind them. He knelt down to his son's level. "Let's go over some rules first, okay?" Jak stood looking at his dad with pursed lips. "Just like you had to be quiet upstairs, you need to use your quietest inside voice down here. The people in the white coats are doing important work, and we mustn't disturb them. Now you already noticed—it's going to smell funny because of the medicine we use to keep animals from feeling pain. At first it'll stink, but your nose will get used to it pretty fast. Okay?" Jak nodded. "Ready to roll?" Jeremy didn't wait for an answer. He punched the code again, and they entered.

Researchers who used to ignore Jeremy when he arrived now greeted him with a chorus of "Hello, Dr. Cramer" and "Evening, Dr. Cramer," and even, "Let me know if you need anything, Dr. Cramer."

Jak stood in the middle of the room surveying its tables, microscopes, and operating lights. He didn't say a word, but Jeremy saw wonder in his eyes. Jeremy walked over to one of the microscopes and pulled out some blank slides. He adjusted the stool and motioned for Jak to sit, which he did. Jeremy ran his hand through Jak's short hair and found a loose strand. He put it on a slide and slid it under the magnifying glass. "Look through here," he said, pointing to the eyepiece. "Tell me when it's clear instead of blurry."

Jak peered through the lens. "Stop! Go back!"

Jeremy adjusted the lens.

"Wow! It's huge!"

Jeremy took a cotton swab from a jar and told Jak to open his mouth. He rubbed the swab against the back of Jak's throat and transferred the sample to a slide. After he placed it under the microscope, they took turns looking through the eyepiece again.

Jak wanted more. Before Jeremy could stop him, he yanked a piece of skin from a hangnail, wincing as he did. Jeremy put it on a slide and stuck it under the microscope. Then he showed Jak how to adjust the focus for himself. Suddenly Jak was more interested in making the eyepiece go up and down than with viewing samples. But then he went back to viewing. He looked first at his fingernail. Then his knuckle. A trace of blood from his hangnail. The scab on his index finger. The lines on his hand.

"Excuse me, Dr. Cramer?" Someone tapped Jeremy's shoulder. Jeremy turned around to see a young assistant with a clipboard. "Sorry to bother you, but we're observing a pattern you might want to see in one of the kidney studies."

Jeremy looked from Jak to the researcher, then back at Jak. "Stay right here," he said sternly. Jak seemed too engrossed in the world beneath him to hear his father, so Jeremy stepped away for a moment.

The researcher led him over to one of the kidneys. He explained that the patient who donated the kidney had received T* after she was brain-dead following a car accident. Only after the patient's body was taken to the morgue did her husband agree to organ donation. "What's amazing," the researcher said, "is that the T* seems to have delayed organ deterioration." It was only an isolated sample, but combined with the suicide case, it indicated a pattern. The possibilities demanded evaluation.

"See, Daddy? I can do what you do!" Hearing Jak's voice behind him, Jeremy spun around. When he saw Jak, he froze. Jak stood with the open end of a surgical glove in his mouth, its five fingers inflated like a balloon. Jeremy had done the same trick dozens of times to entertain his son.

Schooling his voice to hide his alarm, Jeremy asked, "Where'd you get that?" Jak pointed to the receptacle across the room—the one Jeremy's research pod shared with another infectious-disease researcher. The one marked Contaminated.

"Let me have that!" Jeremy insisted. He yanked the glove out of Jak's mouth. The jerking motion caused Jak to bite hard on his tongue. His hand flew up to his mouth and he cried out in pain.

Jeremy gasped. He swept up Jak in his arms and ran to the sink with his assistant trailing behind them.

"O-o-o-w!" Jak wailed, holding a hand on his lip.

Jeremy shoved him under the spigot reserved for ocular chemical burns. The assistant, apparently thinking along the same lines, turned on the water full force. Jeremy held Jak over it. "Open your mouth," he said. "Stick out your tongue, and do *not* swallow."

"Why?" The pitch of Jak's voice revealed his panic.

"Just do it!" Jeremy commanded.

Jak's body went stiff, but he obeyed by opening wide and sticking his tongue in the water.

Jeremy struggled to hide his despair. "That glove was dirty, Jak!" He stood holding his son, his mind racing with a catalog of diseases. There was some blood in the water. Not a lot, Jeremy noticed. But still. Contact with the glove had been brief, but Jeremy thought of the strains and potencies of viruses in the adjoining lab. Tears streamed down Jak's face.

Jeremy called out, "Somebody page Barlow!" Holding his son over the water, Jeremy could feel Jak's little heart pounding. He told himself to calm down and stop terrifying his child. How had Jak gotten a glove out of the closed receptacle? It would've been nearly impossible to open it. *It must have been sticking partway out,* Jeremy thought. He wanted to discipline whoever had left it that way, yet they all did it—including himself. Everybody left gloves half-in, half-out of the disposal containers. Everyone in the lab knew better than to touch one, but how could a child know something like that? The hospital didn't have a policy about children in labs, but common sense told Jeremy they shouldn't have to. It was no place for a kid, especially one young enough to think a skull and crossbones meant pirate play. The lab assistant brought a stool so Jeremy could set Jak down.

"Stand here," Jeremy said. "And keep your tongue in the water. Don't swallow. And breathe through your nose. That glove was dirty, so we need you to keep washing your tongue and your mouth for about fifteen minutes." Jak whimpered. "I know that's a really long time. But it's very important."

Jeremy told himself Jak was in good health. The first line of defense against the threat of viral infection would be Jak's own immune system. Jak struggled, indicating his discomfort. Jeremy patted his son's back.

Ebola. The Asian flu. The bird flu. Hepatitis. Jeremy mentally ran through a list of possible viruses. Measles. Meningitis. Then there were the bacterial infections. Scarlet fever. Whooping cough. TB. Strep. For some of these Jak had been immunized. And if he developed a bacterial infection, antibiotics might help. But the viral infections worried Jeremy. He wanted to pump his son full of antibiotics against the threat of bacteria, but that would weaken Jak's defenses against viral intruders.

All the researchers gathered around. Jeremy pointed in the direction of his research pod. "Anybody who threw away a glove in that receptacle, I want to know what you were working on. And we'll need the list of everybody who's been in and out of here since the last trash pickup." He planned to run his own tests on the glove.

Jeremy looked down at his son and stroked his hair. "You're doing great, buddy." He leaned down and put his cheek on Jak's head. *Please, God, not this one, too.*

One of the researchers said, "They were working on some Hep B research over there earlier today."

The words made Jeremy shudder again. Tears continued to stream down Jak's face. Jeremy leaned down and spoke in his son's ear. "Hey, it's okay. If something like this happens and we clean it super fast—which is what we're doing right now—we'll probably get all the dirt out." Jak started to pull his tongue back into his mouth.

"No, no," Jeremy said. "You need to run water in your mouth for a full fifteen minutes. That's the best thing that will help us make sure to get all the dirt. We start fast and we do it for a long time. You're doing great." Jak held out his tongue as far as he could. There was no more blood. Jeremy wanted to examine his son's tongue as soon as possible, but it would have to wait until the end of the wash protocol.

The assistant who'd distracted Jeremy from his son bore a sheepish expression. "I'm so sorry. It's my fault, Dr. Cramer—I shouldn't have bothered you."

Jeremy ignored his words. There would be time for blame and responsibility later. "We'll need a postcleansing culture," he said. "I swabbed the back of his throat earlier when we were using the microscope. We'll need that sample for a baseline." The assistant disappeared and everyone else dispersed quietly.

As he stood alone with his son in the minutes that followed, Jeremy formulated a plan for beefing up Jak's immune system. He would need great nutrition with supplements. And he'd have to stay adequately hydrated. Jeremy knew he could expect full cooperation from Angie.

Angie! The thought of his wife made Jeremy swallow hard. *She'll never forgive me,* he thought. He knew there was no possible justification he could give her for bringing Jak to the lab. He wondered how he could have been such an idiot.

The lab assistant returned. "Dr. Barlow will be here soon."

NINETY MINUTES LATER as he prolonged the drive home by going way under the speed limit, Jeremy considered what to tell Angie. She'd be glad Barlow took baseline blood samples and wrote a script for preventative medicine. What she didn't need to know was that Jeremy's own impulsive reaction had led to Jak's open wound. It was bad enough that Jak played with a contaminated glove only because Jeremy had been distracted. If she knew the rest ... Jeremy tried to think about something else, anything else.

He pulled into the garage. Looking at Jak in the rearview mirror, he spoke solemnly, "I need you to brush your teeth and get ready for bed while I tell Mommy what happened. Once she and I have a chance to talk, you can tell her all about it. I just need to talk to her first, okay?"

Jak nodded. Once inside he headed for the bathroom and Jeremy found Angie in the den watching a mystery.

Angie muted the TV and nodded dreamily. "How'd it go?"

He didn't answer. Her eyes looked heavy and her hair was disheveled. He wondered if the sound of the garage door opening had just awakened her. He pulled up the rolling ottoman and sat with his knees touching hers. She gave him a curious look.

"How was your night?" he asked.

She sat up and cocked her head. "What's up?"

He sighed. No point in stalling with small talk. "I need to tell you about something that happened."

She raised her eyebrows and sat upright. "During the interview? Or something ... else?"

He hesitated. "The latter."

"What?" She fixed her eyes on him.

"The interview was fine—went really fast. And I got done earlier than I thought. I was going to come home. But Jak didn't want to. He wanted to stay—begged me to stay. So I, uh, I took him ... downstairs."

Angie's expression said she thought he was nuts. "You took Jak to the morgue?"

This was going to be harder than he thought. He shook his head. "The lab."

"The *what?*"

He held up a hand, signaling for her to stay calm. "I know … just let me finish."

"There's more?"

He nodded. "I was showing him some stuff under the microscope, and somebody pulled me away for a moment. I didn't mean to—"

"So what happened, *Jeremy?*" She spoke his name as if it were a disease.

"You know how I sometimes blow up surgical gloves like balloons?" She nodded and blinked. Then blinked again. "Well, he found a glove hanging out of the trash." The words lingered in the air between them like an odor.

"Then you weren't watching him? Tell me he didn't put it in his mouth!" Jeremy looked away. "Tell me he didn't blow it up, Jeremy!" she screamed. "Tell me!" He closed his eyes.

She stood up and railed at him. "How could you? The diseases down there could kill him!"

Jeremy heard a noise behind him and saw Jak standing in the doorway. His toothbrush was on the floor and he held a tube of toothpaste. His lower lip quivered.

"I won't get sick, Mommy. I promise. I put my tongue in the water for a long time like Daddy said."

Angie ran to Jak and scooped him in her arms. "Oh, baby," she said. "Of course. You're right. You'll be fine." She held her son tight, but her eyes locked on Jeremy in a death stare.

CHAPTER 12

The following morning after Angie got Jak off to school, she checked her e-mail. To her surprise she found a message from Portia Barlow:

> *Hi Angie, I asked Jeremy for your e-address. Hope you don't mind. Just wanted to say I'm so sorry about what happened tonight. Nate and I were at the Palace Arms when we got the call. When I found out it was your son who needed him, I was glad Nate could help.*

Angie's resentment grew when she realized Jeremy's idiocy interrupted alone time for the Barlows.

> *Your son is adorable. I know if you'd seen him you would've been so proud of your little man. And your husband—he felt so terrible. I felt bad for him. It must be hard for you to see him beating himself up so much.*

Angie chewed on her tongue when she read that last part. Considering how Jeremy felt right now would take more imagination than she had, but she appreciated Portia's empathy. She read on:

*If you want to do coffee sometime this week, just shoot
me the place, day, and time, and I'll be there. You're in
our thoughts, Portia.*

Angie looked at her watch. It was eight thirty—*too last-minute to
set up something this morning,* she thought. She sent back a message
telling Portia she didn't have any at-home child care options on weekdays, but if Portia wanted to meet at the club's coffee bar, she'd like to
get together in the morning at ten.

The following day as Angie got ready to meet Portia, she took
extra time with her makeup and clothes. She didn't like feeling frumpy
next to the queen of fashion.

Angie had never been to the coffee bar at the club, but she knew
where it was. She took Ainsley to the kids' center and proceeded to the
shop. She spotted Portia, who waved. She already had a table for two
by the window and was nursing a coffee drink.

"Let me grab something and I'll join you," Angie said. She got
some orange juice, and when she returned, Portia scooted out a chair
for her with her foot, and Angie sat.

Portia skipped the small talk. "Tell me straight—how are you?"
Her eyes demanded the truth.

Angie burst into tears. Then she felt stupid. "I'm sorry ..." She
hated that sometimes all it took to make her cry was a little empathy.

"Good grief. Why apologize?" Portia asked. "Nate told me you
already lost a child and now this. I'd be terrified." Angie sat sniffling.
Portia reached into her purse and handed Angie a tissue.

"Thank you." Angie wiped her eyes and nose. "And thanks for
your message."

Portia waved it off. "How's your son?"

"So far so good. Though it didn't help when he heard me tell
Jeremy the diseases in the lab could kill him."

"Oh no!"

"I should've kept my mouth shut till I knew he couldn't hear us. I had a terrible time calming him down. But he finally fell asleep—in our bed. Needless to say, Jeremy slept on the couch."

"I'm so sorry. Must be terrifying," Portia said.

"It was. And is. And I'm also sorry your dinner was cut short by my husband's idiocy. I know you and Nate get so little time."

"That's okay."

The women fell silent, and Angie looked around. "If I'm not mistaken, Jeremy told me you and Nate met here at the club. Is that right?"

"Not exactly," Portia said. "We actually knew each other from way back. Our parents' lake houses were next door to each other, so we had some shared history in the past. But we met again here." Portia pointed in the direction of the courts. "Down there. I worked in the salon, and he came here to work out."

Angie wondered how much Nate knew about Dr. Combs and his handball matches with Portia, but she told herself it was none of her business. "What attracted you to each other?"

"I'm not sure I can speak for Nate—but I suspect he liked the companionship. We knew so many of the same people, which made starting over less painful—his first wife left him because he had a sperm count of zero and she didn't want to adopt."

Angie couldn't believe Portia was telling her so much so soon.

"And I can't have kids—an infection destroyed my tubes years ago. So what attracted me to him? Honestly? Some of the girls I worked with thought he was hot—and he was so oblivious. To this day I don't think he believes me about that, but he certainly didn't mind when I flirted with him. The man is fantastic in the sack—probably because he's totally unselfish. Only problem is it takes an act of Congress—no, more like the UN Security Council—to get him there." Both women laughed.

Portia continued. "Sorry! I can be like a tornado in a trailer park.

I needed someone like Nate to balance me out. And you know what they say about everyone wanting to be with a doctor."

Angie didn't know, and she wasn't sure she wanted to. "Does he come here with you often?"

Portia shook her head and looked dejected. "Not anymore. He injured his knee last year playing beach volleyball." She fell silent. "So what about you and that hotshot researcher of yours? What made you fall in love?"

"I can't remember," Angie said with a mischievous smile.

"Uh-oh." Portia had a hearty laugh.

Angie grew serious. "Sometimes I feel so much anger." She massaged her temples to ease the tension. "I didn't used to be angry—until we lost Ravi. Then I discovered depths of rage I never knew I had. Still, I'm committed to Jeremy—to us. Most of the time, at least," she added with a nervous laugh. "But I hate to keep talking about me. And my problems. What a downer."

"Then why don't you go get your baby and let's go do some mall therapy."

"Yeah?" Normally Angie hated to shop, but suddenly the thought of a new pair of shoes—really, really expensive shoes—sounded perfect.

DURING THE TWO weeks following Jak's mishap, Jeremy was torn up inside by opposing forces. In the media he was a hero. At home he slept in the recliner. Professionally he was worth gold; personally he was—in Angie's words—a butt munch. Time flew at work, where he called Devin daily to check on her and juggled numerous projects in the lab. Everywhere else, minutes crawled. But he could hardly stay away from Jak. Tests on the glove all came back negative, but that convinced Jeremy of nothing.

Angie spoke to Jeremy only in the presence of the children. "Can you pick up some milk?" "How's the weather?" "My mom's getting Jak from school."

The one person who blamed Jeremy more than Angie did was Jeremy himself. When he shaved, he wondered what good it did to come up with a major cure if he put at risk everyone he cared about? When he rode the stationary bike, he reminded himself that he *knew* Angie hated the lab and considered it—and him—responsible for Ravi's death. He wondered how he could have thought even for one moment of taking Jak down there. It all came up so fast. What was he thinking? Was it worth sacrificing his already fragile marriage for the few minutes he'd spent down there? On what? What had been so all-important?

Both Jeremy and Angie watched Jak's every move. Angie fed him extra fruit and vegetables. He took liquid vitamins. Grandma was given orders to keep him to a strict bedtime, even on the weekends. No exceptions.

Every chance he got, Jeremy pumped Jak full of fluids. And he and Angie kept Jak away from Ainsley, just in case. Yet Jak continued to jump, run, interrupt, imagine, and play with boundless energy.

By the end of the second week, Jeremy breathed more easily. Yet at the seventeen-day mark, Jeremy shuddered when he saw their emergency code blinking on his beeper. He was sitting in the makeshift office in Communications. He reached for the phone and punched in his home number. The phone rang only once before Angie picked up. "What's wrong?" Jeremy said.

Angie sucked in deep breaths between sobs and cried out something unintelligible.

"Speak slower," he said, and waited with a racing heart.

She tried again and he struggled to understand. "... school nurse ... called ..." She wailed again. "Jak ... a fever!"

It took a moment for the words to register. Jeremy felt as if he were watching events unfold for someone else.

"Maybe it's just a cold," he said, trying to sound optimistic. He knew she wouldn't believe him any more than he believed himself. Still, it was possible.

Angie wailed. "I knew it … *knew* this would happen."

Jeremy wanted to comfort her, but he couldn't think of anything to say. She had no reason to believe the ending this time would turn out any happier. "Want me to go pick him up?" Jeremy offered.

"Of course not! Are you kidding?" He might have considered her cruel if the same thought hadn't crossed his mind. "Haven't you done enough already?"

"Bring him here, then, okay? I'll find Barlow."

"Okay." Much as Jeremy knew she despised him at this moment, he heard the relief in her voice.

A secretary breezed in and dropped a phone message on the desk in front of Jeremy. It was marked "urgent".

"ER or your office?" Angie asked him.

"The ER. Hey, when they called did they mention what Jak's temperature was?" Jeremy asked.

"No." She hung up without saying good-bye.

He glanced at the phone message. Somebody named Sam Peterson at WP needed him to call back. He started dialing, thinking it might be someone at Jak's school, but then he noticed it was an unfamiliar area code. *Surely this can wait,* he thought, so he pressed the phone's switch hook and immediately called Barlow. Jeremy expected to leave a message, but when he told the pediatric nurse who he was and what he needed, she told him to hold. A minute later Barlow came on the line.

"You need me in the ER?"

"Yes. It's Jak—" the name caught in Jeremy's throat. "He's running a fever. I hate to ask you to drop everything, but—"

"No, no," Barlow assured him. "Meet you down there."

Jeremy quickly called the number for Sam Peterson to find out who he was and what he needed. Upon learning Mr. Peterson was a reporter for the *Washington Post* and that the urgency was the paper's own deadline, Jeremy clenched his teeth. Trying not to sound curt, he promised to have someone else call back soon.

Jeremy sprinted to the nearest elevator and pushed the Down button. When the door opened, Castillo got off, surrounded by a group of doctors. Seeing Jeremy, he gave an obligatory nod.

Perfect, Jeremy thought. He pulled the phone message from his front pocket and handed it to Castillo. "So glad I found you. The *Washington Post* needs to talk to you right away." Jeremy was glad to rid himself of the task and make Castillo look important at the same time. Then he dashed onto the elevator and pressed the button for the ground floor. The doors slid shut. Jeremy tapped his fingers against his leg every time someone stopped the elevator en route. The man who got on with a walker nearly drove Jeremy out of his mind. He considered getting off at the next floor and taking the steps two at a time for the remaining twelve floors.

When Jeremy finally got to the ER, he found Barlow already there prepping the staff. Jeremy appreciated that no matter an employee's rank, the ER team always rallied with an extra measure of professional compassion when a staff member had a friend or family member in need.

An ER station was already set aside for Jak. Upon spotting Jeremy, several doctors and nurses offered their help. Jeremy saw that there was nothing for him to do until his family arrived, so he went to the doctors' station to wait.

He smelled the coffee sitting on the burner and guessed its age at six or seven hours. He dumped it out, put in a fresh filter, and brewed a new pot. As he listened to the drip and smelled the aroma, he thought about what he often termed *the moment*. Normally he was the caregiver in such situations, but several times he'd sat on the receiving end. It never got easier facing those times when people remembered exactly where they were standing, what they were doing, who they were with. No matter what happened at such times, it was never the same afterward—after "she has cancer" or "the chaplain is on his way." Or worse—"he's dead."

When the percolating stopped, Jeremy concentrated to steady his hand as he poured. He took a sip and set his cup on an end table. He grabbed a health magazine the hospital published and thumbed through it. When he saw his own photo and a description of his life-saving work, he felt a wave of nausea.

Barlow came in and sat next to him. "I know you're concerned—*very* concerned—but there's a lot of flu going around."

"Yeah, we admitted Devin with the flu."

"Right. Give me a chance to work him up before making your own diagnosis, okay?" Jeremy looked away. He didn't want his friend to see the moisture clouding his eyes. "So tell me what you know," Barlow said.

Jeremy stared at a scuff on the wall. "Not much. Somebody at the school called Angie and said Jak was sick." He forced himself to make eye contact. "That's it."

"How's she taking it?" Barlow asked. Jeremy looked away again. They sat for a moment, neither speaking.

"Thanks a lot for helping me, man," Jeremy finally said. "I know you have a billion patients of your own."

"The glove deal you called me in to handle—it could have happened to anybody," Barlow said. "It really could have. Try not to be too hard on yourself."

"Dr. Cramer, your wife and son are here." Jeremy and Barlow looked up to see the ER nurse who spoke.

Barlow led the way to the room where Angie and Jak were waiting. When he pulled back the curtain, Jeremy noticed Angie's eyes were too puffy for cosmetics to hide. Jak, who was holding her hand, looked pale. He had on a light jacket, and he wore it zipped with his hood laced tightly around his chin, even though the May weather was warm.

"Hi, Daddy," Jak said, his voice pathetically weak.

Jeremy knelt and wrapped his son in an embrace. "You okay?" he asked, resting a cheek against Jak's. It felt hot, but Jak shivered. "Cold?" he asked. Jak nodded. "We'll try to warm you up as soon as we can." He left his arm on his son's shoulder and stood to face Angie. "And you know Angie," he said to Barlow. They acknowledged each other with solemn nods.

The nurse handed Barlow the chart labeled "Rajak R. Cramer" and disappeared behind the curtain, pulling it shut behind her.

"Jak, you remember Dr. Barlow?" Jeremy asked. Jak pointed to Barlow's Spider-Man tie and gave him a tentative smile.

"You bet," Barlow said. "We're old friends. Let's get you up on the table here and have a look, shall we?" He helped Jak up.

It seemed to Jeremy that Barlow hurried—something he usually did only with critically ill kids. Jeremy hoped Angie, being unfamiliar with the routine, wouldn't notice. He motioned for her to take a seat on one of the stools, and he leaned against the wall with arms crossed trying to look casual.

Barlow turned to Angie. "Everything seem okay to you this morning?"

She nodded. "He left for school around eight, nothing unusual."

Barlow slid a digital thermometer in Jak's ear and waited. Normally the nurse handled such details, making Jeremy wonder if Barlow was doing it as a favor or out of concern.

The thermometer beeped. Barlow removed it and wrote something in the chart. Jeremy glanced over and read the notation. One hundred two point eight. Fahrenheit. Jak coughed. Barlow looked him in the eye. "Been coughing much?"

"A little."

"He coughed some on the way here," Angie said.

Barlow felt Jak's lymph nodes. When he finished, he said, "Let's have a look at your throat." He pulled a tongue depressor from a canister on the counter. "Pretend we're not friends and stick out your tongue at me. Farther. Okay, real wide—good." Dr. Barlow flashed the light in Jak's mouth and peered in. "When did the cough start?" he asked. He removed the depressor and tossed it in the trash.

"In P.E.," Jak said. "I started feeling bad then."

Angie offered, "He has phys-ed at one, right after lunch."

"So it started today. Okay." Barlow made some notations and looked back at Jak. "You say you started feeling bad. What feels bad?"

"My arms and legs hurt. And I'm cold."

Jeremy told himself the flu caused cough, chills, aches, and high fever. But he couldn't stop mentally running through a litany of other troubling possibilities.

"Am I gonna be okay?" Jak asked.

"Yup." Barlow patted Jak's knee. "We're just trying to figure out the best way to make you feel better fast. So we're going to need something from you."

"What?" Jak asked.

"We need you to be as brave as you were the last time I saw you, because we have to take some blood. I'm sorry. I know it's uncomfortable. But it's the only way to make absolutely sure of what you have so we can get you the best stuff."

Jeremy felt a warm glow inside when his son removed his jacket and rolled up his sleeve without so much as a whimper. Barlow poked his head outside the curtain and summoned a nurse. She took Jak to the next station to draw his blood.

While they were gone, Barlow turned to Jeremy and Angie. "I have every reason to think it's just a normal bout of flu." He looked at Jeremy, but his words seemed intended for Angie's benefit. "Considering how quickly you washed his mouth, how long you washed it, and the fact that you called me right after the accident so we could start meds ASAP, I seriously doubt this is related in any way to the lab exposure." He turned to Angie. "From Jeremy's description of what a great mom you are, I'm sure you've had your son on lots of liquids and are watching his nutrition."

She nodded. "Trying."

"Keep that up. And keep him on bed rest. Make sure the symptoms are gone before letting him resume full activity. He'll miss the rest of the week of school. Plenty of Sprite and lots of movies should help. You can use appropriate doses of Tylenol or Motrin to control fever and alleviate the aches. And in the meantime we'll run all the tests necessary to put our minds at ease."

"Thank you, Doctor." Angie blinked quickly but tears streamed down her cheeks nonetheless.

"Now may I speak with you about something before I leave?" Barlow asked Jeremy.

Jeremy said, "Of course," and started to duck out.

Angie grabbed Barlow's arm. "Anything you say to him, you can tell me. I want to know. I can handle the truth."

Barlow took her hand. "Mrs. Cramer, I'm so sorry I frightened you. It's about another patient. Honestly. This has nothing to do with your son. I've told you everything I can about him."

Angie blushed. "I'm sorry. Guess I'm a little jumpy."

Barlow stroked her knuckles. "Quite all right—very understandable."

Jeremy gave her a sympathetic look, but she glanced away. He followed Barlow outside the curtain and moved down the hall. "What is it?" Jeremy asked.

"Something you said. Apparently you've been too tied up in PR to keep up with all the lab reports in infectious diseases," Barlow said. He wore a grave expression that frightened Jeremy.

Seeming to read the terror on Jeremy's face, Barlow assured him. "Really—I'm *not* talking about *that* lab—this has nothing to do with

Jak. It's just that when you said Devin had the flu, it made me wonder if you've been too busy to know."

"Know what?" There it was again—that heavy feeling Jeremy got in his gut.

"Her counts are plummeting. Her T-cell levels."

"AIDS," Jeremy whispered.

Barlow nodded. Jeremy bent over and rested his hands on his knees. "Sorry to be the one to tell you," Barlow said. "Especially now with everything else you have going."

"Better you than Jasper—or Castillo!" Jeremy wanted to go see the labs on Devin right away, but Jak was his first priority. He thanked Barlow and headed back to find Angie. She had Jak with her as she stood at one of the counters signing papers.

"I'll finish up the paperwork, honey," Jeremy told her. "Go ahead and take Jak home. I'm right behind you."

She spun around. "Okay. Thanks." He expected to see angry eyes, but instead he saw gratitude.

After Angie and Jak left, several members of the ER staff stopped to tell Jeremy how cute and smart his son was, how nice his wife was, and that they would be thinking of him and his family. Their kindness seemed out of proportion to a flu diagnosis. *They think it's serious because Barlow handled it personally,* Jeremy thought. He made some last-minute arrangements to be out of the office for a few days, glad to have a legitimate reason to quit taking media calls.

On the way home it occurred to him that he could call Devin. So he dialed the nurse's station and they put him through to her room.

"Hello?" Terren answered.

Jeremy resisted the urge to hang up without saying anything. "Hi, this is Dr. Cramer."

"Oh."

"I guess this is Terren?"

"What do you need?"

"How's your wife feeling today?" Jeremy asked.

"How would anybody feel?"

"I'm sor—"

"Fortunately she's asleep right now," Terren said.

"Okay. Well … would you please tell her I called to check on her?"

"Yeah. Sure." The phone went dead.

At the next red light Jeremy phoned the nurse's station again, and the head nurse answered.

"Do me a favor and pull Devin's chart, will you?" he asked. "I'd like to know her latest labs."

"Sure, Dr. Cramer," she told him. She put him on hold for about a minute and then came back on the line. "I'm afraid the news isn't good," she said. "Her CD4 dropped to fifty, and her viral load is high and climbing."

He'd known Barlow was right about her HIV advancing to full-blown AIDS, but this confirmed it. "Oh great," he said. "Now she's helpless against any and all infections."

"So sorry, Doctor. We've put the isolation sign on her door."

CHAPTER 13

In the middle of the night, Jeremy awoke to see Angie walking past his makeshift bed in the den.

He bolted up. "What is it?"

"Don't worry—he's okay. Just rolled off the bed."

Jeremy felt dizzy. He'd stood up too fast, but he found his bearings.

"I took his temperature," she said, "and it's about the same. So I got him more 7-Up. He drenched his pj's with sweat, so I helped him change." The baby cried, and Angie groaned.

"You go back to bed," Jeremy told her. "I'll take care of her."

"Thanks." Angie sounded immensely grateful.

Aided by a nightlight in the hall, Jeremy made his way to Ainsley's room, where he found her whimpering. "What's wrong, Punkin?" he asked.

She stretched toward him from her canopied crib.

"It's not time to get up yet, baby." She whimpered louder. Jeremy lifted her out and carried her over to the rocker. He leaned his daughter against his chest, but she didn't seem to want to rest. "Lie down," he told her, gently guiding her head until she relaxed it against him. "That's it." He patted her back.

Her thumb came up into her mouth, and she closed her eyes. Moments later she lay sound asleep in his arms. Jeremy sat rocking her, breathing in the aroma of baby powder. He ran his fingernails against the rubber dots on the soles of her footy pajamas and hoped nothing he did would ever hurt her.

Once sure he could move without waking her, he took her back to the crib and laid her down. He stroked her hair and hummed a few bars of a song his mother used to sing about a prince and princess. Then he slipped out.

He tiptoed to Jak's room and stuck his head in the door, listening to his son inhale, exhale, inhale, exhale. The rhythm added to the beauty of his child's face as he lay slumbering peacefully, visible in the glow cast from a Batman nightlight.

Jeremy entered, drawn by the magnetic force of paternal affection. Standing over Jak, he watched his son's rising and falling chest. He reached down and felt the sweaty forehead. It was hotter than normal, but not as hot as Jeremy feared. "Please let it be the flu—nothing worse. Please," he whispered.

The following morning Barlow called Jeremy's cell phone to say Jak's throat culture tested positive for antibodies to one of the Coxsackie viruses. Kids picked it up at school all the time. "Just keep pumping fluids and let me know if symptoms persist—or get worse," he said.

Jeremy found Angie in her office perched in front of her computer, eyes fixed on the window that overlooked the backyard.

"I just talked to Barlow," Jeremy said. Seeing fear in her eyes, he added quickly, "Jak's fine. He tested positive to a common virus—one that kids get at school all the time." Angie got up and hugged Jeremy.

Jeremy knew he should probably go back to work instead of using up all his sick leave, but instead he camped at Jak's side. Angie tended to Ainsley while Jeremy insisted on providing round-the-clock care for his sick boy. The fever lasted about seventy-two hours accompanied by a headache. Jak lay in bed miserable and achy most of the time, and Jeremy sat nearby catching up on a stack of medical journals.

Then suddenly Jak's fever disappeared as fast as it had come. Only after the fever broke did Jeremy realize how much guilt he'd carried. He relaxed his shoulders and let out a huge sigh of relief. The tension in his neck disappeared, and the world seemed lighter—as if a blanket of heaviness had been cast off.

The reprieve lasted only a short while, however. Because when he phoned Devin, Terren told him she was too weak to talk.

In the middle of the following night, Jeremy heard Jak groaning. He made his way down the hall to check on the sound. Placing his hand on Jak's sweaty forehead, he knew at once the fever had returned.

At breakfast Jak cried when he drank his orange juice. Jeremy examined his mouth and found painful red blisters on his son's throat and inside his cheeks. They were also on his palms and soles.

Jeremy logged onto his favorite Internet medical site and entered the symptoms, retyping several times to correct hurried misspellings. He verified that the symptoms were sometimes associated with the Coxsackie virus syndrome. When he read the part about the biphasic fever pattern and blisters, he went back and reread the entire article, this time with painstaking care. When he learned the virus was transmitted person-to-person, usually by contact with the hands, he got up and washed his.

Reading that one strain of the virus caused blisters on the tonsils, the soft palate, and the fleshy back portion of the root of the mouth, Jeremy went into Jak's room with a tongue depressor and a flashlight, and made his son say, "Ah-h-h." But Jak had blisters only on his tongue. That fit more with the hand, foot, and mouth strain of the disease. Another strain affected the eyes, but Jak showed no evidence there, either.

Not wanting to worry Angie, Jeremy took his cell phone to the garage and called Barlow. When his assistant answered, Jeremy asked her to page him.

"I'll have him call you back," she said.

"Do you mind if I hold?" Jeremy asked.

"Not at all, Dr. Cramer," she said. "But it could take awhile."

After about ten minutes Barlow came on the line.

"He's got blisters on his tongue now," Jeremy told him. "His palms and soles, too."

"To be expected. Just do the usual stuff to keep him comfortable. But I think you can relax. Honest! Coxsackie viruses are common—usually picked up at school. They often disappear with no further effects—much like the flu."

That's what the article said too. And Jeremy's experience as a doctor. But he still felt better hearing it from Barlow.

The following day the fever disappeared again. Jeremy stayed home with Jak, concerned that the fever might again return. But this time it didn't. Jak, now feeling normal, was eager to get outside and run. He'd had enough of Jell-O and days in bed.

When Jak was still fine the following morning, he returned to school and Jeremy went back to work.

Going through his in-box, he found a written message from Jasper telling him she wanted to talk to him, so he called her office and the secretary told him to come right up. When he got there, she ushered him in immediately and shut the door behind her.

Jasper sat at her desk with hands folded, smiling. He couldn't tell if her pleasantness was genuine or if she was smirking.

"Glad to see you, Cramer. I've been needing to talk to you. I understand our human AIDS studies are doing fantastic."

Jeremy disliked superlatives. "Better than expected, yes."

"With one notable exception," she said. "Ms. Garrigues. We're not giving any to her."

"Up to this point, she hasn't been sick enough," Jeremy said. "Besides, it's still risky—I'd hate to expose her unnecessarily—"

"Perhaps *you'd* hate to, but Castillo wants it. And he expects you to convince her," she added.

"What?" Rage consumed him. He jumped out of his chair. "I won't do it!"

Jasper remained calm—too calm. "Sit down, Cramer." He complied and she continued, "I know what you're thinking. But let me lay this out for you. As far as Ms. Garrigues is concerned, it's probably her only hope. And as for Castillo, you know the man is consumed with envy to the point of loathing you, but he also knows he stands to gain a lot from your work. If Ms. Garrigues does well, it was his idea. If anyone gives you credit, he leaks that you caused the infection. If she does poorly, it's all your fault, too. So it's a perfect soup—for him. No matter what, he's the hero and you're the schmuck."

Jeremy folded his arms and sat upright. "What if I refuse?"

"You're willing to risk her life to thumb your nose at Castillo? Look at it this way. The stuff's expensive and the hospital is willing to give it to her free. What does she have to lose?"

Jeremy wasn't going to lie to Devin. He'd tell her the truth—that Castillo wanted it. It was her choice, and she deserved to know what was behind it. But Jeremy hoped she'd say no. As far as he knew, she wasn't yet near death, and he needed more time to test it. Besides, if she had a bad reaction, he'd never forgive himself.

DEVIN OPENED ONE eye when she heard her hospital door open. Terren slipped in, pulled a chair close, and sat down. He slid his massive hand into hers, and they sat silently for several minutes.

"One of the neighbor kids made you a present," he told her, reaching into his jacket pocket. He pulled out a cutout heart. He held it for Devin to admire, then got up and pinned it to a bulletin board covered with notes, banners, and posters.

As he did, Devin studied the back of his head. She suspected that unless a miracle happened, she would see that bald spot for only a few more days.

The next thing she knew, she was gazing up at blurry silhouettes.

When they came into focus, she recognized them as the worried faces of medical people staring down at her. She looked around for Terren, but he was gone.

"You had a grand mal seizure." The words were spoken by the doctor with the round face and long, dark eyelashes. She couldn't quite pin down his nationality, but his voice sounded familiar.

Devin listened as the beep indicating her heart rate slowed down. The fuzziness in her brain cleared, and she recognized Jeremy.

"Your son ... okay?" she asked.

Jeremy crossed over to one of the machines. "Just fine, thanks." He gave her shoulder a squeeze. "Now, to take care of *you*. I'm just increasing your oxygen concentration here."

"Where's Terren?" she asked.

Jeremy leaned over her bed and pointed to the door of her bathroom. "Vomiting."

She gave him a weak smile. "I sometimes have that effect."

After a long nap Devin awoke to find Terren sitting beside her with his head bowed and hands folded. "I'm sorry. So sorry. If only I had it all to do over."

At first she thought he was talking to her. Then she thought he must be praying. She tried to turn on her side, but she lacked the energy. She mustered the strength to take his hand, and when her touch reached him, he looked into her eyes. Tears streaked his cheeks.

"You think you're being punished?" she asked, her voice scratchy. He stared off, seemingly unable to meet her eyes. "You're not."

He peered at her. "How would you know?"

"I'm a mother." She tried adjusting her pillow, but couldn't get it to cooperate. He reached over and adjusted it for her. "Remember when Tory was six—how she let it slip to your coach that you'd said he was a jerk?" Devin asked.

Terren chuckled. "My, my. Yeah."

"And remember when we found out she'd been lying to us for a year about Bri—about that miserable excuse for a boyfriend she was sneaking around with?"

Terren's smile disappeared. "I wanted to ground her into the next century. And shoot him."

"Did you quit loving her?" Devin asked. He didn't respond. She stared at the ceiling tiles she'd counted hundreds of times in recent days. "Did you want to punish her forever? Or did you just want to know for sure she'd changed?"

"Maybe a little of both." He chuckled, then grew quiet. "Okay ... just that last part. Still, what I did to you was worse. I wish I'd never met that woman."

Me, too, Devin thought.

After a long silence Terren spoke again, "I can't help but wonder if this ... this thing that's happened to you isn't some kind of ironic justice for that. I mean, I know you got the HIV from that needle, not from me. But still ..."

Devin shook her head.

Terren rubbed the moisture from his eyes. "But then that would make even your sickness all about me, wouldn't it?" He stared at a wall. "Do you ever want to ask why?"

"All the time. And I'll bet the good Lord looks at the mess we've made of this gorgeous planet and wants to ask us, 'Why?' too."

He put his glasses back on and kissed her cheek, then wiped one of her tears. "How you forgave what I did, I'll never know."

She noticed he used the past tense and thought of how she was still forgiving him. It had been no simple, one-time deal. She'd forgiven him thousands of times, and she'd still be forgiving him tomorrow.

THAT EVENING JEREMY knocked on Devin's door. Hearing no answer, he nudged it open and looked inside. He found her alone and sound asleep. He walked over to her bedside and sat, hoping she'd waken soon. Then he studied her bulletin board, reading the sentiments of well-wishers. The cards, messages, kids' drawings—Devin had certainly endeared herself to a lot of people, including him.

The blood pressure cuff pumped into action, and Devin stirred.

"The snake's giving you a hug again," he whispered.

She opened one eye, closed it, and smiled. Then she reached over toward Jeremy and took his hand. She took a deep breath and motioned for him to raise the bed. He pressed some buttons, and she was sitting upright.

"You up for a chat about a single-patient study using the T*?" he asked.

She raised her chin and her face was a study in determination. "Only if I'm the patient."

"You're the patient. Looks like you might get to graduate to serious treatment."

She shrugged. "Told you I was sick. And the cost?"

"Free to you," he said. "But I have no idea what your specific side effects will be, so I can't give you an accurate risk-benefit ratio."

"Side effects are the least of my worries right now," she told him.

"If you want to participate, you're in," he said. "Legal is pulling together some fancy paperwork to make sure we're in compliance. And the ethics committee already approved your case."

When she made no response, he continued, "Talk it over with your husband, and let me know."

"We don't have to talk it over," she said with a shake of her head. "I'm in."

Jeremy decided not to mention Castillo after all. No reason to upset her if she was already sure. "You do have an advantage over all other patients—your doctor really likes you," he said. He squeezed her fingers. "We can start tomorrow."

"Thank you."

He leaned down and kissed her forehead, then started to let go of her fingers, but she held fast.

"I signed a living will today," she said. "I guess we should discuss that, too."

Jeremy wished he could say it was too early for such a discussion— and mean it. When he relaxed and quit trying to pull away from her grip, she let go.

"I talked it over with Terren when you first started working with end-of-life AIDS patients," she said. "But you should know ..." Jeremy waited for her to continue, reminding himself that he didn't have to be anywhere. "You need to know I want a do-not-resuscitate order."

Jeremy tried vainly to suppress the lump growing in his throat. He couldn't believe they were discussing DNRs now.

"You know I'm all for prolonging life," she continued. "But I oppose prolonging death. And forget the feeding tube at the end. I know some courts say a tube isn't medical treatment, but I disagree. It *is* treatment, and it's one I don't want. I've helped lots of people sign living wills, and I'm telling you my wishes while I still have a sound mind. And don't you dare make any wisecracks about my mind."

"I wouldn't think of it." He said it with a good-natured tone, but teasing Devin right now was the furthest thing from his thoughts.

"Wise of you. Now you go handle the paperwork for my infusions, and I'll take another nap." She closed her eyes. Then the sides of her mouth raised themselves into a contented smile, and seconds later she drifted off to sleep.

CHAPTER 14

The next morning Jeremy dropped by the hospital's Legal department and picked up the papers for Devin to sign. He took them to her room, where he found Terren spooning oatmeal into Devin's mouth.

Terren glared at Jeremy, who did his best to ignore it. What could he do? He couldn't really blame Terren. But they both had to be here.

"How are you?" Jeremy asked Devin. He tucked the papers under his arm, picked up her chart, and thumbed through it.

"Been to the bathroom eight times this morning, if that gives you any indication," she said. He glanced at the IV pole. The almost-empty bag told him she wouldn't dehydrate anytime soon.

"I feel better today," she said. "So let's get this over with." She pushed aside the tray.

Jeremy pulled up a chair on the side of the bed opposite Terren and lay the papers in front of her. "The notary should be here any sec," he said.

"Notary?" Devin exhaled loudly. "Two witnesses aren't enough?"

Jeremy shook his head and shifted in his seat. He glanced over at Terren, who fixed his stare in the direction of the window. Devin flipped through the papers. A few minutes later Jeremy got up and finished reading her chart to give himself something to do. The silence made him uncomfortable.

They heard a tap at the door and a robust, gray-haired woman in a too-tight uniform entered. Jeremy introduced her and handed Devin a gold pen.

Legal had been thorough. They assigned a medical history number along with a protocol number. The papers all had Devin's name in the appropriate places. The forms listed Castillo as the doctor directing the research, but Jeremy's name appeared on the forms too.

Jeremy perused the first form and explained. "The purpose of the study is to arrest the development of your HIV/AIDS."

Devin shook her head. "Get real. The purpose is to see whether T* works, increase the status of this institution as a research hospital, and to make somebody a gazillionaire."

Jeremy cleared his throat. "A lovely paraphrase of the hospital's purpose, perhaps. My purpose is for you to get better."

Devin patted Jeremy's hand. "You're kind. But there's no need to sugarcoat this. I know the drill."

"You do need to stick to what's written," the notary told Jeremy.

"All right," he said. "The procedure involves a daily dose of T* in a blood-matched solution. I—uh, Dr. Castillo and I—will collect information about you for the purposes of this research. It will involve daily blood tests and volume analyses to monitor organ function. The duration of the study is unknown, and it will involve long-term follow-up."

"That's the best phrase so far: *long-term*," Devin said.

The notary asked Devin and Terren to initial a series of lines to indicate their agreement with all that had been said so far. Then she turned the page.

"Now for the distasteful stuff," Jeremy said. "The part about risks." Devin took Terren's hand. Jeremy started in on the list of physical and nonphysical risks, which included a litany of horrible side effects. "I have to tell you that because T* is closely related to the type of immune cell HIV attacks, it ought to help," he explained. "But it could also create the perfect environment for HIV to thrive." Devin squirmed, and Terren scrunched up his lips.

"So bottom line—I may get better," Devin said, "but then go downhill, or ... or pass on ... as soon as I get my first treatment." Terren stared at the bedspread.

"I don't expect that to happen," Jeremy said. "But you have to know it could." He lowered his voice. "Of course, all potential risks and benefits are completely hypothetical since no one, including me, has a clue what side effects the treatment might produce."

Devin held the pen resolutely and signed again. Then she handed it to Terren. With a shaky hand, he hesitated, but added his initials.

"And now for the potential benefits," Jeremy said. "I hesitate—"

"I know," Devin said. "You always hate to overpromise. Don't worry. We won't interpret *potential* to mean *promised*."

"Good." He inhaled slowly and launched in. "We have a growing number of AIDS patients in end-stage disease and every last one of them is doing better. We've had some fatalities from the underlying disease, but not from the T* cells, as far as we can determine. So potential benefits include dramatic improvement."

Terren nodded.

"And the hospital will completely cover the cost of the study."

Terren, seemingly against his will, let a full smile slip out.

"You do need to know that federal agencies working for or on behalf of the FDA will have access to your records. They'll want to review and monitor them. But that's to protect you, not invade your privacy." He handed them a list the hospital provided of patients' rights.

Finally they made it to the last page. Devin and Terren had to sign a separate consent form stating that Jeremy had explained everything and they chose to participate of their own free wills. Devin signed and dated it, including the time. Jeremy added his signature to that one. The notary did her part. Then Devin handed the pen back to Jeremy.

"When do we start?" Devin asked. "The sooner the better ..." She reached up and squeezed Jeremy's forearm.

"Tomorrow morning."

———✦———

DURING THE NIGHT Devin worried that the infusion of T* would kill her on the spot. "I'm ready to see you, Jesus," she prayed. "It's not death that scares me, it's dying. Help me to 'fear not.'"

But then she'd open her eyes an hour later, wakened by the same nagging anxiety, and pray all over again.

The next morning she held solemn conversations with each family member. She wrote "good-bye" notes to the girls and Terren, and slipped them into her overnight bag for them to find, just in case.

At her request, Terren, her daughters, and their preacher gathered around her for the first infusion. Her heart raced as she watched the stuff enter her IV and make its way to her arm.

Nothing happened. Five minutes. Nothing. Ten. Nothing. A half hour. Nothing. An hour. Nothing.

With each passing hour she entertained increasing hope that she might beat this thing after all.

By the fourth day she saw improvement in her intestinal symptoms. She and her nurses tried to minimize the significance, chalking it up to some bug wearing off. But at the one-week mark, the pain in her intestines subsided completely and she took fluids orally again. Then by the end of the second week, she went from clear liquids to a soft diet and could walk down the hall. Her weight, urinary output, electrolytes, and blood chemistry all showed slightly more positive signs.

By the first of June, Jeremy signed an order to move her to a non-hospital setting. The whole staff gathered as Terren wheeled her to the curb with strings of helium-filled balloons trailing behind the wheelchair.

After that, Devin came every morning to the infectious disease clinic where Jeremy administered her infusions. Over a period of four weeks that extended into mid-June, Jeremy noted with delight Devin's incremental improvements in color, weight, and energy level. For the first time he had real hope of her recovery, and he found himself day-dreaming about the millions of AIDS patients whose lives he might someday be able to save.

ONE HOT EVENING Jeremy left work early—or at least, early for him—to watch Jak's soccer team play. As he made his way across the park to the ball diamond, he spotted Angie and Ainsley in the stands. When he got closer, Angie waved and scooted over to make room.

Once he got situated, she handed him a white bag. "I picked up some dinner for you," she said. "I'll bet you're hungry."

"Thanks. I am." Opening it, he inhaled the aroma of hamburger and fries. He surveyed the field as he munched on fries. Jak looked bored, standing watch as goalie while the rest of his friends battled it out with the other team at the other end of the lawn. "What did I miss?"

"Nothing. They got started only about ten minutes ago," Angie said. "And they haven't made it to this end of the field yet."

After awhile, Jak sat on the ground and played with the grass. Jeremy yelled, "Jak, stand up, buddy! You have to stay ready."

With a slowness that indicated his reluctance, Jak pulled himself up.

Over the course of the entire game, Jak had to defend the goal only three times—briefly. And his team won seven to nothing.

Afterward he seemed overly winded to Jeremy, but he chalked it up to all the excitement of winning, combined with his own tendency to overanalyze every symptom—one of the down sides to specializing in infectious disease.

The following morning Jeremy and Angie were in the kitchen deliberating over what to eat for breakfast when the alarm clock Angie set in Jak's room began to blare. Jeremy tore in to silence the annoying sound. When he saw that Jak remained asleep, Jeremy looked for the reassuring sign of his son's chest rising and falling.

Jeremy shook him. "Wake up, buddy. You'll be late for school." Jak squinted, and then opened his eyes fully. He grinned at his dad. By the time Jak got up every day, Jeremy was usually gone, but this morning he had an appointment off hospital grounds that allowed him to linger.

"Come on, I'll make you pancakes," Jeremy said. Jak got out of bed.

Jeremy returned to the kitchen and asked Angie, "He doesn't usually sleep so soundly, does he?"

"Never," she said. "But the past day or two he's dragged a bit. Still, he played soccer, right?"

"Hmm." To mask his concern, Jeremy turned toward the pantry and searched for the pancake mix. Her point persuaded him until he remembered Jak spent the entire game standing watch over an empty goal.

WHEN JEREMY ARRIVED home late that night, Angie met him at the door. He read it as a sign of warmth until he saw her expression. Then his mind raced with possibilities. He concentrated on sounding calm. "What's wrong?" She took his coat and hung it in the closet. "Angie? What is it?"

She motioned for him to join her on the couch. "It may be nothing," she whispered. "Maybe I'm overreacting, but Jak spent the afternoon lying on the couch flipping channels. When the neighbor kids asked him to play, he said no." Jeremy's heart pounded and a chill shot through him. "And after dinner he said something felt funny. When I asked what he meant, he couldn't really tell me. He took a nap, and when he woke up, he said he felt better."

"Was he coughing?" Jeremy asked. She shook her head. "Having trouble talking?"

"I'm not sure. He didn't say much."

"Why didn't you call me?" Jeremy felt a squeezing sensation in his stomach.

"I wanted to. But I was afraid you'd think I'm a hovering mother. Maybe I am ..." Angie looked away. "It's probably silly." She shrugged. "A kid sleeps through his alarm and then lies on the couch for a few hours, and his mom has him ... well ..." Jeremy got up and headed toward the hall. She jumped up and followed. "Where are you going?"

"To get my stethoscope."

She grabbed his shoulder. "Wait!"

He turned and recognized the same fear on his wife's face that he saw in brain patients on the way to surgery. It was the same fear he now felt, but he didn't want her to know.

"Let him sleep. Let's not scare him—not yet," she said.

Or ourselves, Jeremy thought.

CHAPTER 15

Jeremy sat in his black suit perched like a crow next to Angie, who had on the same dress she had worn to Ravi's funeral. They shivered on the front row under an awning, their eyes fixed on the hole under Jak's coffin. His tiny coffin. Angie looked smaller to him, as if grief shrunk her.

"I want a divorce." She whispered the words, even though they were alone. "You're like King Midas. Except everything you touch dies."

"Only what I love," Jeremy told her. He kept staring at the dirt. "You're right. Take Ainsley and run. As far away as possible."

A funeral home attendant approached. "You're Dr. Cramer, aren't you?" she asked. Jeremy nodded. She seemed too young for the job. "I read all about you," she continued. Jeremy wished she'd leave. "My mom has HIV," she told him. "Hope you find a cure." She picked up one of the flowering plants from a stand and carried it away.

Jeremy squinted as he watched her. Wasn't that Devin's daughter? It couldn't be.

"How do you do it?" Angie asked. "You always make it look accidental—the people you kill."

"I don't do it on purpose!"

"Yes you do."

"That's not fair, Angie! I don't!"

"You do."

"I can't stop it!"

Angie shook him hard. "Can't stop what?"

Jeremy blinked. Red digits on the digital clock read 3:42. Lying drenched in his own sweat, he exhaled hard and waited for the banging in his chest to subside. *I was dreaming,* he thought. Relief swept over him. Thank God.

"Can't stop what?" she repeated.

He could see the dark form of her face in front of him in the dark. "I must've had a bad dream. Sorry to wake you, hon." He rubbed his eyes to get the sleep out.

"You okay?" she asked.

He wasn't sure yet. He reached over and felt around for her hand until he found it. He needed her touch.

"Want to tell me about it?"

Looking at the clock, he blinked until the numbers came into focus. Then he bolted up. "I need to check on Jak."

"I'll come with you." Angie turned on the bedside light and combed back her hair with her fingernails like she always did as soon as she woke up. She grabbed a fuzzy yellow bathrobe from the closet and threw it over the extra-large men's T-shirt that barely covered her thighs.

Jeremy led the way. In light cast from Jak's Batman nightlight, they could see him on his side with his face to the wall. What little motion Jeremy could make out brought comfort. He reached down and touched Jak's fingers. They felt cool, so Jeremy pulled up the covers and tucked them under his son's chin. Then he cupped his hand over Jak's forehead.

"Fever?" Angie whispered. Jeremy shook his head. She touched her chest. "Whew."

"Shhh. Listen." They both stood still and strained to hear.

"What? What am I listening for?" Angie asked. Jeremy touched his index finger to his lips. In another minute he motioned toward the door.

Out in the hall she asked him again, "What did you hear?"

"Nothing," he lied. No use to scare her when he himself wasn't sure. Jak's breathing level seemed a bit elevated for child sleep, but with the noise from the humidifier down the hall and the heat blowing through the bedroom vent, it was hard to tell.

"What did you *think* you heard?"

He shook his head. "Probably nothing. You're not the only one afraid you're overreacting."

She leaned against him. "I'm glad you're a doctor. I don't know how I'd sleep otherwise."

Once she was asleep again, he planned to go back in with a stethoscope.

Angie returned to the bedroom and slid between the sheets. "Br-r-r, it's cold in here. Hold me until I fall asleep, okay?"

"Okay." He drew her to himself. *What would cause labored breathing?* he wondered. Was he just imagining it? He considered numerous heart and lung options. Then again, maybe Jak was in perfect health. Angie hadn't noticed anything, and she'd listened, too. But if something was wrong with Jak—something seriously wrong—she'd never forgive him. After their past trauma he didn't know if they could survive another blow. She'd forgiven so much already.

As he felt the warmth of her body, a wave of longing came over him. Cradling her head in his hands, he kissed her from her neck to the top of her forehead. "I'll love you all my life," he whispered.

He felt something wet against his cheek.

"You crying?" he asked. She nodded. "What's wrong?"

"Nothing," she said into his ear, then nibbled it. "Just been a long time since I heard you say it like that."

JEREMY LAY STARING into the dark. Angie was curled up beside him with a warm foot planted against his leg. He savored the moment—all four of them under the same roof, with the two of them loving each other. He pulled up the sheet to wipe his eyes. He could barely see Angie in the clock's glowing light.

Worry about Jak's condition finally propelled him out of bed.

He groped his way to the dining room, where he found his lab coat draped across a chair. He turned on the light and pulled the stethoscope from his coat pocket. After tiptoeing to Jak's room, he found his son lying exactly as they left him an hour earlier. Something was amiss—no kid stayed that still. Jak's hands were outside of the covers again, curled up at his sternum.

Jeremy rubbed the chest piece in his palms to warm it. Then he positioned the earpieces, pulled down the sheet, and lifted the back of Jak's pajama top. He set the chest piece against Jak's back, causing him to stir a bit. Jeremy held very still. Jak rubbed his sternum and then lay quiet again.

At first it sounded fine, but then Jeremy's heart kicked into overdrive and he shivered. *This isn't normal ... it's bad!* He listened in a few spots to be sure, but he knew the sound well—a discontinuous rattle like a milkshake sucked through a straw. It meant fluid or mucus in the lung's peripheral portions. Inhalation moved air through the lung's tiny tubules. If they had fluid—which they shouldn't—it made a wet, crackly sound. Rales. Pneumonia sounded like that. So did a host of other horrible possibilities. Jeremy mentally cursed.

He'd worried about Jak's heart. But this didn't fit. The fluid wasn't bad enough to make Jak cough or waken him. So Jeremy assured himself that whatever it was, they'd caught it early. The sound was there. Definitely. But it was intermittent.

Jeremy moved the cold-air humidifier into Jak's room and

returned to the den. It was 5:03—two hours until he had to be at work. Barlow would probably be in at seven, too.

He punched in the number for the ER and asked one of the pediatric residents what time she expected Barlow, just to be sure. When he explained the situation, the coordinator told him they expected Dr. Barlow around 6:30. Jeremy wanted to be waiting with Jak and Angie—and a list of questions—when Barlow arrived. He went back to Jak's room and listened again. No change. He stuffed a couple pairs of Jak's underpants and a change of pajamas into his medical bag—just in case. He didn't want to worry Angie by having her pack anything, which would suggest he expected an overnight stay.

In the kitchen Jeremy started the coffee brewing and rummaged through the boxes of cereal, but nothing sounded good. He forced down a bowl of Cheerios and then hit the shower, his mind turning over the evidence with every passing second.

He put on a pair of green scrub pants and put down the lid on the commode. Sitting with his head in his hands, he tried to figure out what to do next.

After tiptoeing back out to the den, he searched through the bookshelf until he found the two volumes he wanted—one on pediatrics and one on infectious diseases. He pulled them down and scanned through lists of diseases and their symptoms. But Jak's fit so many possibilities. Jeremy knew he couldn't be objective or rational. The patient was his own son.

When six o'clock rolled around, he sat on the bed beside Angie, who still lay curled like a cat. *She looks so tranquil*, he thought. He hated to wake her from her peace—on several levels.

He laid a hand on her shoulder. "Wake up, baby." She opened her eyes. "You need to get up," he said.

She glanced at the clock and groaned. "Why? It's only six. Just have some cereal."

Jeremy took a deep breath. "We need to take Jak to … to see Dr. Barlow."

Angie pulled herself up onto one elbow and squinted. "What did you say?"

"I, uh, I listened to his lungs and they sound kind of funny."

"What-kind-of-funny?"

"Not bad." He spoke slowly. "Just different. A little change."

Angie shot out of bed. She started down the hall, but Jeremy stopped her. "He's still asleep," he said.

She spun around. "I thought you said you listened to his lungs."

"I did—while he slept. Just get yourself and Ainsley ready. I've already showered, so I'll get Jak going."

"You don't mean an office visit at this hour, right? We're going to the ER?" Angie threw open a drawer and grabbed her sweats.

"Right." Even if it weren't so early, Barlow didn't see patients in the office on Saturdays.

He watched her through the open bathroom door as she pulled her hair into a ponytail. "How long you been awake?" she asked.

"I never went back to sleep." He walked down the hall to rouse Jak. He found his son asleep again and laid a hand on his back. "Time to get up, buddy." Jak groaned and turned his face toward the wall. "Too tired, Daddy."

"C'mon, I'll carry you." Jak loved piggyback rides. "The train to the kitchen's leaving right now." Slowly Jak sat up. "Stand on the bed," Jeremy said. He helped his son up onto the mattress. Then he backed up to him and Jak climbed aboard.

Jeremy carried him down the hall saying, "Chugga-chugga," and deposited him in a chair in the kitchen. "Hungry?" Jeremy asked.

"No," his sleepy boy said.

Jeremy fixed some oatmeal and coaxed it down by smothering it in brown sugar. Jeremy thought Jak ate slower than a nurse on a call button, and he also noticed his son taking deep breaths between swallows. "Do I have to ..." Jak took another breath, "... get dressed too?"

Jeremy veiled his alarm. Now Jak couldn't even utter a sentence without needing more air. "No, you don't have to get dressed," he told him. "You can stay in your jammies." Rumpled as they were. Who cared?

"Why are we ..." he took another breath "... going to your office?"

"To see Dr. Barlow." Jeremy knelt down to Jak's level. "It's hard to talk, huh?"

"Kind of." He rubbed his eyes.

"Was it hard to talk yesterday?" Jeremy asked.

"A little."

"But it's harder now?"

Jak nodded. "I don't feel so good, Daddy."

Jeremy went over and put his arm around him. "I know. And I'm sorry. I promise I'll do everything I can to help you feel better."

<hr />

JEREMY DRAGGED IN a couple chairs to the ER room assigned to them, and he and Angie held the kids on their laps. Jak drifted back to sleep in his arms.

Around 6:45, Barlow pulled back the curtain and entered carrying Jak's chart. He gestured for them all to stay seated. Jak yawned and opened his eyes.

Portia was with him. *What's she doing here?* Jeremy wondered. Last time Jeremy saw her, she had red hair. Now she was blonde. She had on less makeup than usual, but even this early she wore stilettos and a denim jacket that matched her jeans. He'd always preferred Angie's natural beauty to the *Cosmo* look.

"The nurse coordinator phoned me at home and gave me the heads-up," Barlow said. His gaze shifted from Jeremy to Portia and he told Angie, "Portia thought you might want a friend—someone to hold the baby or something."

"I didn't want to presume ..." Portia said, sounding as timid as Jeremy had ever heard her.

Tears streamed down Angie's face. "Wow. Thank you." She held Ainsley out to Portia. "How kind ..."

She reached out, fanning manicured fingernails in an awkward attempt to figure out how to take the toddler from Angie. "Do you want us to stay here or shall I take her over to Nate's office?"

"The office would be great. You sure you don't mind?" Angie asked.

"Course not." Nate's office was in the medical building across the street. "Come on over when you finish." Portia adjusted Ainsley so the sixteen-month-old sat on one of her bony hips.

Barlow looked at his wife with adoring eyes. Angie handed her the diaper bag, which Portia slung over her free arm. "I can't thank you enough," Angie said.

Portia patted her shoulder. "Glad to help. Anything I need to know? Is she due for a bottle or anything?"

While the two of them worked out the details, Barlow bent down until he was even with Jak, who was still leaning against Jeremy's chest. Jak's eyes locked onto the doctor's Batman tie.

"It matches your pajamas. Does that make us cousins?" Barlow asked. "How do you feel, big guy? A little tired?"

Jak nodded.

Barlow turned to Angie. "Tell me what you know." He stuck a digital thermometer in Jak's ear.

"He didn't feel like playing yesterday," Angie said. "No fever, but not quite himself. And then Jeremy listened with his stethoscope."

Barlow turned his back to Jak and faced Jeremy. "And ...?"

"Crackly."

Barlow looked at the floor. "Hmm. Anything else?" The thermometer beeped, and he removed it. "Ninety-nine point one. Close enough—that's always a good sign." Barlow wrote in the chart and looked to Jak. "Any coughing?"

Jak shook his head.

Barlow turned and peered over the top of his reading glasses, seeking confirmation from both parents. "Nothing," Angie said.

Barlow felt Jak's lymph nodes. "All's well there. Let's see your throat." He pulled a tongue depressor from his lab coat. "You remember the drill?"

Jak nodded.

"Good. This time I'm the Joker. Stick it out good and hard—that's it—like you really hate me." Barlow looked all around inside Jak's mouth with his light.

"See anything?" Angie asked.

"Yup. I see a mouth, a tongue, and some teeth." He removed the depressor, tossed it in the trash, and gave her a thumbs-up.

"Will I have to … to get a shot?" Jak asked.

Barlow squeezed his knee. "I hope not. But to be honest, buddy, I'm not sure. I'll let you know as soon as I do. And we'll tell each other the truth, okay? Right now—no shots. Does it hurt there?" Barlow focused on Jak's sternum where he was rubbing it.

"Not always."

"Sometimes?"

"Uh-huh."

"When did it start?"

"Yesterday."

Barlow looked first at Angie, then Jeremy. "Has he been doing that for long?"

"I didn't notice." Angie sounded guilty.

Jeremy put his hand on hers. "Me either. Though now that you mention it, he might have been doing that in the night."

Angie stared at him. "Really?"

"Maybe. I'm not sure."

Barlow turned back to Jak. "Okay, let me pull up your shirt and try to find out what your dad heard."

"Daddy has one," Jak said, pointing to the stethoscope.

"Know what he uses it for?"

"To listen to my—" Jak took a deep breath—"thumper."

"Right-o. And he can also hear your air inside—if it's moving like it's supposed to." Barlow lifted Jak's pajama top and placed the chest piece on his back. "We have to stop talking now, okay?"

Jak giggled and bent over. "Is it cold?" Barlow asked. Jak shook his head. "Tickles." He sat up straight again and took a deep breath.

Barlow moved the piece all over Jak's back and chest, patiently enduring the squirms, listening, asking him to inhale, to cough, listening some more.

Angie asked, "What do you think?"

Jeremy shook his head slightly as if to silence her.

Barlow didn't seem to hear her anyway. He removed the stethoscope and returned it to his pocket, then helped Jak lie down. He examined Jak's abdomen. And when he concluded his exam, he helped Jak sit back up and placed a hand on his knee. "I told you I'd be honest, right?"

Jak pursed his lips and nodded.

"Ever been to a slumber party?" Jak shook his head. "It's time you got invited to one. We have slumber parties in my wing here every night. A lot of kids stay overnight. Sometimes parents are there—and *sometimes*"—his eyes grew wide—"they *aren't*. You have to sleep in your own room, but you get to eat the food you like and you only have to sleep when you feel like it."

"Cool!"

"I know our kids would love a visit from Batman. So? How about it? Think you might be able to stay over?"

Jak looked to Angie for reassurance. "Remember how much you love the fish tanks?" she asked. He gave her a tentative nod. "It could be kind of fun," she said. She sounded calm, but Jeremy could see her hand trembling.

"You'll … stay with me?" he asked.

"Of course, honey. One of us will be with you the whole time."

"Okay." He gave his most tentative assent.

Barlow turned to Jeremy and Angie. "Here's the 411. You heard the crackling, Jeremy. I hear it, too. We're looking at shortness of breath at rest, cool extremities, fatigue, possible liver and spleen enlargement …"

Jeremy felt like a moron to have missed some of the symptoms. Diseases were supposed to be *his* specialty. Jeremy didn't want to alarm Jak by spelling it out for Angie, but he knew immediately Barlow was thinking "cardiac." He raised his hand subtly and pointed with his thumb to his chest. Barlow gave the hint of a nod.

"You've got one tough kid here," Barlow said. "We need to run some tests, but at first glance, it looks like lungs. Still, the symptoms *could* fit a cardiac scenario. So let's get him checked in and hooked up to some monitors."

Barlow stuck his head out of the room and called for a nurse. A delicate woman in green scrubs with brown hair entered the room, which by now felt crowded to Jeremy. "I need a pulse ox immediately, along with some nasal oxygen," Barlow told her.

She stepped out for a moment and returned with her hands full. She clipped the clothespinlike oximeter onto Jak's fingertip to measure his blood-oxygen level. Then she strapped little oxygen tubes around his head and ran the feed to his nose. Barlow ordered X-rays, blood-gas levels, CBC, a liver panel, and an EKG—for starters.

Lungs? Heart? Neither option sounded great to Jeremy. Suddenly his eyes felt leaden as his sleepless night caught up with him. And the day was only beginning.

CHAPTER 16

After they got Jak into his "bed on wheels," Jeremy stayed with him in the ER while Angie headed to Admissions to navigate her way through the paper maze.

Tristan, a technician with a goatee and a double chin, entered the ER room. Jeremy knew him well.

"Meet my son, Jak," he said.

Tristan drew closer to see Jak's pajama fabric. "I *love* the look. I want one of those. But I doubt yours would fit me."

Jak seemed unimpressed.

Jeremy turned to Jak. "We need to get your shirt off so we can cover you with stickers."

"The cool thing is," Tristan said, "it doesn't hurt at all, and you get to be like Electric Man with lots of wires." Working his way around the pulse ox and the nasal oxygen with its plastic tubing, he stuck quarter-sized plastic stickers on Jak's chest, arms, and legs. Then he pulled out some long wires.

Jak's eyes grew wide and his lower lip trembled. Jeremy, standing alongside the gurney, stroked his arm. "You won't feel a thing, son. It really doesn't hurt—not at *all*. Not even a pinch."

The tech keyed in Jak's name and birthday. Jeremy wanted to see the cardio pattern as the machine read it, but he kept his focus on Jak. "Stay super still, okay? It'll be over soon."

Jak looked up with trusting eyes and gave a solemn nod. "That's *my* boy!" Jeremy said, pride washing over him. Jak's lips parted as if he had something to say, but Jeremy held up his index finger. "No talking." Jak complied by making a zipping motion across his lips.

Jeremy leaned against the table, craning his neck to see. Suddenly his pager went off. He looked down at the numbers—it was from an unknown source within the hospital. Surely it could wait. He glanced back at the EKG machine as a printer rolled paper off the top of it. From where he stood, on the other side of the bed, Jeremy thought it looked all right. The rate was a little fast—at about 110. But he was pretty sure the EKG would be okay. Maybe there were some subtle changes that the cardiologist would pick up, but they'd be hard to read because of the fast rate. The QRS complexes—the needle deflections with each heartbeat that made the spiky pattern—were close together due to the fast rate. Otherwise it looked normal.

Jeremy's cell phone rang. It was Barlow, calling with a room number and a request to meet him after the EKG and chest X-ray.

"I'll take the printout to Dr. Barlow right now," Tristan said.

"I hafta pee. Bad," Jak said. Jeremy took that as a good sign. "Hang on, son. What do you think?" he asked Tristan.

"Honestly? It looks pretty good. But Dr. Barlow may want a cardiology consult."

"Thanks a lot," Jeremy said.

After Tristan left, Jeremy helped Jak button his pajama top. "Let's get you to the bathroom. I have to come in with you, because we're going to have to save some of your pee in a cup."

Jak giggled. Jeremy helped him slip the nasal oxygen cannula over his head and went into the bathroom with him to get a specimen. Afterward, while Jak washed his hands, Jeremy leaned against the wall outside the door and called the number on his beeper.

"Dr. Castillo's office," a woman announced. He recognized the voice of the chief's secretary.

"Dr. Cramer here. You—or he—paged me?"

"Yes. I did. Thank you for calling back, sir. Hold the line for Dr. Castillo, please."

Jeremy figured the chief would leave him on hold for ten minutes or more, but Castillo picked up immediately. "Cramer, I need you to go with me to Washington D.C. next weekend." Jeremy couldn't imagine why. "Our research on the nurse you infected …"

Jeremy felt his face burn. That nurse had a name and he didn't appreciate the accusation, even if it was partly true.

"She's received a month's worth of T* therapy, correct?"

"Yes, sir."

"I've been talking with Dr. Freudigman at NIH about it. Of course you know him, right?"

"We haven't met, but I'm familiar with his work," Jeremy said.

"Freudigman's coordinating a panel on cutting-edge research next weekend at the National HIV/AIDS Symposium in D.C.," Castillo told him. "And I need you there to explain all the ins and outs of the lab work. Freudigman just had a cancellation so he wants us to fill in talking about our success in treating one of the super-strains."

The word *our* irritated Jeremy. He'd rather have a root canal without anesthesia than spend a weekend with Castillo. Besides, Jak needed his daddy, though Jeremy thought surely he'd be better by then.

Castillo said, "I understand you have a special rotation with call-free weekends, so changing plans should be no problem." Jeremy seethed. "So I'll have my secretary deliver your airline tickets and the itinerary. We'll be staying at the Churchill Hotel. We can talk more about the presentation when we get there."

Jeremy heard a click. He snapped his phone shut and pushed the bathroom door open to check on Jak.

A few minutes later they proceeded to radiology, where Jak got chest X-rays. When the films developed, Jeremy stood reviewing them. Both sides of Jak's lungs showed a cloudy fuzz. And the cardiac shadow concerned him. It always appeared a bit large on kids, but Jeremy knew a problem when he saw one. He stood scratching his head. It looked like congestive heart failure, but that seemed unlikely. He thought of some of the cardiomyopathies, but his mind kept going blank. It frustrated him that he couldn't think straight.

An hour later Jak lay in a private room, sleeping on oxygen and connected to a pulse oximeter. Down in ER his level was 88 percent, but with the nasal oxygen, it topped out at 95. A tech brought in a portable cardiac monitor on a cart like Jeremy's garage tool chest on wheels. Jak's heart beeped a regular pattern with occasional extra beats. Even the minor irregularities unnerved Jeremy and he was glad to step out in the hall to consult with Barlow while Angie stood vigil.

"I know we need more tests," Jeremy said. "But I have to know your working hypothesis—even if it turns out to be something else. Guessing makes me crazy." He rubbed his temples to relieve tension.

"I'm sorry," Barlow said. "This must be awful for you. Here's what I know: Our pediatric cardiologist is out this week, so I called Alex Combs, the cardiologist on call, and he's consulting on the EKG. He should drop by soon. All the parts of the work-up so far suggest a primary cardiac diagnosis with pulmonary complications secondary. I'm not sure yet what the etiology might be."

"So which came first? Do we have a lung problem straining the heart or a heart problem filling the lungs?" Jeremy asked.

Barlow nervously licked his lips. Jeremy understood why he was stalling. He'd do the same. If his hunch ended up worse than the actual diagnosis, he'd have worried Jeremy and Angie needlessly.

"You want the straight story. I get that. I would too," Barlow said. "And I suspect you already know you have one sick little boy. And no, I don't think it's originating with his lungs. After reviewing his chart this morning, I'm thinking the Coxsackie virus he had two months ago could be causing myocarditis."

Jeremy gasped. "Myocarditis?" The words hit him like an emotional aneurism to the center of the brain. It was true—Jak's symptoms did fit an infection of the heart muscle. Jeremy's paternal stupor had kept him from piecing it all together.

Another example of why doctors shouldn't provide the sole care for their own families, Jeremy thought.

A nurse walked by and Jeremy wondered how the world could go on—even just his own corner of it—without stopping, at least momentarily, in reaction to the possible diagnosis. He mentally ran toward the brick wall of bad and worse, crashing with worst—irreversible heart damage, transplant. Or death. "Where do we go from here?" Jeremy steadied himself by placing a hand on the wall. He hoped Barlow wouldn't notice.

"I have to rule out some other conditions that can mimic it," Dr. Barlow said. "I don't want to prescribe heart meds if it's a lung issue. Or vice versa. So we give him oxygen and restrict his fluids—even a touch of diuretic. We keep him stabilized and work him up fully—check everything. I wish his symptoms didn't fit the pattern, but he did have that unusual viral infection."

Jeremy hesitated. "So we keep an eye out for symptoms of heart failure?"

Barlow blinked slowly and nodded. "His heart's working hard to keep up. He's compensating okay—so far. And kids tend to get better if we give them half a chance. So we'll give him every chance we can. It's harder when it's one of your own kids." Barlow pointed down the hall. "Speak of the devil." Jeremy turned to see Portia approaching with Ainsley.

Portia's hair was messed up and her white starched shirt was untucked and wrinkled. As she grew closer, Jeremy saw wet spots where Ainsley must have drooled.

"Thanks so much," he told Portia. "Here, let me take her." Ainsley reached out for him and one whiff told Jeremy she needed a diaper change.

Portia handed Ainsley and her accessories to him. Cheerios spilled as he slung the diaper bag over his shoulder.

"Angie's in the room. You can go on in," he said, gesturing toward the door.

"How's Jak?" Portia asked.

"Don't know yet, but at the moment he's resting," Barlow told her.

"Obviously you admitted him, so it must be super serious," she said.

"Something like that," Jeremy said.

"Not necessarily serious. We just need more information," Barlow said.

She went inside and Barlow shook his head. "Sorry. She means well …"

Jeremy chuckled, remembering that Angie said she could be blunt. "No problem. Excuse me. I need to go change her." He dipped his head to the baby in his arms and started off toward the restroom.

"I'll check back in a few hours," Barlow called after him.

THAT AFTERNOON ANGIE sat watching Jak, hoping Dr. Barlow had the cure for whatever nasty bug had hold of her son. Portia had gone to lunch with her husband, and Jeremy was down taking care of Devin's daily treatment in the clinic.

She was watching her boy sleep, alone in her thoughts of Ravi and fears of losing another child. A tapping at the door brought her back to the present. It creaked open. She expected Portia or Jeremy, but it was someone else. Penetrating gray eyes looked at her and flashed with immediate recognition. "Hello—Mrs. Cramer? Angie, isn't it?"

As the doctor with chestnut-colored hair approached, she stood and extended her hand.

"You remember me—Alex Combs?" he said. "Portia introduced us." He held her hand with both of his.

"You have a good memory," Angie said. His hands felt warm.

"Some faces you don't forget," he told her. "I understand you've had a terrible morning. I'm so sorry. Considering all you've been through, you look amazing."

She stammered. "Uh ... thanks. Um ... have a ... uh ... a seat." She felt like an idiot. She expected him to sit across the room, but he pulled a chair over next to hers. An awkward silence ensued, so Angie looked at her son's IV fluid bag and pretended to read the numbers.

"Mrs. Cr—may I call you Angie?"

"Sure, I guess. Sure."

"All right. And please call me Alex. Angie, I've seen the EKG results and I wanted to talk with you—and your husband, of course—about them."

She glanced at the clock on the wall. "Jeremy's not due back for another hour."

"That's all right," Alex said. "I can tell you, and then you can pass along what I've said." Angie nodded. "I'm not a pediatric cardiologist. Our best one is out until next week. But Dr. Barlow asked me to take a look at the EKG, which I did. And I do have some concerns, but I don't have enough information yet. So with your okay, I'd like to order an echocardiogram on your son."

Angie burst into tears. She wished she were stronger. She hated crying in front of other people, especially people she hardly knew. "I'm sorry."

He lay a comforting hand on the back of her neck. "No reason to apologize. You've been through quite the traumatic—"

When he stopped midsentence and whipped his hand away, Angie looked up to see why. Portia Barlow had walked into the room. She stood frozen.

"Uh ... hello—Dr. Combs," she said icily.

He stood. "Hello, Portia. How've you been? It's been awhile."

"Yes," she said. "It has." She focused intently on Angie. "I need to run, but you call me if you need anything. And I'll phone you later. Promise." She disappeared as quickly as she'd arrived.

"Excuse me," he said. "Be right back." He ducked into the hall, and Angie heard him calling out Portia's name. Angie took the opportunity to blow her nose and wipe her eyes. Alex returned seconds later.

"Already gone?" Angie asked.

He nodded. "Well that was awkward."

At least he's honest, she thought. Angie didn't dare utter a word.

"I beat her the last time we played and I think I bruised her ego," he said. "She hasn't played a match with me since."

So much for honesty. But Angie hardly cared. Especially now, the whole thing seemed so petty.

CHAPTER 17

For the past month Jeremy had spent at least an hour of most days with Devin in the clinic where she received her infusions. He usually looked forward to the daily respite for two reasons—he loved seeing his own research going great, and also because Devin was like a younger, medical version of one of his favorite sages, Maya Angelou. She told engaging stories and found something to affirm in everybody she met—even when she felt rotten. But she felt rotten less and less frequently. And as her energy increased, so did her enthusiasm for Jeremy's work.

But today he didn't feel like talking to anyone. He got off the elevator on the ground floor and passed the fountain at the main entrance. The reception area of the infectious disease clinic, located just off the main hallway, always held what Jeremy considered a fascinating mix of characters, probably because there were so many ways to contract infectious diseases. He entered through a side door to bypass the crowded waiting room.

Lesia, the appointment secretary, was on the phone. If one could be a clotheshorse in medical garb, Lesia mastered the art. Every day she wore a different set of scrubs, always in varying shades and patterns of pink.

Jeremy scanned through the list of patients to find out what room she'd scheduled him to use. He did so slowly, satisfying his curiosity about the challenges facing the team that day—a couple home from vacation with parasitic disease; a fungal infection; bone and joint infections; an infected pacemaker; a TB case; a chronic lung infection; and three college students with STDs.

Lesia punched the Hold button on her phone and asked Jeremy, "You need something, Dr. Cramer?"

He gestured toward her sliding-glass window. "I don't see Devin in the waiting room."

"We've already got her set up in Room D. Ready when you are. Is your son okay?"

"Yeah." He turned his back to her. Having called down to explain his delay, he sure didn't feel like talking about it. He proceeded to the room where Devin was and knocked without waiting for a response.

"Sorry I'm so late," he said when she looked up.

"No problem, man. I hear it's been quite a night." Devin's color was good. "How's—"

"I see you're up to 120 pounds. Fantastic." He plopped down and avoided eye contact by studying her chart. When he saw her date of birth, he calculated her age, and it surprised him. "Hard to believe you're forty-five."

Devin picked up on the hint and didn't press him. "I'm going to assume you think I look younger, not older, than that. I'd say I feel about 95—percent, that is. If the evidence didn't say otherwise, I'd guess I was totally healed."

He kept looking at her chart. "That's great," he mumbled. He got up and hung a bag of the T* solution on the IV pole. "You know the drill. Shall we?"

As he connected the catheter beneath her clavicle to her IV line, she reached out and wrapped thin, gentle fingers around his wrist. He looked down at her.

Her dark hand gave his wrist a squeeze. "I'm sorry. It must be so hard. Too hard to go through alone."

ANGIE HELD A fork up to Jak's lips and coaxed him to taste some beef stroganoff. Suddenly a bar from the "William Tell Overture" blared out from her purse. She fumbled around and retrieved her cell phone on the third ring. Caller ID read "Barlow." She pressed the "talk" button, trying to remember when she'd given Dr. Barlow her cell number. But it wasn't him. It was Portia.

"Sorry to leave like that, Angie."

"That's okay. I appreciated yo—"

"I really should apologize," Portia said. "Talk about casting you in the middle of my awkward drama."

"What do you mean?" Angie shifted to hold the phone in one hand and picked up Jak's fork in the other.

"The little interchange with Dr. Combs. That must've felt awkward."

"A little, now that you mention it," Angie said. "He ran into the hall looking for you, but you were already gone."

"I'll bet he did. Listen, I'd rather not go into anything in detail—not here, anyway. Let me just leave it at this: I'm sure he's a competent cardiologist. Nate certainly thinks so. All I can say is he's consistent. He leaves no stone—or skirt—unturned. Stay away from that man if you can."

"I thought you had a pretty well-matched handball partnership."

"We did—for a while. Before I found out what he's really like. For the past couple of weeks, I've been running the jogging track—alone."

From what Angie had seen, Portia seemed like the sort of woman who would appreciate the kind of attention a man like Combs would offer. But Portia had surprised her before. Angie never would have pegged Portia as the kind to show up and hold a toddler. Angie was curious, but she knew better than to push. "It was kind of you to watch Ainsley. You arrived before I even realized how much help I'd need," Angie said.

"Your baby's really sweet. How are you managing the two kids with Jak in the hospital?"

"My parents live here in Denver, so Mom took off work and came to get Ainsley."

"Good. How long do you think your son's in for?"

Angie had no idea. She wished she knew. Her mother had asked the same question. "Um, I—"

"Sorry. Don't mean to make it sound like prison or something," Portia said.

"I really don't know."

"So you'll be spending the night there tonight?"

"Yeah, probably several nights." Angie hoped that would be all it would take.

"Then you need some stuff, huh? At least an overnight kit—some pajamas? A robe? Toothbrush?"

Angie hadn't even thought ahead that far. "Yeah, guess so," she said.

Portia's voice brightened. "Sounds like a good combo—you have a need, and I love to shop."

"How about if I just give you my house key and a list?" Angie asked.

"I'd rather shop," Portia said. "What size do you wear?"

Angie almost chuckled as she envisioned the sort of stuff a woman like Portia might choose for her. Maybe something skintight? Leopard skin? Glitter? But it was a kind offer. "That would be great—then I could stay with Jak."

"Good. So ... your size?"

"Depends. Something as loose as nightwear and sweats—a ten. Closer-fitting stuff, an eight."

"I'm on it," Portia said. "See you this evening."

JEREMY CARRIED DEVIN'S blood samples to the lab and handed them off. By midmorning he was grateful for a reason to focus on something other than Jak for a while. It seemed like days had passed, not hours, since he listened to Jak's heart in the early morning.

When he got to his pod, he found the airline itinerary Costello had had sent over. Departure was set for late Friday—in six days. No way he could go to Washington. But how could he get out of it?

Jeremy despised Castillo more every day, and on so many levels. As a researcher Jeremy preferred to keep theories to himself until he had solid evidence either way. He liked to verify, verify, verify before he risked giving false hope.

Castillo did the opposite. The minute Jeremy had the hint of a possible breakthrough, Castillo had PR draft a press release and send it to media outlets.

Jeremy didn't know how he'd get out of going, but he could get information together for Castillo, wait on a clear diagnosis for Jak, and then enlist Jasper's help in declining the trip, if necessary.

He fired up his laptop and opened the daily log of Devin's latest results. When he plotted her progress—with weight, blood levels, and energy improving—he congratulated himself that at least something was going right in his life.

He analyzed the data for a few minutes before calling Bonnie Dylan, head of research. Jeremy had postponed a meeting scheduled for that morning, but he told her he had a few minutes now.

He went to the conference room and waited for the team to arrive. When they all got there, he sat at the end of the table and greeted the four students and Dylan. The students had on their usual suit-coat-length lab jackets. Dylan and Jeremy wore the longer coats that marked them as doctors.

Dylan, a woman with ash-blonde hair, tight-set lips, green eyes, and a complexion scarred from acne, had grown increasingly distant of late. Jeremy found out from Jasper that some of the so-called grant money for his own research had actually come from one of Dylan's projects that Castillo defunded. Dylan had never been unkind to him, just strictly business. Jeremy could understand if she resented him. She headed the department; he was a lowly resident. And when Jeremy had added her name to the journal article, Castillo took it off, so sometimes Jeremy felt caught in the middle.

Now she looked at him expectantly. On the center of the table Jeremy placed a cage with five lab rats inside. "Ladies and gentlemen," he said, "I give you Lucy, Ari, Nic, Andy Dorie, and May. Anyone know what their names have in common?" No one ventured a guess. "Let me give you another clue, then. They're short for *Lusitania, Arizona, Titanic, Andrea Doria,* and *Maine.*"

Ted, a bucktoothed assistant with wavy hair and a tattoo of a sword as sharp as his mind ventured a guess. "They all sank?"

"Excellent," Jeremy said. "Yes—all ill-fated sailing vessels. These, my friends, are our test subjects for our next phase of research with T*—drowning experiments. I want you to meet the drowning rats."

"Sounds like a great name for a rock group," Ted said.

THROUGHOUT THE REST of the day, Jeremy would work for about an hour, check on Jak, look into pending test results, and return to the lab, then check on Jak again. Around dinnertime he cycled back through to the check-on-Jak stage and found Angie snoozing in the vinyl chair across from Jak's bed. She looked uncomfortable.

He read Jak's chart, checked his IV, and observed his son for any sign of progress. But the oxygen and pulse rates remained the same. He uncovered Jak's feet to check for swelling when Angie woke up. "What're you doing?" she asked.

He tucked the blanket back in and leaned against Jak's bed. "You know that chair reclines, don't you? You looked uncomfortable."

She shook her head. "No one told me. That woulda been nice."

She reached for the lever on the side of the chair and adjusted it. "You didn't answer my question."

"Just checking for signs. But he's fine."

"What kind of signs?" She sounded worried. Again.

"We need to stay on the lookout for weight loss, swelling of feet, ankles, and abdomen, loss of appetite—"

"Loss of appetite? He already has that!"

Jeremy nodded. "I know. I mean if it gets worse."

"I don't see how it can get much worse. He's hardly eaten all day."

Jeremy had always considered it an insult to patients when doctors withheld information, but it seemed that any information he shared only struck terror in Angie.

They heard a knock and Portia entered wearing a big smile and carrying department-store bags. "Hope I'm not interrupting anything. I brought Christmas." She set down the bags in the middle of the floor.

Both Jeremy and Angie thanked her. "I didn't bring jammies for you," Portia told Jeremy. "If you're anything like my husband, you sleep in scrubs all the time. Now what are you two doing about dinner?"

"Good question," Jeremy said. He looked at Angie. "I guess we can grab something in the cafeteria. But we need to go in shifts."

Angie agreed. "Haven't even thought about it."

Portia waved her forward. "Come on with me. You've been cooped up in here all day." She looked over at Jeremy. "We'll go find something off-campus and bring a doggy-bag back for you."

Jeremy could tell Angie hated to leave Jak, but he was sleeping. "You can stay for a while?" Angie asked him.

"Sure. I might even snooze," he said, pointing a thumb toward the recliner. "Go."

CHAPTER 18

Portia met Angie at the curb in her two-seater BMW. Angie thought they made quite a sight—Portia decked out and smelling like a perfume shop and she in a sweat suit and smelling like an alcohol swab. She told herself she didn't care, but she applied lip gloss in a vain effort to minimize the contrast anyway.

Portia took her to an upscale Italian place a couple of miles from the hospital. Upon entering, Angie salivated when she smelled garlic and cheese. Ebony tables with lacquer finishes were set about the room, which had enormous picture windows draped from ceiling to floor in red velvet. Portia pointed out the table she wanted, one in the back with nobody around. "Better for girl talk," she told Angie in a stage whisper.

A short, dark man with a thick accent took their drink orders. Angie asked for water with lemon, but Portia insisted on a couple glasses of Merlot. He brought them immediately, and by the time Angie took three or four sips, Portia had drained hers. She plopped it down like a stein of beer, put her elbows on the table, and leaned toward Angie. "I know what you're thinking. But we weren't sleeping together." Angie nearly spewed her drink. She thought about denying that the thought had crossed her mind, but why lie?

"Though that was no doubt his fantasy," Portia said.

"Listen, that's your private—"

"What pitiful excuse of an explanation did he give you for our little interchange?"

Angie hesitated, wanting to avoid placing herself in the middle of their tiff. Still, Portia expected an answer. "He told me he beat you at handball and you haven't played since."

At first Portia didn't move. Then she threw back her blond head and laughed. "Oh that's classic! Posh!" She unzipped her coat and turned to wrap it around her chair. Her V-necked sweater accentuated cleavage that Angie recognized as too large and too high to be original equipment. "As far as sports partners, we were well matched," Portia said. "We took turns beating each other all the time. I don't even remember who won that day. This is all too funny."

"Glad you're amused," Angie said, forgetting Jak for the moment.

"It would be funnier if it didn't make me so angry." Portia looked around in an apparent effort to assure that no one could hear her. Angie had to strain to catch her words. "I'll tell you what really happened. He was a total jerk, that's what."

"What happened?" Angie asked.

Portia relaxed a little. "We're both big flirts, but mostly I'm the harmless variety. In my heart of hearts I'm loyal as a collie."

Her words say "loyal" but her body language says "not so much," Angie thought. Either Portia was self-deceived or she had an agenda. Angie suspected the latter, but it made no sense. Why would Portia care what she thought?

"From my perspective our relationship was mostly about exercise with some chemistry to make it interesting," Portia said. "A harmless little ego trip for both. I should have cut things off when Alex started sending text mess—"

The waiter arrived with menus. Angie wanted to give Portia the benefit of the doubt. She knew what neglect could do when an attentive, great-looking alternative came along. Hadn't she asked an editor to take her off a committee once when a handsome colleague started to occupy all her thoughts? She'd flirted plenty before having an attack of conscience. Still, something about Portia's exaggerated protestations failed to ring true.

After they looked over the menus, Portia waved the waiter over and they gave him their selections. For a while they made small talk about Jak and Ainsley. But her dinner partner was determined to take the conversation back around to Alex. "Anyway ... as I was saying, one afternoon we finished our match. He asked me to join him for a drink before he went back to the hospital." She turned her palms upward. "And how much can happen sitting at a bar? So I said okay."

The waiter brought their food, and Portia asked for more wine.

Angie took a bite.

"How is it?" Portia asked, pointing her fork toward Angie's Alfredo.

"M-m. Fine," Angie said, still chewing. "Yours smells good."

Portia picked at her food with the fork. "Looks a little on the dry side. Oh well. Anyway, I started to go to my car so I could meet him there, but he offered to drive. And without thinking I said okay. So I got in with him." The waiter returned with the wine and refilled Portia's glass. He offered more to Angie, but she declined. When he left, Portia made a face at her food and carried on.

"The place had this sultry jazz going. Alex chose a seat in this candlelit booth and patted the bench beside him. But I sat across from him. I mean, how would it look if someone from the hospital came in?"

How, indeed, Angie thought. She wondered again what had attracted a sharp guy like Barlow to a man-eater like Portia.

The waiter returned and asked if everything was okay. When Portia sent her compliments to the chef, Angie observed how smoothly she lied. Portia was definitely too smart and man-savvy to play the naïve girl. Portia turned back to Angie.

"So ... we got to chatting it up. Harmless prattle. After awhile he excused himself to use the restroom. But when he returned, he scooted in close. He kept talking about work. Well, he must've been topping off my drink. Sure, I can drain a glass." She held up the empty one in front of her. "But I never consume more than two. Never. But that day, I just kept going, oblivious to how much I swallowed."

Angie had already grown tired of the one-sided conversation. She just wanted to get back to the hospital. But it seemed the less interest she showed, the more Portia determined to convince her.

"... kiss my neck and talk naughty to me. I should've slapped him then, but I didn't want to make a scene. Apparently he took the absence of objection for a green light, because next thing I knew, his hand made an ascent up my skirt. I insisted I had to use the restroom, but he wouldn't stop. Finally when I made my demand loud enough, he slid over and let me get out. But when I stood, the room spun. So I was stuck. We arrived in his car, and I'd had too much to drink. So I *made* him take me home."

"You didn't call someone to come get you?" Angie asked.

"What? And say I got snockered with a doc who was hitting on me?" Portia shook her head. "I really had no choice. And we couldn't pick up my car at the club because I'd had too much to drink. So when we got to my place, he walked me to the door. I fumbled around for my keys, but kept dropping them. So he took them from me, found the right one—and of course came in when I did."

Of course, Angie thought. She caught the waiter's eye and raised a couple of fingers to call him over. "Could I get an order of lasagna to go?" she asked.

Portia kept on, "Once we got inside, he pinned me to the wall and pressed up against me. But at that point I threw him out. I haven't spoken to him since—until today."

"I see," Angie said. "How'd you get your car back?"

"When I sobered up, I took a cab over and picked it up."

Angie wondered why she hadn't taken a cab home in the first place. But she had a pretty good idea.

"You're the only person who even knows I was meeting him at the club—not that we had anything to hide. It's just a silly little detail I'd hate to worry my husband with. So I'd appreciate it if you didn't mention any of this."

The fuzzy picture snapped into clear focus for Angie. "Got it," she said. How much Jeremy might have already said to Barlow, she didn't know, but she doubted her running into the two at the club had even come up.

"I just couldn't believe Alex would ply me with liquor. He knew better."

Angie thought Alex wasn't the only one who knew better.

AROUND 4:30 SUNDAY morning Angie heard the tinkling of vials. She opened her eyes to see a tech wheeling a bunch of blood samples into Jak's dimly lit room. The light over the sink flickered to life.

"Sorry," the young tech said. "I need to draw some blood so we have the results by the time Dr. Barlow arrives this morning." He checked the band on Jak's wrist and verified that it matched the name on a vial. Then he wrapped a tourniquet around Jak's arm. "Make a fist for me," he said.

Jak obeyed, but—seeing the needle—he started crying. Angie helped by holding him, but his volume and pitch increased until the tech got all he needed and withdrew the needle.

"All done now. I'm sorry," he told Jak.

But Jak was screaming inconsolably. Angie patted his back and said, "It's okay, honey. Mommy's here. Settle down." She leaned down and kissed his forehead. "You need a tissue, don't you?" She took one from his tray table and helped him wipe his nose and eyes. Then she stroked his hair until the wailing turned to sniffling. Blotches dotted his cheeks and his eyes drooped. Angie was glad she'd sent Jeremy down to a call room around midnight to sleep on a real bed. No use in his losing half a night's rest too.

Eventually Jak quieted down and drifted back into a peaceful slumber. But she was too wide-awake to doze off again, though she felt weary. She brushed her teeth with the supplies Portia had brought and washed her face. Looking at her own medium complexion, oval face, and blue eyes, she decided she didn't look half as weary as she felt. Or maybe—she told herself with a smirk—she just looked better having exchanged oversized shirts for fitted red satin pj's. She massaged a crick in her neck.

After lowering the recliner's footrest, she flicked off the light. She plopped back down, drew the blanket up around her, and mindlessly focused on the line of light coming in from under the door.

Concern for Jak captured her thoughts for a while. Then she wondered how Ainsley was. Eventually she considered her marriage. Portia had shaken her. She didn't know why, but something about the exchange made her want to move toward Jeremy, to protect what they had together. She loved him, but sometimes she despised him. If Jeremy asked what he could do to redeem himself, she'd have no answer. How fair was that?

Hadn't she assumed he would keep neglecting them all to do research? Who knew what sort of hoop jumping he'd had to do to keep his promise to be with them twice a week considering the demands of his job.

But there was still Ravi. If only Jeremy had stayed home instead of going to the lab that day. How many times had she thought that? A couple hundred thousand?

In his defense she thought of two times Jak distracted her from starting up at a green light only to keep her from being broadsided when someone ran a red. She'd been lucky. Twice. Was it fair to blame Jeremy for being unlucky?

Someone knocked and she wondered who it could be at this hour.

The door creaked open and a nurse wheeled in a portable blood-pressure machine.

Angie jumped up and flipped on the switch in the bathroom to avoid blasting Jak with the overhead light. With her help, the nurse got the readings she needed without waking him.

"What's the outlook?" Angie asked.

"Temperature fine. Blood pressure's normal."

Angie said thanks and held open the door as the woman wheeled her equipment back out. Then Angie quietly latched the door and returned to Jak's side. She stroked his hair. "Please get better, honey," she whispered. She glanced at the oxygen saturation level on the monitor. It had inched up to ninety-six percent. If only his heart would slow down.

ON MONDAY MORNING Jeremy dropped by to see Jasper to talk to her about ducking out of the Washington D.C. trip, but her secretary told him she was on vacation until the following Tuesday. When he realized he'd have to face Castillo alone, he got a heavy feeling in his gut.

He called to set up an appointment, explaining to Castillo's secretary that he needed less than fifteen minutes. She promised to squeeze him in at 1:30. He arrived five minutes early and bent his way through four paper clips before the chief waved him in, pointed to the leather wingback, and told him to sit down.

Perched in his executive chair behind the mahogany desk, Castillo closed some medical journals and stacked them. Then he folded his hands. "So? What is it, Cramer?"

"My son, sir." Jeremy grasped the arms of the chair for support. "He ... he's here in the hospital." Jeremy hated how wimpy he sounded. Castillo had a reputation for attacking weakness like a lion on an old zebra.

"You infected him, too, right?"

Jeremy thought of a few choice names for Castillo and refused to dignify the question with an answer. "Dr. Barlow admitted him Saturday with some cardiac complications."

"He's in ICU, is he?" Castillo asked.

Jeremy shook his head. "Not in ICU, but we're monitor—"

"Oh. So he's in critical condition, is he?" Castillo pressed his point with sarcasm.

His curled lip reminded Jeremy of a snarling dog.

"Actually, no," Jeremy said. "Not critical. All the labs actually look pretty good. Better now. He's—"

"So let me guess. You've come to tell me you still want to miss the chance of a lifetime—to miss this weekend's conference? And leave me to fend for the hospital without your insights?"

"It's not that I want out, sir. I just—"

"What? The lovely little wife in the powder-blue suit would kill you?" Castillo heaved an exaggerated sigh.

Clenching his teeth to keep from saying something he'd regret, Jeremy took a deep breath. He tightened his grip on the armrest in a vain effort to diffuse his anger.

"You know what, Cramer? You don't have to come. You can certainly stay here with your family." His tone contradicted his words. "I'm asking for only two nights away—at an *important* conference. Is that so much?" He didn't wait for an answer. "You carry a cell phone, right?" Jeremy nodded. "So someone can get in touch with you if anything happens."

Jeremy reached his limit. Rage roared like thunder inside his head. He stood to leave before he said something regrettable.

"Sit back down." The force of the command jolted Jeremy into compliance. "You have a nice job and a nice salary." The chief picked up some forms and threw them on the desk. "I have a stack of résumés here from people eager to take your place. So I suggest you get yourself to Washington if you want to keep the insurance that pays the bills your son's racking up."

Jeremy spoke slowly to keep his voice from shaking. "Thank you for your time, sir." Boldly he rose again—his heart pounding—and turned to leave.

"I'm sorry your son is ill, Dr. Cramer. But you can't do anything for him anyway. Your wife can stay with him while you're gone. And you can be a world of help to our hospital."

"Yessir," Jeremy said. He walked as fast as he could out of the office, past the receptionist and, despite the fact that he was on the eighteenth floor, opted against the elevators and headed straight for the stairs.

FOR THE NEXT three days, except for Jeremy's visits with Devin in the clinic, time dragged by. Jak's elevated heart rate was all that kept him in the hospital. By Thursday Barlow talked of releasing him. Angie's parents took shifts to give Angie and Jeremy a break and allow them time with Ainsley. But they all grew restless for answers. And everyone wanted to get back to normal. Jeremy figured Jak was okay, but he was nervous about leaving Angie alone with the kids. Especially if Jak was going home, Jeremy wanted to keep an eye on him. The conference would make that impossible, but he put off telling Angie about it, hoping he still might find a way out.

Early Friday morning Jeremy called and asked Barlow if they could meet in the doctors' lounge. Barlow entered, pulled up a second chair, and propped his feet on it. "I think your boy's doing well. What-up?"

"I need your help with something," Jeremy said.

"Name it." Barlow laced his fingers behind his head.

"Castillo says I have to go to D.C. this weekend. Leaving tonight." Barlow winced. "What*ever* for?"

"To tell the world we're curing AIDS. We're going together."

"Ew." Barlow snickered. "So how can *I* help? You want me to go tell Castillo that Lincoln freed the slaves?"

"Would you?"

"Listen, I like you, man, but not enough to lay my head on the block. Will that be all, Doctor?" He lowered his feet and shifted forward as if he were getting up, then raised a teasing brow at Jeremy.

Jeremy was glad for Barlow's lighthearted approach. He'd spent a sleepless night worrying about how to leave his son and explain to Angie. She'd been more understanding lately, but he couldn't even convince himself about this one, so how could he convince her?

Barlow asked, "Can I give you some advice?"

"That's why I called this meeting," Jeremy said. "What would you do?"

"I was thinking of releasing your son today," Barlow said. "But I really want my pediatric cardio doc to have a look. She's the best if we need to do any procedures during the study. So—what if we keep Jak here over the weekend, and you fly to D.C. with El Jerko?"

Feeling like a man who'd received a reprieve from the gallows, Jeremy heaved a huge sigh. "Seriously?" He hadn't anticipated this.

Barlow waved him off. "Sure. Batman's lungs are clearing, his weight's normal, his heart's a little elevated, so I can justify keeping him, but I think he's okay."

Finally relieved of the most pressing stresses, Jeremy suddenly became aware of his appetite.

"I'll even help you break it to your bride, if you like. She's a sweetie. We need to keep her happy, don't we? She's been through a lot." He motioned toward the exit and got up.

Jeremy nodded and rose, too. "You and Portia have been so kind. Thanks."

Barlow put a hand on Jeremy's shoulder as they went through the door. "Not kind, buddy. Self-interested. If Castillo fires you, I'd have to break in a new infectious disease guy. And who has the time?"

CHAPTER 19

Later Friday morning Jeremy sat waiting for Barlow, watching morning cartoons with Angie and Jak. Jeremy noticed worry lines on Angie's forehead and bags under her eyes. But Jak seemed okay for the time being. He guffawed every time the road runner blew up the coyote.

Finally around eight, Jeremy heard a knock and Barlow entered, leaving the students and residents accompanying him on rounds outside. He checked Jak's vitals and spent longer than usual eyeing the numbers on his heart monitor.

"What is it?" Angie asked, her glance shifting to Jeremy. "Something wrong?"

Barlow shook his head. "Still the same. Exactly the same." He turned to Jeremy and held out Jak's chart. "Blood work still looks good. You can see the numbers here for yourself."

"So he doesn't get to go home yet?" Angie asked.

"Not yet. Sorry." Barlow leaned against the counter, folded his arms across his chest, and looked at Angie. "I want to keep him hooked up to the monitor and on oxygen over the weekend, though he appears in no imminent danger. If we see no change in his elevated heart rate by Monday, we can see what our pediatric cardiologist recommends. So I imagine your weekend will be uneventful ... but lonely."

She wrinkled up her face. "Lonely?"

Jeremy took over from there. "Castillo's issued a command for me to accompany him to Washington. Leaving tonight, back Sunday. He didn't ask me. He told me."

Angie groaned and her eyes pleaded with Jeremy. "Can't you tell him—"

"You married an optimist here, Cramer," Barlow said, gesturing in Angie's direction. "She thinks you can tell Castillo something! Ha!" He looked at Angie. "Jeremy has a chance to do some real good for the hospital and more importantly for AIDS researchers, and I don't expect anything to change with Jak. I really do think he'll be fine, but I'll check on him more often until Jeremy gets back."

She looked at Jeremy, her eyes growing misty. "Doesn't Castillo even know about Jak?"

"Sure he does," Jeremy said.

"What a jerk!"

Jeremy was relieved to see Angie directing her frustration to Castillo rather than at him. She sighed and looked out the window. Finally she turned back to Barlow. "I appreciate your offer, but it puts more work on you."

"Consider it a favor for a colleague—and a friend." He winked at Jeremy. "I'll find a way for you to pay me back. Don't worry."

SEVERAL HOURS LATER Jeremy sat at a spare desk in the infectious disease clinic while he waited for the nurse to check Devin's weight and vitals. He called down to the lab to get a status report, and one of the researchers told him another of their AIDS patients died. "Morgue wants to know if you'd like to attend the autopsy at two p.m.?" the researcher asked.

"Absolutely," Jeremy said, discouraged by the news and curious about the actual cause of death. Lesia, the appointment secretary, signaled to him that Devin was ready. When he hung up, the pink-clad woman asked, "How's your son, Dr. Cramer?"

"Lots better, thanks. What room today?"

She pointed to Room B and handed him the chart. He scanned it and reread the numbers, just to be sure. Devin had gained another pound, her blood pressure was normal, and all of her blood counts now fell within normal ranges. He slapped his leg with her chart and whistled as he marched down the hall and entered the room where Devin waited.

She looked up when he came in. "Your son must be much better today," she said. "Look at you, all smiley and whistlin'."

Jeremy set her chart on the counter. "Jak's much better ..." He pointed both index fingers at her. "But so are you."

He checked her IV line and hooked up the solution from the lab. It came in the form of an off-white liquid in a 250cc container that looked like a mini-IV bag. It consisted of T* cells mixed with an albumin-rich solution for stability.

"Hey, guess where I get to go this weekend?" Jeremy asked, his voice lilting sarcasm.

"Home with your son, I hope," Devin said.

"Uh, no. Barlow thinks he'll release Jak on Monday. But tonight I get to fly to D.C. with Castillo."

Devin cringed. "Ew!"

"That's exactly what Barlow said, only less emphatically." Jeremy explained his predicament. "I tried to get out of it ..."

"No doubt," Devin said. "But—let me guess. You don't want to file for unemployment?"

"See there? You're smart like that. And besides, who would take care of you if I got tossed out of here?"

"Who *is* taking care of me while you're gone?" Devin asked.

"The weekend doc. But I get back Sunday night, so I'll be here Monday, if all goes as planned."

"*If* all goes as planned ..." Devin said. "Plans! Ha! You didn't used to qualify everything so much, but trauma gives you wisdom, doesn't it? You just never know how life's going to turn out. Tell you what. On Monday we'll celebrate that you survived the weekend and your son's going home. I'll bring the Frappuccino."

THE SOUNDTRACK TO *Saturday Night Fever* playing in the background struck Jeremy as ironic. The Bee Gees sang "Stayin' Alive" as he stood in mask, shoe covers, and double gloves surveying the autopsy room that contained *the wall* with cadavers in refrigeration units. Everything about the place, from its scales and pans to its instruments, drains, and stainless steel tables shone with antiseptic cleanliness.

Wish it smelled like cleanser, Jeremy thought. The combination of formalin and the rank odor of rotting meat tickled his gag reflex.

In her early thirties, Dr. Jackie Glidewall, the deputy medical examiner, was a squat woman with a long face. She had wide-set aquamarine eyes and stringy short hair. "Sorry about the smell," she said from behind her mask. "We just finished a particularly nasty case."

"Apparently so. Br-r-r," Jeremy said, hoping she'd change the subject. Talking about the smell only made it worse.

"Sorry you're so cold. I always wear long johns down here. Even in the summer."

Pointing to one of the speakers, Jeremy asked, "So you're a Bee Gees fan?"

"I like music when I work." She opened the refrigerator with its huge doors and metal trays on rollers that held human remains. Sliding out the one bearing Jeremy's deceased patient, she asked, "Think we can get this or shall we go find somebody else to help?"

"She can't weigh much," Jeremy said.

Glidewall looked down at the corpse. "What're we looking for?"

"I'm doing some research with T cells, and this patient was getting a special solution. She improved, but now this. So I'm curious to know the cause of death."

"An AIDS patient, right?" she asked.

"Affirmative. Acquired HIV from a dirty needle. She was in end-stage disease that reversed enough for her to live independently. But she didn't show up for any of last week's infusions, and her sister found her dead. Yet I honestly question whether AIDS killed her," Jeremy said.

"Overdose maybe?" Glidewall asked.

"That's my hunch."

"Easy to find out." Slowly, carefully she scanned the body in a methodical search for needle marks. "Found 'em!" she said. She pointed out a spot between the cadaver's toes.

Jeremy hated to think of all that T* used on this patient when someone else might have benefited. Such a waste. "I'm also interested—very interested—to see how the organs look."

"In end-stage disease, they usually look pretty beat up," Glidewall said. She held up her scalpel. "Okay, here goes." She made the traditional Y incision—shoulder to midchest on the right, same on the left, and midchest to pubic bone. Taking her handheld tape recorder from her pocket, she dictated: "Forty-three-year-old white female, appears her stated age ..."

When she finished, she looked up at Jeremy. "Let's have a look at the liver." She worked for a few minutes, but then stopped cold. "Well, I'll be ... Will you look at that?"

Jeremy leaned closer. Thrilled to see it with his own eyes, he grinned. "Looks mighty good, doesn't it?"

"You're telling me!" Glidewall said. "I've *transplanted* livers that looked worse than this."

"I don't know too many medical examiners who do transplants."

"Not recently!" She laughed. "I did a rotation through the transplant unit. I helped harvest lots of livers." She pointed with her instrument. "We just saved some length on the vessels for the surgeons to hook up rather than trimming them close, like we do down here. I don't know what you're doing down in the lab, Dr. Cramer, but whatever it is, it's working!"

About an hour later when Jeremy pulled off his mask and shoe covers, he knew the forty-three-year-old AIDS patient who'd probably died of a heroine overdose had organs that looked like those of a twenty-five-year-old. His solution was working. Jeremy envisioned millions cured and dollar signs to match.

As the Bee Gees belted out "More Than a Woman to Me," Jeremy thought, *You got that right. She's more than a woman—she's rock-solid Fort Knox gold.*

SEVERAL HOURS LATER Jeremy waited in the airline terminal for the chief. Jeremy's shoulders tensed when he thought of the flight ahead. *What kind of small talk could he make after an exchange like their last one,* Jeremy wondered. Then it occurred to him that he had a ticket in coach and surely Castillo would fly first class.

Jeremy spent the next hour looking up from his laptop every time he saw feet passing. But the chief never arrived. When it came time to board—still no Castillo. Not that Jeremy wanted him around, but he did wonder what happened.

As the plane pulled away from the gate, the flight attendant directed everyone to turn off cell phones and electronic devices. Jeremy was about to push the Off button on his PDA when a text message came through from Castillo's secretary. It informed him that the chief caught an earlier flight and would meet Jeremy at 7:00 a.m. in the hotel lobby. Jeremy confirmed, powered it off, and leaned his head back into the headrest. The weekend was looking better already.

He arrived well after dark Washington time, but early enough to phone Angie back in Denver. He spoke her name into his phone's microphone and pressed the receiver against his ear. She answered on the first ring.

"Hi, honey," he said. "Just wanted to let you know I got here okay. How's Jak?"

"Fine, as far as I can tell. Nothing eventful going on here. But thanks for checking in. Glad you made it okay. How'd it go with Castillo?"

"I haven't seen him yet—he caught an earlier flight."

"Oh. Pity!" she said cheerfully. "Listen, I didn't get a chance to tell you before you left—but I'm really proud of you. Really proud. I know you'll do great tomorrow. Call me as soon as it's over and let me know how it went."

"Thanks, I will. Good night." He flipped his phone shut and kicked off his shoes. Then he stretched out on the bed and laced his fingers behind his head. He owed one to Barlow.

ON SATURDAY, JEREMY stalled as long as possible before finally heading down to meet the chief. In the lobby he found Castillo already encircled by doctors asking about the research, which suited Jeremy fine. The man treated his employees better with witnesses around.

Castillo gave Jeremy an enthusiastic wave. "Good morning, Dr. Cramer," he said. All eyes turned to Jeremy. Castillo shook his hand and patted his back as if Jeremy were an old golf buddy.

"Morning," Jeremy said, trying to strike a balance between maintaining public relations and being honest.

Castillo fired off introductions. Three men and one woman greeted Jeremy—all with impressive credentials and all of whose names he instantly forgot. Castillo explained that they were the other panelists and the moderator.

They resumed their conversation, and Jeremy stood silently as

Castillo fielded all the questions. Those he couldn't answer, Castillo ignored. After about fifteen minutes Castillo dismissed Jeremy saying, "Let's postpone our meeting until 8:30, shall we? In the meantime, why don't you go scope out the room and let me know the setup."

In any other context Jeremy might have taken offense, but he was glad to have the freedom to leave and was only too happy to wait until later to brief Castillo. He excused himself and went to the front desk to ask the assigned place and time for their session. He confirmed that they were on at eleven, but to his surprise the panel discussion was scheduled for the main ballroom—a room big enough to match the chief's ego.

Jeremy wandered in to check it out. Hotel employees skittered about setting up tables and chairs. And people wearing press badges set up their tripods and tested their microphones.

Knowing he had more than an hour free, Jeremy went back to the room, got his swim trunks, and headed for the pool. Once there, the smell of chlorinated water worked on him like comfort food. He threw back his arms and dove in with all his might. In no time he found his rhythm. The water washed over him, taking with it his cares. So much had changed over the course of a week. Jak's sickness and partial recovery. Devin's improvement. And now he had even more evidence that T* rejuvenated organs, which could translate into diseases cured, lives extended, and enormous financial deals. He reached the other side of the pool and flipped around for another lap.

He knew he should feel content. Wasn't all that enough? Yet questions about T* with submersion victims still nagged him. The "rat pack" as the research team affectionately called them, had responded well. But moving to human subjects with drowning experiments had limits. Serious limits. When he reached the shallow end again he lifted his face out of the water. Droplets rolled off his face, and his worries dripped away with them. He had much to celebrate. Why focus on the obstacles?

When he emerged from the water, he felt euphoric. Even Castillo couldn't get him down, he decided. He rinsed off the chlorine, dried himself, and headed into the dressing room, ready to face the world.

DEVIN SAT IN the infectious disease clinic waiting as she did every day—usually in the morning. Most people spent waiting-room time reading through old magazines, but she preferred people watching. She knew from years of hospital work that every person was a walking story of love, loss, and hope. Some of them added grace to that mix. So she studied patients. She'd observe age, race, general health, how they dressed, how they talked to those who accompanied them, what they read—and imagine the story behind the face.

Once in her girlhood back in Aruba, Devin saw her grandmother clasp her hands together and exclaim "Amen!" when she saw a native shoco owl. Devin had the same response sometimes with people. To her, human beings—even those with no faith—were little pieces of glory walking around. Of all the wonders of the world from which to choose—from Caribbean sunrises to the Alps to Hawaiian sunsets—the ones that made Devin marvel most were human beings.

On Saturday morning at a few minutes after nine, she studied an elderly couple who sat holding hands. The tiny engagement ring on the woman's age-marked hand told Devin she was looking at old love, not a third-time-around relationship. She had a theory that the younger a couple was when they got engaged, the smaller the ring. Great as it was, young love with its intensity and beauty was immature, she thought, compared with the enduring, self-sacrificing kind it took to become "trulyweds." *They've been holding those hands for a long, long time*, she thought.

When Lesia came to the door, she didn't even have to say Devin's name. The receptionist just waved her in. "We've got you in D today," she said, pointing to a room down the hall. "Dr. Reiko just phoned to say he's on his way down."

"Thanks." Devin hopped on the scale, proceeded to the chair at the nurse's station for a blood pressure reading, grabbed a cup for the urine test, and did the finger stick hematocrit. Though she no longer had anemia, they still kept track of her levels.

The weekend nurse stuck Devin's thick chart in the holder outside the door and came in with her to get the IV started. Devin settled into her chair and waited for the doctor. Soon she heard noises outside the door and knew the doctor was scanning Volume Two of her chart. If so, it could take awhile.

That thing could make War and Peace *look like a comic book in comparison*, she thought.

Finally she heard someone rapping, and a young doctor entered. He held her record in one hand. In the other he had her daily dose of T* solution. His hands being full, he nodded. "Hello, I'm Dr. Jeff Reiko. I don't believe we've met." He had frizzy short hair and guileless brown eyes. "I'm rotating through the research department. Dr. Cramer asked me to handle your daily infusion of this." He reached above where she sat and plugged the little bag piggyback alongside a regular IV of Ringer's lactate and hooked it up to her IV. "How do you feel?" he asked.

"Pretty good."

He took her chart, sat down, and opened it. "That's great."

Devin coughed. If they were going to spend an hour together, she might as well make his acquaintance. "So … tell me about yourself," she said. "How'd you end up choosing … to specialize … in infectious disease?" She felt a tightening in her airways and involuntarily clutched her throat.

Dr. Reiko stared. "What? What's …? Son of a …" He jumped up and stopped the infusion.

Devin's throat slammed shut and she gasped for breath, but no air filled her lungs. Reiko yelled "Code 13!" and something about an allergic reaction. The room became as frantic as a kicked ant mound. Dr. Reiko barked orders, demanded a crash cart. Several nurses flew into the room. He punched the call button, and one nurse helped him pull Devin to the floor for CPR.

The swelling happened so fast Devin could feel it. Straining with all her might, she tried to suck in air. Nothing.

Another nurse careened in with the crash cart, equipped with a defibrillator, IV medications, and supplies. She gave her a quick shot of Benadryl according to Dr. Reiko's orders. Devin heard "Code 13" over the hospital's PA system. She was choking to death.

"Load the epinephrine. I need an IV push," Dr. Reiko demanded. Devin hoped the adrenaline would help. It *had* to—and fast. She tried to keep herself from thrashing around, wanting to cooperate, but desperate for breath. She would scream from the pain—and terror—if she could. But her lungs were locked, shut tight.

Someone shoved an oxygen mask over her face, jerked her head back, and tried to force the air in. She felt herself losing consciousness. *God, please help me!* Faces grew fuzzier as a voice tried to soothe her. She struggled with every ounce of strength she had. Then everything went black.

REIKO HAD JUST infused an apparently lethal substance into Cramer's prize patient. He knew he had to cover himself. He ordered everything he could. Seeing one of the nurses still holding a full needle, he couldn't believe she hadn't given the injection yet. "What're you waiting for? Shoot the epinephrine!"

"I can't!" she screamed. "She's DNR!"

Everyone froze.

She pointed to the front of the chart on the counter, and sure enough—there it was in bold, red letters: DNR. Reiko cursed, grabbed the needle from her, and shot it into the vein anyway.

"Patient's wishes!" the nurse pleaded. "We have a living will. She's got HIV/AIDS." Tears welled in her eyes. "Legally we ..."

Reiko knew he had to follow the patient's expressed wishes, but he wasn't letting her die on his watch. He took the gamble that she'd signed the DNR only because death seemed imminent at the time. He had to keep trying. "Call her husband! We can put in a tube if he gives the okay."

One of the nurses scrambled to find the emergency contact information in the chart and punched the numbers on the wall phone. Another worked to ventilate Devin using a mask and Ambu bag.

Nice try. But Reiko knew it was pointless. No way to get air in—the airway squeezes tighter than a tourniquet.

Once she lost consciousness, he worked to slide in a plastic airway.

"What? You're going to bring her back so she can die of AIDS?" one of the nurses asked. He gritted his teeth and kept at it.

"I got a machine at both phone numbers, sir," the other nurse, holding her chart, told him. By now Devin had not moved for three minutes.

Down on his knees and panting, Dr. Reiko peeked at her pupils. Fixed and dilated. He cursed again. No sense in proceeding. He leaned back on his heels, snapped off the gloves he had on for the infusion, and looked up at the clock. "Time of death, 9:47."

CHAPTER 20

Jeremy hoped Castillo would never again ask him to attend a public meeting on behalf of the hospital. He sat fuming, wishing this so-called panel discussion—which started more like *The Castillo Show*—would end. Though Jeremy planned to keep quiet about the autopsy until he could further substantiate their findings, Castillo went and announced it. About halfway through the ninety-minute session, the moderator appeared to clue in that Jeremy handled the hands-on research, because he quit asking Castillo anything and started firing questions at Jeremy. That made both Jeremy and Castillo squirm.

Most of the discussion sounded like a repeat of the hospital press conference, but this time they faced a larger crowd and higher stakes. And last time Angie had come with him as moral support. Though honored before a crowd of his peers, today Jeremy felt more alone.

Castillo had claimed their hospital would find a cure for AIDS. Everybody wanted a piece of that. Though he thought the chief was pompous to say it, Jeremy had to concede—judging by all the journalists surrounding him—that it would land their hospital in the news.

Castillo said other things that bothered Jeremy. He made it sound like T* was a cure for AIDS. T* held promise for extending the life spans of AIDS patients, but it didn't eliminate the virus.

When the meeting broke up and Jeremy left the stage, a crowd mobbed him. Doctors wanted protocol details. Reporters clamored for sound bites. One by one, Jeremy systematically worked his way through the crowd of pathologists, researchers, and journalists from all over the world.

He glanced around self-consciously, looking for Castillo. The group surrounding the chief looked smaller, but at least he wasn't watching Jeremy with a green eye. As Jeremy scanned, he noticed someone in the back of his own group—a tall man who looked to be in his early fifties. He had dark hair with a smattering of gray, and he wore scrubs—unusual attire when everyone else had on suits. He stood out like a Goth at a ballet recital.

Jeremy exchanged business cards and brief bits of conversation with those around him. He promised to send information to e-mail addresses. And when the crowd thinned a bit, he extended his hand to meet the tall physician. But the man shook his head. "I'll wait till you're finished," he said. "It's personal—I'm a friend of Mic Justine's."

Mic was the chaplain at Jeremy's hospital. But Mic was no close friend—not by any means. Jeremy didn't think Mic even knew he was here. *Why would he send a friend to see me here?* Jeremy wondered.

"Suit yourself," Jeremy said, and moved on to the next person.

When five or six people still remained in his circle, Jeremy saw Castillo talking on his cell. Jeremy knew he'd better hurry up. He felt a little guilty when he practically brushed off three people who'd waited so long to talk with him.

He glanced over at Castillo again. Now the chief looked upset. The color had drained from his face and he was talking fast. *Whoever he called must've angered him,* Jeremy thought. After Jeremy rushed his way through two more conversations, he saw Castillo pacing, apparently impatient for him to finish so he could regale him for something.

He turned to the man in scrubs. "So ... you're a friend of Mic, eh? How do you know him?"

The man extended his hand. "I'm a chaplain like he is—only

part-time." Jeremy looked at his scrubs. Something didn't add up. "Name's Ben McKay. I'm also a part-time ob-gyn here in D.C."

"Nice to meet you." *Strange,* Jeremy thought. *If his specialty wasn't even infectious disease, why come here?*

"I'd like to speak privately for a minute," McKay said, his voice low and sober. He gestured toward the ballroom doors. "I've secured a room down the hall where we can talk."

Jeremy blinked. "Something wrong?"

Dr. McKay's voice coaxed gently. "Mic phoned and asked me to come find you." He motioned for Jeremy to follow.

As Jeremy started to go, Castillo called after him. "Where do you think you're going, Cramer? I need to talk to you!"

"Be right back," Jeremy said, avoiding eye contact. Then it hit him. Something must be wrong with Jak. But why didn't Angie call herself? Or Barlow? Then he remembered—he'd turned off the volume on his phone!

When a chaplain wants to speak to you alone, Jeremy thought, *it always means bad news.* He quickened his pace to catch up with McKay. "Is it my son? Is Jak okay?"

"Your son's fine," McKay said.

Then what could it be? Jeremy wondered. The next fifteen yards went by in slow motion. He couldn't imagine, and wasn't sure he wanted to. Dr. McKay slid a card key in a door and they entered a small breakout room. Twenty to thirty chairs were set up classroom style with a podium and a flip chart at the front.

"Have a seat," the chaplain said, motioning toward one of the chairs. He brought one and sat across from Jeremy. Whatever it was, Jeremy could tell from his expression that it was serious. His heart pounded.

"What is it?" Jeremy asked.

"Sorry to keep you in suspense," he said. "Mic asked me to come in person to break some difficult news." Jeremy clutched the sides of the seat bottom to brace himself. "It's your nurse friend Devin Garrigues."

"Devin? What about her?"

"She passed away this morning."

"Wh-hhat?" How could she be gone? He'd seen her only yesterday. "Are you *sure?*"

McKay pursed his lips and gave the slightest of nods. "I'm so sorry."

"H-how?"

"She was getting an infusion."

A tremor of fear started as a shiver and gained strength until it shook Jeremy like an earthquake. He tried to absorb the shock, but failed. "She died getting her infusion?"

"Correct," McKay said.

Jeremy covered his mouth. She was his friend. His patient. And it was his fault. It couldn't possibly be true. His emotions pinballed from grief and sadness to panic. What now?

Conscious of the pattern on the carpet he'd been staring at, he remembered he wasn't alone and looked up.

McKay's brown eyes glistened. "I understand you were good friends," he said.

"We are—were. What else did Mic tell you?"

"That it's too early to know much. But she had some sort of allergic reaction and her airway closed."

"They couldn't get a tube in?"

McKay shook his head. "I don't know many details. Mic said they tried to revive her, but from what he heard, they hesitated to go full-court press because of a DNR order."

"They didn't do a tracheotomy?" Jeremy asked.

McKay shook his head.

Jeremy stared. They hadn't thought to update her record when she got better. "They didn't even try?" He smacked his hand against his forehead, angry at the world. What a waste! They didn't even *try.*

"If there's something I can do …" McKay offered. He touched Jeremy on the shoulder.

Jeremy thought of Castillo and wanted to avoid him at all costs. He couldn't face him—not now. The chief must already know, Jeremy concluded. He must've phoned the office, and they told him.

The chaplain sat with him for a bit longer, then he offered to pray with him, but Jeremy declined. What good were prayers now? He just wanted to get out of there.

"Anyone you'd like me to call … or have Mic call?"

"No thanks." Jeremy regathered his professional persona. His thoughts ricocheted off the inside of his head. Making a decision of any kind, even something as simple as determining whom to call or whether to return to his room, felt overwhelming. But he had to.

"I need to go home," Jeremy said, resigned to his fate. "Thanks for coming." Jeremy envisioned what a disaster it would've been to hear the bad news from Castillo—and then to have to join him on the return. But right now what mattered most was Devin … and her family. Terren. The girls.

"Mic's been trying to call you himself," McKay said. Jeremy pulled his phone from his pocket. He scrolled through eight messages—six from general numbers at the hospital, another from Barlow's office, and one from Angie—and turned up the volume. He'd return the calls when he got to his room.

Jeremy stood. "Thank you so much for coming, Doctor, uh … Chaplain …"

"Ben."

"Thank you, Ben. I'm grateful." They shook hands and Jeremy exited as fast as he could. When he got to the elevator bank, he had to think hard to recall what floor his room was on. When he arrived at the right hall, he had to concentrate to remember his room number. Finally he found his door and stepped inside.

He threw himself across the bed, his head aflame with heat and then numb. Was this how a stroke felt? Or catatonic shock? He lay stiff, unable to move, frozen by the reality of what had passed.

"Devin ..." He repeated her name. "It's all my fault." He'd stuck her with the needle. His T* had poisoned her. And he hadn't thought to change the DNR. "All my fault ... Devin, I've really failed you!"

Maybe he'd mixed up the wrong solution. No, he'd been careful. Very careful.

Could she have developed an allergy? Possible, but highly unlikely.

His mind lumbered through the options. How could T* have done that? She'd had numerous infusions with great results. Did she get the wrong cells? The wrong mix? What could possibly explain a fatal reaction?

What if all their research was a total waste? Maybe it didn't work long-term for humans. What if all he'd accomplished was to temporarily improve the organ function of rodents and some AIDS patients only to have them die suddenly?

And what about Devin's family? She had two girls—motherless now. He'd never forgive himself for that. Not to mention Terren. If Terren was angry before, he'd be murderous with rage now. What if he sued the hospital? Or worse—pressed charges against Jeremy himself?

Would the hospital fire him? Would anyone ever hire him again? If only he hadn't stuck her with that needle ...

How would Castillo react? How would the media report it? And what about the rest of his colleagues? No one would ever respect him again.

He gasped when he thought of Angie. What would she say? He'd killed Ravi, and now Devin, and maybe Jak wasn't far behind. If she didn't already hate him for that, she would soon.

SHORTLY AFTER TEN o'clock Mountain Time on Saturday night, Jeremy poked his head in the door of Jak's room and saw his son sleeping soundly. When he opened the door wider, his eyes met Angie's. She jumped up to meet him. "Jeremy!" she whispered. "Honey!" She pulled him inside and wrapped her arms around his waist. "I'm so sorry, sweetheart."

Jeremy rested his cheek against hers, at home in her welcoming arms. She held him tight. He heard her mumbling, her face against his chest. He pulled back and looked at her. "What did you say?"

"I thought you'd never get here."

He looked into her eyes. He had proved himself an absolute failure, yet here she stood looking at him that way. He pressed his lips against hers and then whispered, "Longest trip of my life."

She intertwined fingers with his and pulled him farther into the room. "You must be exhausted—in every way." She gestured toward the recliner, but he declined.

"I've been sitting at the airport, on the plane, in the car … I need to stand awhile." He leaned against the counter by Jak's bed and looked down on his son. "How is he?"

"Another good day," Angie said. "Uneventful—the way we like it."

He checked the monitors, which confirmed what Angie said. "Glad somebody had an uneventful day," Jeremy muttered, looking away. "You know what all this means, don't you?"

She raised her brows.

"I've brought all sorts of media attention to our hospital at the worst possible time; I've killed Devin; my research is destroyed; and to top it off, I blew off my boss. Oh, yeah, and my son's in the hospital."

Angie was thoughtful. "Maybe that's how you see it. But let me tell you how it looks from here," she said. "You tried every way possible to slow the avalanche of media attention, but your boss forced you to go anyway—so he gets to pay for being a jerk. You don't know what killed Devin. Your son's better. And the best thing you did all weekend was blow off that idiot and fly home!"

"I didn't totally blow him off," Jeremy said. "I left him a message at the front desk."

"Close enough," she said. "If I didn't already love you, I'd love you just for coming home when it was time. If you have to lose your job, at least you have your dignity intact."

This was the Angie he married. Warm but feisty, and ever on his side. For a few seconds he thought of something other than his pain. But then the grief hit with a new wave. "I just can't believe ..." his voice cracked and he lowered it to a near whisper. "She's gone, Angie." He turned his head away so she couldn't see. "Devin's gone."

"Oh, honey," Angie said, drawing close and slipping into his arms again. "What a shock." They stood like that for a while, with his head resting against hers, only the dim lights from monitors and the sound of the machines filling the room.

"I need to go down to the lab," Jeremy said.

"What?"

"I have to find out what went wrong. You're right. I don't know what killed Devin. But I have to find out."

CHAPTER 21

On Sunday Jak remained stable. That bit of good news helped. But it came as no surprise, either. As Barlow said, if given half a chance kids got better on their own. Once the pediatric cardiologist checked Jak out, Jeremy felt sure they could make a rapid departure. He missed Ainsley and was ready to have his family home again.

Jeremy spent most of the day in the lab trying to figure out what killed Devin. All of the coworkers who knew her seemed to operate in a similar eyes-glazed-over lethargic state, functioning as if on autopilot.

Interaction with Barlow comforted Jeremy the most, probably because he said the least. No platitudes. No pat answers. Just a pat on the shoulder and "I'm so sorry." But it frustrated Jeremy that none of the evidence—not one test or piece of research—uncovered a clue about what caused her death.

He was standing with a beaker in his hand when it dawned on him that the lab had gone strangely quiet. He looked up and saw a man with black hair staring across the counter at him. Jeremy recognized him from another context. It took a second to register that it was Castillo.

All the researchers had either disappeared into their pods or sat caught where they were, with their heads ducked as if deeply engrossed in their work.

"I hope you're proud of yourself," the chief said with a studied calm. "It takes a lot of talent to single-handedly destroy in one morning the reputation this hospital has worked for years to build."

This is it, Jeremy thought. *He's going to fire me.*

"Perhaps I could understand if you had stayed on like a true professional to help with damage control. But you skulked off like a scared cat."

Jeremy's cheeks felt hot.

"If you know what's good for you, Dr. Cramer, you will immediately get to the bottom of what caused this shame on our good name. And you'll rectify it." Without waiting for a response, he turned and marched through the door.

His words burned in Jeremy's ears. He looked around and surveyed the room, wondering who had heard. Jeremy drew little comfort from the fact that Castillo hadn't fired him. At least then he would've been free from his control.

The phone rang and Ted, one of his research assistants, sprang up to answer it. Jeremy looked at the beaker he was still holding and tried to remember what to do with it.

"It's for you," Ted said, holding up the receiver. "Glidewall's asking if you want to attend Devin Garrigues's autopsy on Monday afternoon." Ted cocked his head. "Seems the least you can do is attend the post to see what your precious crap did to her."

"Her words or yours?" Jeremy asked.

"I'm just sayin' what everyone else is thinking." Ted gave a flippant shrug and held out the receiver.

The research assistant had never had a bone to pick with Jeremy before. But Jeremy recognized in Ted the human impulse to distance oneself from failure. Jeremy suppressed the urge to remind Ted of where he fell in the lab's food chain. He took the phone and put the receiver to his ear.

"Dr. Cramer, I'm so sorry—I know this is a tough call, her being your friend and all," Glidewall said. "I just thought I should offer you the choice."

Hard as it was, he had to go. He was ultimately responsible for this. And how else could he exhaust every possible option? "Yeah, I'll be there. Thanks."

The call brought his thoughts back to Devin. Though people could develop allergies at any time, Jeremy suspected something in the serum itself caused Devin's reaction—something different from previous doses. Did she get the wrong cells? Were they mixed wrong? Lab error? He had to find out whether the T* itself caused the reaction or if some wild-hare proteins got into the serum he grew it in. If only he'd been there. Even if he couldn't have saved her, he'd know firsthand what happened. And he could have told them to ignore the DNR. Devin signed it to keep from prolonging her death, not from extending her life.

FIRST THING MONDAY morning Jeremy was relieved that he and Barlow could finally meet with the pediatric cardiologist. She studied Jak's latest EKG and ordered a more complex procedure. Her schedule for Monday was already crammed, and Devin's funeral was set for Tuesday morning, so they agreed on 1:00 p.m. Tuesday.

After a quick lunch with Angie up in Jak's room, Jeremy slipped into the basement to join Dr. Glidewall after the autopsy started. Much as he dreaded it, he needed to watch as she excised Devin's organs for evaluation.

Glidewall dictated: "Forty-five-year-old black female, appears her stated age ..."

He braced himself as Glidewall made the traditional Y incision, and he told himself the body was just the shell, not the person.

Jeremy's stomach lurched. He wished he hadn't eaten. He concentrated to relax his muscles.

Glidewall worked away for a few minutes to get to the liver. Normally Jeremy could separate relationships and medicine, relegating them to their own compartments. But as he stood watching, this one crossed over too much. The "friendship" drawer wouldn't stay shut. It kept kicking itself open and spilling its contents into the "doctor" drawer. He'd never participated in an autopsy on a good friend, and he hoped he never again had to.

He avoided looking at her face and tried to focus on her corpse as a research specimen. Glancing down, he saw her hands—hands that had curved around his wrist and told him his problems were too diffi-cult to face alone.

"Once again, you have an AIDS patient with amazingly healthy organs, Dr. Cramer," Glidewall said.

Jeremy leaned in to see better. Sure enough, it was just like the last autopsy. But Devin's apparent good health raised more questions than it answered.

It seemed so unreal. *Oh, Devin*, he thought. *I'm sorry. Really sorry.* Then he couldn't help himself. He glanced up at her face. When he did, he felt a wave of heat and the nausea hit again with full force. He had to get out of there. He needed to clear his head. And going back to the lab wouldn't cut it.

He excused himself. Then he peeled off the gloves and mask, deposited them in the trash, and headed for the garage.

He got in his Saab, drove away from the hospital, and made his way to I-76. From there he headed northeast from Denver. It was all so unfair. Devin was too young to die, and so tragically. The suddenness still shocked him. He tried not to think about the horror of her body sprawled out and cut open on the table, but he couldn't stop himself.

Using his GPS, he located Barr Lake State Park about twenty miles away. When he arrived, he walked to the trailhead of a path leading around the lake's perimeter. The late-June sun shone on the dirt laced with pine needles and last fall's decaying leaves. He inhaled the rich odors of the earth. Mature cottonwoods lifted massive limbs overhead in an arching roof.

As he walked, he focused on the trees, the path, the leaves, working to concentrate only on what his senses encountered. Before long he stopped to watch canoes glide by. He inhaled deeply as if clean air could somehow purge him of the guilt and grief he felt. And the creepy feeling he had about the autopsy. He didn't want to remember Devin with her body laid out and devoid of life. He wanted to remember her calling him a flatliner, or telling him in her island accent that she was a yellow-dog Democrat, or saying how much she loved Frappuccinos. But she would never again call him or wake him from sleep to say she needed him in the ER.

Her death seemed a random, senseless tragedy. He considered how she herself might explain it if she were here. As one of those mysterious gaps between what God allows and what we understand? As one of the unspeakable evils that passes through permitting hands?

A couple on horseback passed him, laughing and talking. He couldn't believe the world had the nerve to go on without her. He marveled that in the midst of such anguish, others could pass him without detecting his loss. The agony permeated his whole world, yet it stopped at the perimeters of his body.

It was the same life-must-go-on feeling he had when Ravi had died. Part of him felt relieved that the world didn't need him, that his pain didn't weigh down and stop everyone else. Less depended on him that way. Too much was resting on his shoulders anyway.

He considered his responses, pondering how he might have done better. Maybe Castillo was right that a true professional would have stayed in D.C. to answer questions. But he wondered if Castillo had ever lost a friend, or if he'd even *had* one.

Jeremy passed a half hour walking and stopping and pondering, then walking some more. Eventually he told himself it was time to get back. But he felt ready. Or at least as ready as he was going to be.

As he drove back toward Denver, he hit rush-hour traffic. Cutting through the maze of cars, he reentered the hospital world in his mind.

By the time he pulled into the doctors' garage, he had a few new questions for Jak's cardiologist, and a couple more pieces of evidence to track down in the lab regarding Devin.

He worked in the lab until 2:00 a.m., and then spent the rest of Monday night sleeping fitfully. He had several nightmares. The only one he remembered was the one in which Devin came back to life during her autopsy. But that was enough.

WHEN JEREMY AWOKE Tuesday morning in a call room, he felt exhausted. He dragged himself upstairs to see Jak and Angie. Jak was still the same, but they decided Angie would stay with him rather than going with Jeremy to the funeral.

He went home to shower and put on a suit. The hot water helped ease his tension, but he dreaded the service. If it weren't for his mistake, Devin would be at work today. And how awful to face Terren and the girls—especially in their time of rawest grief. He considered not going, but he wanted to pay his respects to Devin—and she'd made it clear that she'd expected him to go.

All the way to the church, Jeremy had second thoughts about going. The service was for the living, not the dead. How would those who blamed him feel when he showed up? Most murderers didn't attend their victims' funerals.

Still filled with doubt, he pulled into the parking lot at 9:45 for the ten o'clock service. He joined himself to a group walking in, hoping to be less conspicuous that way.

Standing in his dark suit, he waited his turn to sign the guest book. His turn came, and he noticed—to his relief—that Nate and Portia had already signed in. When he peeked inside the sanctuary doors to find them, he inhaled the aroma of fresh-cut flowers. He guessed the place could hold about three hundred, and it was filling fast. A cross hung front and center, flanked by banners that said "King of Kings" and "Lord of Lords." He looked around to locate his friends in the room filled with sprays of roses, carnations, and all number of flowering plants. He spotted the Barlows near the back on the right side.

An usher handed him a program, and he made his way to the Barlows. "Mind if I join you?" he asked. Nate lifted sympathetic eyes, as did Portia. They scooted over to make room. He slid in next to Nate and offered a brief greeting, then studied his program. A picture of Devin's face on the front made him blink fast. Jeremy was glad Nate didn't try to make conversation. He didn't feel like chatting. He brushed off the thought that people were staring at him, accusing him with their gazes.

An organ prelude drowned out the sounds of muffled voices and Jeremy ventured a look around. He scoped out the crowd and saw plenty of people he knew, though it took a few seconds to recognize some of them in nonmedical clothes. He figured he must look different to them, too.

While most in attendance wore the traditional black or charcoal-gray his mother taught him to wear to funerals, some of the women wore bright colors. And hats. Some even had feathers. And he'd never seen so many sequined blazers, except in Vegas.

According to the program, the funeral looked pretty standard except for "Testimonies from the Community." He had a few stories of his own he could tell about Devin, but no way ...

When he looked more closely at the front of the room, he saw the coffin. He had to swallow back the lump in his throat. He'd overlooked the closed coffin earlier because it rested on the floor rather than up on the platform. Seeing it brought a wave of fresh disbelief that Devin was gone. Really gone. He strained to remember her last words to him. All he could recall was something about trauma and wisdom and how life had a way of surprising a person.

He pushed his cuticles back as he thought about the autopsy results. They sure didn't tell him anything new.

A voice interrupted his thoughts. "… Pastor of Mount Ebenezer Church. We are gathered today to celebrate the life of Devin Garrigues. Beloved wife, mother, sister, fellow Christian, and friend." A large black man in a dark, flowing robe and a booming voice stood behind the podium. He opened a large book and read, "Jesus said, 'I am the resurrection and the life. Everyone who believes in me shall live even if he dies.'" He bowed his head and the crowd followed his lead. "Let us pray. Almighty God, look on this your servant lying in great weakness, and comfort her with the promise of life everlasting given in the resurrection …"

Soft organ music continued while he spoke. Jeremy bowed his head, but his meditation remained locked on the previous day. Devin's lifeless, cold body lay stretched out on the table and split wide open. Another chill ran up his back and out to his fingers and toes. He tried to think of something else, but the only other thought pressing into his consciousness was the memory of the needle accident.

He wished he hadn't come. He didn't want to attend, but staying away seemed worse. He looked around, certain that people were blaming him. Seeing their heads bowed down, he remembered he was supposed to pray. But as soon as he bowed his head, the preacher said, "Amen."

The man delivered a short message from the text quoted earlier, leading in with a story of how, a decade earlier, "Devin placed her faith in Jesus Christ alone to save her, not because of her good works, but by grace." The organist segued to "Amazing Grace," and Jeremy was glad he at least knew the tune. He found the words on the back of the program but he couldn't find his voice, so he pretended to sing. To his surprise, he heard the melody sounding forth next to him in a beautiful, baritone voice. *Who knew Barlow had pipes?* he thought. He was even more startled when Barlow sang with some vigor. So, it seemed, did nearly everyone but Jeremy. His experience with funeral singing had been that people mumbled or hummed halfheartedly, but not this crowd.

When they sat again, the robed choir stood. It comprised Devin's friends, some of whom Jeremy recognized from work. He expected something somber to match the mood, but instead, the choir swayed back and forth as they sang a rousing number—the minister called it a "special"—identified in the program as, "Ride On, King Jesus." People clapped to the beat as if attending a celebration. The only words he understood were the words that matched the title and something about a "great gettin'-up mornin'." Or was it "mournin'"?

When everyone took their seats again, a man identified in the bulletin as Devin's brother stood behind the pulpit to deliver the eulogy. He spoke in an accent more pronounced than hers.

"Forty-five years ago, my little sister, Devin Alida Dekkens Garrigues was born in the city of Sasakiweg, Aruba, in the heart of the southern Caribbean. Our little island off the coast of Venezuela offered few options for higher education for the daughter and son of a physician, so she chose to follow me abroad to study." He took a moment to gain his composure. "Because we grew up on the beach, we wanted the adventure of living with mountains in view. So Devvie joined me studying in Denver. She applied for a University of Colorado Health Sciences Center School of Nursing scholarship." He looked at the congregation over the top of his bifocals. "She, being the smarter of the two of us, received a full scholarship." Gentle laughter rippled through the crowd. "And though English was her second language, our native tongue being Dutch, she graduated salutatorian of her college class."

It surprised Jeremy to learn English had been her second language. It seemed strange to learn something so significant about her when he thought he knew her so well.

Her brother talked about her career, her family, her civic involvements, and her church membership. Then he concluded with, "She is survived by her husband and daughters from Denver, and myself, her brother, Gregor, from Santa Cruz, Aruba."

As Devin's brother returned to his seat, Jeremy stared at the backs of the girls' heads and remembered the day Devin got her first bad-news results. "I have a husband and girls at home," she'd said. *Now, thanks to me, those girls have no mother,* Jeremy thought.

The time for testimonies proved an interesting mix. First a man with eyes deep in their sockets hobbled up to the microphone stand in the aisle. He leaned on his cane, and in a fragile voice spoke. "Many days Devin dropped by after work to check on me because I couldn't afford good medical care, and what the government paid for, I couldn't easily drive to." Jeremy felt a stab of grief when he saw a tear track the man's wrinkled cheek. "Can't believe she went before I did," he said. The man shook his head, and the crowd murmured their agreement. "I'm going to miss that girl," he added, before shuffling back to his seat.

It was so like Devin to do something like that, Jeremy thought.

Heads nodded when a large woman got up and said, "Devin organized a mother/daughter trip to Aruba to introduce some of us here to *real* sunsets." Knowing laughter broke out when another of her friends said, "Devin is responsible for my addiction—to specialty coffee drinks."

A few storytellers didn't seem to know how to wind down, and Jeremy's mind wandered to Jak. He hoped the heart catheter with electrophysiological studies later would help them find some easy-to-treat cause so their lives could return to normal. Soon.

A petite brown-haired preteen moved up to the microphone, drawing Jeremy's attention back to the service. She leaned in and began to speak in a shaky voice. "I live down the street from the Garrigueses." She took a deep, calming breath. "My mom had heart pain last year, and Mrs. Garrigues was at work when we came in the ambulance. She stayed with me until my dad got there. And after Mom died ..." Her voice wavered, and she stopped to compose herself. "Since then ... Mrs. Garrigues has called me every Wednesday to

ask how I am. But now she won't call me tomorrow." Jeremy blinked
fast and swallowed hard. "And I'll be the one calling her daughters,"
the girl added. She covered her mouth to muffle the sound and she
returned to her seat. Jeremy lamented that the devastation reached so
far. Devastation he himself could have prevented.

Next everyone stood for the Lord's Prayer. Jeremy knew it better
than he thought he would. When he was small, his family went to
church with his dad's parents whenever they visited, which was several
times a year. Jeremy's throat caught on "… as we forgive those who
trespass against us …" *What if the one you have to forgive is yourself?* he
wondered.

Jeremy wanted to bolt. He loosened his tie, hoping that might
help him breathe more easily. The choir did another special, this one
called "No More Night," which the program said was based on an
excerpt from The Revelation of St. John the Divine. Jeremy understood the lyrics clearly: "No more night, no more pain, no more sin,
never dying again …" The words reminded him of Devin's own words:
"When that day comes, please don't sit there beating yourself up. You
can grieve for my family. But don't you grieve for me."

At the end, one of the pallbearers opened the casket, and row by
row everyone filed out of their seats and down past the body.
Normally Jeremy looked away when he approached a body at funerals. He preferred to remember the person as they were when living.
But he had to replace his last memory of Devin with a less haunting
vision.

When his turn came, he looked at her face. It was a good face—
the face of someone he considered wonderful. She looked peaceful. He
sighed deeply.

All right, Devin, he thought, *I'll try not to grieve for you—just like
you said. I know if there's truly such a thing as a better place, you of all
people are there. But it'll be pretty hard, because I'm really going to miss
you.*

———❈———

"I KNOW THAT my Redeemer liveth!" The preacher boomed out the words so loudly they startled Jeremy as he stood behind the rest of the mourners at the graveside.

The late-June sun beat down on the back of Jeremy's neck, and the voice continued, "He shalt stand at the latter day upon the earth. And though worms destroy this body, yet in my flesh shall I see God. The Book of Job, chapter nineteen. This is the word of the Lord."

The Book of Job? Jeremy wondered. He had thought the preacher was quoting a line from Handel's *Messiah*. Some of the mourners uttered in unison, "Thanks be to God."

Heads in front of Jeremy partially blocked his view, but he could see that the preacher held a small, black book marked with a number of ribbons. Rising behind him the Denver skyline sparkled, and beyond that Jeremy gazed at the sweeping vista of snowcapped mountains. Conscious of his own frailty in the face of death and timeless majesty, Jeremy felt minutely small. He was self-conscious about being there, too. He hadn't wanted to come. But Devin's words kept coming back— not "*if* you attend," but "*when.*" Still, he wondered if his standing there made it worse for Terren—if he even knew. Jeremy intended to stay as far back as possible to keep from being seen. He wished Nate and Portia had come, but Nate had gone back to work after the funeral.

The preacher kept reading and Jeremy focused on his "thous" and "haths." He'd heard his in-laws complain about preachers who used such old-fashioned words, but Jeremy liked them. The elevated language seemed to better express the sense of otherworldliness in the midst of the surreal. His eyes bore into the side of the casket and the hole under it, wishing with all his might this were a dream.

Suddenly all heads bowed, and Jeremy realized the preacher had said, "Let us pray." He looked down at his well-shined shoes.

"Forasmuch as it hath pleased Almighty God of his great mercy to take unto himself the soul of our dear sister here departed," the preacher said slowly, deliberately, "we therefore commit her body to the ground; earth to earth, ashes to ashes, dust to dust; in sure and certain hope of the Resurrection to eternal life, through our Lord Jesus Christ who shall change our vile body …"

Our vile body, Jeremy thought. That certainly fit the image of Devin in the autopsy room. He imagined her alive again in a better place and wondered if the Christian heaven served Frappuccinos. The thought made him smile.

Shortly after that, the minister concluded with another prayer and invited mourners to file past the family and express their condolences. Jeremy wandered off about fifty yards until he found a stone bench. Sitting with his head buried in his hands, he tried to empty his mind. It hurt too much to think. But he had to pull himself together.

The sight of the hole in the earth where they would lay Devin's body evoked a sense of horror. He flashed back to the hole under his father's casket. And his mother's. And Ravi's. And now back to Devin's. Three of those four deaths had been at least partially his fault.

Yes, forgive us our debts.

He didn't know how long he sat like that, but he suddenly became aware of someone approaching. He looked up and saw Terren. The huge black man strode toward him. He was now only about ten feet away. Pain like a nail stabbed Jeremy's heart, and he jumped up. "Terren! Please know—"

Terren took a few more steps toward Jeremy. Then he stopped, squared his shoulders, and shoved him hard. By grabbing a gravestone on the way down, Jeremy kept from hitting the ground with full force. But he was down and he tasted blood. He'd bitten the inside of his cheek.

Terren held up his fists. "You got a lotta nerve coming here."

Jeremy found his balance and scrambled backward like a crab. He used another gravestone to help himself to his feet. He was stunned speechless. He took another step backward to increase the distance between himself and the angry hulk of a man.

Standing there with bloodshot eyes, Terren spewed forth a host of profane names at Jeremy. He kept his fists up, prepared to strike.

"I don't blame you," Jeremy said weakly. He rubbed his elbow where it had hit stone.

Terren screamed. "She trusted you. And you killed her!"

Jeremy didn't know what to do. He deserved it. He wished Terren had knocked him out. Maybe he should get closer and let him really take a swing.

"I oughtta return the favor and kill you right here. Don't think I couldn't."

"I—"

"Shut up!" Terren yelled. "My family's already heard too much from you." He dropped his fists. "And don't think you've heard the last from me."

Jeremy moved behind the headstone, placing a barrier between himself and Terren. Suddenly lightheaded, Jeremy braced himself by grasping it. He took a couple of deep breaths.

"I hope you have a good lawyer. You're gonna need one. I know a few myself, and they'll be calling you. It'll be my personal pleasure to see them eat you alive."

As quickly as he'd arrived, Terren turned and stormed off, fists still clinched.

Jeremy's heart pounded as he watched Terren go. Jeremy couldn't really blame him. If somebody killed Angie with a contaminated needle, he'd be livid, too. It *was* his fault.

Still, he wasn't going to hang around for more punishment. He hurried to his car, fired up the engine, and shifted the transmission into gear. Then he sped out of the cemetery as fast as he could.

ngie held Jak's hand and walked alongside his bed as the tech wheeled him toward the cardiac care center. The electrophysiology studies would start in fifteen minutes. She looked around for Jeremy, hoping to see him sprinting toward her. Why wasn't he here? She had expected him back by noon—nearly an hour ago. She figured he might have slipped down to the lab on his way in from the funeral because his cell phone went into voice mail when she tried to reach him. The basement had terrible cell reception.

Though Angie had yet to meet the pediatric cardiologist, Jeremy held his colleague in highest regard. Still, Angie felt nervous. Jeremy said that fewer than one in a hundred patients undergoing such heart studies developed complications, but those odds sounded lousy. She hoped the stats lumped all ages together, and that first-graders did better than seventy-five-year-olds.

The tech asked Angie to remain in the empty waiting area for the duration of the test. That was her signal that she'd have to part with Jak. Angie nuzzled her boy's cheek, which smelled of rubbing alcohol. "I'll be waiting for you when you get finished," she told him. He grabbed on to her neck and clung to her. The tech waited as reflexively she wrapped her arms around Jak and held tight. "You'll be fine, honey," she whispered in his ear. "Daddy will be here soon, and he'll stay with you the whole time."

"Why can't you come in with me, Mommy?"

She had to look away from his dark eyes before they destroyed her composure. "I'm not a doctor or a nurse, honey. Besides, you'll be asleep." She wanted to stay with him, but Barlow told her that liability concerns prohibited nonmedical personnel from standing in on this procedure.

Eventually she had to pry Jak loose and watch the tech wheel him through the door, wailing and stretched out toward her as he went. She wanted to cry too, but she smiled and waved, trying to communicate courage by wearing a confident face.

Seconds later Dr. Ludmilla Vorobyova came out to meet her. Vorobyova looked only a few years older than her. She was of average height and wore her straight brown hair pulled back in a taut ponytail. She had angular features and naturally red lips, and she wore no makeup.

Standing in scrubs with a face mask pulled down around her neck, she took Angie's hand and spoke with a thick Russian accent. "Mrs. Cramer, glad to meet you, finally." She spread hands apart as if beholding a thing of beauty. "You are as lovely as your husband said." She looked around in vain. "He is here, no?"

"I expect him any moment."

"Ah, well … good man, your husband. Smart. Very smart. Almost smart as me." She chuckled at her own humor, which Angie found amusing.

"He went to a funeral."

"Nurse Devin's?" Dr. Vorobyova asked. Angie nodded, and the doctor cocked her head. "Strange." She motioned toward the door through which the tech had taken Jak. "Dr. Barlow returned some time ago. Perhaps your husband was detained. Anyways, no need to fear." She motioned for Angie to sit and took the chair next to her. "The mama has questions, yes?"

"You attach electrodes … directly to the heart?"

"Correct." Vorobyova looked at her in earnest. "We get precise maps." She held her thumb and forefinger closely together. "Very precise—of the pathways electrical impulses travel." She continued talking with her hands. "We take long, thin tube and wires, and place them in blood vessel—leg blood vessel—then snake them up to his heart. We inject dye through a catheter and measure how heart valves and heart muscles function. Okay?" She slapped her thigh. "Nothing to worry about."

All that detail gave Angie *more* to worry about. "How long will it take?"

Vorobyova's hands went palms-up. "Kind of long. Maybe four hours, maybe less."

Angie chewed on a fingernail. Still, Jak had been in the hospital for ten days and they had no answers.

Seeming to sense her anxiety, the doctor patted her arm. "Any procedure has risk, but I expect no problem. *Nyet*. Once catheter is in place, I stimulate your son's heart with tiny impulses he cannot feel. No pain. They can trigger irregular beat. These help me know where they happen and why."

If Jak seemed well enough to go home, why risk it? Still, something was causing the elevated heart rate.

"As I told your husband, some details on EKG puzzle me. With children—sometimes hard to tell. But I must be honest. I see more than elevated rate. Perhaps a little left-axis strain. But don't you worry. We take good care of your little b—"

The door opened and Jeremy burst through. "So sorry I'm late, honey." The women stood. "Hello, Luda. I see you've met my wife." He reached out and shook Vorobyova's hand, then turned back to Angie.

"Dr. Vorobyova was just telling me about the procedure," Angie said.

"I go get started now," Vorobyova said, pointing to the door with her thumb. "Your wife—a lovely person, Jeremy." She turned to Angie. "So nice to meet you." She clasped her hands together and held them against her heart. "I promise—I take very good care of your little one. Don't worry, Mama." She faced Jeremy. "Come back soon as you like."

"Be right there," he said.

Jeremy's eyes followed her out. Angie took a seat and Jeremy joined her.

"Sorry I'm late."

"How was the funeral?" Angie asked.

"Tough. But on the way back I got a call from the lab, and I actually have some good news. No, great news!" he said. "I think I know what happened to Devin. It wasn't the T* at all."

"What?" Curious as she was about Devin, right now all Angie could think about was Jak.

"The bag that held the solution Devin was getting when she died? I just got the results back. And the albumin in it was tainted!"

That made no sense to Angie. "Which means ...?"

When a couple entered the reception area, Jeremy motioned toward the door so he and Angie could talk in private. Out in the hall, he continued, "The problem wasn't with the T* cells at all. The culture we used for Devin was clean, pure, pristine. Great news, because it means we can continue with the research. But we had to suspend those cells in a fluid to keep them viable—alive, right?" So far she tracked with him. "That requires a little sugar, a little protein."

"So you're saying something was wrong with the fluid?"

"Yes! Devin had a severe egg allergy, and it looks like there was some albumin from an egg source—chicken egg, specifically. Not unusual. But not what we'd been getting. We recently changed providers—probably due to cost. And the doc of the day may not have noticed. That's what I need to look into."

"And that's good news ... how?"

"When Devin died, we had to stop all the infusions on humans.

But we can probably start them again now. I always mixed the T* with albumin. And the tests on the solution used the day Devin died showed it was the albumin, not the T* that was the likely source of the violent reaction. The albumin came from sources that included eggs. And Devin had a severe egg allergy."

"They didn't know she was allergic?"

"I knew. And it's all over the lab protocol specific for Devin. I'm still looking into that. The important thing—Devin didn't die of AIDS, and she didn't die from the T*. She died of a common but violent allergic reaction. That explains why her autopsy showed such remarkable healing from the damage done by AIDS, yet she still died. In fact, she had such a massive reaction precisely because she was doing so well. That's the sad irony." Jeremy grew more reflective. "Her eosinophils … um, white blood cells … uh … her body mounted such a huge allergic response—because her immune system was so strong."

"I see. So what happens to the manufacturer?"

"Probably nothing. They disclosed the ingredients. I need to find out where the mess-up happened, but I suspect it was the doc on duty." Jeremy leaned against the wall. He was more relaxed than she'd seen him in days, even though he had dark bags under his eyes. "I don't know. Nothing like this has ever happened. But I'm guessing we get the details together and turn all the evidence over to Legal."

"You must be so rel … relieved." Angie's voice cracked.

Jeremy's head tilted and he gazed into her eyes. "You okay?"

She shook her head and looked away. She knew if she saw any sympathy in his eyes, she'd break down. "Worried about Jak." She looked at his shoes. "I'm sorry … I know—"

He took a step toward her and lowered his voice. "Aw, sweetheart, he'll be fine. The cath itself takes only about half an hour. We'll spend most of the time in prep—draw a blood sample, discuss the details of the procedure."

She wished he'd shut up and hold her.

"He's already had an EKG and an Echo, so we don't even have to do those," he continued. "He'll get an IV line and some anesthesia. And when he wakes up, he won't remember a thing. The docs are just talking right now, or I'd be in there."

"I know all that. I'm just worried." When Jeremy stood there motionless, Angie realized he wasn't going to clue in. She'd have to ask for what she needed. "Hold me?"

"Sure." Jeremy wrapped her in his arms, and she felt his head resting on hers. A middle-aged woman passed them on her way in, and for a moment Angie felt stupid. But she decided she didn't care.

"Sorry you got stuck by yourself," Jeremy told her. "I planned to come straight here, but I got the call when I was on my way in."

"I'm just so scared." Angie wiped the tears that had escaped her lashes.

He leaned back and looked at her. "What scares you most?"

"That he'll have a heart attack or something during the procedure."

Jeremy's eyes were kind. He took her hand and told her, "I'll be there the whole time watching. I'll go in right now. And I'm sure he'll be fine. Just fine."

ONCE THE WAITING room filled up with the postlunch appointments, Angie walked up to the reception window. She waited until the young black-haired receptionist looked up. "I think I'll make myself crazy if I stay here leafing through magazines for four hours," Angie said, rubbing clammy hands together. "When my husband gets finished, just have him call my cell, and I'll come right down."

She dragged her feet all the way back to Jak's room, chiding herself for her choice, but knowing she could do nothing if she stayed. Back in the room, she punched in her parents' number to check on

Ainsley. She briefly talked with her mom, who offered to bring Ainsley up after dinner. Angie said that sounded good. After she hung up, she glanced at her watch. That had taken all of seven minutes.

She picked up her laptop, turned it on, and typed "electrophysiology studies" into the search engine. Then she narrowed her exploration to "risks," and skipped right over the part that said side effects were rare.

She read the dangers slowly: bleeding around the point of puncture. Blood clots. Perforation of a blood vessel. Abnormal heart rhythms.

She felt paralyzed as a statue as she imagined Jak's heart rate beating violently out of control. She knew she shouldn't, but she read on.

Stroke. Heart attack. Shortness of breath. Fainting. Palpitations. Chest pain. Low blood pressure.

Those were bad enough. But consuming fear exploded into terror when she read the last two: perforation of the heart. And death.

THREE DREAD-FILLED hours later, her cell rang. She answered with trepidation.

"Come on down," Jeremy said, flatly. "He's in recovery."

She held the cell phone with both hands. "How is he? You sound upset. Is he okay?"

Jeremy hesitated. "Luda isn't saying much. Come down and we'll talk more. You can see Jak now, though he's still out of it."

She hurried to the Recovery room and spotted Jeremy by Jak's side. Jeremy looked worn out. He glanced up when she saw her approach.

"How is he? Okay?" Angie asked.

"We need to keep him quiet for about six hours, but right now, he's still pretty zonked," Jeremy said.

She gazed down at her child and stroked his hair. Then she pulled up a chair and sat across the bed from Jeremy.

Vorobyova burst through the door with her lab coat unbuttoned and rippling behind her. As they stood to greet her, Jeremy mumbled to Angie, "She waited for you to get here. She wants to talk to us together. Barlow, too." To Angie that sounded like bad news.

Vorobyova waved them to their seats without looking at them. "Please sit down." *Something's definitely wrong*, Angie thought. Her heart pounded. Vorobyova turned and looked expectantly at the double doors through which she had just entered. After a few seconds Barlow came through wearing a somber expression.

He pulled up a chair, but Vorobyova remained standing. She crossed her arms and tapped her lips with her index finger. It seemed she still couldn't face them. "Procedure went fine—no complications. I took specimens to pathology myself and ordered a quick read. So we know as soon as possible. I will call you when I know."

"But …?" Jeremy asked. Vorobyova lifted her eyes slowly to meet his. "What are your hunches?" Jeremy prompted. "What do you think it might be?"

"Ah." A long silence ensued as Vorobyova chewed on her lower lip.

Angie could tell it was the inevitable question the doctor clearly wished to avoid.

"Maybe I have not-so-good news." She shifted her weight and looked over to Barlow, apparently for moral support. "I have concern about muscles. So I took biopsy of his muscle during procedure, and now we wait."

"Biopsy of the heart muscle? Something serious? Something permanent?" Angie asked. "Or something that will heal?"

When the doctor's eyes grew misty, Angie felt faint. Vorobyova said, "I fear he has dilated cardiomyopathy." From the fallen look on Jeremy's face, Angie knew it was bad. Really, really bad.

Jeremy spoke quietly, his eyes pleading. "Seriously? You think Jak may have ..." He almost couldn't say it. *"DCM?"* Jeremy stared at his son, now starting to stir on the bed. Barlow put a hand on Jeremy's shoulder.

"That is my fear," Vorobyova said.

Angie hated being the only one present with no clue what DCM was. "What does that mean?" No one spoke. She looked at her husband. "Jeremy! Give me a worst-case scenario."

He looked at her and hesitated, but she glared. She hated it when he kept her in the dark, even out of compassion. Vorobyova came to his rescue. "Worst-case scenario? Could be heart transpla—"

"Hey, let's not go worst-case before we know what the pathology shows," Barlow said. "Jak may fully recover without it coming to that."

But it was too late. Angie heard the word *transplant,* and fear punctured her heart, ripped through her, and tore into her brain. She heard nothing else of the discussion that followed. She'd lost one son, and now the other needed a heart transplant.

CHAPTER 23

When they returned to Jak's room, Angie pulled Jeremy into the bathroom. He shut the door so Jak couldn't hear and Angie sobbed in his arms. Her body shook with grief. He held her tightly and wept, too, overcome with the shock and pain of it all. How could it have come to this? Jeremy pictured his boy standing in the lab with that glove in his mouth, and parental guilt piled itself on top of grief. Jeremy had no proof of a link between the two events, but it had to be his fault.

He reminded himself that Jak was on the other side of the door. They didn't have the luxury of giving in to their grief. Besides, Angie's parents were on their way. He handed Angie a tissue and took one for himself. They blew their noses, washed their faces, and exited the bathroom.

Within a few minutes they heard a knock at the door. Jeremy, sitting nearest, opened it. "Gramps, Grandma," he said. Joan, with her too-made-up lips, handed Ainsley to Angie and embraced Jeremy. Then Tom proffered his hand and pulled Jeremy into a hug.

They took turns giving Angie and Jak hugs and kisses. Joan hovered over Jak. "How do you feel, sweetie pie?"

Jak, still groggy from anesthesia, said a faint "okay." He pointed to his groin, where the pressure dressing was. "Kinda sore."

She tousled his hair and kept smiling down on him, a grandparent's adoration in her toothy grin. "I brought you some gingerbread cookies!"

Angie sat down and placed Ainsley in her lap, and Jeremy leaned down to give Ainsley a kiss. Angie cooed, made silly noises at their fat-cheeked cherub, and played a game with her toes. It was the happiest Jeremy had seen her in more than a week, yet he knew inside she felt anything but happy. He was glad for the momentary distraction. "How was she today?" Angie asked.

Her mom hesitated. "Let's just say I think Ainsley's ready to be home." She turned to Jeremy. "So how'd today go for Jak?"

Jeremy and Angie planned to tell them, but they wanted to wait for the right time and place. Not in front of Jak.

"Uh ... it went ... the procedure went okay." Jeremy and Angie exchanged glances.

The lighthearted mood in the room vanished. Joan looked at them sideways and Angie's eyes begged Jeremy to handle it. He said, "The pediatric cardiologist has ... some concerns ... but I think Jak'll be just fine." He spoke with false cheeriness, walked to the other side of the bed, and squeezed his son's hand.

"What kind of concerns?" Tom asked.

Joan touched her husband's forearm. "Maybe we should talk about this later. Out there, dear." She motioned toward the door with her head, and Tom clued in.

"Jak'll be fine," Jeremy repeated. "Won't you, sport?" Looking frail and pale, Jak nodded up at him.

The next half hour passed slowly as the question about Jak's health hung over them like smoke, permeating everything and stifling easy conversation. Jeremy dragged in more chairs so they could all sit, but he worried that the commotion might wear Jak out. He wished his in-laws would leave. He lacked the energy to keep up the pretense. But he wanted time with Ainsley. He and Angie had seen so little of her since Jak was admitted to the hospital. If only his fragile family could have some privacy.

As soon as Jak drifted off, the room grew quiet. Angie bounced

Ainsley on her leg and gestured for Jeremy to pull his chair closer. She spoke to her parents in a near-whisper. "It's been a tough day." She turned to Jeremy expectantly.

"This afternoon Jak's cardiologist ran some tests." He stated the obvious in hopes that the more difficult words might magically form as he stalled.

"What did he find?" Tom asked.

Not wanting to blatantly correct his father-in-law on the cardiologist's gender, Jeremy rephrased his answer. "The doctor suspects Jak may have a condition called *cardiomyopathy.*"

"Cardio?" Joan wrung her bejeweled hands.

"What is it?" Tom asked, looking between Jeremy and Angie, concern filling his face.

Jeremy had no choice but to come out with it. "An abnormality in the structure or—in this case—the function of the heart muscle."

"Sounds serious," Joan said.

Jeremy moderated his voice to sound more casual than he felt. "It could be."

"They call it DCM," Angie said.

Tom made a funny face. "How do you get DCM out of cardio-whatever-it-is?" His *out* sounded like *oat.*

"Cardio*myopathy,*" Jeremy said. "*Dilated* cardiomyopathy."

"Dilated? He has a dilated heart? What does that mean?"

"The concern with DCM is that, um, the heart slowly loses its efficiency as a pump," Jeremy said.

"My word," Tom whispered. "So it's serious?"

"Serious enough to require expert medical care. But we're certainly getting that," Jeremy said. "The pediatric intensivist almost sent him home over the weekend, he was doing so well. If that tells you anything."

"How do you catch something like that?" Tom asked. Jeremy avoided looking at Angie on that one. "Is it hereditary?" Tom continued.

Suddenly Jeremy felt defensive. "Sometimes. But lots of things can trigger it. In older patients alcohol abuse and even pregnancy can bring it on."

"And younger patients?" Joan asked.

Jeremy still couldn't look at Angie. "We see it with connective tissue diseases. And exposure to certain drugs and toxins. Infections. Nutritional deficiencies. Even cancer and autoimmune conditions." He hoped he'd made the list of possibilities broad enough to warrant her giving him the benefit of the doubt—though that was more than he was giving himself at the moment.

AN HOUR LATER Angie walked her parents and Ainsley down to the car while Jeremy stayed in the room with Jak. As he watched his son sleep, he mulled over the day's events, still in a state of disbelief. Suddenly his cell phone vibrated. It was Dr. Glidewall from the morgue.

She talked faster than usual. "You at home or the hospital?"

"Up in the children's cardio wing. Why?"

"I'm working late too—on a postmortem. And I have something down here you have to see."

"What is it?" He sat upright in the chair.

"You have to see it to believe it."

Her evasiveness annoyed Jeremy. He tried coaxing an answer out of her, but she refused. "It'll be another five or ten minutes before I can get away," he told her.

"Just come on down when you can. You can let yourself in. The access code's seven-five-nine-seven. Like you're making a triangle on the keypad."

Once downstairs Jeremy donned his gown and shoe covers as quickly as possible, glad the place smelled only of Formalin this time. Air Supply blared from the boom box when he entered. He walked over to her, but the music blasted so loudly that he had to repeat himself twice when he asked her a question. Finally he went over to the boom box and turned down the volume.

"Sorry. I guess it was loud enough to wake the dead," she said with a giggle from behind her mask. "When I turned it on, I didn't expect company."

He stood beside her and pulled his mask over his mouth. "So what do we have here?"

"One of your former T* patients fresh outta hospice."

Jeremy surveyed the corpse and was taken aback when he recognized the body as that of a twenty-three-year-old hemophilia patient who had contracted HIV as a child. "Sad," Jeremy said. The patient had been doing so well—until they stopped his T* treatments.

"Died about five hours ago."

"We lost one today, huh?" he said, trying to sound emotionally detached. *Why hadn't anyone told him*, he wondered. Then he calculated the time of death at about the time they wheeled Jak into Recovery. "So what's all the mystery about?"

"See these organs?" she asked. "They look fantastic for an end-stage patient, right?"

Jeremy agreed. It was good, but this was nothing new. They'd been seeing a pattern of great-looking organs on corpses.

"Okay. Now, see that?" She pointed with her scalpel.

"Looks like a healthy kidney," Jeremy said, his tone reflecting his so-what attitude.

"Yes, it does, Dr. Cramer. So healthy, in fact, that—in my amazement—I decided just for fun to inject a little saline into the renal artery." She pointed to the blood vessel supplying the kidney.

"I don't suppose the patient got up," Jeremy said dryly.

"Not exactly. But watch this." Something about her eyes told him she wasn't kidding. She injected 50 cc's of normal saline, and in a matter of seconds the dead-for-five-hours kidney secreted a tiny flow of urine.

Behind Jeremy's mask, his jaw fell slack. The kidney functioned.

"Dr. Cramer," she said, her voice hushed almost as if she were afraid, "this patient died *five hours ago*. I have cut him open from stem to stern and that kidney still secretes. Brought back to service—*hours* after death."

Jeremy snapped his mouth shut. The evidence was right there in front of him. But it couldn't be. Cadaver kidneys had produced urine before, but only immediately after death. Never this long after the patient expired. If he was really seeing what he thought he was seeing, Jeremy realized he could possibly prolong cell life or at least slow the process of cell death. That meant an organ's viability could be maintained for much longer than previously possible in the absence of a blood supply.

"I hope you have a way to keep your findings quiet until you can patent them," she warned.

Jeremy was so focused on the discovery that it took him a few seconds to realize she'd spoken and to comprehend her words. "We can't patent cells," he told her.

"Whatever. But you of all people recognize the ramifications, right? We're talking about more than HIV here—which would be awesome by itself. But we're talking about the potential to reverse the effects of heart attacks, electrocutions, underwater submersions ..."

"I need to sit down," he said.

"Me, too!"

WEDNESDAY MORNING WHEN Barlow stopped in Jak's room, he told Angie and Jeremy that their son's condition was stable. And on his way out he invited Jeremy to join him for a donut in the doctor's lounge after rounds.

At the appointed time Jeremy picked up some pastries and found a free table.

The lounge was the size of a small coffee shop and had an intimate atmosphere. On one side were high-end tables and chairs. On the other were finely appointed couches and armchairs that some designer had chosen and arranged. Doctors sat reading the news or gathered in small groups talking in low voices. Jeremy recognized most of them, though he knew only about half by name. Several stopped and asked about his son.

He was just licking his lips to get the chocolate frosting off when Barlow entered. Jeremy wondered if the new Batman tie he had on was for Jak's benefit.

"Let me grab something and I'll be right there," Barlow told him. He got a plate of steaming French toast, with butter and syrup in small dishes on the side, and returned. He motioned for Jeremy to join him at a more private table across the room. Jeremy followed and they took their seats.

"Something specific you wanted to talk to me about?" he asked.

Barlow pretended to choke on his juice. "Just like my wife—blow past the niceties and get right down to it," he said with a kind smile. "Sure, I wanted to talk to you, but mostly I want to see how you're doing."

"Does that make you my personal pediatrician?" Jeremy asked, smiling.

"Wait! Did you …? Did you … *crack a smile?*" Barlow asked.

"Shocking, huh?" Jeremy took a big bite out of his second donut.

Barlow leaned forward on his elbows, and Jeremy noticed that he looked older somehow, and tired. "Seriously, how're you holding up?" Barlow asked. The sincerity in the senior doctor's gaze caught him up short and the lightness of the moment fell away.

Jeremy didn't answer. How could he? Other than infecting a good friend with a needle that led to her death and putting his son at serious risk, he felt swell—like a thumb he'd just smashed with a hammer. And—wait—that was after the wreck that killed Ravi. Sure, the research was going well. Far better than four days ago. And learning that Devin's cause of death was due to something other than T* made for some good news. But who really cared about helping all the strangers in the world if he couldn't protect the people he loved? He didn't know how to answer, so he didn't.

Barlow took a long drink on his juice and set down the glass. "Let me ask you something." He hesitated, seeming to select his words with care. "You're not blaming this ... Jak's health ... on the glove incident, are you?"

"Of *course* I am." Jeremy couldn't believe Barlow had asked.

"I thought as much. But I'm not convinced they're related."

"Are you serious?" He searched his colleague's face for a hint of deception, but found none.

Barlow stopped buttering his French toast. "Yes, I'm serious. First of all, back when we checked the glove your son blew up—to see what grew off it—you found *nada*, right?" He resumed buttering, dipped a square in maple syrup, and took a bite.

Jeremy shook his head. "So what? Most of the nasty viruses are nearly impossible to culture if a glove's been sitting in the trash for a while. We both know a negative culture means next to nothing."

"And the bacteria came back negative, too, right?"

"So?"

"And nobody in the lab confessed to leaving a glove hanging out ..."

Jeremy sputtered. "Course not."

"So even though the evidence doesn't condemn you, you condemn yourself?" Barlow sat back as if he'd just made his case and won.

"Listen, man, I appreciate you trying to make me feel better. I really do." Barlow started to argue, but Jeremy held up a hand and kept going. "But let's be honest here. We both know if my son had never come to the lab with me, he'd be playing baseball and catching salamanders instead of lying up there." He gestured in the direction of the pediatric wing. "He wouldn't be ... hooked up ..." His voice cracked as he choked out, "… hooked up to oxygen with a monitor on his heart."

The vigor with which Barlow shook his head surprised Jeremy. Barlow pointed for emphasis as he spoke. "*You* of all people should know better! You take a kid in the highest-risk age bracket in a school full of germs and expose him to the highly contagious Coxsackie virus … and you think it was the *glove?* Yes, the complication he developed is rare," Barlow said. "But it's a well-documented one. You know what fragile creatures we all are. There are bad bugs everywhere. Most people handle them fine. But once in a while, somebody gets one that goes bonkers. Or their genetic makeup puts them at risk. Or something lowers their resistance. Don't you dare blame this on yourself! This is exactly why a doctor can't treat his own kids. What happened to your great objectivity?"

Jeremy couldn't believe what he was hearing. "You really believe yourself, don't you?"

"Of course I do. I don't lie to patients, and I won't lie to you. I told you in the ER and I'm telling you again now—I think they're unrelated. You have a right to know the truth."

Jeremy looked away and blinked back the tears that threatened to cloud his vision. He formed his words with difficulty. "I made him bite his tongue."

"So what?"

Jeremy blinked faster as a tear threatened. "I wish I could believe you," he finally said.

"Why *can't* you, Jeremy? You know good evidence when you see it. Why can't you *see* this?"

Jeremy kept his focus on the wall near them. "I think …" He couldn't finish the sentence.

Barlow was patient, but he expected an answer. "You think … what?"

"Because of the timing. It was too close to the glove incident."

"It was past the typical incubation period ..."

"Barely. And besides ..." Jeremy looked around and made sure no one could hear him. He didn't want *himself* to hear it. "Angie would never believe it wasn't my fault." He took a deep breath and blurted out the rest. "If I don't take responsibility, she'll be even angrier, like I contaminated my kid and then wouldn't own up to it. That would be worse to her than causing it." Tears nearly blinded him now. "I've already lost my parents and my son—not to mention Devin—and now I'm afraid of losing it all."

They sat silently for a long time, Jeremy continuing to look off at the wall and Barlow staring at the floor. Then quietly under his breath Jeremy asked, "You *sure* you don't think it was caused by the glove incident?"

"I really don't think so. Certainly the history we've developed on your son's case doesn't support that. Look at me, Jeremy."

Their eyes met.

"Hear me well. This is *not* your fault."

CHAPTER 24

Jeremy tossed his trash and exited the lounge behind Barlow. As they walked to the elevators, their beepers went off simultaneously. Jeremy didn't recognize the number, but Barlow did. "It's Luda Vorobyova."

Jeremy made the call for both of them. Vorobyova's assistant told him they had Jak's test results and wanted the doctors to meet in the doctor's office up on the cardiac floor immediately before her next appointment.

Once the men arrived, the receptionist ushered them straight back to her office. Vorobyova, who was sitting at her desk with a receiver against her ear, waved them in. She kept talking, and Jeremy drummed his fingers on the arm of the chair, wishing she'd hurry up. If she was in such a big hurry, why was she taking so long? The suspense made the seconds drag. Barlow took the opportunity to check his PDA.

If Jeremy didn't already know Vorobyova came from Belarus, he might have figured it out from her office décor. The watercolor paintings of Orthodox onion-shaped domes suggested she was Russian, but plaques under the pictures identified them as churches in Minsk.

When her call finally ended, she quietly opened Jak's file on her desk. She held up a sheet of paper. Her expression was one of grave concern. "As feared, Jeremy, tissue samples from your boy's heart muscle confirm my prognosis: dilated cardiomyopathy."

Jeremy had the same sensation he always got with devastating news—at first a sharp pain in his head like a punch or a stroke and then the room spinning and shrinking as reality set in.

"Of course you know what this means," Vorobyova continued. "I am sorry. His heart—not strong enough. Not enough cardiac output. Probably will get worse. Maybe soon. Probably soon."

Jeremy held fast to the arms of the chair, trying to anchor himself as the room twirled.

She continued, "The body demands too much of the heart. So … you have questions?" She lifted kind brown eyes to Jeremy.

That was it? That was all she planned to say? Jeremy was in too much shock to formulate words.

Barlow jumped in, "How widespread is the inflammation? What's the current cardiac output and ejection fraction? And what course of action are you recommending?"

She twisted her lips before answering. "Cardiac function is adequate for now—at bed rest—but barely. Sometimes they turn around and improve with supportive care. Rest. Oxygen. Medicine as needed. But sometimes … often … medicines do not work. Cardiac dilation reaches point of no return. It can take weeks. Or days. But we see steady decline. I'm sorry."

She thought for a few seconds and began again. "What to do? We continue bed rest and I order no-salt diet. We can probably maintain oxygen levels for little while … only because he stays on oxygen. But this is no way for little boy to live." She looked at Jeremy. "You want child to run, play, go to school, of course."

"What are you saying?" Jeremy asked.

She bit her upper lip, pausing before she answered him. "Even if I wanted, I could not lie to you. You are smart man. You know prognosis for long-term survival in pediatric DCM. We hope, we pray to God he gets better. But we plan for worst, yes? That way we are prepared. If good news makes our plans useless, we rejoice that we wasted time wisely."

"What's the next step, then?" Barlow asked.

She directed her words to Jeremy. "I notified head of cardiothoracic transplant team so we can start process to put your son on the list. You will want to consult with him and his group of physicians, nurses, counselors … the chaplain. Many people available to help you."

It took Jeremy a moment for that to sink in. He felt as if someone had just whacked him in the stomach with a two-by-four. "I have to tell Angie."

"I'll go with you," Barlow said.

Jeremy stood and extended his hand. "Thank you, Luda."

She received it with both of hers. "I am sorry."

Jeremy exited with Barlow following close behind, and they proceeded down the hall in stunned silence. When they reached the men's restroom, Jeremy said, "Excuse me for a minute."

Finding the room empty, he entered a stall, leaned his forehead against the door, and panted. Jak might die. They'd already lost Ravi. They'd just lost Devin. And now this? He knew his marriage couldn't survive more devastation. Emotionally he didn't think he could either. *Please, God, if you're there, don't let me lose another child!*

He worried that they'd never find a match for Jak's heart. The horrors of transplant and everything that could go wrong weighed heavily as his weary mind considered possible scenarios.

Not wanting to keep Barlow waiting, he whipped some toilet paper from the roll, wiped his eyes, and blew his nose. Though he dreaded telling Angie, he couldn't keep Barlow waiting. He had to pull it together. Splashing water on his face didn't take the redness from his eyes, but it helped.

Out in the hall Barlow was engrossed in a phone call, much to Jeremy's relief. He wouldn't have to say anything. Or even look at him. Or be looked at. As Jeremy listened, he realized Barlow was talking to the head of the transplant team. Barlow had started the ball rolling already. While still talking, he motioned for them to proceed toward Jak's room.

Jeremy knew Angie was anxious for any news. And sometimes even bad news was better than waiting; at least when people knew something for certain, they could begin to face it. Or that's what he'd always thought. But maybe not with such grim news like this. Jeremy dragged his feet. Waiting with hope would be better than knowing with despair.

When they arrived, Jeremy stood outside the door and took a deep breath, trying to summon the courage to do what he had to do. Mercifully, Barlow seemed in no rush, despite the fact that Jak's needs had consumed so much of his time. Barlow crossed his hands and studied a square on the floor, apparently waiting for Jeremy to signal readiness.

"Can you tell her?" Jeremy asked. "Probably better that way."

Barlow nodded and Jeremy took another deep breath before giving the door a weak tap and opening it.

Angie sat in her usual post at the end of the bed. Jak was asleep. When her eyes met Barlow's, she jumped up. "You're back—so soon. What's up?"

"Can you come out in the hall a sec, honey?" Jeremy asked.

She gave him a puzzled look, then turned to make sure Jak was still asleep. When she joined them outside she asked Barlow, "You have some results?" He nodded. "So what do you know?" Looking from Barlow to Jeremy, she seemed to read their faces. "Bad news?"

Jeremy recognized in Barlow's voice the same soothing tone Jeremy adopted for the most calming effect. "We just came from Luda's office. Jak's cardiac function is adequate for now—at bed rest. She said sometimes these cases turn around and improve with supportive care alone."

"But ...?" Angie asked.

Barlow swallowed and took a deep breath. "But her diagnosis confirms dilated cardiomyopathy." Jeremy saw a sudden glittering of tears in Angie's eyes. Barlow continued, "She wants to continue bed rest.

And she's ordered a no-salt diet. She also wants to keep a close eye on him for signs of improvement."

"But he's going to be okay, right?" Angie whispered. She looked from Barlow to Jeremy, seemingly searching for hints in their expressions.

"We don't know for sure," Barlow said. "But we'll watch closely for signs of deterioration. And just in case—we can't rule out transplant."

Angie covered her face, turned her back to them, and sobbed as only a mother could.

———

WHILE JEREMY'S BOSS, Dr. Jasper, was out of town, Jeremy had kept her informed by e-mail of all the developments in Devin's case. He requested a meeting with her as soon as she returned from her cruise, and that was the only message she answered. Because of the funeral on Tuesday, the earliest they could meet was Wednesday.

When Jeremy arrived at her office around lunchtime with a few minutes to spare, the secretary told him Jasper was waiting and sent Jeremy on in. He found Dr. Reiko sitting in one of the high-back chairs that faced Jasper's desk. Jeremy assumed Jasper summoned Reiko so she could hear from the only eyewitness what happened with Devin's infusion.

Seeing them together, Jeremy noticed for the first time that Jeff Reiko could be Jasper's son—no, her grandson. Both had fuzzy hair—hers, frizzy and shoulder-length; his, much shorter. Both had round cheeks. His gave him a baby-faced look, though Jeremy suspected that had more to do with too many vending-machine meals than innocence. Her face was suntanned and her cheeks red, as usual. Reiko looked tired and his scrubs were wrinkled.

Jeremy didn't often see Reiko on weekdays, since he was a week-end doc. He assumed Jasper would excuse him, but she didn't, and he didn't stand.

"Have a seat, Cramer. We were just finishing here. But I asked Dr. Reiko to stay for a moment because I want you to hear something he told me."

Reiko was on Jeremy's list of people to consult. The two had spoken briefly on Sunday night, but that was before Jeremy knew Devin's actual cause of death. He was glad Jasper saved him the trouble of tracking Reiko down.

Jeremy started in, "It looks like there was some albumin—"

Jasper shushed him by shaking her head and holding up a hand. "Hang on, Cramer. Reiko, tell him what you told me—exactly what you just said."

He looked at Jeremy. "Your notes said to take albumin from the special storage refrigerator—the fridge marked for Garrigues, right?" Jeremy nodded. "But that fridge was locked." That didn't make sense to Jeremy. Reiko continued, "So I checked in the main fridge where you keep the unmixed T*, and I took one of the bags of albumin from in there."

The idiot! Jeremy lunged forward and opened his mouth to berate him when Jasper reprimanded him. "Shut up and listen, Cramer." She turned to Reiko. "You didn't ask around for a key, right?"

He shook his head. "I'd already made the patient wait ..."

Jeremy was furious. This lazy manatee of a doc killed Devin with his sheer lack of initiative.

"And besides," he continued, "I didn't think I needed one after I opened the other refrigerator. I just used the bag with her name on it." He looked at Jeremy. "I figured you put it in there for me."

What? He's trying to cover what he did, and now he wants to pin the results of his negligence on me, Jeremy thought. He couldn't believe it. "What bag marked with her name?"

Reiko shrugged. "The one in the general fridge. I assumed you prepared it, Cramer."

Jeremy stared at Reiko. "And what exactly did *my* note say?" Jeremy asked, his tone dripping sarcasm.

"The only thing on it was 'Garrigues.' Like I said, I assumed you stuck it on there for me." He explained to Jasper, "It was one of those little yellow square sticky notes—the kind that peel off easily."

Jeremy had never in his entire life labeled anything with a yellow sticky note—let alone something in a lab.

"Thank you, Dr. Reiko," Jasper said. "That will be all for now." He got halfway across the room when she stopped him. "Do me a favor and let's keep these details among the three of us until we get to the bottom of this. Okay?"

"Absolutely," he said. He seemed glad not to talk about it.

As soon as Jeremy was sure he was out of earshot, he insisted, "You know he's ly—"

"Hold your horses, Cramer," Jasper demanded.

He pounded the desk. "But he's lying. I e-mailed the instructions to him from my Blackberry at the airport. I'll forward you a copy." He stood to make his words more emphatic. "Check the security records and you'll see I didn't return after I sent it. I didn't put anything for Devin in that refrigerator!"

She glared up at him. "Siddown! Would you get a grip, Cramer?" Jeremy sat and fumed. "Save your steam," she said. "We're just getting started."

"There's more?" He could only imagine the tale Reiko had devised. It was going to be one doctor's word against another's, and though she said otherwise, it felt like Jasper had already made up her mind to believe Reiko.

"The results you told me about ..." she asked. "The egg tainting? Where'd you get the data?"

"Singular Labs."

An "aha" look came over her. "So you sent it outside for testing too?"

"Sure."

"And you know what our lab found ..."

"Actually, no, I haven't had a chance to get down there yet today. But I assume they'll show the same results. I ordered both internal and external tests on everything in this case. I know it costs more, but I did it in the hospital's interest. For redundancy. I figured in case we get sued, the manufacturer will demand testing from a disinterested party."

Jasper beamed. "Got to hand it to you. It'll save us work when it's time for the little conference we have to hold when exploring negligence or iatrogenic death. Maybe in a few weeks. Could be a few months. But the more we can learn, the better. Does anyone in our own lab know about the testing redundancy?"

Jeremy thought a minute and shrugged. "I don't know. If they do, I doubt they care." He didn't like the sound of "iatrogenic." *Doctor-caused.* Yet her tone was affirming, not accusing.

"Let me make absolutely certain I understand you. It is your contention that you didn't put any albumin-laced T* in the general refrigerator?"

"Absolutely!"

"Okay, okay. And you haven't yet received the results from our friends here?" she asked.

"I may have." Jeremy shrugged. "I just haven't made it downstairs yet today."

Jasper handed him a lab report. "Perhaps this will interest you." It was from Ted, Jeremy's assistant, with appropriate supervisory signatures. And it said the results found ... nothing. Jeremy stared up at her.

"Do you have more of the sample that killed her?" she asked.

It didn't add up. Why would two tests on the same sample reveal different results?

"Cramer! I asked you a question. Do you still have the bag?"

He nodded.

"Where is it?" she asked.

"Down in the general fridge where Reiko put it afterward."

"Let's go down and have a look."

CHAPTER 25

Waiting with Jasper in the elevator banks, Jeremy tried to fit together the facts. He had some puzzle pieces, but so far they made an incomplete picture. He was sure Reiko was lying. But why would Reiko go so far as to tamper with lab results to show nothing was wrong? His story depended on Jeremy mislabeling a *tainted* bag. But surely Ted had no reason to mess with a sample. Maybe he made a mistake. Unlikely, but possible.

Perhaps the outside lab made a mistake, he reasoned. Also unlikely—especially because their findings matched Devin's reaction. Still, Jeremy would ask for a retest.

He and Jasper boarded the empty elevator and stood side-by-side facing the doors. When they shut, Jasper folded her arms and rocked on her heels. "You sure hacked off Castillo." In the reflection he could see the skin around her eyes crinkling and the corner of a smile tugging at her mouth.

"Guess you heard all about it when you returned yesterday," he said.

"Yesterday? Ha! How about my entire vacation?" she asked. "Next time I'll book a cruise where I can't get cell service."

"Sorry."

But Jasper seemed amused more than anything. She gave him a sideways jab. "You rascal. Kind of served him right for forcing you to go. I told him not to."

She's really clueless about what I'm going through right now, Jeremy thought.

"Marching up there to try talking him out of making you go," she continued. "Ha! I gotta hand it to ya, Cramer. That took nerve. And then to leave D.C. without him!" She chuckled and clucked her tongue.

"I shouldn't …" He was going to say he shouldn't have left D.C., to express regret, but he didn't want to lie.

"Amazing he didn't fire you on the spot when he got back. That says he has more stock invested in you than he lets on." She gave Jeremy a hearty slap on the back. "And just for the record, so do I. I heard about the big discovery in the morgue last night. Spectacular." When Jeremy merely grunted, she seemed to pick up on his mood. "Hey, sorry to hear you've had your son up here. Hope he's getting better."

"Thanks." Jeremy wished the elevator didn't have mirrors. He looked down so she couldn't see in the reflection his disconsolate expression. Time to change the subject.

"Other than your calls from Castillo," he said, "I hope you had a good time on your cruise. I do appreciate your trying to run interference for me, especially from afar—even if he didn't take your advice."

"You're welcome. Big part of my job description, running interference with Castillo." She whistled. "You're not the only one. If you only knew the half of it."

When they arrived at the lab, they went straight to Jeremy's pod. On his desk lay a report that matched the one Jasper showed him. It said the in-house lab found no evidence of a problem in the sample.

Jeremy located the bag in the refrigerator. He reached out to pick it up, but Jasper grabbed his arm. "How about we put on some gloves first?"

Their eyes locked and Jeremy understood. "Gloves. Right."

ANGIE SAT STARING at her child. The news seemed incongruent with Jak's improving energy level. He was sitting up, the effects of the anesthesia appearing to have completely worn off. As she watched him play a handheld game, it seemed that his color had improved, too. Was he really getting worse? Had he contracted some dread disease? If so, what? And why would God let something like this happen? *Not this child, too. Please! Wasn't the loss of one child bad enough?* She mused that all this time to sit and think would surely make her a philosopher—or crazy.

"Mommy, look!" He tilted his game in her direction to show off his high score. His spirits lifted hers a bit. "That's great, sweetie," she said, trying to sound enthusiastic.

He powered off the machine and laid it beside him on the bed. "When can we go home?"

She went to his side and laid a hand on his upper arm. "You miss your friends at school?"

"A little maybe."

She could tell by his unenthusiastic answer that wasn't it at all. "Your stuff?"

"And sissy."

"I miss her too."

"Plus my toys. And Jon-Jon and Brian and Julia." The neighborhood kids had signed and sent a banner now draped across the wall under his TV, but that only seemed to make his loneliness worse. His friends got to hang out together while he was stuck in the hospital.

"I don't know how long, honey."

"A long time?" His sweet little eyes pleaded for her to say no.

"Maybe. But maybe the doctor will let us go home if we take oxygen with us." She'd done some Internet searching about home equipment, but most of the information had been for adults. She didn't know about pediatric monitors. She knew she shouldn't have offered hope without checking with Jeremy first. The words slipped out.

Tears clouded Jak's eyes. "Oxygen at home, too?"

So much for offering hope, she thought. "I don't know. We'll ask the doctor."

"Am I going to die, Mommy?"

"Oh, honey! Of course not!" The words caught her completely by surprise. She remembered Barlow telling her that kids were more perceptive about these things than most parents expected, but nothing she or Jeremy said should have given Jak that impression. She was unprepared, but she had to say something. "Why do you ask?"

"I've been here a long time. And this." He pulled at the tube that led to his nose. "What's heaven like, Mommy?"

She gasped, and then tried to cover it by coughing. "I don't know, sweetheart." She thought of Dante's description in *Paradiso*. And Milton's. She realized she'd never actually read what the Bible said about heaven, though the Sayers book was based on the Gospels. In Sayers' version Jesus talked a lot about heaven and the kingdom of heaven and the kingdom of God, but he never described it. "They say it's a good place. A happy place full of light. But I don't expect you to go there anytime soon."

He seemed to ignore her assurance. "Ravi's there."

"Yes," Angie said wistfully.

"And you know what?" he asked. "Instead of this tube to breathe, I'll wear a space suit! That's how astronauts breathe." Delight danced in his eyes. "I'm asking the president of heaven for a space suit."

After Jasper left, Jeremy sat in his pod and took out a legal pad. Maybe writing a few notes would help him organize all the details he was trying to mentally keep track of.

Jak first. If Jak needed a transplant, Jeremy had to know at what point. Transplant lists moved slowly—notoriously so. Jeremy knew the stages of grief well, and he liked denial best. But in this case, he didn't have the luxury of indulging himself. He knew proactive investigation could save valuable time. He had to explore the options. At least if they had to do a heart transplant, they could do it here rather than changing hospitals. And he knew the key players. That could only help. Awful as it was, he needed to meet with the team. Jak couldn't even get on the list until that happened.

In the meantime he wondered about getting Jak home. Though Jeremy had an easier time of it with Angie and Jak nearby, and Jeremy felt better with Jak close to his medical team, some transplant patients waited at home. He made a note to talk to Barlow and Vorobyova about options.

And what about T* where Jak was concerned? Might it improve his chances? No way Angie or Barlow would ever agree to it. But could it improve Jak's heart function? Probably not. Jeremy had no evidence whatsoever that T* improved muscle function, and even less that it could repair muscle damaged by infection. Besides—Jak was a child and children already had T*. Nothing had ever given Jeremy reason to believe that more was better. He crossed that option off the list.

As for the research, they needed to determine that the albumin solution that killed Devin was tainted. If they could establish an egg-allergy connection, the T* human trials could get back on track. If not, they had to start all over. But Jasper was handling that for the time being. Nothing he could do there.

Ted poked his head in. He started to say something but Jeremy interrupted, "Hey, c'mere." He jumped up and pointed to the conference room. "Got a question for you." Ted followed him in and Jeremy shut the door. "Have a seat."

"What's up, man?" Ted sat down and smoothed back his dark, wavy hair.

"I got the results from the albumin test you did."

"Yeah, what's up with that? I just got the third-degree from Jasper." He seemed exasperated.

"I have some questions about your research."

"Sorry, man. She told me not to talk to anybody about it. I guess that means you, too. I'm sure you were hoping it was a problem with the new lab's albumin we've been getting, but the evidence just wasn't there. Really too bad, too, considering what I was coming to tell you...."

"What?"

He shifted in his seat and talked with his hands. "It's our water-logged rats. We submerged Ari and Nic for five full minutes after the test group quit their underwater struggle. Test group all bit the dust. But ..." He leaned forward for dramatic effect. "But Ari and Nic survived."

The news rendered him speechless. Jeremy had longed for this moment. He'd worked for it, sacrificed time with his family for it, spent his life preparing for it. It should be fantastic—a once-in-a-lifetime joy. Followed by a party with champagne. Instead the news amounted to little more than a private comment in a dusty lab conference room. His hope faded as he realized it would probably never make a real difference in anyone's life. It totally stunk.

"Sort of good news/bad news, huh?" Ted, with his bucktoothed grin, seemed oblivious to Jeremy's mood. "Your stuff works. But what kind of market do you think there is for animal resuscitations? Ha! So what do you think it is, Dr. Cramer?"

"What do you mean?"

"You're trying to isolate what was in the T* that caused the adverse reaction. What's your hunch?" Either Ted was a great actor or Jasper had not mentioned the contradicting lab reports to him.

"Frankly I have no clue."

IN THE EARLY evening Jeremy made his way to Jak's room. When Barlow came for rounds, Jeremy wanted to be there. He found Angie asleep in the chair. Jak was sitting up watching a PBS animal show with the sound muted.

Jeremy bent to pick up the book Angie had apparently dropped when she'd fallen asleep. "How you feeling, sport?" he whispered.

"Hi, Daddy!" Jak reached out for a hug and Jeremy obliged.

"Did you and Mommy have a fun day?"

"Bor-ing!" Jak blurted out the word a little too loudly, causing Angie to stir. She rubbed her eyes and sat up. Recognition flashed on her face when she saw Jeremy. "Oh, hi. Sorry. I must have dozed off."

"So does this mean you didn't make dinner?" Jeremy asked, trying to keep the mood light. She said something in reply, but it didn't register because he glanced at Jak's oxygen rate and saw that it had dropped to 95 percent. Jak had been lying down lately, so Jeremy thought perhaps he should attribute the drop to Jak's upright position. Still—not good news. Certainly not an improvement.

Jeremy fingered the oxygen tube. "Jak, honey, did you take this off while Mommy was asleep?" Jak shook his head. Jeremy wondered if his son had somehow pinched it. "Were you lying on it, maybe?"

Jak didn't answer. He just looked up at his dad and said, "Mommy says maybe I can go home soon."

"Did she now?" He looked to Angie for an explanation.

She held up a hand in defense. "I said *maybe*. I just thought if all he needs for a while is extra oxygen, some meds, and a low-salt diet, we could talk to—"

"We can always ask." He turned to Jak. "I don't know, sport. I doubt it. But we'll try."

Angie stood and put her hands on her hips. "I can go down to the cafeteria and bring us something for dinner. Or we can order out. Or

I'll go out and pick us up something. What sounds good?" They were trying to choose between Chinese and Italian when Barlow arrived.

After the usual courtesies and a glance at the equipment, he assumed a kid-friendly persona, as Jeremy had seen him do with Ninette, the thymoma patient who was now doing well. "'ello Batman. 'Ow are we this evenin', gov'nor?" Barlow shook Jak's hand. "Been sittin' up long?"

Captivated by this new caricature, Jak couldn't seem to formulate an answer. Angie filled in the blanks. "He's been sitting up most of the afternoon."

"Let's 'ave ye lie down a bit, shall we?" Barlow pressed the button on the automatic bed and moved Jak to a reclining position.

"When can I go home?" Jak asked.

"Want to go 'ome, do ye?" Barlow pulled back as if shocked, then peered into Jak's eyes as if he'd asked to house an elephant in his room. "Now, why would yer want t' do that?" He held up a finger. "I know what it is. Food's bad, is it? I could order ye some kidney pie. Put hair on your chest, it will." Jak giggled. "Can't compete with yer mum's mac and cheese, though. So's that it? Yer wantin' kidney pie?"

"Ble-ech!" Jak said. Barlow recoiled as if stunned. Jak loved the reaction, so he repeated it with more enthusiasm: "Blee-e-ch!"

"Well then, suit yerself. But don't say I didn't offer." Barlow held out a hand and shook Jak's. "I best be goin', gov'nor. Need to talk to your folks, now. Be seein' ye tomorrow."

Barlow led the way and Jeremy and Angie followed him out the door. Once in the hall Jeremy asked, "So was that a British gent or a pirate?"

"Hey, gimme a break. I went to med school, not acting school."

Angie got straight to business. "What's up?"

"I took the liberty of setting up a meeting with the transplant team for tomorrow morning at nine. It would be best if you can both make it."

"Transplant team? This is happening so fast," Angie said. "Is that necessary? Jak's not even on a transplant list yet." Jeremy intertwined his fingers with hers and looked to Barlow to fill her in.

"This is the way we get him on the list," Barlow said. "The first step is to find a transplant team that will treat him. Fortunately your husband here has some connections. We're not saying your son definitely has to have one, at this point. But we're taking every precaution and planning for every possible eventuality."

"I see," Angie said. "And what does a meeting like that involve?"

"You meet with a group of surgeons, nurses, counselors, and the chaplain, if you wish. They determine if Jak's a good candidate. That involves assessing his physical condition and his attitude, among other factors."

"Other factors?" Angie was growing more intense. "Like what? What other factors?"

"Um, like if he's willing to give up drinking and drugs."

Angie smiled, and Jeremy saw a twitch in the corner of Barlow's mouth. "With a dad who's a complete lunatic," Barlow continued, "that could be a problem. I'll do my best to cover for you, man. But you're gonna owe me. Big time."

CHAPTER 26

Angie's mom agreed to come sit with Jak so Angie and Jeremy could meet with the transplant team. Angie had just put the last touches on her makeup when her mom arrived with Ainsley. Angie melted when her toddler's brown eyes met hers and little arms stretched out. "Mama!" Ainsley leaned so hard out of her grandmother's arms that Angie quickly grabbed her lest she fall. Mother and child held each other in a tight embrace, and Ainsley wrapped dimpled fingers around her mother's thumb.

"Where's Jeremy?" her mom asked.

"Working. I expect him any minute."

"Do I have time to run down to the car and get the playpen?" she asked.

Angie looked at her watch. "Yes, but hurry." The thought of a sixteen-month-old toddling around in a hospital room with all those germs made Angie nervous. She wasn't keen on exposing Jak to anything Ainsley might be carrying, either, but her concern for Jak being left alone outweighed her other reservations.

After her mother slipped out, Angie sat Ainsley on her lap. She played pat-a-cake for a while, and then she bounced her wildly. "This is the way the ladies ride!"

"Looks more like the way jockeys ride."

They looked up to see Jeremy. Ainsley reached out and squealed. "Dad-dee!"

"Hi, baby. C'mere." He took her from Angie's arms and gave her a big squeeze. "How's my girl? You're getting so big!" With Ainsley perched on his hip, he walked her over to Jak's bedside. "How's your brother today, huh?" He looked again at the oxygen level and stared.

"What is it?" Angie asked.

He turned around. "What do you mean?"

"Something wrong?" She motioned with her head toward the monitor.

"Has he been coughing or anything?"

Angie shook her head. "It hasn't changed, has it? It's still between ninety-five and a hundred, right?"

"We can talk about it later." Jeremy clearly didn't want to say anything in front of Jak. That set off all sorts of alarms for Angie.

The minutes dragged as she waited for her mother to return with the playpen. While Jeremy entertained the kids, anxiety consumed her. Why had Jeremy put her off? What was going on with Jak's oxygen?

Ten minutes later they shut the door behind them. "What is it, Jeremy? It said 95 percent, right?"

"Sure. Ninety-five's okay if you're breathing on your own and you have a normal heart rate. But if you're on oxygen with an elevated heart rate ..."

"We need to tell Barlow," she said.

They walked to the conference room in silence. Barlow greeted them when they arrived, and Jeremy pulled him aside. "Jak's oxygen dropped to ninety-five," he said.

Barlow stroked his chin and looked at the floor. "I'm not surprised."

"You're not concerned about it?" Jeremy asked.

"That's not what I said."

A doctor Jeremy didn't know interrupted them and asked for a word with Barlow, and Jeremy excused himself gracefully. Spotting the chaplain, Mic Justine, he found Angie, and introduced him to her. A man of average height and build, Mic had hazel eyes, a shock of snarled red hair, and a nose that had come in contact with a foul ball. "I've been meaning to thank you," Jeremy said. Mic waved off his words as if whatever he'd done were nothing. Jeremy turned to Angie. "Mic's the one who sent his friend in D.C. to tell me about Devin. He saved me from a dose of Castillo's bedside manner."

Mic told Jeremy, "I meant to say hello when I saw you at the graveside service. I'm sorry about what happened."

"I don't remember seeing you," Jeremy said.

"You were talking with the bereaved husband. Didn't seem like the best time for greetings," Mic said. As Angie watched, an unspoken understanding seemed to pass between them. She wondered what it was.

"Appreciate that," Jeremy said.

Barlow called for everyone to have a seat at the table and made the introductions. Angie had met nearly everyone present—Jeremy, Barlow, Vorobyova, and now Mic. But she'd never seen several of them—the counselor, the dietician, the transplant coordinator, and one of the doctors. He introduced himself as Dr. Bailando, head of the transplant team, before taking over from Barlow.

Angie sat half-dazed through most of the meeting. She could handle *cardiovascular* and *immunosuppressants*. But when they threw around words like *orthotopic* and *perfusionist*—especially when Vorobyova and the head surgeon interacted with each other—they lost her. Fortunately the counselor and Mic sometimes asked for "help with translation." She suspected they did that more for her than for themselves.

Though she missed some of their meaning, in the end she knew the bottom line: Jak qualified for the transplant list and this was his team. Any relief she felt about getting the green light to start a search—which could take days, weeks or even years—was tempered by the fact that nobody put a healthy child on a transplant list. She could hardly believe only two weeks had passed since his last soccer game. And now this. She had to face it: She had a gravely ill child.

———※———

THAT AFTERNOON JEREMY sat in his pod calling every doctor he knew to get out the word about Jak's need. It seemed morbid to ask colleagues to keep an eye out for a kid on a ventilator who could go on to donate a heart. Yet the evidence suggested Jak might need one—maybe even soon—to survive. When weighing his own squeamishness about asking against his son's life hanging in the balance, Jeremy considered the choice a no-brainer.

As he was talking with a cardiologist across town, he noticed a light blinking on the phone to signal he had a message waiting. When he hung up, he listened to it. Jasper was summoning him to her office. He phoned to tell her he'd be right there and hurried to find out what she wanted.

He found her out in her reception area waiting for him. She waved him into her office and shut the door behind them. Then she handed him a lab report. It came from Northam Labronics, an independent laboratory out of Phoenix. Jeremy stared at the results, which made no sense. "Two tainted samples? And another that isn't?" he asked. "Where'd the third come from?"

Jasper traced a pattern in the wood on her desk. "The first, which shows albumin tainted with egg product, is a retest from the sample you sent to Singular. The second, which confirms *no* egg product, is a retest of the sample Ted tested. The third is from the bag you gave me out of the refrigerator."

"That's so strange. I gave Ted a sample from the same solution I sent out." How could three samples from the same bag turn up different results? They couldn't. And how could an outside lab confirm Ted's finding? No way both Ted and an independent lab made the same mistake. "Reiko has to be behind this. But maybe Ted's involved, too."

"Or maybe not."

"Are you suggesting that I—?"

She waved off his concern. "No. That's why we're having this conversation. If I suspected you, do you think I'd show you that report?"

She had a point. Jeremy sat with slumped shoulders. "It makes no sense." He hated how much the stress of Jak's illness impaired his ability to analyze.

"Let me help." Jasper seemed to be enjoying herself. "I suspect foul play. Not necessarily the murderous kind. But someone's covering. And you are the *least* likely suspect."

"I don't understand …"

"Let me tell you how I see it. First, you and Ms. Garrigues had a congenial relationship. No hanky-panky as far as anyone knows. You exerted great effort to save her life after you … uh … after she contracted HIV." Jeremy would have worded it differently, but she spoke the truth. "You had every reason to try to restore her to health," she continued. "For the sake of your reputation."

"O … kay."

She took a deep breath and launched in again. "And you handle smallpox and Ebola viruses. If you wanted to hurt somebody, we would've seen something more creative than egg tainting. If you want to engage in foul play, why tank your own serum?"

It made him uncomfortable that she'd given so much thought to his guilt or innocence. And the very idea that someone would want to hurt Devin made him feel ill. Still, Jasper trusted him. That was good.

"Let's say you fouled up and tried to cover up," Jasper said. "Why send samples to an outside lab? Or allow a tainted sample to go to either place?"

"So what did happen? And why?" Jeremy asked.

"I'm not finished with your part yet," she said. "I can think of only one good reason why you'd want to cover up what you did. If a solution without egg took Ms. Garrigues's life, something's wrong with the T* itself. And that kills your research."

That option made Jeremy nervous. It seemed plausible—other than the fact that he knew it wasn't true!

"Problem with that theory—again, why send a sample to an outside lab? Whether by accident or on purpose, the evidence doesn't point to you. Frankly I'm not sure what this all means," she said. "But I have some sneaking suspicions. And that's why I called you up here. I need your help." Jasper leaned back in her executive chair making the coils squeak. "Your turn."

"What do you mean?"

"What does the evidence tell you?"

"Pretty much the same thing it tells you," he said. But he decided to give it his best shot. "Let's assume the most likely probability—an accident," Jeremy said. "Assume someone messed up by mistake. After Devin's death, I took samples from the bag. I gave a sample to Ted to test and sent the other off. I know I didn't tamper with it. And the inside one came back clean. Now the only reason to 'untaint' a sample would be if Ted had something against me. Or my research."

Suddenly, Jeremy thought of Ted's remark about his "precious" research and wondered if he should read more into it.

"What about Reiko?" Jasper asked.

"If he tampered with evidence," Jeremy said, "why mess with what exonerates him? He would want the hospital lab report to confirm egg tainting, not show it to be clean. And it came back clean. The in-hospital report—the only one he had access to—is the one that came back clean."

"Precisely. So maybe Reiko told the truth."

Jeremy reviewed what Reiko told them through new eyes. "He said Devin's refrigerator was locked when he got there."

"Who has keys to refrigerators?"

"Everybody has the key to the general refrigerator. But I have the only one to Devin's."

"No. I myself have a master key," Jasper said.

"Okay, right. Everybody higher up the food chain has one of those. But none of the other researchers like me do. Nor the assistants or students." He thought he might see where this was leading.

"What about the bag?"

"He said it had Devin's name on it—with a yellow sticky note." That was the part Jeremy considered most lame. Such notes were too easily lost, and what intelligent lab employee would take such a risk?

"Okay, I have an assignment for you. Scope out the lab and see who uses yellow sticky notes. If I show up down there snooping around, everybody gets suspicious. But for you—a piece of cake. It's a long shot, but worth checking."

When Jeremy got back to the lab he meandered through the pods looking for sticky notes. But by the time he finished, he realized he was apparently only one of two researchers who *didn't* use them.

CHAPTER 27

A few days later on Monday morning, Angie sat in her usual spot at the end of Jak's bed. More and more it seemed all Jak did was sleep. Though he remained in stable condition, Angie could see that, without a new heart, he'd spend his life lying quietly near oxygen. Getting up to go potty wore him out. Even his cleansing routine, which demanded little energy, required a postsponge nap. Something would have to change drastically. And soon. Even a heart transplant started sounding better than this.

She picked up the day's menu and realized it was July fourth. It felt strange. She'd lost track of weekdays not to mention days of the month. Hours passed not by ticking seconds on her wrist but by the routine arrival of people who drew blood and changed IVs. Rather than eating when they felt hungry, she and Jeremy ate according to the food delivery schedule. Jak's meal arrived, so they thought about making a cafeteria run.

The staff in the pediatric ward dressed up for holidays, and she wondered what costumes would parade through Jak's room in the hours to follow. She glanced again at the menu. Jak would love the hamburger, but unsalted fries? And he'd miss the fireworks. She thought back to a year ago on Independence Day. Ainsley still had a toothless grin. Jeremy had to work. And the needle accident with Devin had just happened, so he was in a funk. But Angie's parents took her and Jak to

Denver's biggest fireworks display at Broncos' stadium at Mile High. Jak vacillated between yelling "Wow!" when the fireworks burst into color and clinging to her after every boom.

Now Devin was dead. Jeremy's amazing discovery might come to nothing. And Jak needed a new heart.

The already-long-term hospital stay was taking its toll with no end in sight. Ainsley, who previously made progress with self-feeding, now refused to cooperate for her grandmother. All Angie's clients granted extensions, but it meant their second income dwindled as she made a full-time occupation of sitting with Jak. She didn't even want to think about the hospital bills.

And besides Jak's ailing health, all human subjects had stopped receiving T*. Until they reached some sort of resolution on incongruent test results, Jeremy had to limit his research to animals. Some of the terminal patients who had improved while receiving T* had reversed and were going downhill fast. Two had already died. What a waste.

Her thoughts returned, as they always did, to why all this had to happen. If only Jeremy had been more careful. It amazed her how much could change in one quick, thoughtless moment.

BEATRICE JASPER SAT in the chair she had ordered for its intimidating size. A no-nonsense kind of woman, she came up through the ranks when only the most assertive women made it into management. She had few qualms about winning through intimidation. Still, she bullied only when she felt she had to. And she hoped today would not turn into one of those days. She suspected it might.

Across the desk from her sat the head of research, Dr. Bonnie Dylan, whom Jasper had summoned. Dylan wore no makeup and her thin blonde hair looked as though she might have forgotten to brush it.

Jasper surveyed Dylan's body language as she sat before her. She normally assumed an open posture, but today she sat twisted pretzel-like with legs and arms crossed. And she was turned to the side rather than facing Jasper. Something was up.

Take it slowly, Jasper told herself. Affirm. Assume the best. Act shrewdly. Much was at stake—the hospital's reputation, Jeremy's research, and the fate of so many who stood to benefit. She leaned back and interlaced her fingers across her stomach, hoping to help Dylan relax. "So what's the mood like in the basement since we've had to halt the research?"

"Not so bad," Dylan said. "We're still doing animal trials—with some encouraging results."

"Really sad about Ms. Garrigues, though, isn't it?"

Dylan shifted around and seemed to be avoiding eye contact. "I didn't really know her."

"Sure. But do you have to know her to consider her death a tragedy?"

Dylan was defensive. "Of course not!" She changed the subject. "What did you want to talk about?"

Jasper studied her, trying to avoid reading too much into her reaction. "How much do you know about the AIDS patients we've lost since we had to stop human trials?"

Dylan recoiled at the question and took awhile to answer. "You mean ... as a researcher? Their blood levels? That sort of thing?"

Jasper slid two files forward. Each had a photo of the deceased affixed to the front with a paper clip. In one, a slender young man in a jean jacket smiled out at them. In the other, a pudgy woman in her fifties wearing a crimson dress looked like she was posing for a mug shot. "I mean their personal lives. Who their parents were. Or their children." She pointed to the young man. "This one strikes me as particularly sad. Matthew Thompson. Twenty-three. Leaves behind both parents and two sisters. He graduated from the University of Denver last year."

Dylan looked confused. "O-kay …" Her tone suggested, *And your point is …?* "I don't generally look into their personal lives."

"Maybe you should sometimes. This guy—" Jasper tapped at his photo—"a real winner. Born with hemophilia and contracted HIV as a child through a blood transfusion before donor-screened, heat-treated products. He responded wonderfully to T*. But went downhill fast—passed away—shortly after we took him out of T* therapy." Dylan swallowed and lifted her blonde eyebrows. Jasper continued, "You went into research to help people like this. Right?"

"Well, sure." Dylan squinted as if she'd just stepped from a dark room into daylight.

Everything was working as planned. Jasper scooted the files so they were right in front of Dylan and left the photos staring up at her from the edge of the desk. She pulled back her hand and leaned on her armrest. "Both of us chose the careers we did because we hoped to make a difference. Which is why I'm so glad we'll probably soon return to using human subjects for T* research."

Dylan shot straight up and a flush rose in her cheeks. "What? How? We just had a patient *die*. How can we resume human trials?"

"You don't seem very happy."

Dylan stammered and finally pulled a sentence together. "It's not *that*. I just … just … don't see *how*." Her green eyes hinted at some unspoken terror going on inside.

Jasper had her right where she wanted her. Like a hunter who has an animal in scope at close range, she let the words fall. "It turns out she didn't die from the T*, at all. She died because of an egg-tainted albumin mix."

The two women sat, their eyes fixed on each other. "That will be all," Jasper said.

Dylan threw up her hands. "That's it? That's all you're going to say?"

"For now. I'll give you forty-eight hours to let me know whether you want me to be your advocate or whether I'll be ripping apart your testimony in court."

———————✦———————

THE NEXT MORNING Jeremy was in his pod, filing test results when a call came in from Barlow. "Are you sitting down?" Barlow asked.

"Should I be?" The last thing Jeremy needed now was bad news. He wondered how much more he could take.

"Probably."

"I'm sitting."

"I just want to give you the heads-up on something. We may have a match."

"You don't mean—a transplant match?" Jeremy felt a rush of adrenalin.

"I do. Maybe. Did you happen to read today's paper?"

Jeremy got his information—mostly national and international news—off the Internet. "No. Why?"

"Front-page story. You might want to pick it up. Last night a nine-year-old kid took a bottle rocket through the eye."

Jeremy had actually read about that tragedy along with other Fourth of July disasters. But he hadn't realized the family was local. *How awful for the kid—and the parents*, he thought.

Barlow continued, "Apparently his big brother set off a bottle rocket that didn't go. The kid leaned down to see what was wrong, and now he's on a respirator. No brain function."

Jeremy wondered how that brother must feel right now—especially since bottle rockets were illegal in Colorado. But his thoughts quickly returned to Jak's needs. "So what next?"

"We wait. The mom's willing to sign, but she wants to talk to her husband first. Problem is, he's overseas on military assignment and out of contact."

Jeremy wanted to groan. "Does anyone know how long that might take?" Immediately he felt a stab of guilt for thinking of his own inconvenience before feeling empathy for a woman whose son died while her husband served his country overseas. He imagined the agony of having to break it to Angie over the phone that Ravi had died. How awful.

"We have no idea. So since both Mom and Pop have to give consent, we sit tight. As soon as they can track down the dad and get his okay, we have to be ready to move."

"Do we even know if the blood types match?"

"Blood types match. But that's all we've verified so far."

Jeremy processed aloud. "So still some big unknowns ... size match ... major antigens."

"Right. The kid was admitted at Denver General, and they're keeping him on the respirator until they can get a signature. They'll transfer him here if everything matches so we can proceed as soon as the dad gives his okay. I don't want to get your hopes up, but I thought you should know."

"It seems amazing for the kid to be right here in the area," Jeremy said.

"Um, not exactly. Maybe I should have clarified—this connection didn't come from either of the registers. Apparently one of your researcher friends at D.G. knew about Jak from a mass e-mail you sent, and when the accident happened, he contacted the pediatrician."

ANGIE BOUGHT A baked potato for lunch and turned to leave the hospital food court when she spotted Portia with a woman she didn't recognize. Neither Angie nor Jeremy had seen Portia for a while, and she wondered why. Angie waved, but it seemed Portia didn't see her. Not wanting to interrupt, Angie left without greeting her.

In the middle of the afternoon Angie heard a gentle rap at the door. When she went to open it, she inhaled the fragrance of "Classic" before she saw her visitor, but she knew immediately it was Portia. Sure enough, Portia stood wearing a flattering businesslike shirt-dress, but her manner exuded less confidence than her apparel.

"How've you been?" Angie asked.

She could hardly hear Portia's reply. "I've been better. Is this a good time to talk?" Portia glimpsed inside the room.

"Jak's sleeping, but we can whisper." Angie opened the door wider and motioned to one of the chairs.

Portia walked in, plopped down, and looked at the ceiling. "I saw you in the cafeteria. And I guess I owe you an apology."

Angie waved it off and took the other seat.

"I've been trying to work up the nerve to talk to you."

Angie thought Portia was surely overreacting. Why make such a big deal about not waving?

"Sorry … for falsely accusing you … in my mind, at least." Angie wondered what she was talking about. Portia's eyes traveled down the wall, met Angie's briefly, and glanced toward the window. "I assumed you told Jeremy everything, and you know what happens when people assume."

Angie had told Jeremy about running into Dr. Combs and Portia together at the club, but that was all she'd said. She wondered if Jeremy had mentioned it to Barlow.

"I spent a few days vowing never to speak to you again before I found out it wasn't your fault." Finally Portia looked at her. "We're doing better now—Nate and I—though we sure had a couple of rough days there."

Angie knew if she just kept quiet, Portia would come out with the story.

"Nate went for a final checkup on his knee, and when he got back from seeing the doc, he told Jeremy he got the all clear. So …"

Angie connected the dots and cringed. "Let me guess. Jeremy asked if he'd be replacing Alex Combs as your partner at the club."

"You guessed it. So Nate with his visceral intelligence comes home that night and goes fishing with me. He says, 'My knee's all better, so I'm wondering if you want to meet me at the club … or keep my replacement?'"

Angie grimaced.

Portia pulled at one of her buttons and shifted in her seat. "I asked what he meant, knowing—fearing—I knew exactly what he meant. But he doesn't answer me, right? Instead he asks, 'If I were to tell you I was on Google Earth looking at our neighborhood and I saw Alex's Jeep parked in front of our house a couple of afternoons, what would you say?' He didn't lie, of course," Portia said. "He just laid a trap."

"A couple of afternoons?"

"Yes." Portia waited, seemingly to let the implications sink in. "I found out later he was totally guessing on the Google part. He's never even used Google Earth! But he sure hit his mark, didn't he?"

If it weren't so pathetic, Angie might have snickered. She had to admire Barlow's cunning.

"And thinking you'd blabbed and tipped him off, I assumed he knew more than he did and fell right into it. Did it ever get ugly after that." Angie saw misery staring out of Portia's eyes. "At first I got super defensive, but he was so wounded. And kind. Not at all what I deserved."

Angie hadn't noticed any change in Barlow. She wondered how much of others' pain she failed to notice as she lived in her in own self-focused world.

"But you feel like the two of you are working it out?" Angie asked, hopefully. "You said things were better."

"It'll take time." Portia sighed. "Lots of time. A lifetime, maybe. But yeah. I hate that I've hurt him *so* deeply." She got a faraway look. "The good part—if there can be such a thing—was that it forced one of those deep talks you don't choose to have because they hurt, but once you have them ..."

It occurred to Angie that she and Jeremy needed one of those. On the surface her relationship with Jeremy was improving, but deep down she still hadn't forgiven him. She looked over at Jak and knew nothing Jeremy did or said could ever compensate for what happened to both of their sons.

"I'm on my way to work here in a few minutes. I got a part-time job." She waved her hand down the front of her buttons as if to explain her outfit. "I need to do something other than decorate the house and play at the club and shop all day. Nate encouraged me to find something to do with myself."

"Where do you work?" Angie asked.

"I'm the volunteer coordinator for the pediatric unit's new animal-assisted therapy program. Anyway, I actually have a reason for telling you all this ..." She took a deep breath, as though what she was going to say took some effort. "I think you need to know something Nate said to me in the middle of it all—something about you and Jeremy. I realize I'm on iffy ground here, but I think it's important that you know. Important enough to risk it."

A knock at the door interrupted their conversation. Angie's mom arrived with Ainsley for a visit. Portia jumped up and offered her seat. Angie made introductions, and then Portia bowed out.

"Guess we'll have to talk again later," she said. "Sorry!" And with a quick wave she was gone.

CHAPTER 28

That night Jeremy was sleeping in a call room when the phone jarred him. The clock said 3:15 a.m. It was Angie, her voice full of alarm. "Jak's oxygen dropped to ninety!"

"Be right there," Jeremy said, his heart pounding. He was fully awake now. Jak clearly needed a new heart. The realization hit him like a backhanded slap. Then a measure of calm fell. It seemed odd, actually, that he wasn't panicking. But the thought of his talk with Barlow about the boy on life support brought a measure of hope. He was glad the boy was now under Barlow's care. He paged Barlow's answering service. To his surprise Barlow himself answered.

"Word gets around fast," he told Jeremy. "How'd you know I was up here with your potential donor?"

"I didn't. What's happened that you're here so late?"

"Decreased liver function. He stopped breathing for a while after the accident, and by the time the paramedics got to him, he'd been out for an undetermined period. We're dealing with the after-effects now."

Jeremy processed the words with a sinking heart. "Actually I didn't know. I'm calling because Angie just phoned to say Jak's oxygen level dropped again." There was no reply. "Hello?"

"I'm here. Sorry. Just thinking. Wish we could proceed with transplant."

The words seemed to come so easily for Barlow, but they hit Jeremy like another slap.

"In the meantime," Barlow continued, "maybe the mom will give consent to infuse the T*. What do you think? Worth a try? She wants some good to come from the tragedy. Perhaps if I explain what we know about it, she'd agree."

Jeremy wondered if extra T* in a child—which was yet untested—would even offer any benefit. "I don't suppose we've got consent yet from her husband?" Jeremy asked.

"No. Anyway, be right there."

Barlow beat Jeremy to Jak's room. When Jeremy arrived, Jak was sitting patiently as Barlow checked vitals. He didn't even try to calm Jak with cartoonish antics this time.

Only when Barlow turned to Angie did Jeremy really see her standing there in her new satin robe. She wiped her red nose with a tissue and her face looked ashen. He drew her into a hug and they stood holding each other and watching Barlow. As he held Angie, Jeremy admitted to himself that Jak would not recover. What had probably been apparent to Barlow for several days was finally sinking in.

Barlow asked Angie, "So he was asleep when you woke up and saw the monitor?"

"Not exactly. I heard him messing with the controls on the bed, making it go up and down. The sound woke me."

Barlow finished his exam and asked them to join him in the hall. In the brighter lights Jeremy noticed his gray stubble and fatigued eyes. "It's not as bad as I feared," he said. "If he'd been sound asleep at 90 to 91 percent, I'd be alarmed. But he was apparently awake and perhaps even playing a bit. That's a good sign. But frankly, even *that's* not great. If we can't get consent for transplant in the next twenty-four hours, we might need to consider going with a left ventricular assist device."

"Would that require an operation?" Angie asked.

Barlow nodded. "It would help the heart pump and give it time to rest until we can give him a healthy heart."

"He's definitely going to need a transplant, isn't he?"

When Angie asked the question, Jeremy realized they'd both been in denial. Maybe it was good that the donor's father hadn't been immediately available. The short delay gave them time to face reality. He wondered how serious the donor's liver problems were and—more importantly—if the child's heart had suffered discernible damage. He didn't think he should ask. Better to wait on Barlow to tell them. He finally saw the utter urgency of getting Jak a heart.

Standing with arms crossed and staring at the floor, Barlow spoke soothingly. "He definitely needs a transplant. I'm sorry. But until we can get the okay to proceed, we'll keep him as stable as we can. I'd prefer not to intervene with a temporizing procedure if we're set to go with the transplant. It'd be much easier on Jak if we only have to go in once. But we might have to. This wait could take awhile."

"What do you mean?" The distress in Angie's voice spoke for both of them.

"I just talked to your potential donor's mom. Her military contacts aren't telling her much, but she suspects her husband's in deep cover and may remain unreachable for up to two weeks. I'm moving Jak up from second to top priority status on the transplant list. We'll see if that can generate a match."

"You mean look for another donor?" Angie sounded horrified.

"Two weeks may be too long."

"But this one seems so perfect!"

"I know," Barlow said. "We've got compatible blood, an ideal geographic setup, and we received confirmation this afternoon that the size is just right. But no way can we proceed without both parents. We're not even sure the dad is going to say okay."

"Does the mom think he will?"

"She says *probably*. But she's not positive. So we need to pursue every possible option. We can hope this works, but we can't shut any doors. I'll be back around eight to check on your son. You two hang in there. You're not alone, okay?" He drew them both into a bear hug.

BEATRICE JASPER SPENT most of the day at her desk wondering if she'd hear from Bonnie Dylan. In the last forty-eight hours both Ted and Jeremy had informed her that Dylan was nosing around asking questions, but they'd kept mum. Both seemed eager to know what was going on, but she'd put them off. Jasper even had pizza brought in at lunch the past two days—something she never did—so she could remain at her post just in case Dylan showed up.

At 4:30 on Thursday she finally got her answer. While sitting with her head down, writing, Jasper sensed a presence at her door. She glanced up and there stood Dylan looking haggard and puffy-eyed. "Come on in," Jasper said. She laid her pen on the desk and folded her hands.

Dylan shut the door behind her, groped for the back of the chair, and sat down. She intertwined her long, wiry fingers and fidgeted before she spoke. "I want to know how you knew it was me."

Jasper steadied herself to keep from visibly expressing her relief. That one sentence gave her the confidence to proceed unimpeded by any doubt. Jasper hadn't even talked to Legal yet. But she'd been careful not to accuse. And she wanted to give Dylan every opportunity to do the right thing. "How'd I know? Sorry. Can't tell you. We have to save revelations for discovery." It was as close to a legal threat as she felt she could go. "That is, unless …"

"Unless what?"

"You decide to confess. Take the initiative. You'll find the court more sympathetic. And, as I said yesterday, you'll find me more supportive too."

What a loss this was for the hospital, Jasper thought. Dylan was a first-class researcher absolutely devoted to her work. Though gladdened at the prospect of getting back to human trials on AIDS research, Jasper felt a pang of sadness. How would they replace Dylan? And what would become of her?

In all their years as colleagues Jasper had never seen Dylan cry, but now tears welled up and overflowed. "I didn't *mean* for her to die!"

"What did you mean?"

"I hate Castillo! That—" She cut loose with a long string of expletives. "He's ruined my life!"

Jasper lowered her voice in inverse relation to Dylan's rising volume. "I know he has. That's why I recommend confession over denial."

Dylan's demeanor changed, as if somehow infused by hope. "What do you mean?"

Jasper regretted cutting off Dylan before she'd finished. The more Jasper knew, the easier time she'd have gathering evidence, if necessary. "I mean, if the truth comes out, you don't have to take the fall alone."

"But I did act alone."

"No doubt. But your reasons for doing what you did will become a matter of the public record." Jasper saw a twitch in the corner of Dylan's mouth that told her Dylan followed her reasoning. If hatred of Castillo motivated Dylan enough to drive her to drastic measures, Jasper intended to use that same hatred to get at the facts she needed.

Dylan squinted and Jasper saw loathing in her eyes. "You know what an *über*-jerk he is to everyone, but especially me," Dylan said. "The D.C. trip was the last straw. I got invited. I made plans to go. I set up meetings with colleagues. Then he got me uninvited and took the superstar instead. Sure, Cramer's a good researcher. But he's just a resident, and I'm head of the research department!"

"What difference did you think the death of an AIDS patient would make?"

"I didn't mean for her die! She was stronger than I thought, so her body launched a more impressive reaction than I expected. And that blasted DNR! I had no idea she was still DNR. I just wanted to knock Castillo off his high horse with all his 'my research is curing AIDS' crap. I figured at worst an adverse reaction to the T* could set back human trials for six months, but the humiliation might shut him up for a whole year." Her lips parted in a nefarious smile. "Maybe I still wouldn't get credit for my work, but at least he wouldn't either."

It occurred to Jasper that killing someone, even if accidentally, was a high price to pay for refusing to share credit. There was the loss of human life with possible jail time. And even if Dylan avoided that, no hospital would ever employ her again.

"So when things went worse than planned, you had to cover your tracks," Jasper said.

Dylan looked at her lap and nodded. "You know I'm not the kind of person who would kill someone. But … you're saying if I have to go down, I can take Castillo with me?"

"I'm saying if you tell the truth about what you did and why, the court will certainly read and consider your testimony—as will the hospital board."

To Jasper's amazement Dylan seemed resolute. She sat up straight and seemed relieved. "What do I need to do?"

"I guess wait outside while I make a call." As soon as Dylan stepped out, Jasper called one of the hospital attorneys and filled him in. Jasper had a sneaking suspicion that Dylan might bolt. But when Jasper emerged, Dylan was still sitting there. Jasper brought her back into the office and shut the door again.

Jasper spent the next two hours in meetings with members of the Legal department. Then Jasper, a hospital attorney, and a member of law enforcement accompanied Dylan to her office to retrieve her personal items. The hospital had a policy of making such scenes public to impress on employees the importance of law keeping. Afterward the three of them walked Dylan to the front door. She handed her car keys to Jasper. "Can you get it to my house?"

Jasper nodded. Dylan bent down and slid into the backseat of the police cruiser. She stared straight ahead as the car pulled away from the curb and headed down the street.

JEREMY SAT PICKING at his omelet in the cafeteria at 7:30 the next morning. He was trying to remember the last time he and Angie had eaten a normal meal—the kind they used to have in the dining room with Jak—when his cell phone rang. It was Jasper's secretary. "Dr. Jasper's holding a meeting with the lab staff. Can you be there in fifteen minutes?"

"I can." Wondering what was up, he shoved the last few bites into his mouth, washed them down with a long swallow of black coffee, and grabbed his lab coat off the back of the chair.

When he got downstairs the place was buzzing like a hive. One of the researchers filled him in on the previous evening's events. Everyone was talking about it. Jeremy wondered exactly what Jasper knew, but he figured with the clues he had, he could formulate a likely hypothesis.

Soon Jasper arrived accompanied by representatives from Legal. The research staff of about fifteen doctors—no students allowed—had gathered in small groups. Some stood in the aisles, others leaned on the black counters, but all speculated in muffled tones about what Jasper would tell them.

When she said, "Good morning," everyone grew quiet. "I know we all have plenty to do, so I'll keep this brief. I have bad news and good news. First the bad. Effective yesterday, Dr. Dylan has resigned." Only the hum of refrigerators cut the silence.

She gestured toward her companions. "I've been advised to limit my remarks on that subject, so that's all I plan to say for now. We'll appoint an interim research director as soon as possible—hopefully by

Monday. If anyone should contact you about it, please limit your comments and direct all calls to my office."

"And now for the good news," she continued. "We've learned that the patient death that led us to suspend human testing with T* was due to a problem with the albumin mix, not with the T* itself. So we're resuming tests on human subjects. Immediately." She clasped her hands together signaling she'd said all she planned to. "Obviously we have lots to do, so let's do it. Thank you." She turned on her rubber-soled shoes and marched out.

Jeremy felt a swirl of emotions. Devin's death had been a complete waste. But he now had the all-clear to use T* again—maybe even on Jak's potential donor, though they hadn't tested it on children. And then there was the melancholy of seeing a good researcher like Bonnie Dylan leave under suspicion. On top of that, Jak. He sank into his chair.

Jasper had piqued his curiosity. What was the exact connection between Dylan leaving and human trials resuming? He knew more than most, but he still had questions. Lots of them. Answers would no doubt come in time, but he hated to wait.

He swiveled around and eyed his to-do list, knowing the lab employees would be as active as a morgue at midnight while everybody speculated about what Dylan did and who would kiss up to Castillo to snatch her job.

Jeremy called Barlow and filled him in. At the end he added, "I don't know what's up with our potential donor's liver, so forgive me for butting in, but since you mentioned it earlier …"

"You haven't actually done trials on children …" Barlow said. "Still," he continued, "without it, the organs will be useless soon anyway. So I guess the question is whether you're willing to take the risk with Jak."

"What do you mean?"

"If you have that level of confidence in your discovery, I think I could convince the mother that it might save the life of another youngster."

That was a tough one. But what harm could it do? And it might actually help. Jeremy wished he felt more confident. "If we don't get another donor, what choice do we have?"

"Right. I'll see about getting the mom's consent."

ANGIE WAS JUST emerging from the shower in the restroom adjacent to Jak's room when she heard her phone ring. After she dried off and dressed, she picked up the message. It was from Portia.

"I'd like to finish our conversation soon, if we can," Portia said. "So call me."

Angie had gone over their last conversation numerous times, and she couldn't imagine what Portia planned to say. Lately she found herself replaying everything people said—whether Barlow or the nurses or her mother—every conversation. Boredom made it worse. She had so little else to occupy her besides Jak's condition and the kids' shows he watched nonstop.

She phoned Portia back. "Hi there. It's Angie."

"Sorry to leave you hanging the other day."

"That's okay. I figured you preferred not to talk in front of my mom."

"Right. Is now a good time for me to come back?" she asked.

"Jak's due for a nap in about thirty minutes. Can you come up then?"

"Sure."

At the appointed time Portia stood at the door. The solid red tank top she had on with her red plaid capri pants was tighter than what Angie would wear with such a busty figure, but for Portia it was more modest than usual.

Portia came in, her fragrance filling the room, and quietly moved a second chair close to Angie's. She sat in it, leaned toward Angie, and spoke barely above a whisper. "I'll get straight to the point. Believe me,

I took no pleasure in telling you what I did. I'm not proud of myself. But I actually had a reason for burdening you with all that—and it wasn't to relieve my conscience."

Angie simply nodded and leaned back in her chair.

"I realize we haven't known each other all that long or well. So you should know, normally even I wouldn't dare tell you what I'm about to say. But I don't see much of a choice. There's too much at stake and not much time."

"What is it?" For once Angie wished Portia would get to it.

"You think your husband infected your son—I mean—that the glove accident ... the one in the lab ... led to all this." She gestured toward Jak's bed, the IV pole, and the monitors. "Right?"

Taken aback, Angie blinked at her. She blinked again. She was speechless.

"Well, Nate doesn't think that had one thing to do with this. Not at all. But you've somehow convinced both of our husbands that they don't dare say so. It's the little piece of good news nobody talks about for fear you'll think they're lying. As if Nate would even consider covering for somebody on something like that!"

"I-I—" Angie didn't know what to say.

"I took the risk of telling you what I did about Alex and me so you would know I've come clean on stretching the truth with you, because you have to believe me about this. Your husband loves you, he loves his kids, he's smart, he's not an arrogant jerk like Castillo—though he actually has every reason to be—and you're missing it! Jeremy's half destroyed himself with guilt. He's just destroying himself. He knows you blame him. We know you blame him. And right now Jeremy needs more than anything in his life to know you won't pin the outcome of your child's health on him no matter what happens."

At first Angie was boiling with rage. But she forced herself to consider whether even a fraction of Portia's words rang true. The fact was, she did blame Jeremy. Was it that obvious? She knew Portia believed what she was saying—there was no other logical explanation for her behavior.

"You know what's really sad?" Portia asked. "I confess … I destroyed the trust in my marriage. But, girl, there are many ways to destroy trust in a marriage. And you know what else? The outcome's the same. So in a sense, your approach is not really any different in effect as my indiscretion. I'll bet you think I fooled around with Alex because of some deficiency in Nate."

"You did say he's never home."

"But I knew that when I married him! See … you look for these simple cause-and-effect relationships and they mess you up. You look at your son's condition and you feel you have to have somebody to blame. That way, if you can keep them from messing up again, you can make sure it never happens again. Your world stays safe."

What does she think she is, a therapist?

"If that were true, every sexually abused kid could have prevented her predator's advances," Portia continued. "Believe me, I know a thing or two about that. And it's not true. But now I have gone and said more than I needed to." She got up and looked Angie squarely in the eyes. "I hope you can appreciate that what I'm doing is an act of friendship. And I'll make you a deal—I'll get my act together with my man and you get your act together with yours."

She walked out and shut the door behind her.

Angie was glad she didn't hang around for a thank-you. But afterward Angie sat pondering her words. Maybe Jeremy wasn't totally responsible for Ravi's death, but he bore some responsibility. And they'd probably never know if Jeremy's decision to take Jak to the lab was behind their present circumstances. What if it wasn't? But what if it was?

Could she forgive him? Would she?

So it all came down to one question: "Will I forgive?"

She thought of how Dorothy Sayers ended *The Man Born to Be King*. Following three fireside denials, the one denied stood by a charcoal fire on the beach and offered three fresh chances to declare love. Three times guilty, three times forgiven.

She knew she had to do the same for Jeremy.

AT ABOUT HALF-PAST four that afternoon, Jeremy was in the infectious disease clinic administering a T* infusion for one of his late-stage AIDS patients when Lesia called him to the door. "Dr. Barlow's looking for you," she said.

He checked his cell phone and found it still half-powered. He wondered why Barlow hadn't called. "Okay, I'll phone him. Thanks."

"No. I mean he's here."

Jeremy dropped his pen. "Where?" She pointed to one of the examination rooms. Jeremy stammered. "I ... I can't leave this patient alone. Get me a nurse. Quick!"

It took less than thirty seconds for Lesia to scurry off and send a nurse hustling to help, but in that short span Jeremy envisioned Jak's oxygen level dropping, the donor dying, Jak dying!

As soon as the nurse took over, he dashed out and burst into the room where Barlow stood waiting. Jeremy found him leaning against the counter, arms folded, looking pleased. Seeing him relaxed, Jeremy scaled back his anxiety a notch. "What is it?"

"Sorry. You look terrified. It's not about Jak, if that's what you're worried about."

Jeremy clutched his chest and heaved a great sigh. "Something like that."

"Sorry—really. But we do have to act fast. We got a call from El Paso. They have a donor match for us."

Jeremy's pulse quickened again. "That ... that's great."

Barlow said, "They've got a patient with minimal brain function, no brain-stem reflexes. On a ventilator. Blood group, height, weight—

all a close match. When they ran the data, Jak topped the list, so we got the call. Bailando reviewed the case and declared the heart suitable for transplant."

"Bailando? Already?" Jeremy asked. This was happening so fast— and completely apart from his knowledge.

"You bet. Protocol, buddy. We've even notified El Paso that we'll accept it. And our ICU and admitting teams have jumped into action."

"So ... the next step?" Jeremy asked, glad to have Barlow in charge.

"Notify the parents. And that would be you. So here I am."

"Angie doesn't know yet?"

"Nope. See? We haven't done *everything* yet. Come on. I'll tell you the rest on the way." He opened the door.

Jeremy followed him blindly, but hesitated when he remembered his AIDS patient. Pointing to the room he'd just left, he said, "But I need—"

Barlow tugged at his arm. "I talked to Dr. Zoan already. As soon as he finishes up with a patient, he's on his way to cover for you."

"Thanks. Appreciate that." Jeremy had to hurry to keep pace with Barlow, who kept unfolding details as they passed the fountain in the lobby. "El Paso ran into a snafu with jet transportation, though. Bailando says it might go faster if we take the hospital helo to his hangar out at Front Range Airport and use his Learjet to go pick up the heart. We really have no time to waste. Jak's borderline, and they've already set up for the retrieval in El Paso. All the family and medical issues there require some haste to coordinate everything."

Jeremy stopped. "You mean fly Denver-El Paso-Denver instead of a round trip from there?"

Barlow dipped his head. "Affirmative." Barlow pulled on Jeremy's sleeve again to make him keep walking. "If El Paso can arrange dependable transport, Bailando's plane can turn around and come back. If not, you haven't lost any time." Vorobyova's words about wasting time wisely came to Jeremy's mind. Barlow kept on, "The plane's already there. The pilot just has to do preflight checks and get proper coordinates. Bailando already set it up. It should be ready to go in about thirty minutes."

"Nice of him."

"Whatever else you do, keep your phone on."

"Got it."

"And something else I should tell you—though maybe a moot point now. Earlier this afternoon, before all this shook loose, I got consent from the local donor's—"

"But if we have consent, why go—?"

"Lemme finish. Consent to give him an infusion of T*."

"Oh. Guess we won't do *that* now," Jeremy said.

"Too late."

Jeremy stopped short. "What do you mean?"

They reached the elevator banks and Barlow pushed the UP button. "I figured you're dealing with enough guilt … in case anything goes wrong. So I went over your head and got Jasper's okay. Zoan handled the infusion. That's where we were when I got Bailando's call."

Jeremy was momentarily struck dumb. But then it dawned on him how stupid it would be to himself infuse his own son's heart donor with an experimental substance, confident as he was of its efficacy. "So how'd it go with the kid?" Jeremy asked.

Barlow mocked with a playful grin. "Considering I left before we finished the infusion, it might be a little too soon to tell."

Jeremy laughed at himself. They boarded the elevator and Barlow punched the top button. "Hey, that's not Jak's floor." Jeremy reached to press a different button.

Barlow grabbed his hand and stopped him. "That's because we're going up to the helipad."

"You're going to get the heart yourself?"

"No. You are."

CHAPTER 29

W hen Jeremy and Barlow arrived on the roof, the helicopter roared, ready for flight. The odor of fuel filled Jeremy's nostrils. Blades overhead whipped the July air, making his eyes water and tossing his hair in great pulses.

Barlow pantomimed a telephone and yelled above the deafening noise. "Call me when you can hear me!"

The pilot, seeing them, threw open the door for Jeremy and motioned for him to board. Jeremy jumped in, situated himself on the passenger's side, and fastened his seat belt. *This is it*, he thought, his heart pounding. He felt both excited and nervous. As the pilot secured the door, Barlow gave Jeremy a thumbs-up.

Jeremy waved and the copter lifted off. Within seconds it soared over Denver's streets that led like arteries to the heart of the city. Observing the vehicles as he peered down on traffic Jeremy appreciated his private flight service to the airport. The twenty-five miles by car could take over an hour in even prerush-hour congestion, but in the helicopter it would take only five, seven minutes tops. The higher they went, the better the panorama. How beautiful to see Denver from the air—smoggy as it was—against its backdrop of majestic peaks.

Within minutes the runway came into view and grew larger as they approached. After the pilot landed the copter near the Learjet, he pointed out to the plane. "There's your bird," he yelled. "Just the two of you." Jeremy could see the navigator through the front window of the glistening silver craft. He thanked the copter pilot, jumped out, and ran for the Learjet, feeling the heat of the tarmac beneath his feet. As he approached, the jet-engine noise replaced that of the copter.

Jeremy hopped in the open door and pulled it shut behind him, leaving the thunder behind. The bird was a beauty, and it smelled like a new car. He surveyed the interior, which was about the size of a travel trailer—but much more luxurious. It seated six in the main cabin with two pairs of leather swivel chairs that faced each other and a two-seater couch to match. The loveseat was situated opposite a bar with a marble counter. Jeremy took a seat on the couch.

The pilot opened the cockpit door. An older gentleman with silver hair, he smelled of pipe tobacco. "You ready?" he asked. Jeremy nodded, but the pilot pointed to the seat belt. "No, you're not. Fasten in."

As Jeremy pulled the belt around his middle and locked it, the pilot secured the door. Then he returned to the cockpit, and in seconds they taxied down the runway, gained speed, and took flight. Jeremy arched his neck to watch out the window as the mountains came into view again. The late-afternoon sun cast long shadows.

His thoughts quickly returned to Jak. Realizing he had no idea what to do next, Jeremy pulled out his phone. When he flipped it open, he saw the time: 5:08 p.m. A mere thirty minutes earlier he'd infused a patient with T* and now he sat gliding south a thousand feet or more over Denver's foothills.

He called Barlow, who answered on the first ring. "Bailando wants to know how you like his little toy," he told Jeremy.

"Some toy!"

"He said to tell you to help yourself to what's in the cabinets—snacks, drinks. Some Sudoku books to keep you occupied. Oh, and he said to use the cabin phone rather than running down your cell battery."

"Thanks. Will do. How's Angie holding up?"

"I just came from there. She was a little stunned, as you can imagine. Nervous. But mostly glad."

"I'll call her when I get off the phone with you."

"I'm in the transplant unit now. We'll bring Jak down any minute for pre-op tests and preparation. You know the score—exam, blood work, chest X-ray. The transplant coordinator has verified that the donor's condition is stable, so El Paso's proceeding with surgery."

"How long does it take to get there in one of these babies?" Jeremy asked.

"Bailando says about two hours. Commercial airlines have a flight time of about an hour and forty-five minutes from here to there. So I'm estimating your return at around 9:00 p.m. At this point it looks like we'll bring Jak to the pre-op area around eight, targeting the OR for nine to nine thirty. We'll assemble the team and have everybody ready well before then. Of course I'll stay with Jak every minute."

It occurred to Jeremy that he'd missed his chance to hug Jak and tell him a final "I love you." He had to call soon if he planned to at least speak the words.

"I'll keep you posted, and you do the same for me," Barlow said.

"Will do." Jeremy hung up and hunted for the cabin's communication system. In a box flush with the paneled wall over the counter he found a set of earphones and a keypad. He used the equipment to call Angie's cell. "How're you holding up?"

"Jeremy! I'm so glad it's you!" she said. "But I can't really talk. They're getting ready to wheel Jak out."

"Let me speak to him first, okay?"

She didn't answer, but he heard her saying, "Honey, it's Daddy. He wants to talk to you."

Jak's frail voice came on, "Hi, Daddy. Mommy said you got a helicopter ride."

"I did. But it would've been more fun with you there. When this

is over and you're all better, we'll take a helicopter ride together."
Jeremy took a deep breath. So much at stake. So little in his control.

"Mommy says I'm getting a new heart tonight." Jak sounded frightened.

"It's true." Grateful as Jeremy felt about getting a donor, he also knew the risks. "I know you'll be brave. I wish I could be there—and I will be. I'll be with you as soon as I get back. Don't worry, son. It's going to be fine."

"I'm scared."

Jeremy felt like saying, "Me, too," but he knew better. "It's okay. You can be scared and brave at the same time. Mommy and I will be there waiting the minute you open your eyes. It's just like going to sleep."

"Mommy says I have to go now."

"I love you, Jak."

"You, too, Daddy."

Angie came back on the line. "Sorry, hon. They're waiting for us."

"It's okay." Jeremy wiped his eyes with his fingertips. "Wish I were there."

"Me, too," Angie said. "But I'm also glad—really glad—you're there. I love you." How long had it been since he'd heard those words? "I'll always love you," she said, her voice breathy.

"I love you, too, Angie. I'll be back soon. We can hold each other while we wait for Jak to get to Recovery. Sorry you have to do this alone."

"Thanks. Gotta go."

Jeremy hung up and made his way aft in search of tissues.

Back in his seat he wondered how he'd pass all that time. Four hours! The waiting would drive him crazy.

He wished he could go under the knife in Jak's place. He remembered the conversation with Devin about death, how she asked if Jeremy could imagine the love it would take to sacrifice an only son.

Not a chance. He already knew how it felt to lose one. Never, ever would he give up his son for someone else. He couldn't imagine what kind of love such a sacrifice would require. He half-prayed, half-thought, "God if you're there, I know I'm nothing like you. But if you gave up your only Son, you know how I feel. Please, please make a way."

He pondered an assortment of potential disasters. A slip of the scalpel. Infection. Organ rejection. Maybe it was good the next few hours would drag. The endpoint could be so awful, so life-changing in the worst ways.

Forcing himself to think of positive outcomes, he pictured Jak going to school. And running on a soccer field. Eating French fries. Hiking up Pikes Peak. Splashing in the pool. The thoughts brought peace for a moment. But the doctor part of him kept butting in, reminding him that it often didn't turn out that way.

Jeremy rifled through the cabinets. He found a stack of cardiothoracic journals. He scanned the indexes and read what he could on last year's transplant advances, approaches to immunosuppression, and ways to take patients off the heart pump. That took an hour. Having exhausted anything that interested him, he stared out the window and worried about Jak.

Thirty minutes later Jeremy phoned Barlow to say they were getting close. "I take it El Paso didn't come up with a faster way to get the heart to Denver," Jeremy said.

"No. Looks like we made the right move. I gave the team there your cell number in case you need to talk directly. And let me give you some contact info for them." He gave Jeremy the requisite details. "Oh, and one more thing before you hang up—it looks like the infusion we did for your potential donor improved his liver function within the hour, but he developed complications."

"What kind of complications?"

"Not related to T*. He was anoxic for some time after the accident and apparently developed some clotting in his legs—and flipped some to his lungs. He went into shock and we had to let him go. Even with him on the ventilator, we couldn't keep up his blood pressure. And why resuscitate? He was already clinically dead. The only reason to drag it out was for potential transplant. They still haven't located the dad."

Imagining how that mother must have felt, Jeremy could hardly speak. "Wow. I'm … so sorry. How terribly sad."

"Yes it is. And it's a good thing you're where you are, isn't it?"

Jeremy imagined how he'd feel right now without the second donor coming through. He shuddered at the thought of the boy's death without consent and no alternate plan. Stressed as he was, he was glad to be sitting in the seat of a Learjet on his way to El Paso. He wondered if this was in answer to his plea. That would require events to be set in motion before he even asked. The question ripped at the curtain of his understanding. He had no way of knowing for sure.

He passed the next twenty minutes on the phone with the lab arranging details so he could stay nonstop with Angie in the pediatric ICU over the weekend. As he talked, he sensed the plane descending and knew they were getting close. He wrapped up his business and gazed out the window at the Franklin Mountains jutting up out of the landscape. The imposing sight of Mt. Franklin grew larger as the plane approached and landed with a bump.

Once they taxied and came to a stop, the plane sat idling at a gate. He opened the door and was met with a blast of searing humid wind. A man in a blue uniform ran toward him, his ID photo bobbing on his pocket as he trotted out to the plane. He carried a cooler the size of a six-pack. Jeremy took the container, thanked him, and shut the door. Everything was on schedule at a few minutes after seven. Back in his seat he waited until the Learjet did an about-face before they taxied up the runway and, with a whoosh, they were airborne again.

Curiosity drove him to open the treasure chest. Inside, packed in an icy saline solution lay a plastic-wrapped human heart. It was the most marvelous site Jeremy had ever seen—more precious than everything he ever could or would own. He sat there in wonder, feeling terror and awe until he reminded himself it needed to stay cold, so he shut the lid reverently. Then he used the plane's phone to call Angie and leave her a message: "We have a heart!"

He returned to his place on the couch and buckled in again. But after a few minutes, he got up and found one of the puzzle books. It took little time to see how useless it was even to try working a Sudoku puzzle when his son's life hung in the balance. Jeremy returned to his post at the window and sat pushing his cuticles back, wondering how Jak's body would respond to a new heart.

Thirty minutes later Jeremy's phone rang. It was one of the lab assistants. "You know Jasper authorized an infusion this afternoon, right?" he asked.

"Uh-huh."

"Well, they just took the kid off the respirator. Don't worry, though. It's probably unrelated to T*. It looks like he threw some massive clots and shocked out so they took him off and pronounced him dead. So what I need to know … will you want to do a postmortem?"

"Yes. Just not tonight."

"Of course not. It's just—" a beep interrupted whatever he said "—plan to cremate otherwise."

Jeremy saw that Barlow was calling. "I gotta run. Yes, send the kid to the morgue. We'll do a post on Monday."

"Okay. Have a great weekend."

Jeremy hurried to catch the call from Barlow before he hung up, but it was too late. As he was pressing the numbers, a ring tone signaled that he had a message waiting. He accessed it and heard Barlow's voice. "Nothing urgent or emergent. But call me back on the flight phone."

Jeremy phoned right back using the unit on the wall.

Barlow told him, "I just wanted to let you know the transplant coordinator has informed the OR staff, anesthesia, blood bank, and the bio and pulmonary labs. She's getting the equipment together now. Normally she would have accompanied you, but we truly thought she'd need to be here in case a team from El Paso arrived. Looks like we'll wheel Jak into OR in about thirty minutes. But we won't open anything until we hear you've hit the ground, okay? That's still looking like it'll be nine-ish."

"Great. Thanks. I guess you've had a busy night there," Jeremy said.

"Kind of."

"Sorry to hear about …" He realized he didn't even know the boy's name. "About the other boy. Letting him go. The lab just called to ask if I wanted to do a post."

"What did you tell them?"

"I said probably not tonight."

CHAPTER 30

At 8:45, Jeremy's phone rang again. He was glad he'd conserved as much power as possible, because the one bar left indicated the battery level was low. It was Barlow. The first words out of his mouth were, "Everything's okay …" Yet he sounded tentative.

"But …?"

"But we've had a little change in plans on transport. Helo just got called on a life-and-death accident, so we can't send it to pick you up. We're dispatching an ambulance instead to get you at Front Range Airport. That sets us back only about thirty minutes, so we're still fine. Doing great timewise, actually."

Thirty minutes sounded eternal to Jeremy, but he reminded himself that it wasn't worth someone dying for him to have faster transport. If this was the worst obstacle, they'd done well.

"Call me when you get to Denver, okay?" Barlow said.

"Will do."

"Now … you need to know—we've got Jak in the OR with the anesthesiologist standing by," Barlow said. There was a long pause.

"And …?"

"To be honest, his oxygen's dropped." Jeremy gasped. "Probably with all the excitement," Barlow quickly added. "And we've had to move him around a lot. But if we can put him on the pump, we can get control while you're coming with the heart. So I think we're going to go ahead and get started."

ANGIE SAT NEXT to Jak's bed-on-wheels in the pre-op room. All tests were finished, and the anesthesiologist had just wrapped up his pre-op visit. This was it. July seventh would always be a day to remember in the Cramer household—one way or the other.

She took her boy in her arms, stroked his forehead, careful to avoid disturbing the plastic tube that provided oxygen through his nose and kept him comfortable. She looked into the black circles in the center of his brown eyes. "I love you," she said. She kissed his cheek. While she felt anything but calm inside, she tried to form soothing words. But she was mute. What good could words do? And what words would she use, anyhow? Words were supposed to be her gift. Her profession was looking for and finding meaning in them. But she had none for this moment.

She wished she could infuse peace like one of Jeremy's solutions. If only she could pour her spirit into Jak's, to take all his illness on herself and bear it instead.

Barlow came and stood by her.

"It's time, isn't it?" she asked.

He pursed his lips but didn't answer. He didn't have to. She knew.

"But Jeremy's not back yet," Angie pleaded. "Can't we wait until he gets here?"

Barlow shook his head. "I'm sorry."

Mother and child clung to each other, both of them helpless. She had never felt so close to Jak. And she might never hold him again. If something went wrong, she felt certain she wouldn't survive. She wiped his tears and then her own. "I love you, sweetheart." She tried to make her voice sound stronger than she was. "You'll do fine. I'll be right here—Daddy and I will be—when you wake up. We'll be the first thing you see!"

"He's in good hands—the best," Barlow said. "He'll be fine." He gave her hand a squeeze. "You'll see."

Her son kept his eyes locked on her as they wheeled him backward through the great double doors. "I love you," she mouthed. When they swung shut, she bent half over and bawled.

AFTER BARLOW'S CALL, even the seconds dragged. Jeremy checked his watch every three or four minutes, certain each time at least ten had passed. He could no longer think of anything but Jak. Watching out the window, he wished he could will the plane to go faster. But instead dusk settled in slowly, and almost imperceptibly trees yielded their identities to a unified outline. Against the silhouette, the city came into view, its lights like flecks of glitter. It seemed that the jet crawled rather than flew through the sky as they made their slow-motion descent. Eventually wheels met runway and Jeremy could see the ambulance waiting. He flipped open his phone to call Barlow. He felt so glad to be back in Denver that he wanted to cheer. The time was 9:11 p.m.

"I'll have someone check the Internet for an updated traffic report," Barlow said. "We'll reroute you if we have to. We don't want you getting stuck in traffic somewhere. But at nine on a Friday night, you should be fine."

"If I don't hear from you, I'll see you in about thirty minutes," Jeremy said.

The pilot accompanied Jeremy as he transported the cooler across the tarmac to the ambulance. With a hearty handshake and a "Glad to help!" the pilot departed. The driver's assistant occupied the passenger seat, so Jeremy climbed in the back, situated the precious cargo in his lap, and fastened his belt.

Jeremy braced himself for the slow twenty-four-mile trip. But he hadn't counted on the siren and the speed. Even though the plane moved faster, it felt slower. In the rescue wagon it seemed as if he was actually making progress. He had to brace himself every time they took a corner. The driver careened down the highway, and cars got out of the way to let him pass. This was more like it!

About fifteen minutes later Jeremy's phone rang. Hearing it, he expected to learn about some highway obstacle. But he didn't recognize the number. The caller identified herself as the El Paso Hospital transplant coordinator. He assumed she was checking on his progress.

"We're doing great here. Almost there. Maybe another ten minutes," he said.

"Oh! I'm so glad I caught you in time," she said. "I have terrible news."

Despite the blur of cars out the window, Jeremy's world screeched to a dead stop. "What kind of news?"

"The heart we gave you—the patient had Hepatitis E."

That was all Jeremy heard. He didn't have to hear more—the implications were unmistakable. Unusable. She couldn't possibly be right. If Terren had slugged him square in the jaw, his fist would have hit with less impact than her words. Hep E caused liver failure in a healthy patient, and Jak's immune system was suppressed. That beautiful heart was rotten. Worthless. "But ... how?" How was it possible?

"We're so sorry. The donor was shot in a drive-by shooting a couple of days ago, and at that time we thought he'd survive. We didn't run the tests required for transplant until we put him on the list. And we just got these results."

"Are you sure? This changes *everything*." Jeremy felt as though he'd sprinted twenty miles in the wrong direction. "It can't be ..."

"I'm sorry. So sorry."

No way Jak could receive a heart infected with Hep E. Jeremy wanted to spike the heart onto the pavement. All that effort wasted.

The stress. And now they were out of options. He gritted his teeth and punched the seat.

"We're so sorr—" The phone went silent. Jeremy looked at it and saw that all its lights were out. Out of power.

He sat there, shoulders slumped. They'd been so close and now this. His son probably wouldn't make it. No way they would find a third donor in time. Jeremy wanted to lie down and die with Jak.

He had to call Barlow. He glanced at his watch. He estimated he'd arrive at the hospital in five to seven minutes. And he figured Jak was probably already under anesthesia. The team might have even started the case, preparing to put Jak on the pump to expedite transplant. Jeremy didn't know. But when his phone died, he lost his address book with all the numbers. By the time he borrowed a phone from the driver or contacted the hospital through the ambulance dispatch and tracked down the needed numbers, they'd be there. He stuffed the phone into his pocket.

He had to make a choice.

Now.

What about the donor in the morgue? He had been infused only hours earlier with T*.

But they hadn't tested T* on children.

Still, it did seem to improve the donor's liver function.

Yet what kind of a test group was that? A vast sampling of ... one? Besides, a liver wasn't a heart. Far too risky. He wiped sweaty palms on his scrubs. No way he could do it. And even if he *could* do it, what chance did it have of working?

But he couldn't let Jak die. The potential donor died only a few hours earlier. Hadn't the other cadaver's kidney still worked great after *five* hours—and that was an AIDS patient. This kid had no infectious diseases. All evidence said he had a perfectly healthy heart. Jeremy considered the unthinkable—the outrageousness of this opportunity.

But harvest an organ without donor consent? How would he feel if someone did that to his kid?

Yet the mom had been willing. The dad probably would've been too. Who knew? If only they could've found him.

This was different from sneaking an organ without anyone's knowledge. He'd probably lose his license. No more practicing medicine. His career ruined. Everything he'd worked for. Everything he loved. But he loved his son more. What a no-brainer choice: his son or medicine? Easy.

He felt discomfort in his foot and realized he was tapping it rapidly.

He didn't have to decide now. He could go to the morgue and have a look first. A calm washed over him.

He got the driver's attention. "When we get close," he said, "I need you to turn off the siren. And instead of taking me to the ER entrance, drop me at the doctors' door."

"Really? You sure?"

"Absolutely."

Jeremy spent the next few minutes formulating his plan. It was as risky as Russian roulette with five bullets in six chambers. Angie would divorce him if it didn't work. But she might if he didn't try too. He had to try. Maybe he could never make up for what happened with Ravi, but he could try to save the child they would otherwise lose. Jeremy knew he was the only one in the world who could do it. And it just might work.

When the siren went silent, he took a deep breath. They were within two blocks. The next twenty minutes might be the most important of his life. He would have to use every single brain cell he possessed. He couldn't think about Angie. Or Jak. Or anything except what he had to do. Focus. He'd need a scalpel, a bone saw, some fresh cold saline solution to transport …

At 9:32, the ambulance slowed and rolled to a stop. Jeremy hopped out, removed the cooler, and called out "Thank you!" Then he waved the driver on and ran for the elevator designated for doctors, which provided access both to the morgue in the basement and the OR upstairs. He whipped out his key.

He was taking a big risk. No—an enormous one. How did he know the heart in the morgue was still viable? He didn't. But he was pretty sure. Removing the heart would be fast and relatively easy. Though he'd never actually performed an autopsy by himself, he'd attended plenty. And he knew the heart had only a couple of connections—aorta, inferior and superior vena cava, pulmonary trunk. *Voila!* It would be out. If he really hurried, it would take fifteen minutes. What had Glidewall said? She trimmed vessels close for autopsies, but CT surgeons left them as long as possible for transplant.

He reached the morgue and realized he needed the code. For a moment he despaired—he was locked out. Then he remembered. Glidewall had given him a mnemonic device: The code made a triangle on the keypad. He punched in 7-5-9-7 and heard the lock click. He opened the door and turned on the lights.

A few terror-filled minutes later, he had pulled the cadaver from the refrigerator, made the Y-incision, and was staring at the perfectly healthy heart. He had to rush if he planned to proceed, but raging internal conflict made him hesitate. Either way he did the wrong thing—harvest a heart without permission or let his son die when he had half a chance. Yet harvesting the heart was the *right* thing— what any loving father would do: everything in his power to save his child.

But maybe it was a suicidal leap. He could lose both child and career.

Yet the heart sure looked good.

Was it a foolhardy choice? Maybe wisdom drove him. He didn't know. How could he weigh the limits of his own knowledge and experience against his son's only chance to survive?

No choice.

He knew.

He lifted the scalpel and cut.

AT 9:48, CARRYING the cooler close to his chest, Jeremy calmly strode to the OR. He handed it to one of Dr. Bailando's surgical nurses as his heart raced.

Seeing him, Barlow came over. "Where you been, man? I've been trying to reach you!"

"Sorry. My cell died."

"I was afraid of that." Barlow motioned to the OR. "Any chance you want to stay?" Jeremy shook his head. "I understand," Barlow said.

Jeremy excused himself, but he left through the doctors' exit rather than going through the waiting area where he'd risk running into Angie. He still had to go tell the ER crew they could quit waiting for him, return to the morgue to finish what he'd started, and *then* go find his bride.

CHAPTER 31

Jeremy swung by the lab on his way back from the OR to snatch his phone charger. When he returned to the morgue, he plugged it in and connected his phone. Listening to his messages, he heard Barlow and Angie in increasingly desperate voices trying to reach him. The last call came from the transplant coordinator in El Paso telling him they should just dispose of the heart. No need for any microscopic work.

It took about forty boom-box-free minutes to complete what he needed of the autopsy, taking samples from kidneys and liver. He left the body appropriately prepared for the pathologist, with the heart from El Paso and the cadaver's dissected organs in plastic bags after recording their weights. He wondered how long it would take for the pathologist to figure out something was amiss and realize what he'd had done. He scrubbed the room until it shone, careful to return everything exactly as he found it. Then he phoned Angie.

"Why haven't you answered your phone?" she asked.

"Battery ran out."

"Of all times!"

"Tell me about it. Be right there." When he arrived at the OR waiting room, he went to open the door, but hesitated. He knew he must tell her what he'd done—no matter the outcome. But not now. This surely wasn't the time. The pathology department handled noth-ing but emergencies on weekends, so he had until Monday before anyone would even begin to find anything out of the ordinary—if they ever would.

He glanced at his watch. Almost 10:30. He opened the door a crack and saw her there—sitting all by herself seemingly lost in thought. *She told me she'd love me always*, he reminded himself. Ah, promises made in the heat of desperation. He wished it were true. He suspected if the heart didn't work, she'd change her mind. He wondered what would become of his family of four after tonight.

Her eyes met his. "Jeremy!" She jumped up to greet him. They clung to each other and wept. He buried his face in her hair, inhaled her herbal fragrance, and hoped with everything in him that she would soon hold the living, breathing form of their son. "I thought you'd never get here," she choked out. "I'm so scared."

He held her tighter and looped her hair behind her ear in gentle strokes. Then he took her hand, led her to the chairs, and turned toward her. "The heart looks fantastic. I think he'll be fine."

Her shoulders relaxed at the words. "Really?" Her eyes glistened with hope.

"Uh-huh."

She heaved a great sigh. He imagined what he might be saying to her right now if he hadn't made the choice he had. It made him feel better about the load weighing on him.

"How long do you think surgery will take?"

"Depends on how it goes. Probably about six hours."

"Six hours?" She groaned.

"Yeah. Have you been by yourself all this time?" he asked. She looked pale and he wondered how long it had been since she'd had any food.

"Yeah. Mom and Dad are on their way. I told them to stay at home, especially since they'd put Ainsley to bed already, but they called a neighbor who agreed to watch her. And I asked Portia, too. She's on her way. But the important thing is that you're here now."

They settled in for the wait. He filled her in on the details of his trip—leaving out some essentials. Then she gave him a minute-by-minute rundown of the afternoon. He was glad she was doing most of the talking instead of asking details of his timings and whereabouts.

Mic, the chaplain, paid a visit, as did a number of Jeremy's colleagues. Portia arrived close to midnight with snacks, sandwiches, and drinks. When Angie actually ate a Reuben, Jeremy quit worrying so much about her.

Not long after that, Angie's parents dragged in carrying a stack of magazines with a stash of freshly baked peanut butter cookies.

They took turns surfing channels on the waiting room's television, munching, and flipping through magazines, always with an eye on the clock's ticking seconds. They talked in quiet tones. A mood of nervous optimism permeated. Whenever anyone opened the door leading from the OR, which Barlow did every hour, they all jumped. He would wander out to deliver updates such as "so far so good" and "uneventful" and "all's well."

Rather than gowning and entering the OR, Jeremy stayed with Angie. She'd suffered alone enough. Besides, she seemed to be feeling kindly toward him, and he wanted to enjoy it while it lasted.

Finally at 4:10 a.m., Barlow and Bailando appeared. Bailando was a tall, gentle man in his early fifties with brown eyes and blond eyelashes. He had the physique of a football player and a winsome smile. Standing with his hands folded, he announced, "Congratulations! It's a boy!" His gaze fell on Angie. "Your son's doing great."

Angie's hand flew to her mouth and she started to cry. Jeremy wrapped his arms around her as the doctor delivered hugs all around.

"We'll move Jak to a special cardiac care unit," Bailando finally said to Jeremy. "We need to keep him sedated and on the ventilator for a few hours." They all gathered around the doctor to catch the details as he continued. "We hope to get him extubated by noon. For now he's got a tube in his nose, a couple coming from his chest, a line in his neck, and the tube down his trachea. You'll see all sorts of wires and electrodes. Hear lots of beeping. And a warming blanket on him that looks like an air mattress. All of that's normal. The main thing he needs now is rest. But he has a great-looking ticker, and he did fantastic. As soon as we circulated the blood to warm up the heart, it started beating in perfect rhythm. It still amazes me every time I see it happen." He turned to Angie and, with a twinkle in his eye, warned, "You may have trouble keeping him down."

"The least of my worries! When can we see him?" she asked.

"Soon. But it'll take a day to sleep off the anesthetic, so don't expect much from him. And you'll have to scrub and wear masks, gloves, gowns, and caps for at least the first twenty-four hours—until we remove all the lines and tubes."

They thanked him profusely. And then they went to scrub while the team got Jak situated in Recovery. Finally Angie and Jeremy received the okay to go see him. They hurried to his bedside and looked into the face of their child.

Jeremy locked his eyes on his son lying there alive with the aid of a dead child's heart. It stuck him as nothing short of a miracle. A healthy pink replaced the pale cheeks of the previous weeks. His chest rose and fell in perfect rhythm. Jeremy had never seen such a thrilling sight.

Jeremy glanced at Jak's oxygen level and read 99 percent. Jeremy looked back at Jak and then at Angie, whose eyes met his. "Amazing, isn't he?" Jeremy whispered. He reached across the bed and squeezed her hand.

They stood on either side of Jak, each taking one of his hands, as they marveled at the sight of his face and rejoiced that his heart monitor registered perfect beats at ideal intervals. Eventually Jeremy looked up and stared at his beautiful wife adoring their child before signaling with his head that it was time to go.

Only as they removed their garb did Jeremy realize how bone-tired he felt. He didn't remember ever feeling so exhausted—and he'd pulled a few all-nighters in his day. Having earlier secured a key to one of the hospital's overnight housing units, Angie went up to Jak's room and retrieved their overnight bags.

For the first time in weeks Jeremy held her in his arms and fell soundly asleep. Five hours later they rose, dressed, and returned to Jak's side. For the next ninety minutes they jumped every time he stirred. But he kept breathing the slow rhythm of deep sleep. Looking up every time Jak so much as licked his lips, Jeremy wished his boy would wake up. He needed to see his eyes, to hear his voice, to know he would be okay. Jeremy vacillated between relief that Jak was still alive and terror of the new heart's unknowns. He knew he'd probably saved Jak's life, but what if the heart had hidden risks. No one had ever tried what Jeremy had just done. How could he have done it to his own child?

Another thirty minutes passed, and Angie and Jeremy watched as Jak slowly opened his eyes. When they jumped up and came to his side, he smiled. Angie leaned over him and kissed his forehead. "Hi, Mommy," he said in a groggy little voice.

"Hello, honey," she said, smiling down at him. "Daddy's here now." She motioned to Jeremy.

"Daddy!" Jak said with a little more energy.

"Hi, buddy. You did great. I'm so proud of you," Jeremy said. He hugged Jak as best he could through all the wires and tubes, but the motion made Jak wince.

"We'll have to take it easy. You'll be sore for a while," Jeremy said, "but you did great. How do you like your new ticker?"

"Okay," Jak said, his eyes already heavy again.

Jeremy stood there holding Jak's hand, and in another minute he fell back asleep. Several minutes later he woke again and exclaimed, "Daddy!" Jeremy repeated his previous words, aware that Jak would probably forget this time, too.

As expected, Jak drifted in and out of sleep for most of the day. Jeremy and Angie spent the hours donning gowns and visiting Jak at strictly monitored intervals. Though his breathing improved, it hurt to take deep breaths, and his eyes watered when he moved or twisted.

They watched for signs of rejection. But Jeremy told himself to cast off worry for another day. Right now life was sweet. Their boy was on the mend.

The following morning Jeremy awoke feeling the gravity of what he'd done. His conscience exploded with the reality. On the one hand, he had no regrets. On the other, it would mean giving up research. What a loss! And who knew what the ramifications would be for their health insurance coverage. With more expenses to come. The one thing that encouraged Jeremy, besides Jak thriving, was the thought of the transplant implications for T*, even without his ongoing involvement. Jeremy thought of other parents like himself, of spouses and family members, whose loved ones had better chances of survival now.

By nine o'clock Sunday night, Jeremy felt driven to talk to Angie. He had to tell her before the morgue opened on Monday. She had to hear it from him. And so did Barlow. And Jasper.

To Jeremy's surprise, he didn't have to coax Angie away from Jak. She seemed eager to get back to the hospital's housing.

When they returned to their hotel-like accommodations, Angie said, "We need to talk."

"What about?" Jeremy stretched out on the king-sized bed.

"About us." She sounded nervous.

He sat back up. "What about us?" When Angie burst into tears, a tremor of fear shook him. "What is it?" he asked.

"I'm so sorry, Jeremy! So sorry! I've punished you for things you couldn't control. And for trying to keep living. I've wanted you to stop taking any risks. But where does that end? Quarry stones and you might get injured. Drive and you might have a wreck. But you have to keep working and driving. I can see that now."

Much as he wanted to hold on to each one, the exact words blurred in his memory as soon as she said them.

"You probably think I'm apologizing and saying I love you because Jak's doing well. But that's not true. You have to believe me." She seemed desperate. "Tell me you believe me!"

"I do." He didn't know if that was because he wanted to so much or because he heard it in her voice back when he'd been on the plane. He drew her next to him on the bed.

"Forgive me, Jeremy," she said. She'd never used those words. Never asked him for that. It went beyond a mere, "I'm sorry." It required a response.

"Of course I forgive you." As he said it, he knew he was about to test her words to the limit. He longed to keep the sweetness of this moment, but she had to know—now. "I have something I need to tell you, too," he said.

She propped herself on her elbow, worry in her eyes. "What?"

"Jak's heart … it's not … it's not from El Paso." She squinted at him. "It's from the potential donor," he said. "The one here who … uh …"

She shot straight up. "But he *died* before you got back."

"Right, I—"

Sweetness faded to horror. "What did you do?" she demanded. "And why?" The muscle in her jaw tightened and Jeremy could see the distrust in her eyes. As he struggled to find the words, he could see her tears welling. He had to explain. Fast.

"Remember how I said I had to take the ambulance?" He looked away from her eyes, which bored into him. She didn't say a word. "Well, while I was in the wagon, I got a call from El Paso telling me the donor was infected. Hepatitis E." He glanced over and saw her eyes had grown yet wider.

"Hepatitis E? Never heard of it!"

"We don't see it much in the States. It usually involves a contaminated water supply. But believe me, it's one dread infectious disease for a kid on major immunosuppressants."

"How could that happen?"

He could see her mind working to fit details together. "They didn't get the results until it was too late." Angie groaned. "And then my phone died as I was talking to her, but I had enough info to know." As he retold the events—about going to the morgue and exchanging hearts—Angie relaxed.

"I'm glad you didn't tell me until now—now that he's improving!" Angie said. "So nobody knows?" He shook his head. "You're not going to try to hide it—are you?"

"No. I've certainly considered it! So much is at stake. I'm sure I'll lose my job. But even if they don't figure it out in the morgue, which they might, there's too much interaction with El Paso to keep it under cover for long. And when the donor's parents find out, they'll be livid. I feel bad about that."

She thought for a while about that and slowly her tight muscles relaxed and formed a smile. Then with a burst of energy, she threw her arms around him.

Much as he liked—no, loved—the response he was getting, he wasn't sure Angie understood fully. He peeled her off himself. "I'm sure I'll lose my medical license." The reality hit him again. "I'm finished as a doctor."

She sat cross-legged on the bed with a smile on her face. "But don't you see what you've done?" He wasn't sure what she meant. "You gave up your career so Jak could survive!"

Jeremy nodded and picked at a piece of lint on the bedspread. "But we'll probably get sued. Maybe for millions."

"Listen to me! If they drag you into court, throw the book at you, and strip you of your license, they can tell you you're unfit to collect garbage, but I'll still love you for what you did." She threw her arms around him again, knocking him so hard he fell backward on the bed. "You saved his life!"

CHAPTER 32

On Monday morning Jeremy called Barlow's cell phone at seven. Nate didn't even bother with a greeting. "Everything okay, buddy?"

"Pretty good," Jeremy said. "But I need to talk with you. Think you might have some time in your morning?"

"Sure. We can meet for breakfast after rounds. I'll visit Jak last and we can head down from there." If Barlow was curious, he didn't show it.

Around 7:45, Barlow arrived. He checked Jak's vitals, chatted with him for a few minutes, and then motioned to Jeremy that he was ready to go.

"Your boy looks good," he said as they headed down the hall. "Right where he should be—maybe even a little ahead of the curve. You and Angie must be so relieved. I sure am!"

"Very," Jeremy said.

When they arrived in the cafeteria, Barlow waited for the cook to make his French toast, and Jeremy grabbed some cereal. He headed for the table where they'd last met.

"Uh-oh. We need privacy, huh?" Barlow teased from across the room. But Jeremy didn't laugh.

As they ate, Jeremy talked about the weather. And sports scores. And Dylan's departure. But he couldn't seem to bring up what he needed to say.

And Barlow seemed in no hurry. He'd peeled and eaten an orange and was starting in on his French toast, yet Jeremy hadn't even broached the subject. If he was going to come out with it, he'd have to do so without any prompting.

"I have a confession," Jeremy said.

Barlow dropped his fork under the table. He bent to retrieve it, and when he lifted his head, he looked anemic.

"You okay, man?" Jeremy asked. He'd turned so pale and so suddenly.

"What is it?" Barlow asked, terror in his eyes.

Jeremy thought Barlow was sure jumpy. He decided to switch strategies. "The heart from El Paso ... the patient had Hepatitis E."

"Hep E?" Barlow looked surprised, then laughed. "That's what you wanted to tell me?" He seemed hugely relieved. "Very funny. I'm so sure an infectious disease guy would let us give his kid an infected heart. You had me going for a second, man." He got up and retrieved a replacement fork.

This would be more difficult than Jeremy thought.

When Barlow returned, Jeremy tried again. "Um ... I didn't give Bailando the El Paso heart. I took the one ... from here. The patient we—you—infused."

Barlow couldn't have looked more stunned if Jeremy had hauled off and hit him. "You what?" He stared, then glared. "You're serious." Jeremy nodded. "The one in the morgue?" Barlow asked.

"Uh. Yeah. Look, I'm in the ambulance almost back to the hospital when El Paso calls to say they've made a mistake."

Jeremy saw the muscles working in Barlow's neck and it made him more nervous.

"Y-you've already started the surgery. You've got my son's chest open, and I'm headed to the OR with a heart you can't use."

Jeremy paused for Barlow to say something, but he just squinted. Feeling compelled to fill the void, Jeremy continued, "My phone goes dead, so I can't even talk to you about it. I see no choice but to try to save my son's life."

"But … you didn't have consent." Barlow's bewildered tone matched his expression. "They never gave consent."

"I know. I know how you feel about unethical organ harvesting. And about informed consent. I agree with you!" He figured it would go better if he didn't try to justify it. "And I realize I'll lose my medical license."

"You sure will." Barlow moved his jaw from side to side, seeming to take it all in, perhaps weighing all angles. "So … what do you want from me, Doctor?" he asked. His tone had an unpleasant edge.

"I respect you enough that I wanted you to hear it here first."

"Appreciate that." The words carried no warmth, and Barlow's lips were pressed tightly together.

"What do you think I should do now?" Jeremy asked.

"You want my *advice* now?" Barlow sucked on his lower lip and the veins in his neck stood out like cords. With hands rested on the table, he worked his thumbs in circles around each other. Disapproval shrieked from a cold silence that enfolded him.

Jeremy regretted the question. He should've just informed him and left it at that.

Finally Barlow lifted wary eyebrows. "Meet me over in my office in two hours. I need time to think through what … what you've done here." He got up, tossed his still-full tray of food in the trash, and disappeared through the door.

Jeremy didn't know what he'd expected from Barlow. Certainly not approval. But he hoped for at least a hint of understanding. If nothing else, the man was consistent on the question of informed consent. Jeremy picked at his food for a while and then dragged his feet as he returned to Jak's room.

When the appointed time came, Jeremy made the trek across the hospital skywalk to the office complex. He'd been to Barlow's office only a couple of times. An Alice-in-Wonderland mural decorated the walls in the reception area, and in the middle of the room was an enormous tank filled with rainbow fish. Jeremy sat and studied them, mesmerized by their unhurried motion while he waited.

About two minutes after he arrived, a nurse came to the door and directed him to proceed to Barlow's office. She pointed to the room. Jeremy found Barlow seated, hands folded on the desk, apparently deep in thought. In front of him was a list. Jeremy slid into the seat and their eyes met briefly.

"We need to consider three things," Barlow said solemnly. "The family, the law, and lastly your career. First the law."

Jeremy nodded.

"I won't lecture you, at least not much, other than to remind you that the law is a good thing. Tell me again—what was the name of the child you lost?"

"Ravi."

"All right. Imagine getting a call from someone saying they took Ravi's heart without your permission because they needed it to save their own child's life."

"I know." Jeremy looked at the floor.

"You'd feel violated—deeply violated. Outraged. Wouldn't you?" Jeremy nodded. "Yet, knowing how it felt to lose a child, you'd understand the love that would drive someone to do such a thing."

"Yes."

"Having never had a child, I can't fully understand, but I can imagine. So how much do you know about Colorado law when it comes to organ donation?"

"Not much."

"Well I'm not positive you've broken it. But if not, you've come close. Fortunately for you, though, we have more lenient laws than some other states. The U.S. generally operates under informed consent, so would-be donors have to sign a card signaling their wishes.

But then, without additional legal documentation, the family gets the last word. Unlike most states, Colorado has *presumed* consent. That is, we assume willingness to donate unless it's expressly stated otherwise."

That sounded hopeful to Jeremy.

"Still, at the hospital we would never, *ever* take an organ—especially from a minor—without permission. And that brings us to the family. The *victims*, if you will."

The word stung.

"It'll tear them up when they hear what you've done. You violated the body of their child without their knowledge or consent. Now, Greta Stephenson—that's the mom—she was unwilling to give consent without her husband's okay. Assuming his, she probably would have agreed. Otherwise why drag it out by keeping her boy going on the ventilator? Still, it feels different when you consent. It's not the same as having the choice taken from you. But she did want some good to come of their tragedy, and she found Jak's story compelling. So we have that going for us."

Jeremy liked the sound of "us." It sounded better than "you."

"But it's still going to be difficult." He exhaled with a hard sigh. "In a sense, Jeremy, you're only one signature away from *Oprah*."

Not getting Barlow's meaning, Jeremy squinted. "What do you mean?"

"If you had consent, you'd be a hero—paraded for all to applaud. It appears you proved there's a way to use an organ from a corpse already in the morgue, which might mean thousands of people sitting on transplant lists finally get the organs they need. And yet … without that one little signature, your career as a doc is charbroiled. Who knows how this will go? I'd advise you to go straight from here to Legal," Barlow said. "Tell them I'm willing to act as a liaison to the Stephenson family to try to do some damage control for the hospital and for you."

Jeremy felt terrible. He'd put Barlow in an unenviable position, yet Barlow was willing to help him. What a friend. "Thank you."

"They just *cannot* hear this in the news."

Jeremy could imagine the headlines: "Heart from Corpse Dead 3 Hours Saves Child."

"And it'll eventually make it to primetime," Barlow continued, "because you just made transplant history." Jeremy saw the hint of a smile on one side of his mouth.

"Now," Barlow continued, "I think it's safe to say that for the time being, your career as a medical doc is toast. You'll get your license suspended. But nobody revokes a PhD, so you'll have to find work as a researcher ... though I doubt anybody will let you near a morgue—and you'd better prepare yourself to get sued. Royally." Barlow sniffed and shook his head. "You've just discovered a way to keep organs pristine and usable for several hours after death. So that part is thrilling."

"Thanks," Jeremy said.

"But I don't envy you." Barlow shook his head slowly. "You get to tell Jasper, who'll get to face Castillo. And won't the chief enjoy hanging you so he can watch you twist and twitch? Except, like I said, you just made transplant history." A flash of insight crossed his face. "Now *there's* a perfect dilemma for Castillo!" He leaned back, touched his fingers together, and grinned at the prospect. "Having to choose between the savory prospect of publicly eating you for lunch—which he'd relish like a connoisseur—and keeping mum about your big discovery when he could claim it as his own since you're silent. But silence would downright violate his own nature."

The smile slowly disappeared, and Barlow looked at Jeremy with penetrating eyes. He leaned forward and gripped the edge of his desk. "Just know this. For a while you're in for some rough sailing. I can't say I like what you did, but I'll do what I can to help from here."

"Thanks. I appreciate that more than I can say."

—※—

Jeremy sat across the desk from Sherry Cravens, a professional-looking woman in her late thirties with light brown hair that she wore cropped at the chin. She was one of the hospital attorneys who had accompanied Jasper when she announced Dylan's departure.

"So what did you think of my message?" she asked.

Her words puzzled him. "Your message?" Jeremy said.

"Isn't that why you're here? My e-mail about the lawsuit?" she asked. Jeremy's heart jumped. How could the boy's parents already know—and have a suit in motion? "The papers we received this morning from Terren Garrigues …?" Seeing his blank look she asked, "Then why *are* you here?"

Jeremy sat up straighter. "Guess you'd better tell me about the papers."

"I wrote this all to you in my message, but basically Mr. Garrigues has named both the hospital and you in a legal suit." She pressed her lips tightly, and he wondered if the disapproving look was intended for Terren or for him. "Yet because someone else has confessed to tampering with his wife's T* solution, we hope to get him to drop—or at least to shift—the charges. I didn't notify you to worry you. I just thought you should know." She picked up her pen and doodled with it as she continued, "Even if he goes through with it, this is exactly why we provide insurance as part of your employee benefits package. As long as you don't break the law, you're covered."

"Appreciate that. What if I do break the law …?" he asked.

"But you didn't. Did you?" She looked up and peered at him over the top of her half-glasses.

"Um, I'm not sure …" He drew a deep breath and launched in, laying it out as succinctly as possible.

When he finished, she condemned him with her eyes. "Let me make sure I understand perfectly, Dr. Cramer," she said. "You removed a heart from a deceased minor without the express written permission of the parents?" The coldness in her voice made him shudder.

Looking down at his lap, he said, "Yes, ma'am."

"You do realize your malpractice insurance will likely be of no help on this one." Her eyes bored into him like a drill. "So you might want to transfer all your assets to your wife's name alone. And I hope you have a good attorney, because I expect the parents—once they learn what you did—to sue. For millions. And win."

Jeremy imagined himself unemployed and his family homeless. He hadn't thought that far. But what if he had? Would it have made a difference? He knew the answer was no.

"You need to seek legal counsel—get your own personal attorney," she continued. "You might start with the malpractice insurance supplier. They'll likely want to appoint someone to help protect their interests."

Jeremy realized that even if, by some miracle, he retained his medical license, no insurance carrier would ever cover him again.

"Now I can't speak for Dr. Jasper," she said, "but I assure you that she will be advised—in the strongest possible terms—to give you fifteen minutes to remove your personal items from your desk and ask you to leave the premises."

JEREMY PROCEEDED SLOWLY to Jasper's office, brooding over the conversation he'd just had. When she saw him standing in her doorway, she waved him in. "Heard about your son," she said. "I had no idea how serious it was. I hope he's improving."

"He is," Jeremy said. "Thanks."

"What's on your mind?" She motioned for him to take a seat. "I guess you heard we're getting sued."

"Yes. I just came from Legal," he said.

She waved it off. "Aw, don't fret over it, Cramer. Sure, you infected her, but Dylan will probably take the fall."

He ignored her words. "Dr. Jasper, I have something I need to tell you. And you're not going to like it."

Jeremy told his story for the third time. As he did so, she sat expressionless with her arms folded across her chest.

When he finished, she shook her head. "In the course of one week my entire research team has been torpedoed. And obliterated."

What could he say?

"I just came from talking with the board about Dr. Dylan. Now I'll have to go back to them with this mess? What were you thinking?" She paused and heaved an enormous sigh. Then she pondered what he'd told her. Eventually her lines softened. "I suppose I would have done what you did, to tell the truth."

At least she empathized.

"So what are my options?" Jeremy said.

She scratched the side of her chin. "It's complicated. When I tell Castillo about this—and you know I'll have to—he will *so* want to nail your butt to the back fence and use it for a dartboard." She leaned forward on her elbows. "*But* if we fire you straight out, you pack up your research toys and go play in somebody else's laboratory."

"So you don't want me to resign?" he asked.

She shook her head. "The hospital will have to distance ourselves from you initially. But really, it mostly depends on whether the boy's family wants to press charges. If so, you're definitely out of here. If not, we can suspend hospital privileges pending a full inquiry and recommend suspension of your medical license—which buys time and hurts nobody. Such a course allows us a good defense if the whole thing blows up in court, but it still allows you to freelance as a researcher. And you might even make more than residents' pay that way. If you wanted to set up your own company, we could probably even outsource the lab to you."

"You think Castillo would agree?"

She shrugged. "What choice does he have? You're the one who really understands T*. And even if the boy's parents sue for millions, if we let you go, we lose the potential for a multimillion-dollar pharmaceutical deal. Maybe even multibillion. You held four aces," she said. "Now you hold three. The card you'll no longer have is a medical license. But you're still holding a major research breakthrough, a rep as a major research wizard, and a PhD behind your name. Three aces is still a pretty good hand."

The contrast between this conversation and the one in Legal left Jeremy confused. "So what should I do?"

"Go sit with your son. We'll put you on a leave of absence effective immediately until the board makes a decision. I'll keep you posted."

"Okay. Thanks." Jeremy rose to leave.

"Wait. But before you go, I may as well bring you up to speed about Dylan."

Jeremy had virtually forgotten. He sat back down. "What's the deal?"

"It was Castillo. I've watched him abuse her for years. And she couldn't take it anymore. But all she did in the end was batter herself. You know what he's like. Legal helped her write out a statement for the board, so they're taking a look at his tactics. But—fact is—treating someone like your personal porcelain throne isn't against the law. And to our board, Castillo's the *rainmaker* when it comes to money and grants."

"So she used the egg-tainted mix on purpose?"

Jasper nodded. "Knowing of Ms. Garrigues allergy, Dylan used the egg-tainted albumin. And after the disaster, when you gave the sample to Ted for testing, she switched it out with a clean one—underestimating your system of checks and balance. But I'll say this in her defense—she didn't set out to kill anybody."

"But she *did* kill somebody." Jeremy was furious.

"The world's full of lowlife insects, Jeremy. And always, like roaches, they survive by ducking out of the light. Dylan will probably get a light sentence. And our board probably won't even reprimand Castillo. He's their big fish, and there's no policy that prohibits him from being a bottom-dwelling scum-sucker. That's life in the big-city hospital."

CHAPTER 33

For most of the two weeks that followed, Jeremy tended to Jak's medical needs. But a dark cloud hung over Jeremy, and at night it unleashed a storm inside.

All he knew from Barlow was that the donor's family was devastated, and they wanted time to think through what they planned to do. The father had apparently been located, but Barlow wouldn't discuss any details.

Jeremy felt terrible, but he couldn't apologize. How could he be sorry? He was sorry for their pain—so sorry for that. He asked Barlow to at least communicate that much.

It felt strange to spend the day at the hospital but stay out of the lab. As for Jak's condition, Barlow said his hospital stay could last up to four weeks, but Jeremy suspected Barlow would discharge him by the middle of week three. Jak was thriving and antsy to get home—as they all were.

Barlow kept his distance, but he expressed to Jeremy that he wasn't trying to punish him. He had ongoing contact with the family, and to protect their confidentiality, he couldn't discuss the case. Besides, he'd been advised by Legal to avoid in any way appearing to condone Jeremy's actions.

Yet whenever the stress of it all was too much for Jeremy, he'd go to Jak's room and watch his boy play with the controls on the bed or listen wide-eyed as his mom read to him. Jeremy had only to remind himself of the alternative to put circumstances into perspective. Besides, he knew his father would have approved of his choices. Maybe he hadn't fulfilled his dream of helping submersion victims, but he'd sacrificed it all for his child. Maybe that was the better legacy, after all.

DAY SEVENTEEN FOLLOWING the transplant fell on a Monday. And on that morning Barlow showed up for early rounds as usual. He had no residents or students with him that day, and he hung around Jak's room afterward. Angie was out meeting with a client, so it was just the two men and Jak.

"I have something to give you," Barlow said. "Is this a good time?"

Jeremy motioned for him to take a seat, but instead Barlow leaned against the wall and removed a piece of yellow paper from the pocket of his scrubs. He handed it to Jeremy. "It's from Greta and Bryan Stephenson."

The name didn't register.

Barlow pointed to Jak. "Parents of Ethan—the heart."

Jeremy took the piece of legal paper, which was folded numerous times. He shook it until it opened and read its contents:

Dear Dr. Cramer,

I am the mother of Ethan Stephenson, the boy whose heart you removed to save your son. About the time Ethan was killed, insurgents shot down my husband's helicopter in the Middle East. As he parachuted, gunfire wounded him. He hid alone for days before the Marines recovered him. Now he's home facing multiple surgeries.

Our son's doctor, Dr. Barlow, has been wonderful. He came out to our home to tell us what you did. On a second visit, he gave us more details about Jak than he'd given us earlier. We understand you and your wife have already lost one child, and we can't imagine losing two.

Still, I'll never again tell my husband "you've stolen my heart." What used to sound romantic now makes me ill. When Ethan died, I thought nothing could make our grief worse. I was wrong.

But a few days after we heard what you'd done, we asked each other if we'd do the same to save Ethan. And we would. My husband said he probably would have consented to organ donation if we'd reached him earlier. But that doesn't change the fact that you acted without our permission.

Still, Dr. Barlow said that because of Ethan, more lives can now be saved. It doesn't remove our pain, but it comforts us to know his life made a difference.

We do have one request. We would like to meet your son and listen to his heart. In a strange way it feels as if a part of Ethan remains with us. Yet we'd prefer you were not present. Would you permit a visit with Dr. Barlow there?

Greta and Bryan Stephenson

Jeremy refolded the paper. "Did you read it?" he asked Barlow. He looked at the floor and nodded. Jeremy didn't say anything.

"Is there some question?" Barlow asked.

"Is that really all they want—to meet Jak? That's it? The end of the legal story?" He imagined restful nights, no more nagging fears about the future. Even the possibility of retaining his license. He felt shaky. A little tearful.

"I can't make any guarantees here. But hopefully so."

Amazing. "It might be a little weird for Jak if these strangers show up wanting to hear his heart."

Barlow winked. "I'll bet we can find a couple of white med student coats they could borrow. Besides, Jak loves his new heart, right? I'll bet he won't mind letting them hear the heart of their little hero."

CHAPTER 34

Two and a Half Years Later

Jeremy leaned on the counter at the nurse's station in the pediatric intensive care unit. As he waited for Barlow to show up, he drank black coffee and studied the ornaments on the Christmas tree atop the counter. It was decorated with cartoon characters.

Before long, Barlow rounded the corner. "Hey, hey!" he said, seemingly pleased to see his old friend. They shook hands. "Congrats on getting FDA approval."

"Thanks," Jeremy said, studying his shoes. He felt a little self-conscious about T* in Barlow's presence.

"So how's the freelance life?" Barlow asked.

"All right. But I miss some of the perks of hospital life."

"What? There are *perks?* You mean the food? Or residents' pay?" Barlow asked. Without expecting an answer, he continued, "I got the notice to attend your reinstatement hearing in January. I'll be there to put in a good word."

Jeremy felt even more self-conscious. "Thanks. But I have no illusions about them reversing it anytime soon. And I'm okay with that."

"Coming to our New Year's party next week?" Barlow changed the subject.

"Wouldn't miss it. Now—you're a busy man. So what's up?"

"Someone I want you to meet—the parent of a patient." Barlow motioned for Jeremy to come with him and led the way to the elevator bank. He got off on the fifth-floor wing, reserved for adult asthma and lung patients. Upon reaching a private room, Barlow knocked.

Inside they found a balding man. Jeremy guessed his age at about forty-eight. He was heavyset with brown hair, small blue eyes, and a face full of brown whiskers. When he saw the men enter, the patient pressed the button on the automatic bed so he could sit up.

Barlow introduced Jeremy and then told the patient, "Dr. Cramer's an undercover doc—a researcher. And I need you to tell him how you ended up here."

The man drank from the straw in front of him and began. "My son and I was ice-fishing yesterday. Ice broke and we fell through. Somebody saw and pulled us out. I don't remember that part." He hacked and cleared his lungs. "When we got to the hospital, we was both unconscious. My son came to right away, but I was in bad shape."

Barlow looked at Jeremy, a gleam in his eyes.

The man continued, "The ambulance folks carry stuff they said they just started using for people like us. ER doc told me later it was developed by some guy here at the hospital. They say if it'd happened three years ago, I'd-a been a goner. I guess you could say he saved my life." He hacked again. "Maybe in a hundred years nobody'll visit my tomb, but my wife thinks I'm more important than the president— know what I mean? She's the kind who believes the fate of the world is half owing to unfamous folks like me."

Barlow smiled proudly and pointed to Jeremy. "Dr. Cramer here—"

Jeremy shook his head and stopped him. "So you feel okay now?" Jeremy asked the patient.

"Uh-huh."

"And your son?" Jeremy asked. "He's doing well?"

The man gestured toward Barlow. "Doc here released him last night. They say kids always do better in dunkings than grown-ups."

Jeremy and Barlow exchanged knowing smiles. "So I've heard," Jeremy said. He shook the man's hand. "Tell me again your name, sir."

"Henry Wade."

"Wonderful to meet you, Henry. Really wonderful."

AT TWILIGHT THAT evening Jeremy slipped his arm around Angie's shoulder. Outside their back door they stood in the snow watching the kids. Huge flakes made light tapping noises against the glass on the sliding window and covered their neighborhood in a coat of white ermine. Jak was pulling a sled carrying his four-year-old sister.

Jeremy watched his children and reminded himself to savor the moment. Angie apparently had the same thought. "Hard to believe he'll turn ten soon," she said, her eyes on Jak. "They sure grow up fast. I miss the baby stage." Jeremy knew it was a hint, but he enjoyed keeping her in suspense.

They stood watching, content to see their darlings chortling and giggling and playing. Jeremy looked up at the stars. *Guess I never said thanks.*

"So are you going to tell me?" she asked.

Jeremy smiled. "Sure. Your HCG level was fifty-five."

She mock slugged him. "You're driving me crazy!" She muttered something about the aggravation of being married to a researcher and how there was just something *wrong* about a husband giving test results to his wife instead of vice versa. "And fifty-five means …?"

"It means … if it's a boy, we're naming him Henry Wade."

Angie squealed. "Jeremy Cramer!"

He wrapped her in a hug. "Congratulations to us!" He gave her another hug and a kiss.

"Who's Henry Wade?" she asked.

"Someone Barlow introduced me to at the hospital today." He filled Angie in on the details.

She slipped a hand into his. "Imagine," she said. "A wife and four kids. Think of the heartache you've prevented."

"Oh I love it when you talk like that," he said, as if she'd said something deeply seductive.

"Talk like what?"

"Like you believe in me."

"Of course I believe." She stood on her tiptoes and kissed his nose.

Jeremy pulled her close, held her tight, and looked up at the stars. "I believe too," he said, knowing she'd miss his double meaning. "Maybe it's highly contagious."

... a little more ...

When a delightful concert comes to an end,

the orchestra might offer an encore.

When a fine meal comes to an end,

it's always nice to savor a bit of dessert.

When a great story comes to an end,

we think you may want to linger.

And so, we offer ...

AfterWords—just a little something more after you

have finished a David C. Cook novel.

We invite you to stay awhile in the story.

Thanks for reading!

Turn the page for ...

• **Angie Cramer Interviews the Author**

• **For Further Exploration**

• **Discussion Questions**

Angie Cramer Interviews the Author

Angie: You obviously know Jeremy and me and our worlds quite well. But I don't know you at all. Tell me about yourself.
Sandra: I'm glad you're speaking to me. After what I've put you through, I realize you'd probably like to punch me.

Anyway, to answer your question, I thrive on variety. I'm a freelance journalist teaching grad-level classes on writing, women, and oral communication; I edit a magazine, *Kindred Spirit,* for Dallas Seminary, which has about thirty-thousand readers (www.dts.edu/ks); and I'm working on a PhD in Aesthetic Studies at the University of Texas at Dallas. I'm also a fifth-generation Oregonian transplanted for the past couple of decades in Texas.

Angie: Aesthetic Studies?
Sandra: Yes. Lots of folks ask what a degree in Aesthetic Studies is. Since I write medical thrillers, one reader thought it meant I was majoring in anesthesiology. But the Aesthetic Studies emphasis falls under the Arts and Humanities Department. My studies are part fiction-writing, part history, part philosophy, and part art. I'm not a visual artist. Seriously. I draw stick people. But I take classes about art such as "Women of the Renaissance." I appreciate art. I try to understand it. And I love the program. Because I teach writing to artsy grad students (last semester I had one with pink glow-in-the-dark hair that my daughter thought was *the coolest*), I need a PhD to equip me to better help them.

During the time I wrote *Informed Consent*, I took a course in the works of Dante. That influenced me to include in my characters' lives five of the seven deadly sins.

Angie: Which ones?
Sandra: That's for you to figure out.

Angie: Would you please translate the quotation from Dante at the beginning of the book?
Sandra: Sorry, but no. That's for you to discover. But it shouldn't be hard. A simple web search is all you need.

Angie: What do you hope readers will gain from *Informed Consent*?

Sandra: What does every fiction writer want? I want to so engross readers in my story that the laundry waits, the bills go unpaid, and they bite their nails off. I can always dream, right? As for themes I explored some topics that are far too complex to handle in a sound bite—informed consent, end-of-life and patient autonomy issues, a compassionate response to AIDS, choosing between overworking and family life, grace. I hope readers will feel they've enjoyed the story and in the process thought about bigger issues confronting us on this fragile planet. I guess it's a form of edutainment.

Angie: How would you describe informed consent—not the book but the phrase as it's used in conversation?

Sandra: As a patient I give consent to a treatment or I take medicine based on my understanding of the facts and the implications of my actions. Let's say I need synthroid for a thyroid problem. I should read about risks and benefits and decide if I want to take it. Now, if my friend sneaks synthroid into my applesauce, I have not given informed consent. For individuals who can't give informed consent, legal guardians or caregivers must be authorized to give consent on their behalf. Yet giving or getting consent can get complicated—as life often is. Sometimes you have two ethical ideals that crash into each other—in this story, life and death of a child vs. the choice of the deceased's parents. When two ethical ideals collide, you have to make imperfect choices and then live with the consequences, and there will be some.

Angie: Are you a swimmer?

Sandra: Yes and no. Never competitively. But I do swim for physical therapy, and I often think about plot twists as I do laps. The phone never interrupts, and nobody ever stops me to ask a question.

My connection to the world of competitive swimming is less direct: My sister's best friend post-college was Matt Biondi's sister, Annie. Before the Seoul Olympics in which Matt won seven medals, his father—Captain Nick, as they called him—extended an invitation to my husband and me to go yachting with some of his friends and with my sister and her husband in San Francisco Bay. If you can believe it, I said no because I wouldn't know more than two people. After Seoul I kicked myself. Repeatedly. But the captain was gracious enough to offer again a year later, and the second time we said yes. But of course that time Matt wasn't with them, so I never got to meet him. Through that I learned a lot about risk-taking.

Angie: Why did you give Devin Garrigues such a terrible disease?
Sandra: Shortly after I graduated from college, I took a job in downtown Dallas, and there I had lunch every day with a group of young professionals. Two of my friends in that group were practicing homosexuals, and they both died of AIDS. One contracted HIV after surviving a knifing. As he walked to his car one night, he got jumped by some guys who felt they were "doing society a favor." They sliced his kidney and he told me he didn't even realize it until he got in the shower and looked down. The water around his feet was red.

That same year we buried the husband of a friend from church. And in another church, one that often partnered with ours, the music pastor died of AIDS. He'd contracted HIV years earlier from a dirty needle. All that was just the beginning.

Fifteen years and millions and millions of deaths later, it's easy to get compassion fatigue. But we can't afford to.

My more specific interest, which is why Devin is a person of faith, lies in the response of the faith community to the pandemic. If you haven't seen the *Frontline* documentary, "The Age of AIDS," which you can watch on the web, I recommend doing so. The film itself is about the virus, but I think it also captures well the faith community's opposing responses to the pandemic.

The first is judgment. My niece is a spiritual person, but to my knowledge she does not profess faith exclusively in Jesus Christ. And sadly, in her work with AIDS patients, she has encountered Christians who have the attitude that "AIDS patients deserve to die because their disease is their own fault."

The second is compassion. Contrast my niece's experience with a conversation I had. A now-retired general who directed one of the world's largest international aid organizations, having just returned from a tour of something like thirty-eight countries, gave me a much different perspective. When I asked, "What's the most exciting thing you see happening worldwide?" he surprised me with, "The response of Christians in Africa to the AIDS crisis." He went on to tell how denominational hospitals and relief organizations were working with governments, pharmaceutical companies, and local pastors to lead the way in working for education, free medication, and support for the afflicted and their families.

A few months later I read virtually the same assessment from Nicholas Kristof in one of his *New York Times* columns.

The contrast between the North American church's response in the past (it's changing now) and the African church's response troubled me. That's why I gave this horrible, wasting disease to a Christ-following character. We need to keep rethinking the stereotypes and lack of compassion.

I consider what my niece encountered to be a graceless response. And I think a lack of grace is a lack of imagination—the inability to imagine how easy it would be to find ourselves in someone else's shoes given that person's set of circumstances.

A second reason I "ruined Devin's life" relates to another area where I believe we need a course correction—in processing end-of-life issues. Certainly I had concerns with how the general media dealt with the Schiavo case, but I also had serious concerns with how the religious press treated it. The biases on both sides sickened me. Sometimes I agreed with the conclusions of both sets of journalists, yet I vehemently disagreed with *how* they reached their conclusions. Devin's character allowed me to explore the difference between prolonging life and prolonging death.

I once attended a workshop for religion journalists on writing about bioethics. The presenter argued for what he called the "Little House on the Prairie" defense. That is, he said if Dr. Hiram Baker, the doc in *Little House*, didn't have something at his disposal, it's probably "medical treatment." Later, I was told other bioethicists often use that same argument. Yet other religious people want to argue that a feeding tube is not medical treatment.

Of course when I tried to weave that into the manuscript, one of my writing advisors said the reference to *Little House* was too "precious," so I axed it. The story was more important than shoehorning "talking points" into the text.

Angie: What else did you want to communicate?
Sandra: I wanted to explore lots of ideas. Doesn't every author want that? Specifically, the value of good cross-gender friendships; the importance of families spending time together; how easy it is to be bitter; how life has inherent risk; the complexity of ethical choices. Some of the dynamics in Geneva at WHO with AIDS research. Fun stuff, too—the Canyon of Heroes, for example. Far, far too much to list here.

Angie: Choose one.
Sandra: Okay. Take you for example—I thought you needed to fall in love with Jeremy again. Often people think romantic stories are only about the unmarried. But as the population ages, one good trend I see is in movies such as *Spanglish* and *Shall We Dance?* that affirm renewing the love that drew couples together rather than cashing in that love for something new.

Two years ago I fell headfirst down eight steps and destroyed my left clavicle (among other injuries). When that happened, the first question out of my husband's mouth after he rushed home was, "Where do you want me to take you?" In that moment I fell in love with him all over again. He gave me a choice. One was a scary hospital five minutes from our house, and the other was one I trusted, but it was twenty minutes away. He understood that only *I* knew how much pain I could endure and whether it was worth the tradeoff in security. I opted for the hospital I trusted, but I was glad he didn't make that choice for me. Sounds like informed consent, huh?

Angie: Why, then, would you use Portia, who cheated on her husband, to confront me about protecting my marriage? Isn't that hypocritical?
Sandra: Sure. But sometimes people who have failed are in the best position to understand the importance of what they've sacrificed—and of the value of grace.

Angie: Like Peter in the Sayers book I read …
Sandra: Precisely. Sayers took her ending right out of the Gospels. What isn't included in that scene is that at the end of his life Peter wrote, "Grow in grace.…" If anybody knew what it felt like to receive grace—undeserved kindness—it was Peter. Judas needed forgiveness, too, but he took the opposite approach from that of Peter, and Judas ended up committing suicide.

I confess that I did get my foundation for storytelling technique from the Bible, complete with examples of those redeemed after messing up. There's a reason it's the best-selling, most-translated book in the world and the foundation for western lit.

When my husband and I went with a medical team to Russia in 1992, representatives from their equivalent to N.O.W. approached us and asked if we'd teach them the Bible. When we picked ourselves up off the floor, they explained: Their educations were truncated by being prohibited from reading it for seventy years. They would hear expressions such as "a David-and-Goliath scenario" or "the handwriting on the wall" or read Melville's references to Jonah or Tolstoy's references to other biblical stories, and they had no idea what those stories were.

In both the first and second testaments, we find love and failure and betrayal and hope and redemption. And we also find great use of motifs. Think of the tree image beginning in Eden, then again at the cross, and finally with the tree of life at the end.

So back to the initial question—is Portia a hypocrite? Sure she is. But sometimes a hypocrite can do a fine job of telling the truth. Aren't we all hypocrites, after all? We all know kindness is better than selfishness, but how kind are we when people cut us off in traffic? Yet does our frustration, if expressed, disqualify us from saying it's better to stay calm?

Angie: So why do you write? To communicate some grand truth?
Sandra: I write for the same reason Eric Little ran. I can't not write. I'd curl up into the fetal position if I couldn't write. I have to do it. I love it. And writing is the closest I'll ever get to creating *ex nihilo*. I write and worlds appear. I can speak places and characters into being. Like you.

Angie: Which raises a question … Why did you allow Ravi to die?
Sandra: It grieved me to hurt you. I do care about your feelings. But it's a mystery you'll never understand because you can't see a world beyond your own. I had to for the greater good.

Angie: Where can readers find you on the web?
Sandra: I rant and pontificate regularly, often with a touch of humor, on my blog at aspire2.blogspot.com.

It's been great talking with you, Angie. I'll miss you. And I hope someday you'll find it in your heart to trust me.

For Further Exploration:
Recommended Resources

Documentary: *Frontline's* "The Age of AIDS"
    Available on video or at www.pbs.org/wgbh/pages/frontline/aids/
Book: *The Skeptic's Guide to the Global AIDS Crisis* (Authentic, 2004), by
    Dale Hanson Bourke
Web site: Organ Donation
    www.organdonor.gov
Web site: Christian Medical and Dental Associations
    www.cmdahome.org
Web site: Do No Harm–The Coalition of Americans for Research Ethics
    www.stemcellresearch.org
Web site: The Center for Bioethics & Human Dignity
    www.cbhd.org
Sandra Glahn's Web site
    Aspire2.com